Blood and Wisdom

by

Verlin Darrow

This is a work of fiction. Names, characters, places, and incidents are either the product of the author's imagination or are used fictitiously, and any resemblance to actual persons living or dead, business establishments, events, or locales, is entirely coincidental.

Blood and Wisdom

Cover Art by *Kim Mendoza*

The Wild Rose Press, Inc.
PO Box 708
Adams Basin, NY 14410-0708
Visit us at www.thewildrosepress.com

Publishing History
First Mainstream Mystery Rose Edition, 2018
Print ISBN 978-1-5092-2086-1
Digital ISBN 978-1-5092-2087-8

Published in the United States of America

I heard a shot and hit the deck. "Get down!"
I shouted to Jerry and the others. Most of them did. The next shot kicked up the sand by my hip. The guy was zeroing in on me with a rifle from up on the cliff. The altitude made it a tough shot, but any decent marksman was going to nail me soon.

There was no cover at all on the beach. I sprinted for the freezing water as more shots rang out. Then I ran awkwardly through the shallow water and dove in under a crashing wave. I had to fight my way through to deeper water. Already, my clothes felt like they weighed forty pounds. A moment later, while I hid underwater as long as I could, I sensed a big body near me. When I came up to the surface about ten yards from where I'd plunged in, I saw Larry the dog next to me, paddling for all he was worth. I heard another shot and submerged again.

I was suddenly aware of how cold the water was. No one swam or surfed in the Monterey Bay without a wetsuit in April. I wouldn't last long.

I don't know if Larry was trying to save me or he thought we were playing a new game, but he swam directly overhead and started scratching the hell out of my shoulders. If the bullets or the water temperature didn't kill me, my dog might.

Praise for *Blood and Wisdom*

"The story has great pace, fun characters who you care about, plenty of twists, and narrative 'personality,' especially with all of the psychology and spiritual references.

Many good zingers, taut scenes, and punchy, believable dialogue.

The mixture of a hard-boiled story line with a soft-boiled private investigator works well and the psychology-spiritualism element grabbed and held my interest."

~C.I. Dennis, author of the Vince Tanzi series

~*~

"Verlin Darrow has a sense of plot and style that carries the reader forward into that special place of anxious expectation, the place where putting the book down is unthinkable...Darrow gets us into the minds of people you wouldn't want to invite for dinner. Fascinating."

~Richard House MD, author of Between Now and When

Dedication

To everyone. We're all in this life thing together, aren't we?

Chapter One

As I was finishing my initial research for my latest client, Aria Piper, I received a call from her. "Can you come down here right away?"

"Why? What's going on?"

"There's a man in our well." She expelled her breath in a whoosh and then inhaled as if she were about to dive under water.

"A man in your well?" I had no idea what she was talking about.

"A dead man. A dismembered dead man."

Two hours earlier, my assistant Matt had escorted Aria into my office at nine on a foggy spring morning. I'd always felt drawn to Aria's chocolate brown eyes. She seemed to be living right there—where she met the world with those eyes. They undoubtedly observed the world more calmly and clearly than mine, but the way they expressed her essence set them apart. Aria radiated authenticity. She always had. Back when we'd been colleagues—interns at a downtown Santa Cruz counseling center—I'd been intimidated by her and kept my distance. I was curious to see how I'd feel now that I'd been a private investigator for twelve years.

"Good morning," I said.

She wore a simple cream-colored tunic, black jeans, and navy running shoes. She'd pulled her dark brown hair back in a ponytail and wore no makeup or jewelry. Tall, dark, and slim, Aria Piper could've been an Italian movie star if you imported her into a more voluptuous body. The years hadn't done her much harm either, unlike yours truly. She probably didn't sport any knife scars, and her smooth, clear skin demonstrated a level of clean living I could only aspire to. Well, I would if I were more sensible.

Her smile was complex. The middle of her lips seemed pleased to see me, and there was generic cheerfulness surrounding that, but the corners of her wide mouth quivered. Was she holding back tears? No, it was fear.

"Hi, Karl," Aria said in a lower voice than I remembered. "It's great to see you." She offered her hand, and I shook it. Soft skin overlay taut muscles. She smelled like cookie dough.

"Tea?" Matt piped up. "Coffee?" I'd forgotten he was there.

"Tea would be lovely," Aria told him as she settled into the green armchair in front of my elderly oak desk.

Matt wandered out of the office to the reception area. You couldn't call it a waiting room. It was too cramped, and no one besides my landlord ever waited in it. I always seemed to be a little too busy—and a lot too poor—to see him.

I settled into my supposedly cushy desk chair. An hour into my day, my butt ached already from sitting around so much lately.

So far, I wasn't intimidated by Aria. I was intrigued. What could have brought her to me? What had scared her?

"Are you still a psychotherapist?" I asked.

"Yes and no. I've kept a small private practice, but

mainly I teach now." She unfurled a hand in my direction, as though she were demonstrating a teaching method.

"Up at the university?" I could see her there. Half her students probably fell in love with her.

"No, at a small spiritual center I founded. We're in the redwoods behind the hospital," she said. She wriggled a bit to get comfortable in her chair, and I struggled to keep my eyes on hers. Wriggling women awakened the adolescent in me.

"No kidding? That's great. Are you a Christian?" As soon as I uttered this, I felt stupid. What I'd asked usually constituted an insult in ultraliberal Santa Cruz. If she hadn't wriggled…

"No. Closer to a Buddhist, but we're not religious per se." Aria smiled again, and this time it spread across the full spectrum of her lips. She'd relaxed a bit, and clearly she hadn't been insulted.

"Spiritual, but not religious," I said. "I think that's one of the categories on Match.com."

"It is. Before my awakening, I tried all of those sites."

What did she mean by "awakening"? Full-blown Eastern-style enlightenment? Really?

"You?" I said. There'd be time for a more in-depth chat later. Or if I didn't take her case, there wouldn't be and it wouldn't matter.

"Yes, me." Aria crossed her legs and leaned back a bit. "And for some reason, I mostly received responses from tech engineers." She shook her head and tucked a loose, black hair behind her ear. For such a centered person, I figured this demonstrated a modicum of agitation, and not about bad dates.

"Bummer," I said. I had nothing against engineers, but I could see that it was time to give her a chance to get to the meat and potatoes of her visit. Whatever else I thought of saying in that moment would've extended our small talk.

Then we were both silent. I tilted forward and shifted my weight onto my thighs as I watched Aria. She watched me back. It didn't feel like a staring contest.

I liked the way her cheekbones created contour and shading on her face. Higher than most people's, they hinted at an exotic ethnicity somewhere in her family tree. And her nose was completely unobjectionable. I objected to most people's. I'd had to grow into mine and still avoided looking directly at it in the mirror, which wasn't easy.

Matt finally strode in with Aria's drink—a grocery store teabag in a microwaved white mug. I'd spoken to him several times about the impression this kind of low-end hospitality made. I'd hired friends before, though, and I knew the drill. Matt's diagnosable wife had dumped him eight months earlier (I'm going with borderline personality disorder), and he'd served as her CEO father's cyber-security consultant. Matt's subsequent unemployment and his predecessor's pregnancy had coincided nicely, so it had worked out for all of us. For the most part.

"So what brings you in?" I asked Aria once Matt ambled to the outer office.

"I'm being threatened." Her calm voice was belied by the trembling corners of her mouth.

"By whom?"

"I think it's Reverend Gary Crowder. He wants to

buy our property, and he won't take no for an answer. If it's not him, it's probably one of his followers."

"Does he run a center, too?" Crowder was a familiar name, but I couldn't think why.

"A church. Well, a cult, really," Aria said, playing with her hair again. "It's currently in a converted warehouse on the west side of town—by the farmers' market. But to be clear, I have no proof of this. It may be someone else." She caught sight of the dark hair curled around her finger, paused a moment, and then gently lowered her hand to form a steeple with her other one, which struck me as appropriate.

"What kind of threats are they?" It was one thing for a bully to sling around nasty words and another for a bona fide villain to threaten credible violence.

"Phone calls on the landline in my office," Aria said. "A man says he'll kill me if I don't stop doing Satan's work." Aria gazed at me intently, holding herself absolutely still.

"What's the voice like?"

"It's low and rough, and he uses an ersatz Southern accent," Aria said after some thought. All her answers were measured and thoughtful. She started to imitate the voice and began coughing. "Sorry," she added when she'd gathered herself. "I can't go that low."

"In many senses of the word, I imagine." I thought for a moment. "You're a therapist, Aria," I said. "And a much better one than I ever was. What's your take on the guy? Is he serious?"

"At first, he sounded harmless."

"Now you're not so sure?" I knew she wasn't, but when I coaxed my clients into telling me what I already knew, then they could be certain I knew. At this point in the process, most people wanted to be heard and understood above all else.

"No, I'm not," Aria confirmed. "He's called three times, escalating the scope and intensity of his threats each time. Yesterday morning—the third call—he stayed on the line, and I was able to converse with him." She paused and sipped her tea for the first time.

I felt impatient—a ruinous quality in a would-be therapist and not particularly helpful in an investigator either. "And?" I asked.

"He's serious. I won't repeat what he said—it's too vile. But he meant every word of it." Aria's lips curled in disgust, revealing gleaming white teeth. Would a spiritual teacher use whitener?

"Why are you here? Why not go to the police?" I've heard a variety of responses to this boilerplate question, which often determined whether I accepted a case. I'd learned the hard way that even when I was strapped for cash, I still needed to be careful who I worked for. My scars could attest to that.

Sometimes the potential client was mixed up in something illegal. These were the most dangerous cases, made worse by clients' attempts to hide the shady aspects of the investigation. I often found myself in the dark when I most needed illumination. Other times, potential clients requested impossible tasks— find the man who stole her necklace in 1989 or please prove the absence of something. I clued these folks into reality and saved them a lot of money. The proposition that irritated me the most was when an investigation was driven by sheer revenge or spite—"Karl, go dig up something damaging so I can inflict suffering on some poor schmo because I'm mad at him." These people were often fifty going on fourteen. I felt like telling them to grow up, and I didn't take their cases anymore. I wish this list was comprehensive, but unfortunately for my bank account, I'd suffered many more reasons to turn down cases than to take them.

"Crowder's brother is the chief of police," Aria said. "They were no help." She shifted in her seat and frowned.

Maybe her butt hurt too? I immediately dismissed that stray thought. Frowning Aria was a completely different person. Now I saw a sensitive, wounded woman. Perhaps she was a trauma survivor, triggered by the threats.

"Oh, that's right—Jim Crowder," I said. That was why I'd known the name. "How'd you find that out?"

"I called the police after the second threat. When the officer I spoke to heard Pastor Gary's name, he transferred me to the chief. Crowder's brother told me not to worry—that public figures receive threats all the time. He said he'd had two in the last week. I should just go about my business and…well, the gist of it was he had his mind made up before he took the call. And he's wrong—I'm not a public figure. I keep a very low profile."

"Why's that?"

"There are several occupational hazards in spiritual teaching. If you're not careful, your group devolves into a personality cult. I'm not a guru. I'm just a teacher."

"They could do worse," I said, smiling.

Aria didn't smile back, which surprised me. "Also," she continued, "I don't want to attract students based on superficial elements such as my looks. For that matter, I don't want to attract students at all. The ones that need to find me, find me. I trust the universe."

This struck me as an odd thing to say. Surely Aria wasn't as naïve as that. Did she think the whole system was self-regulating—we played no role in how anything worked out? She observed me digest what she'd said, and I saw myself through her eyes for a moment.

I was thicker and more wrinkled than the Karl Gatlin she'd known. And I'd had a nasty skin cancer carved out of my temple several weeks earlier, creating a discolored dent with a scab in the center. Otherwise, I could still pass as a character in a *Law and Order* rerun—maybe an Irish terrorist or a defense attorney from the wrong side of the tracks. Anyone craggy-looking, really.

"So the threats continued after you called the police?" I asked, mostly to get her talking again. I'd thought myself into becoming self-conscious.

"Yes. I tried to contact the sheriff's office after the third time too, but they just referred me back to the city police."

"Okay, so how do you see my role in this? And are you sure you can afford me?" Gurus were rich. Teachers weren't.

"We have money," she said. "That's not a problem. What I'm hoping is you can find out who's calling and either dissuade him from continuing or gather enough evidence so he can be arrested, brother or not."

I thought it over, clasping my hands behind my head. I always stared up at the ceiling when I was deciding whether to take a case. I don't know why. It was an easy call in this instance—I knew I would help Aria. But somehow the ritual seemed necessary. At one point, I peeked at Aria, who was finishing her now-tepid tea and peering around the room with a bemused expression on her face.

The local Goodwill store probably wasn't the best place to buy furniture. And I guess I'd watched too many 1950s detective movies. My desk, filing cabinet, and bookshelf reflected my preference for wood over metal, but all of them were so worn and battered, you felt sorry for the poor trees who gave up their lives for them. The file drawers sat askew in their slots, one tilting to the right, the other to the left. Black and white movie posters clung to the once-white walls, none of them at the same level.

On the other hand, I'd hung a one-of-a-kind Ansel Adams print of the Grand Tetons on the wall behind my desk. It had been a gift from one of his granddaughters, whom I'd rescued from an abusive boyfriend. And one of my area rugs was worth more than my car, not that you could tell. Whatever pattern was still detectable bore only a passing resemblance to whatever its weaver had fashioned. To me, it looked like geometric geese. Matt contended it began life as a floral design. What made it rare was the type of silk and dye that had been the norm in a particular corner of China in the seventeenth century. What made it mine was my late uncle, the founder of the business I now ran.

"I'm willing to take your case and see what I can do," I finally told her, gazing into those alert brown eyes. "But I think you need protection while I explore this. These may just be idle threats, but it's better to be safe than sorry. If I find the creep after you're dead, what good does that do us?"

"What do you mean by protection? Security

guards?" Aria frowned again.

I felt a strong urge to only say things that elicited her warm smile. "A bodyguard. I know the right guy. You'll like him."

"I'm not sure that's a good idea."

"No?"

"No. I need to tell you a little bit about my work to explain why." She leaned forward, closing the distance between us in a way that felt good. Not sexual, just generically good. I could see she wanted to explain herself regardless of the circumstances, perhaps to spread her gospel and "help" me, although I certainly wasn't ripe for the spiritual picking. In fact, I probably would've been voted both least likely to become a therapist and least likely to drink New Age Kool-Aid in my high school yearbook.

"Sure. Go ahead," I said, sitting up straighter and shifting my weight to my left buttock. Maybe a new desk chair was on Santa's list this year. Since I served as my own Santa, I could probably arrange it. I needed to work on the merry thing, though.

"I open people up," Aria said. She paused to see if I knew what she meant. I didn't and she could see that. "I help my spiritual students develop a more straightforward relationship to reality. Together, we dismantle defense mechanisms. Then, when someone's ready, I strip away whatever still stands between them and their direct experience."

"Aria, this is fascinating, but what in the world does it have to do with hiring a bodyguard?" My impatience had gotten the best of me again.

"Because of the way I work, a certain percentage of my people will be raw and vulnerable at any given time. They stay at the center during this phase of their development—where it's safe for them. If I allowed a man with violent energy on the property, it could be quite damaging."

"John's not going to hurt anyone," I told her. "He's a nice guy, Aria." The energy part was too weird to address. I judged people by their behavior, not some imaginary force inside them.

"I'm talking about energy, Karl—not behavior."

I thought things over for a moment. "Okay, fine. How about this? He and I can stop by later today to see the center. You can warn all the vulnerable people to hide or something. That way, you'll get an idea of what it's like having him there."

It was her turn to ponder. "All right," she finally agreed, although I could see by her body posture that she wasn't happy with this compromise. She sank a bit in her seat, and her hands steepled again. Probably she'd muster some pretext to bar John once we visited.

"How does this work?" she asked. "Do you need a check today?"

I told her my fee structure, and Aria wrote a check for the retainer while I was still talking. Irrespective of history or looks, anyone that eager to pay became my new favorite client.

"Thank you," I said, as she handed me her check. I noticed that her hand was vibrating. Not shaking. Vibrating. "Is there anything else I need to know before I get to work?"

"Yes, but let's save it until we're at the center." Aria glanced at me. Is that okay? her look asked.

"Fine," I told her. "I can get going on the Internet in the meantime. I have access to all sorts of sites that are reserved for professionals." I smiled as reassuringly as I could manage.

Probably all I'd find was public information about Crowder, the property, and, of course, Aria herself. I researched my clients just as much as everyone else on a case. I was frequently amazed by what they didn't tell me based on their self-serving ideas about what was relevant. Your husband's missing? Gee, I think the fact that you were having an affair might be germane. There's money missing from your office? Yeah, maybe the fact that your ex-con cousin works there might have something to do with it. They feared my moral judgement about their lives. But who was I to them?

Once Aria had departed—and she looked just as good going as she had coming—Matt ran into my office and began dancing a jig. "I'm getting paid!" he sang to the tune of "Happy Birthday." Matt was the world's worse singer and probably in the bottom ten as a dancer.

I gave John Ratu a call once I'd shooed my assistant back to his desk. Matt was supposed to be making debt-collection calls. He liked to tell people I had a puppy with Parkinson's disease or that I owed money to vicious loan sharks. I usually left my door ajar to listen to him.

"Hi, it's Karl Gatlin," I told John.

"Hi, Karl. Have you got some work for me?" His deep baritone voice boomed at me. John was still working at developing an "inside voice," as my sister called it. It was just one of the eighteen million traits she'd demanded he modify. He'd changed about one and a half of them.

"I do have some work," I said. "Bodyguarding. But

let's pretend we're polite and ask each other how we're doing first. You're going to need good manners for this one."

"Sure, mate. How's it going?" John spoke with a strong New Zealand accent. He was a huge Maori man—a former rugby star and my sister's ex-husband. She'd met him on a vacation over there. It was just like her to bring home a human souvenir instead of a T-shirt.

"Fine," I said. "And you?"

"No worries."

"Was that so hard, John?"

"You're as bad as your sister, Karl. Now tell me about the job."

So I did, emphasizing that he had to audition for it. Or his energy did.

"Oh, that's all right then," he said. "I've got terrific energy. Dogs love me."

I could easily imagine that. "Good. Can you be here at 2:30 so we can drive down to Aria's together?"

"Sure. You still got that dinky little car? You know I don't fit in that."

"You drive, then. I'll see you later."

"Okay, mate."

I got on the computer and started earning my check. Between the databases I subscribed to and the ones that Matt hacked into, practically everything I needed to know was online somewhere. Well, at least for run of the mill cases—running background checks, locating deadbeat dads. That kind of thing.

I discovered Reverend Crowder was a local who'd attended a small Bible college in Oklahoma. After his graduation, he'd served as an assistant pastor in

Flagstaff, Arizona, and then taught at a Christian high school in a small town just east of San Diego. His church in Santa Cruz—"Jesus Is Everything"—was a sizable operation, with a slick website that featured videos of contented-looking people giving testimonials: "Reverend Gary helped me turn into the person I always longed to be." "My kids love their pastor. He's a true prophet." "Finally! A values-driven community guided by a true leader." This last guy looked like a serial killer.

There was a lot more Crowder on the site than there was Jesus. If the Son of God was Everything, then apparently the reverend was Everything plus even more Everything.

God Himself had apparently told Gary religious secrets, but "he couldn't reveal them at this time" because "Satan's forces surround us and they would use these sacred truths against all mankind if given the chance." When the time was right to reveal his prophecies, Crowder promised he'd tell his ministry's supporters first. You could send your support by snail mail, and they accepted credit cards and PayPal, as well.

The paranoid tone of the text and Crowder's narcissism were alarming. Us-against-them organizations were capable of dangerous acts. Like fear-biting dogs, they lashed out when they became panicky.

Gary Crowder himself was photogenic. He wore fitted western suits and held himself ramrod stiff—like a Confederate general in an antique photograph. With his jet black, wavy hair and his annoyingly regular features, he could've modeled camouflage gear in a hunting catalog. I pictured him shooting a baby deer or maybe a neighbor's cat.

Crowder's eyes betrayed him. They weren't compassionate or particularly self-aware. If your average dog's eyes reached a nine on a kindness scale, Gary Crowder's dwelt in the three to four range. I also saw Type A ambition in his eyes. A lot of it.

His police chief brother—Jim—had worked his way up from sergeant after two tours in the military police. He was forty-eight, three years younger than the reverend. He'd been a third baseman at Fresno State, was married with three kids, and served on the board of several charities. There was no hint of scandal.

The ease of finding Jim Crowder's personal data made me realize I hadn't found comparable information about Gary on the Everything Church's website. Was he married? Did he have kids? In my experience, his type of sect stressed traditional family values.

I dug a little deeper. Reverend Crowder had been married in Oklahoma right after college, but only for a couple of years. They'd never officially divorced, and no record existed of any other relationships. He raised Airedale terriers and always had at least three or four at his ranch in Corralitos—a rural community south of town. Crowder played the clarinet and liked to mountain bike.

I only found one disparaging item, a newspaper article in which a female university student accused Crowder of groping her three years earlier. The police had dismissed her case for lack of evidence, so she'd gone public. Apparently, Leanne Atkinson had been a member of the Jesus Is Everything church, and she'd weathered one-on-one pastoral counseling with

Crowder. She stated that she was willing to "put her reputation on the line to stop this evil hypocrite from preying on vulnerable congregants." I made a note. She was someone worth talking to.

I looked up Aria's organization next. The Santa Cruz Spiritual Center—could she have come up with a more generic name?—was represented by a sophisticated website as well. It listed the center's meditation and activities schedules and displayed professional-looking photos of the property. Tin-roofed, one-story dark green buildings sat in a meadow beside a redwood forest. It could've been a small private school or an artists' cooperative. A section of the website detailed the community's mission statement and goals, which didn't entice me into abandoning my current life paradigm. Mostly the message was live in the moment, love everybody, and let go of ego-based concerns. Nothing new there.

Then the phone rang, and the game changed.

Chapter Two

When I finished talking to Aria, I called John Ratu and told him to meet me at the center. If there was a murder, there was going to be a bodyguard—whether Aria liked it or not.

As I drove the five or six miles to Aria's place, I periodically glanced at the conspicuously empty passenger seat. My ex had custody of my dog for another day, which rankled me the most when I ventured out of the office on a case. Larry and I were a team.

The sun cut through the usual morning fog—a gift from Monterey Bay—patchily transforming a gloomy, late spring day into a luminous spectacle. I reminded myself how lucky I was to live in a resort town with mountains, redwood forests, and beaches all within a ten-minute drive.

I was also aware thoughts like these represented an attempt to postpone facing whatever feelings had been stirred up by the murder. The previous two murder cases I'd investigated had both ended poorly, and not just for me. I knew there was a gunky goulash of emotions buried beneath my internal travelogue.

John beat me to the center and stood next to our client as I pulled into the gravel parking lot beside the largest building. He made Aria look like a grade school kid. John was twice as wide and a head taller. He wore black shorts and a bright green polo shirt.

In terms of coloring and facial features, John resembled a cross between an African-American and a Samoan. His nose was both long and wide, but the surface of his face was so expansive that it didn't dominate. His other similarly oversized features always seemed to be a beat away from smiling. He smiled with his whole face, although his broad mouth led the way, initiating an upward ripple. The overall effect wasn't quite handsome, but people tended to like and trust him right off the bat.

Unlike a football lineman or another variety of refrigerator-sized American, John's body tapered from the shoulders down to the waist, bulked up again at the thighs, and then stayed in scale on down the line. He wasn't obese—quite the opposite. His percentage of body fat must've been way lower than mine, and I'm quite fit, due more to genetics than self-discipline. John appeared to be all muscle—coordinated muscle. He'd been a world-class athlete.

"I see you've met," I said as I approached them. I looked at Aria and raised an eyebrow. How was John's energy?

"He's a delight," she said. She wore the same outfit as she had in my office—cream and black. Her stress was obvious, despite her effort to hold herself still and speak in a normal tone. Her brows furrowed, and I could hear a burr in her throat that hadn't been there before. I had one of my magic-eight-ball thoughts—God knows where they float up from. Aria was probably innocent. There was no blood on her. Of course she was innocent, I told myself. What a ridiculous notion.

"I like her, too," John said. "Is she single? I'm too shy to ask her myself."

Aria and I smiled. John was about as shy as I was rich. Aria's genuine smile escaped through the veneer of calm that overlay whatever else was going on, and then almost immediately morphed into a tight-lipped imitation of the real thing, lips held against her teeth in an unnatural position. She held it a tad too long too, but that was understandable, given the circumstances.

"Where are the police?" I asked. None of this was real enough yet to trigger any conscious emotions. I was just going about my business as usual.

"They're parked around back," she told me. "By the patio—where the wishing well is."

"A wishing well?" I hadn't seen one of those in years.

"It's from when the property was a boarding school. Now it's just decorative. I don't encourage any wishing. It devalues the moment."

Her pronouncement bounced off me. If I stopped to consider every snippet of philosophy that came my way, I'd never get anywhere. "Well, I guess we better head over there," I said.

John spoke up. "It's pretty rough, Karl. Get yourself ready."

I glanced at him. I hadn't noticed that his earlier flirting had been an effort. John had a haunted look in his eyes now, and both of his hands were shaking. I'd never seen him like that.

"You've already seen the body, John? How long have you been here?"

"I was nearby, and I drove fast. Here's the thing—there's no head and there's no hands either."

"Oh, God," I said. The words sank into in my gut, which tensed and seemed to drop. There was always a point where the idea of a crime left off and the reality took over, often when I experienced the fallout from it firsthand—a grieving widow or a beat-up kid. Other times, a sudden shift blindsided me in the middle of asking somebody a question.

I soldiered on, ignoring the churning. We walked around the building, Aria between us. No one was in a rush. When we turned the corner, the layout of the center was clearer. Most of the dark green, clapboard buildings were narrow and long. Perhaps the place had once been a sash mill. The buildings grouped around an expansive central courtyard and the covered limestone well sat in the middle of it. The peak of the well's roof sported a strip of copper flashing, and its sides were covered with weathered wood shingles—the kind you saw on New England beach houses. The thing cost about as much to build as a week's stay at an upscale Maui resort.

Terra-cotta tiles paved the courtyard, and a random array of wrought-iron tables and chairs could've accommodated a couple of dozen people. It looked like the backyard of a South American drug dealer in a film. All it needed was an immense swimming pool ringed with bikini-clad starlets and a few muscular henchmen with machine guns.

About a dozen cops milled around the well, waiting for someone to tell them what to do next. A Hispanic man in his forties peeled off and approached us as we stepped onto the sprawling patio.

"You're Gatlin?"

I nodded.

He held out his hand. "Detective Luis Cardenas."

I shook it. A sturdy-looking guy, he wore khakis and a blue Oxford shirt. The staid clothes looked out of place on him. For one thing, he was a fairly dark-skinned fortyish Latino. For another, his features conspired to intimidate whoever he aimed them at. Individually, they were ordinary enough. Together, they were fierce. His eyebrows angled downward as though they were angry about something on their own. And his eyes held defiance. I'd hate to be his boss. I got a whiff of musky aftershave as he moved past me and forced me to turn to keep him in view.

"Frank Meyer says you're all right," Cardenas said, looking me squarely in the eye, all emotion leached out of him now. "So I'm going to assume that's true unless you give me a reason to think otherwise." His anger and all the rest were tucked away. I imagined Cardenas practiced that look to rev up the intimidation he naturally radiated. It was overkill, but he was good at it. If you haven't been to prison, where it's on the syllabus of Survival 101, it's hard to master.

"Fair enough," I said with a slight smile. "I guess I'll do the same with you, even without a reference."

He gave me a hard look now, angling his head and bringing his eyes to bear at a sharp angle. This was an alpha male cop—not my favorite variety. "Look, I'm doing you a courtesy here because Ms. Piper asked me to," he said, his voice edged with impatience. "She and I already had a very productive interview. And there's a big push in the department lately to cooperate with people like you. I don't know why, to tell you the truth. So let me remind you that you're at a crime scene. Touch anything and you're history. Give me crap again and you're history. Do you understand?"

"Sure. What about my associate, John?"

"Are you kidding?" Cardenas turned and high-fived the big Maori. "This is my main man. John and I play softball together. You ever see this dude at the plate? He hits a home run practically every time he's up."

Cardenas was suddenly a totally different guy. I liked this one better. And now I liked softball, too, which had hitherto seemed like nothing more than an excuse to drink beer on a hard wooden bench between bouts of standing around waiting to drink beer again.

I looked at John, who shrugged. "I was recruited by the police team," he said. "It's a really easy sport. I figure it's good to know policemen. You never know."

"No, you don't," I agreed.

"Let's not forget there's a dead body here," Aria said with an edge to her tone. I glanced at her. She'd tightened her lips again and narrowed her eyes. I felt as though she were addressing her comment to me, but she was staring at the redwoods beyond the meadow. I wondered what was going on in her head. Were her religious beliefs being tested by the murder? Did she still trust the universe?

"Yes, there certainly is," the detective said. "Follow me." He gestured with his head and we set off.

I asked Aria where the center's residents were. The place was deserted except for the cops.

"There's a team of officers interviewing everyone in the dining hall. Apparently, we're all suspects to begin with."

By now, it was one o'clock. Her mention of the dining hall reminded me I hadn't eaten lunch and I was hungry.

"You wanna see the body?" Cardenas asked me once he'd stopped at one of the tables near the center of the courtyard. We weren't quite within earshot of the other cops, which wasn't an accident. He didn't want me overhearing anything.

"Not especially." I hadn't considered avoiding the awful sight, but once Cardenas offered the option, I found myself answering without hesitation. What was the point? I wasn't a scientist or a cop. Let them do their job. And how could I keep a lid on my feelings with the image of a headless corpse seared into my mind?

"Sit over there, then." He pointed to the wrought iron chair facing away from the well.

"Sure. Thanks."

We all sat down and looked at the detective. John's chair flexed and groaned under his bulk. An odd chemical smell seared my nostrils, a cross between glue and paint—a gift from the forensics team.

"Ask me questions," Cardenas said. "That's the cooperation part of this. Then I'll ask some."

Aria spoke up. "Thank you for taking the time to talk to us. I know you're very busy."

He nodded.

"Do you know who the poor man is?" she asked.

"We do not. As you know, the perp removed the identifying portions of the body. We know he's Caucasian and he's wearing a Keep Santa Cruz Weird T-shirt and a pair of old jeans, which doesn't tell us much. Maybe the shirt means he's a local. Maybe it means he's a tourist. Everybody likes that stupid shirt. But don't worry. We'll find out who our victim is.

23

Nobody stays a John Doe for more than a few days on my watch."

"Do you think this is likely to be connected to the threats I told you about?" she asked.

"I don't believe in coincidence," Cardenas told her.

"I don't either." Aria shook her head, emphasizing her agreement.

I was content to sit back and let the conversation unfold without me. I could pay attention to the details better when I wasn't thinking about what I was going to say next.

"What's your version of what it is instead of coincidence?" Cardenas asked Aria. He slid his chair forward slightly, and I wondered why he cared. Before Aria could speak, he continued. "What's your cult all about, Ms. Piper? Start with the no-coincidence thing."

"First of all, we're not a cult, a church, or a religion, Luis. May I call you Luis?"

"Make it Lou."

"Thank you. Please call me Aria."

He nodded.

"This is an educational center," she continued. "I'm a teacher, and the residents here are my students. One of the principles I stress is there are no accidents—no coincidences." This was her teacher voice. The words flowed out of her effortlessly, with conviction and authority. Her mouth relaxed, and the very present eyes were back. Maybe explaining something helped her recover from trauma. "All we need to do is pay attention, putting aside our conditioning and old patterns, and there it is to see—the perfect connectedness of everything."

"So," Cardenas replied, "you think the whole

world's just fine the way it is?" Clearly, he thought this was ridiculous. He raised his eyebrows, and his tone was an invitation to argue.

"Yes, and there's tremendous room for improvement, too."

He shook his big square head. "That doesn't make any sense. How can the world be perfect and also need improvement?"

I shot a look at John to see how he was taking this. He'd get a snootful more if he stayed and protected Aria.

John was rapt, zeroed in on Aria's face. Apparently, she'd struck a chord with him. That was good.

"It's not something that's going to make sense to you today, Lou," Aria said. "But we eventually have to learn how to accommodate paradox if we want to know truth."

"What about dead babies?" he asked, lingering on the last two words.

I had no idea what he was driving at. I was still puzzling out the paradox thing. Aria responded right away. Personally, I couldn't see the point of all this chatting, especially since Cardenas had given us permission to ask questions, which would've been much more useful. But it wasn't my place to direct things. Yet.

"Who are we to second guess what happens?" Aria said. "We can only perceive the world from our limited vantage points."

The detective shook his head again and pointed to the nearest building. "So this place is some kind of wacky metaphysics school, then. Am I right?"

Aria smiled. "From your vantage point, yes. Let's call it a wacky metaphysical school."

"So where was I?" Cardenas said, looking up and to the left.

"You think the threats and the murder are connected," I reminded him, "because you don't believe in coincidences."

"Yeah. Odds are they are. Let me ask you this, Gatlin…"

"Karl."

"Karl. You've been on this case for a few hours. Did you find out anything yet—anything that might help us out here?"

"Aria told you about the phone threats and her experience with your chief?"

Cardenas nodded.

"Did you notice the guy on the phone mentioned Satan?" I asked. "That's also on Reverend Crowder's website."

"No shit, Sherlock." Cardenas glanced at Aria. "Sorry."

"That's all right," she said. "We're all under a great deal of stress here. This is truly horrifying."

Her face was placid, though. She'd recovered for now. Perhaps she'd reminded herself of her faith by outlining some of her philosophy to Cardenas. I could see how a belief that everything was connected and always going the way it needed to go would be consoling in the face of a murder. Sometimes I wished I had an outlook that helped in that department, but I couldn't just graft on something that didn't make sense to me.

"All the fundamentalists talk about Satan."

Cardenas spit out the words as though these were terms he didn't even want in his head. "That's their deal. And don't worry about the chief. Nobody's managed to slap a muzzle on me yet. If his own mother murdered the guy, I'd nail her ass."

John glared at him. "That's twice, now. Let's watch the language, mate."

"Oh yeah. Sorry again, Aria."

Apparently, John's bodyguarding now included vocabulary guarding as well.

"What was the time of death?" I asked.

"It looks like about twelve hours ago—sometime in the middle of the night. When the forensic guys finish up, the coroner will give us something more exact."

"And the cause of death?"

"Unknown at this time. There's no trauma to the torso, so it was probably a blow or a shot to the head. And he was killed somewhere else and brought here." Cardenas shifted in his chair like he had hemorrhoids. Maybe I was projecting onto him. I'd had a nasty bout with them about six months earlier—an occupational hazard since modern investigating was mostly desk work now.

"Will you need to find the head to determine the cause of death?" I asked.

"I don't know. That's not my area. But disposing of body parts isn't much easier than getting rid of whole ones. Somebody's dog will probably find them in the woods or something."

"Will you use police dogs to sniff around in the forest here?" Aria asked. Her eyes focused on where the tree line started again. It was a ragged border, interrupted by a few scraggly shrubs and a shed or two.

Fifty yards from the trees, the redwood scent was still strong enough that, when I tried, I could pick it out amidst the chemical smell.

"We're doing that, but I doubt they'll find anything." Cardenas shook his head vigorously. "Why go to all the trouble of dismembering somebody if you're going to leave the parts nearby? And whoever did this made really clean cuts. Amateurs are the only ones who'd be stupid enough to discard anything nearby."

"So are you're thinking it's a gang hit?" I asked. I couldn't think of who else qualified as a professional dismemberer.

"Yeah, maybe. The Watsonville gangs haven't graduated to this kind of thing—yet. But there are some Hondurans moving into Salinas. They call themselves the Hombres. It seems like the newcomers are always the most brutal."

"Why would they come all the way up here to Santa Cruz and pick this well to dump the body in?" Salinas was a working-class agricultural town about an hour south of us. "And I thought you said this was likely to be related to the threatening phone calls."

"Hey, I'm just talking here. It's early," Cardenas protested. He held his palms up and shoved them toward me. It was both a concession and a pushback against what I'd said. He was a complicated guy. There was more to him than just the machismo.

"Sorry." I thought a moment. "Who found the body?"

Cardenas pulled out a tablet and tapped on it a few times. "It was a Ms. Sue Motti."

"Sumati," Aria said. "It's a spiritual name. Her

original name is Joyce Palacio."

"You give them new names?" Cardenas asked. He seemed more surprised by this than I would've expected. Lots of ex-hippies and spiritual seekers in town had weird names. He must've run into this a score of times.

"No. She'd already taken that name before I met her," Aria told him.

Cardenas nodded. "What's her role here?"

"She's one of my earliest students—from before we acquired this property. And she's an administrative assistant, as well." Fear and something else were creeping back onto her face. Resignation. She was beginning to accept the situation. I could see it in her beautiful brown eyes. Throughout my time spent with her, Aria's beauty stood out, sometimes distracting me, sometimes on the back burner of my attention. Now I looked away to break the spell.

I glanced at John again, who'd been uncharacteristically quiet. He was slouched down, shading his eyes from the sun. He winked at me as though that were a meaningful response.

"I talked to Sumati," the detective said. "Her background's pretty rough. What can you tell me about that?"

"Why don't you and I discuss that later, Lou?" Aria said gently. "I don't think it's any of these gentlemen's business."

"Yeah, you're right." He paused and then scowled at me as though I were judging him for what he'd asked.

"I have a few more questions," I said as sweetly as I could. "Is that all right?" Cardenas nodded again. This time it was one sharp motion. "How many men are going to be put on this case? And what assurance can you give my client that you'll be making a timely arrest?"

I'd pushed him too far. I could see that immediately. I usually antagonized alpha males sooner or later. It was in my DNA.

"That's it. That's all I'm going to tell you," Cardenas said with heat. His face flushed red, which wasn't easy given his skin tone. I put my hands up and leaned backward. Cardenas made an effort to control himself, but he glared at me as though I'd sucker punched his sister. This guy needed some anger management classes. And maybe a sedative.

"Karl's a good guy," John told Cardenas. "Don't worry about him. He's my ex-brother-in-law. We go way back."

"That's great, John. But I know you as a fun guy who hits home runs." He'd regained control of himself. "You could be the least reliable person in the world when it comes to vouching for people."

"I agree with John," Aria said. "And I've known Karl for fourteen years."

"All right, all right." Cardenas waved his arms around as though he were being attacked by bees. Then he looked at me appraisingly. "Maybe we got off on the wrong foot." He reached his hand out across the black wrought iron tabletop. "No hard feelings?"

"None at all." I weathered his viselike grip again. "I'm just grateful you're willing to talk to us. And obviously there are aspects of the case that you can't discuss." We both paused, which suited me. I needed the time to figure out how to get a little further onto his good side. "In terms of my investigation," I said, "so far I've been immersing myself in background information."

"Immersing, huh?" Cardenas said.

"That's right. But I did find a newspaper article about a woman who said she was assaulted by Reverend Crowder. I don't know if that has anything to do with this."

The detective grunted. "I'll check into it. What's her name?"

"Leanne Atkinson." I thought I saw Aria react to this, but I couldn't be sure. My peripheral vision was better than average, but hardly reliable.

"Anything else?" Cardenas asked.

"No."

"Okay, now that we're on the case, Aria won't be needing your services anymore. Thank you for your cooperation."

Aria spoke up immediately. "That's between Karl and me. And I certainly do need him."

Cardenas gestured with his arm again. I had no idea what this motion meant. It mimicked a man casting a fishing rod.

"I think I need John as well," Aria said, "and I imagine your budget doesn't allow you to provide protection for someone like me."

"No, it certainly doesn't." Cardenas turned and spoke to John. "Are you good at this? Can you handle yourself? I thought you were a welder."

"I'm good at lots of things." John threw his shoulders back and sat up straighter. "Wanna see me in action? Wanna fight?"

Cardenas almost smiled. "No, thank you."

Then he turned to face me. "Just stay out of our way, Gatlin. This is the nastiest crime in the county in a long time. This perp should not be running around thinking about who he wants to cut up next. And the media scrutiny is gonna be a major pain."

"Of course I won't interfere. You're preaching to the choir here. I'm guessing you had problems with Monterey Bay Investigations and you think we're all alike. We're not."

"Okay. Fair enough. Now I've got other things to do, so why don't the three of you make yourselves scarce?"

"We'd be happy to," Aria told him. "Come on, gentlemen. I'll show you around the property."

"That's a strange man," John said once we were out of earshot. "One minute, he's your friend. The next—who knows?"

"Shall we diagnose him?" I asked Aria.

"Let's not."

Chapter Three

More compact than it looked in the online photos, the property was also prettier. A redwood forest surrounded the six buildings on three sides. Most of the trees looked to be second growth, making them about a hundred years old. They weren't as massive as the ones in national parks, but some were just as tall. The meadow we walked through to get from one building to another was well landscaped, with groupings of flowers and shrubs.

Hand-lettered wooden signs sat at ankle height beside several of the gravel paths: "Find a way to cooperate with how things need to be." "Give yourself permission to be where you're at." And "You can count on impermanence."

Otherwise, the center looked like what it was—a school.

Our tour was cut short when we ran into Aria's head administrator, Paul, on the porch of her office, which adjoined her studio apartment. Unlike the rest of the buildings, it sported all the outward trappings of a cozy home, including a wood-shingled roof and elaborate eaves that reminded me of a witch's house in a storybook.

About my age—early forties—Paul wore a gray fedora that could've been on steroids. All the dimensions were exaggerated. If this style of hat had ever been in fashion, it wasn't now. For a moment, I had a fantasy that Aria made all her students wear silly hats—to stay humble or something. That didn't make much sense.

"Aria!" he called, without acknowledging our presence. How in the world could you ignore John?

"Yes?"

"It's the press. They're here, and they want to talk to you," Paul said with urgency. "This kind of scandal could ruin us. I can see the headlines now: 'Cult Murder Rocks County.' Or maybe 'Religious Weirdos Find Headless Corpse.' "

"It's the hat that's weird, mate." John pointed to it with a meaty hand.

"Whoa!" Paul stepped back involuntarily. "Who the hell are you? You're the biggest guy I've ever seen."

"I'm Aria's bodyguard. Who the hell are you?" That interested me. John didn't like the guy, and he liked pretty much everyone.

"Oh, I'm sorry." He put out his hand. "Paul Webb. I handle all the practical stuff around here."

The two men shook hands, and then Paul turned to me. He may have had a limited field of view, but when he focused on you, his gaze was powerful. The left corner of his mouth drooped just a bit. I wondered if he had Bell's palsy or some other neurological disorder.

"You must be Karl Gatlin," he said. "I'm glad you're on board. The world needs Aria. We have to get to the bottom of this to keep her safe."

"Of course."

For some reason, he didn't try to shake hands with me, so I didn't offer to either. He was quite handsome in a dissolute kind of way—as though he hadn't taken care of himself most of his life. Even so, his high, prominent cheekbones and big hazel eyes were striking.

He aimed himself at Aria again. "This really is imperative, Aria. We have to get a hold of the story before it gets defined by every Tom, Dick, and Harry in the tabloids."

"That's fine, Paul. I'm happy to talk to them."

"I don't get it," John said. "Who are these Tom and Dick guys?"

"It's just an idiom," I explained. "Aria, why don't I wander around and talk to people while you and Paul handle this? John will go with you, of course. That's how it works. He'll be your shadow."

"You can tell people I'm your fiancé." The Maori pointed again, this time to his ring finger.

She smiled at him. I couldn't tell if she was genuinely amused or just indulging him. I saw tension beneath the surface, though. Her grip on her feelings was still tenuous.

"Good plan," she said. "Let's meet back at my office in an hour or so. If you get here first, Karl, make yourself at home. And feel free to visit the dining hall. I imagine you've missed lunch."

"My stomach thanks you."

At the dining hall, after a brisk walk by several serious-looking adult students, I lunched on a quinoa salad, a kale salad, and a fruit salad. This put me way over my annual salad allotment. No matter what was in a salad, I always felt hungry an hour later.

A large, spare, well-lit room with rows of antique oak tables and an incongruous crystal chandelier, the dining hall echoed every sound that came its way, even silverware and footsteps.

Garrulous to a fault, Aldo the cook perfectly fit the bill for my purposes. Once I filtered out pure gossip, a report on his startling spiritual progress, and a robust salad endorsement, I found out a great deal about day-to-day life at the center. At this stage, it was hard to know what mattered, so I was happy to gather all the general information I could.

Aldo looked like a cook—or a chef, actually. He was plump. Not obese. And he wore a stained white apron over his white clothes, with a yellow baseball cap perched on his curly black hair. He'd managed to stain the cap as well. Pesto sauce, I figured.

He told me about forty full-time students lived at the center, and another seventy or eighty visited on the weekends. Most of these were local—from around the Monterey Bay. But some students drove from as far away as San Francisco, an hour and a half north. And others commuted from Silicon Valley, which was a forty-minute trip over the coastal mountains.

The daily schedule didn't sound like much fun. Up at six. An hour of meditation. Breakfast. Then two hours of chores—mostly ordinary things like washing dishes and sweeping. But the residents also took turns performing what Aldo described as "esoteric spiritual activities that you wouldn't understand." Once a week, students met with Aria one-on-one during their chore hours.

After a similar early afternoon schedule, students had four hours of free time, starting an hour before their salad-infested dinner. There were films and hobby clubs they could attend in the evenings. I was curious about what hobbies these people might be interested in. The cook showed me fliers for a knitting club, a book club, and a genealogy club. Pretty standard stuff.

On the weekends, when all the day-trippers showed up, Aria gave talks and met with these students. Everyone meditated a lot, too. And a committee organized special events—family day, field trips to various parks, and even a western swing dance once.

On Thursday mornings, Aria saw therapy patients somewhere else—Aldo the cook didn't know where. He seemed embarrassed that he didn't know everything there was to know, looking down and shuffling his feet like a schoolboy caught with contraband.

I left the dining hall and wandered around the grounds. More of the residents were out and about now. From the looks I received, they apparently thought I was a policeman. I get that a lot. Policemen are apt to be craggy, too.

Aria's students tended to be white, with a sprinkling of Hispanic and Asian men and women mixed in. I spied clusters of young adults, a rickety senior leaning on an aluminum walker, and every age in between. They could've been shoppers at a farmer's market or a ceramics class at a community college. No special spiritual qualities stood out.

I approached a young woman who was smoking in the shade of a live oak. She could've been going to a costume party dressed as a 1960s flower child. She had on raggedy denim overalls over a purple tie-dyed shirt, and she'd braided flowers into her blond pigtails. She was cute, with small, pointed features and a bow of a mouth.

"Are you supposed to be smoking?" I asked. As I drew closer, I could smell that it was pot. "Plus, there are cops all over the place."

"I've got a medical card." She ostentatiously took a drag on her joint and blew smoke at me. "And it's legal now, anyway. Mind your own business."

"Hey, do you want me to tell Aria you're being rude to her old friend?"

She squinted at me. I got the impression she usually wore glasses. "Did anyone ever tell you look like a younger version of that drunk, broken-down actor? Nick Somebody?"

"Nolte, yeah."

"Don't get me wrong. You're smushier-looking—and much uglier."

"Thank you," I responded, as though I'd received a particularly pleasing compliment. "I'll refrain from commenting on *your* appearance. Let's just say you're making a statement, although I'm not sure what it is. Fuck you, world?"

She smiled despite herself. "Yeah, basically. What do you want?"

"Can you help me find Sumati? I need to talk to her."

"She's probably over in the group room." The girl pointed to one of the smaller buildings close to the edge of the forest. Its tin roof glinted in the sunlight. "It's easy to pick her out. She's fat, and she has frizzy hair. She teaches the rules to newcomers."

"Do you think she's meeting with them today? Is it business as usual around here even with the murder?"

"Probably. They're all so fucking gung-ho." She shook her head and scrunched up her features, bringing her eyes, nose, and mouth together like a facial Pangaea.

"I take it you're not so enthusiastic?"

She snorted. I hadn't heard a good snort in a long time. "I can't wait to get out of here, but I've got no place to go, and I'm not hitting the streets again. Not after what happened last time."

I let that pass. Although we were getting along splendidly now, I had no interest in mining for personal history, and I doubted she'd want to tell me. "What's wrong with being here?" I asked. "It seems like a nice place."

I was treated to another snort. This one was more muted. Then she took another hit on her joint before looking away and answering me. "Aria's okay, but most of the other people here are total losers. They end up at a place like this because they're too screwed up to be anywhere else. And what they make you do here is ridiculous—all the meditation and everything."

"How'd you end up at the center?"

"My mother. She's been coming on Saturdays for years. She got Aria to take me. But believe me, I'm leaving soon. Next week at the latest." She said this with no heat, and I got the impression she'd proclaimed the same thing plenty of other times.

"Okay, thanks for your help."

She shrugged and turned her back on me. I was glad *I* wasn't trying to teach her anything.

Sumati sat by herself on a round, cotton candy pink cushion on the polished maple floor of the group room. As advertised, wild frizzy hair tumbled down her shoulders, and she must've been eighty pounds overweight. Her hair hid part of her face. What I could see was well-worn, with a scar over one hazel eye. I guessed she was thirty.

"You're Karl Gatlin? I'm Sumati. I heard you wanted to talk to me."

"Yes. Do you mind?"

She patted the cushion next to her, which was bright purple. A dozen cushions created a circle, each one a color rarely found in nature. The rest of the room was almost bare, with just a smattering of photos of indeterminate mountains on one of the light green walls.

I hunkered down, my bad knee complaining. I tolerated chairs. I didn't like cushions. "I won't take up too much of your time," I told her. "I know you've got a class to teach."

"It's more like an orientation." She looked up at me, her eyes expressing an unknown stew of emotions. "I'm not qualified to teach anything. And the new students are still talking to the police, anyway."

Sumati's voice was a rich alto. I figured she was a singer, and I wondered if there was a choir at the center. It was easy to picture her belting out old-time gospel tunes. Then I remembered that Jesus was not the protagonist of this particular narrative.

"How'd it go for you when you had your turn with the police detective?" I asked.

"Okay, I guess. That guy has a short fuse, though, doesn't he?"

"He yelled at you?"

"No, at some other cop. But it scared me. I've had some really bad experiences with men."

That might explain her weight and her face-obscuring hairdo. Sometimes abused women took themselves out of the game that way. I looked at her more closely, although I knew that might make her uncomfortable. She was very fair—like a country girl in an Irish movie. Perhaps girls over there looked like that in real life too. I wouldn't know. The closest I'd ever gotten to Ireland was cultural, not geographic—drunk on Guinness on the floor of an Irish pub in San Francisco.

"I was wondering," I said to Sumati, "why you were looking down into the fake well where the body was in the first place. Did you have a special reason?"

"It's not fake, exactly."

"Whatever." I've never had much patience for people who sidestep perfectly straightforward questions. I used to think that avoiding answering was a tip off about who was hiding something until I realized that virtually everyone hid something. Usually plural somethings, actually. It might be a lowly motive, a drinking problem, or something more sinister. There were lots of ways to differentiate between the innocent and the guilty. Avoidance wasn't one of them.

"Well," Sumati began hesitantly, "I got a phone call at the office that said 'Go look in the well,' so I did."

"On Aria's landline?"

"Yeah. She lets me use her desk when I'm doing the payroll and stuff." She was looking past me at the blank wall. I got the feeling this was her standard modus operandi, not a behavior stemming from the topic of our conversation.

"How many paid employees are there?" I asked, following my nose. It was an opportunity to find out more about how the center operated.

"Four. June the gardener, Paul, me, and the cook—Aldo. You should talk to him. He knows everybody."

41

"Thanks. You're a part-time employee? And a student of Aria's, too?"

"Yeah, both. I'm not a very good student, though. I should be a lot further along by now. But Aria says that if I just put one foot in front of the other and keep going, everything will work out." She looked me in the eye for the first time. She really wanted to believe what Aria had told her was true, but I could see she wasn't quite sure.

"That sounds like good advice," I said, throwing her a bone. "Can you describe the voice on the phone?"

"It was a baritone and creepy."

"Did he think you were Aria?"

"I guess so. I don't know." She leaned toward me so quickly, I thought she might fall. "What's it like being a private eye? Is it like in the movies?"

"Sure. Only everybody in real life is even better-looking than the movie stars. Especially me."

She laughed, and liquid waves of sound tore loose from deep within her, unlike like any laugh I'd ever heard before. It wasn't just loud, mellifluous, and continuous. It seemed to be bubbling up from deep within her—a primal laugh, if you will.

"I've gotta go see your boss," I told her when she'd returned to this world. "I'm late. Thanks for your help."

As I climbed down the front steps, I spied two middle-aged women shuffling toward the building. They must've been recruits heading for their orientation. One of them was crying, and the other held her head low. They'd given up their ordinary lives and hauled themselves to a spiritual center, ostensibly to find peace of mind. What they'd found instead was a murder investigation.

Chapter Four

Aria, Paul, and John were waiting for me inside Aria's rather ordinary office. She hadn't shopped at Goodwill, but wherever it was, the store hadn't been too far up the retail food chain from there. More photos of mountains sprinkled the light-yellow walls. What was with all the mountains?

I felt peaceful in the room. Perhaps it was simply my proximity to Aria.

"Sit, sit," Paul said. John winked at me. Aria smiled a real smile.

She sat behind her uncluttered red oak desk, and John and Paul shared an oversized brown love seat. I entertained a fantasy that John's weight would turn the thing into a seesaw and he'd launch his seat mate into the air. I took the only remaining chair, which faced all of them. I guess they'd been saving it for me.

"How'd it go?" I asked.

"She did great!" Paul reported.

I studied him. He was beaming as though he'd won a hat contest with that ridiculous fedora he was still wearing. I suddenly realized none of the people I'd talked to had uttered a word about him. Why was that? Was it because Paul was gay? He certainly seemed gay. Maybe he was just a nonentity compared to Aria. Or it could be something more relevant to my investigation.

"Are you a student here as well as an

administrator?" I asked him.

"Sort of." His eyes shifted down, and he crossed his legs elaborately, self-consciously.

Aria spoke up. "Paul's an old friend from before I became a teacher. He's the only one here who doesn't defer to me about everything. He keeps me honest. But the rigors of the spiritual life don't suit him. He lives offsite and participates on alternate weekends."

"She's too strict for me." Paul smirked at his friend. "Anyway, I've already got an internal critic that keeps me in line."

"Which reporters did you talk to?" I asked Aria.

"There were five of them. Two had video-camera operators with them. I guess they were local TV people. We're big news."

"We didn't let them take any images of Aria," Paul said. "But I think that's going to be a problem. When people in criminal investigations insist on privacy, it's suspicious."

Aria shook her head. "I explained my reasons for keeping a low profile. The same ones I told Karl earlier."

"Still," Paul responded. He finally took his hat off, an act he performed slowly, almost ritualistically. I think he'd forgotten he was wearing it. His completely bald head gleamed in the overhead light, which gave him more of a spiritual look, although I imagine people on the street assumed he was getting chemo.

I glanced at John and realized he probably hadn't eaten, either. I asked him if he needed to.

"Yeah, calories are where it's at for a big guy like me."

"Why don't you go down to the dining hall and see

if you can find Aldo," Aria said. "Tell him I sent you."

"Try the kale salad," I suggested.

He made a face.

"Maybe you'll like the quinoa salad better."

"Seriously?" He looked at Aria with concern. "Is he serious? Salad?"

She nodded, amused.

"Oh, God. The things I do for a paycheck. Are you sure you're gonna be safe here without me? Karl couldn't punch his way out of a paper bag."

John was aware I carried a compact Sig Sauer .380 in a hip holster. Ever since brawling with the rapist who'd given me my shoulder scar with his stiletto, I keep it handy. And I could street fight, too—just not as well as the big Maori could.

"The police are still on the grounds. I saw a few on my way up," I said, taking him at face value, although I knew he was teasing me. I didn't want our client to think we weren't serious about a gruesome murder.

"Okay, then."

He leapt to his feet, and we all flinched. He was amazingly quick for a man his size. For any man, for that matter. It was easy to imagine him rampaging on a rugby pitch.

When he'd gone, I asked Aria how he was working out.

"John's perfect. I love his energy."

"He's kind of a cross between a kid, a dog, and a man," I said. "And he's got the full spectrum of positive traits from all three."

She smiled again. I loved her smile. I found myself over-focused on her sensuous lips, ignoring all the body posture and other clues to understanding her. Aria was just achingly beautiful. And kind. And smart. If I wasn't careful...

The first day I'd interned with my Uncle Bud—in the midst of his passing on the PI business to me after I'd flamed out as a would-be therapist—he'd told me his cardinal rule: never sleep with a client. He'd also told me I wasn't suited to the detective business. He was old school—like the protagonist in a pulp novel. As far as he was concerned, if you ever talked about feelings, backed down from anyone, or "dressed like a fruit," you were "a pussy who oughta go write poetry, for fuck's sake." On the other hand, he was damned good at his job, very generous with his time and money, and endlessly patient with me. In the end, I won him over after I became proficient with a handgun, charmed several of his clients into bigger retainers, and bought him a double-wide mobile home in Bisbee, Arizona. Thank God, he retired to it a few weeks later.

"So what did you tell the reporters?" I asked Aria. "I'm curious."

"I said we were shocked and disheartened by someone bringing violence onto the tranquil grounds of our peaceful community. And I answered questions. Most of them were irrelevant to the matter at hand, but I did my best to satisfy the reporters. Paul had written up what he called 'sound bites,' and he shared those as well. They'll have a variety of quotations to choose from when they compose their stories."

"Were you an English major?" I asked.

"Yes, I was. Is it obvious?"

"Only to a trained investigator like myself." God, I was showing off. I quickly got us back on topic. "In every one of my cases that made the news, the reporters got all the important facts wrong. Don't expect much. That's my advice. Plus, they skew everything to play to people's fears. They want the public worrying about the murderer, and maybe worrying about a mysterious guru, too."

"Well, we'll see," Aria said.

I glanced over at Paul. He was asleep. "Does he do that a lot?"

"Yes."

Chapter Five

I headed home instead of back to the office. I needed to relax and just be by myself for a while. Like many introverts, I could playact as though I were an extrovert, as the situation called for, but the effort drained my energy. Some years ago, I'd endured a remarkably extroverted girlfriend who charged up from socializing, which would've been strictly her business and not mine, except then she demanded sex immediately afterward when I most coveted a nap.

I tried not to think about the case, which I was reasonably good at for someone who wasn't developmentally challenged, on drugs, or a Buddhist monk. If I let my early experience on a case percolate and then bubble up, it usually worked out better than trying to analyze things before I'd gathered enough data to warrant any conclusions. I used to continuously generate screwy theories as I worked to untie the knots of a case, but all this amounted to was a complex bias when I finally encountered the truth. Or I didn't. I even remember thinking "fuck the truth" one time when I was inordinately satisfied with an elegant theory I'd refined while chasing a bail jumper through Nevada. I remember the guy better than most. He'd stolen nearly two hundred thousand from a synagogue, and then when I caught him, he'd tried to justify his actions by arguing that Jews had killed Christ, so "those arrogant bastards" had it coming. Thank God most of my cases didn't expose me to lowlifes like that.

Matt brought Larry over around six. I had fifty-fifty custody of the most beautiful dog in the world. Lately, Matt was taking a turn as the buffer between Adele and me. It had been five months since our divorce was final, and she still hadn't calmed down. This was both a major pain in the ass and an ongoing reminder of why I'd needed to leave her. Like I needed any reminders.

Larry was a three-year-old mix of indeterminate breeds, but one of them was definitely Rhodesian ridgeback. He was big and muscular, with reddish-brownish short hair. Most people thought he was an exotic breed they'd never seen before. I told them he was an Albanian funhound.

It was great to see my pup—and he was mine, even if an idiot judge made me share him with Adele. Larry went nuts when he raced in, careening from room to room—all four of them. Then he tried to jump into me. Not onto me—into me. He had a strong urge to merge, as my mother used to say about her very Catholic brother. If Larry ever figured out how to do it, the Karl/Larry amalgam would probably be a major upgrade.

Matt stayed for what passed for dinner at my condo. I made cheesy rice burritos for all three of us—extra salsa on Larry's—and Matt and I discussed the case. He was a lot smarter than I was, a handy trait in an assistant.

"I agree with Cardenas," Matt said after I'd reported everything I could remember. "Forget about the threats for now. They've been trumped by the murder, and it totally sounds like a gang thing."

"Why do you say that?"

"Don't you?"

"Never mind about that. I want to know your reasoning, Matt."

"Well, the most common murders are between intimate partners, right?"

I nodded.

"I don't see a spouse getting so worked up they'd do something as gory as cutting off partner's head and hands. I know it obscures the identity of the victim, but it takes a certain kind of person to be able to do that."

"I'm with you, but suppose someone was a butcher or a surgeon. Or they could be delusional or psychopathic. Those people get married, too."

"Sure, but that's a really thin slice of demographic, Karl. None of those scenarios are very likely." He took a bite of his burrito and chewed it hurriedly. "So who else murders people? Pastors interested in making real estate deals? Squabbling spiritual groups? Anonymous phone callers? No, the next most common murderer is a gang member, and lo and behold, the ones around here deal drugs, too. That's number three on the list. So I've got my money on one of the three basic gang motives— a turf war, a respect issue, or a drug deal gone bad."

He paused to catch his breath. When Matt became excited, he talked faster than he could breathe. He wasn't eating much, either, although this was probably due to the cuisine.

Matt would've been a good-looking guy if he'd been born to different parents and possessed any sense of style. His dirty blond buzz cut accentuated the pointiness of his narrow face. His eyes were dark and deep-set. At work, he wore skinny black jeans and a faded, blue chambray button-down shirt. It was like a uniform. And no matter the temperature, he always wore black rubber flip-flops. Santa Cruz was a beach town, but that didn't keep the temperature from dipping down into the thirties in the winter. Matt wasn't self-conscious about his appearance, though. He felt good about himself, and he didn't care what other people thought.

We'd met on a case a few years earlier when his aunt had needed my help with a sexual harassment case. He'd worked for the same asshole as she had, and he'd helped me set up the harasser by planting a video camera in his office.

"You've done some reading today, haven't you?" I asked.

"Yeah. Quite a bit. We haven't had a murder since I've been here. So let me ask you this, Karl. Based on what you've found out so far, is there any group in this area that fits the bill? I'm talking about drugs, gang activity, and people horning in on other people's territory."

"Yup."

"Bingo. The Hondurans. And they like to dump bodies all over the place. In Texas, they left one in a men's room at the state capitol."

"What's the point of that?"

"Hey, I don't know. I guess to make sure everybody noticed what they did," Matt said.

"You're making a good case, but something doesn't fit."

"What?"

"I don't know. It's just a feeling I have from being

down at the center today. There's something else going on there. I'm not saying you're wrong, but it's not the whole story."

"Well, I've learned to trust your intuition, Karl, but that's kind of a conversation stopper. What am I supposed to say to that?"

"Don't say anything. Eat your burrito. I slaved over a grungy microwave for two and a half minutes so you could have a nice hot meal."

While Matt ate, Larry tried to climb onto my lap. He'd finished his own food in about ten seconds.

"That dog has no idea how big he is," Matt said.

"Yeah, he has a distorted body image. Maybe he should be in therapy. What's your take on Aria?"

"Well, it's clear she made quite an impression on you, but I couldn't tell much from meeting her." He took a few more bites of his dinner. Then he spoke again, more softly now. "Tell me what you think Aria looks like. I want to check something out here."

I started with a police-style description and then switched over to more of a personal take on her. "It's her eyes that are something special," I finished. "I mean, she's a striking woman all the way around, but I think I know why she attracts all those students. They want to have eyes like hers. It's like she really sees you, and everything she sees is okay with her. It's hard to explain."

"You're in love," he said. "It's obvious from the way you're describing her. It's been so long, you've forgotten what it's like. How many years were you with Adele?"

"Sixteen."

"And no one since?"

I shook my head.

"You're a goddamned ascetic, Karl. I don't know how you do it."

He took a few more bites of his burrito, which decided to spurt rice onto the floor, sending Larry sprawling across the white linoleum.

I'd been meaning to upgrade my place. The kitchen floor matched the elderly Formica countertops, and the faucet in the small sink had needed two new washers since I'd moved in six months before. The rest of the condo was more of the same. My complex had been one of the first in town, which made it affordable. Well, relatively affordable, given its proximity to the beach.

"Hold on," Matt said. "I thought you said you knew Aria years ago. Why didn't you fall in love with her then if she's so wonderful?"

"We both had partners and I was a moron—look who I married. Aria was different then, too."

"Different how?"

"Well, she looked great and she was a no-bullshit type, but she wasn't as evolved."

"Evolved? You mean, like spiritually?"

"More or less. Or maybe emotionally. She always looked at you in a real way—you know, with her full attention. But she struck me as someone who'd gotten by on her looks up until that point. I mean, why bother developing a personality if you don't have to? Anyway, I kept my distance. That wasn't a self-confident era of my life. I was a lousy counseling intern, and my girlfriend had me three-quarters convinced I was damaged goods."

"Why weren't you good at doing therapy?" Matt asked. "I mean, aside from being an insensitive clod who consistently ignores his employee's needs, you seem like you would be."

I ignored the barb. I enjoyed his sense of humor, but I was afraid if I encouraged him, he'd go overboard. I'd seen him with his brother, and it was brutal. "Well, I could figure out what was up with my clients, but I was damned if I could move them from point A to point Z," I said. "I mean, I knew how *I* went about things—how I changed. But it turns out most people are different from me. So everyone was a black box to me, with inner workings they weren't aware of enough to clue me in. I guess I was supposed to know already."

"What's different about the way you do things—how you change? I've never noticed anything."

"I'm a quantum-leap guy. It's never gradual—it's always a revolution, not an evolution." I realized this sounded rehearsed. Actually, it was a small-scale example of my process. Suddenly, I knew something well enough to fully and concisely explain it. The day before my conversation with Matt, I might've noodled around for a half hour and never stumbled onto anything coherent.

"Ah," Matt said. "So getting back to Aria. She's different now? Is that what you're saying?"

"Definitely. You need to spend some time with her. She has a presence—a poise. No, that's the wrong word. It's equanimity. That's what she has."

"It sounds like you want it too."

"Well, sure."

"Maybe you should join up—do whatever she did to get this way," Matt suggested.

"First, I've got to keep her alive and find out what's going on."

"What's your plan?" He fidgeted as though waiting for me to tell him was some sort of torment.

"I don't have one yet. You'll be the first one to know. How'd it go with the collection calls?"

Once I got him talking about that, he was off and running. The upshot was I was eight hundred dollars richer than I'd been the day before.

"You deserve a raise," I told him.

"Karl, you know I've got much more money than you do. And anyway, you can't afford it. I'll let you know when you can."

"All right." I picked up our plates and marched them to the dishwasher. "Larry needs another walk. You want to come?"

"Nah. I've got to get moving. I'm meeting Rachel at her mom's."

"Really? Her mom's?" Rachel was the woman Matt wasn't in a relationship with. Their partnership had every quality of a relationship that I could think of, but neither of them were willing to call it that.

"I love her mom. She's a hoot. Take care, bro."

He got up and tried to give me a hug, which was a game we'd been playing for weeks. I'd told him I didn't like to hug guys and now he was trying to "desensitize me." I sidestepped him this time, but Larry tried to get in on the abortive hug. He scratched my back, but hey, love hurts.

Chapter Six

I slept a little better than usual. Larry's a restless sleeper, and when he's chasing critters in dreamland, he lets out a continuous stream of muffled barks and growls. But he'd had a quiet night.

After our morning routine, which included a long walk—this time to Twin Lakes Beach—we drove to my office on the edge of downtown, next to one of the six health-food groceries in the area. One thing I'd liked about my previous location was the pizzeria next door. A developer had razed the entire strip mall to make a giant hole in the ground, still there three years later. Now my snacks were devoid of all the additives the kid inside me craved.

The office perched in the second-story corner of a newer stucco building, which some fool had painted baby shit brown. I had a view, if you count looking at a low-end Chinese restaurant and an battered black pickup truck eternally parked in the same space. An unsuccessful accountant, two chiropractors, and a physical therapist practiced in the other small office suites. The best thing about the building was the parking—six covered spots with a portico to the back door. And the shared bathrooms had been remodeled just prior to my moving in. They looked like something you'd find in the lobby of a four-star hotel, replete with marble countertops and fine art photos of God knows what. One looked like a barn on fire as seen by someone on acid. Another had been doctored to resemble a purple galaxy, but I could see ferns and a cat wearing sunglasses in there, too. I guess the photos constituted a Rorschach test of sorts. I'd hesitate to share my perceptions with a decent therapist.

Santa Cruz is perched on the northern tip of the horseshoe-shaped Monterey Bay, so the Pacific is to the south, not the west, and inland is north. Culturally, everything's rotated a quarter-turn sideways, too. The Keep Santa Cruz Weird T-shirts—plagiarized from Austin, Texas, by the way—were wholly unnecessary. It was weird and it would stay weird. Not only did we have multiple iterations of every conceivable type of alternative retail business, we spawned more tattoo artists and psychotherapists per capita than anywhere else in the country.

New Agers swear Santa Cruz is an energy vortex—whatever that is. If vortices attract people who think outside the box, then maybe we do. We also have a ton of surfers, many of whom don't think much at all.

Matt had beaten me to the office and was clacking away on his laptop at the desk in the outer office. He could type about eight thousand words a minute. Larry charged him but pulled up before a full-speed collision, settling for a hockey-style hip check.

"Good morning, Larry," Matt said. "Good morning, boss."

I returned the greeting. "Have you unearthed any startling new statistics that probably don't apply to our case?" I asked.

"Maybe, but if you're going to adopt that attitude, I'll just keep them to myself."

"You do that. I'll be in my office drawing up a plan of action. Once I get something on paper, I'd appreciate your feedback."

"Sure."

Theoretically, I could do stuff like this at home. But I never did. There were too many distractions. Larry settled on the carpet by my side as I slid into my oversized desk chair and pulled a legal pad out of a drawer. I'd percolated as much as I was going to at this stage; now I needed to enlist the logical part of my brain.

I decided to delineate the focus of the investigation—should it be the threats or the murder? As a one-and-a-half man show, I couldn't afford to stretch myself too thin. Early in my career, I'd taken on big cases and tried to run concurrent investigations. Not only were the clients disappointed in the results—there weren't any—but someone had gotten badly hurt (me).

Since Aria had hired me because of the nasty phone calls and the police were much better equipped to hunt down killers, I decided to stick to the original mandate for now. The threats were probably tied in with the murder, but I'd cross that bridge if the evidence led me to it. It was probably a moot point, anyway, since most murders were solved in the first forty-eight hours—gang killings included.

I could start in various ways. I could track down the groped university student, I could go meet Gary Crowder, I could head back down to the center and dig around, or I could do more research online.

I brainstormed a few more options, trying not to evaluate them until I'd made a comprehensive list. I could also go see the police chief, pretend to be a new spiritual student at the spiritual center (only a few people down there knew who I was), talk to Cardenas again to see how his investigation was going, go find some Hombres—the Honduran gang—and see what they had to say, or look into Sumati's past. Maybe it wasn't an accident that she'd been the one to find the body. We only had her word that there had been a phone call about the well, and apparently she had a sketchy past.

I could hardly call my list a plan of action, and I'd already strayed away from the threats over to the murder. I decided to see what Matt thought. I gave him a yell, and he strolled in a moment later.

"Karl, I've told you, all you need to do is press that button on your phone if you want me. I don't like the yelling."

"Personally, I don't like all the complaining. I guess we both have our crosses to bear. Have a seat, and see what you think of these ideas." I read them aloud and waited. As fast as Matt assimilated some things, I knew I needed to give him time with this. He was weighing an array of elements I probably hadn't considered.

"Well," he finally said, rubbing his hands together, "obviously, some of these ideas are stupid. Do not go find any Hondurans. And do you really think you could pass for a spiritual seeker? You?"

"There was that thing I said yesterday."

He studied my face. "You don't even have anything specific in mind, do you?"

"Well, no. But I remember it was something way spiritual. And you can't live in Santa Cruz without picking up the lingo."

"Yeah, but it helps if you know what the words mean, Karl. Anyway, the ideas I like are finding the coed and checking Sumati's story. If you approach either one of the Crowders prematurely, you'll just tip them off that you're sniffing around."

"Yeah, I was thinking that, too."

"Then why'd you put that one on the list?"

"I was brainstorming, Matt."

"Well, you didn't say that, did you? How was I supposed to know?"

I sighed. Matt felt free to blurt out all sorts of unproductive stuff, switching into a friend role when it suited him and retreating into an employee role when it didn't. On the other hand, my former receptionist Ruth hadn't been the sharpest pencil in the box, and the gal before that had stolen my car.

"I'll tell you what," I said. "You find out everything you can about Sumati, whose slave name is Joyce Palacio, by the way, and I'll try to hunt up Leanne Atkinson."

"That's the university student?"

"Well, she was back then."

"I'll get right on it." Matt jumped up, reminding me of John's much more athletic move the day before. Larry barked, thinking someone new had shown up. "It's just me," Matt told him from the doorway.

Larry went back to sleep.

I found Leanne's photo first. I liked to be able to visualize whoever I was researching. Apparently, Reverend Crowder had excellent taste in gropees. She was a peppy-looking blonde—a head cheerleader type. Her best feature was a full-lipped mouth, which didn't quite obscure her perfect teeth.

Ms. Atkinson had moved up in the world. She'd graduated with honors from UC Santa Cruz, and was now working on a doctorate at Stanford in holistic environmental studies, whatever that was. It sounded like the degree you needed in Silicon Valley to become a janitor. She'd also married to a guy who ran a nonprofit that provided healthcare to farm workers.

Stanford had given her a teaching assistantship as part of her financial package, so a perusal of the online school catalog let me know where she'd be later that morning—teaching a section of Introductory Ecology in Building 320. Palo Alto was an hour north. I liked it up there—great restaurants, a dog-friendly vibe, and thousands of extremely smart young people.

"Road trip!" I called out.

"What are you—sixteen?" Matt called back.

I could've phoned Leanne. But it was easy to say no to someone in my line of work on the phone. I could be quite charming in person. With Larry as my wingman, we'd jollied many a recalcitrant witness into hours of careless chatter.

Most of the trip up was picturesque. The first leg of Highway 17 wound through the forested mountains between the coast and the Santa Clara Valley. Larry lay on the passenger seat of my Mazda during this stretch. The blind curves, steep grades, and narrow lanes served as a filter that kept the Santa Cruz county's population down. You had to be intrepid to commute on the road, which at one time—before they installed concrete dividers—had been nicknamed Killer 17.

From there, we inched along a freeway that slipped between all the high-tech campuses of Silicon Valley. Now Larry sat up, fascinated by the lack of scenery.

Then on the latter part of Interstate 280, we both watched a slew of luxury cars zoom by us as we passed through rolling hills and huge estates. This was a wonderful part of the country if you were rich. Otherwise, you commuted in horrible traffic from someplace a lot crappier than where you worked.

You can't park on the Stanford campus. There are about three spaces for visitors, and they're always full. If you're a student, ruthless parking officers tow your car before you can run into your professor's office, argue a grade, and run out again.

So we parked off campus and hiked in. I outfitted Larry with his green service-animal vest so we could go wherever we wanted. I only did this on the job, and even then it stretched my ethics. Larry hated the vest. He knew it made him look dorky, and I think he suspected it cut down on his action with the ladies. He's always been in denial about having been neutered.

Quite a few students stopped us to meet Larry and ask what breed he was. This was par for the course, and I'd left enough time for it. I got one laugh about his being an Albanian funhound, but all the others took me seriously. I could never decide if this was a litmus test of people's sense of humor, self-absorption, or gullibility.

We arrived early to the classroom building, so we sat on a wooden bench across the alley from it. I enjoyed the people watching—well, half the people. My watching has always been markedly gender-biased.

A campus cop snuck up on us from behind. "Sir?

"Yes?"

He strode around in front of us. He was an imposing older African-American with a beige band-aid on the side of his nose. Didn't they make darker ones now? I grabbed Larry's leash and held on tight. I could tell he wanted to go jump on the nice stranger.

"You'll have to get that dog down from there. These benches are for people." He wasn't worked up about it. He was just delivering news.

"Sure. Sorry." I persuaded Larry to move, and he sat upright on the sidewalk in front of me, watching the cop.

"May I ask what your disability is, sir?" He glanced at Larry's green vest.

"Actually, you may not."

"Excuse me?"

I pulled out my copy of the federal ADA statutes and handed it to him. "Check out the highlighted part."

He took a minute and read it at least twice. Students starting streaming out of the building across the street. "Oh, I'm sorry. We should've gotten a training on this."

"Yes. There are a lot of litigious people out there. And you have very deep pockets here, don't you?"

"I suppose so. You have yourself a good day." He pivoted military style and strode away.

I almost missed my quarry. She strode out of the front door just as the cop departed. He'd ruined plan A, so I went with plan B.

"Excuse me," I called. "Do you have a minute?"

I could see her glance at me momentarily and then focus on Larry. "Oh, what a beautiful dog."

We strolled over to her. "I think he's the most wonderful creature in the world," I told her.

She was shorter than I expected, and her smile was even more radiant than in her photos. She wore navy corduroy pants, a white shirt, and a black blazer. Unlike all the women at Aria's center, she'd enhanced herself with makeup and several pieces of jewelry beyond her wedding ring—silver half-moon earrings and an opal pendant. I upgraded her from head cheerleader to homecoming queen. In person, she reminded me of an actress in a popular sitcom. Most people remind me of someone else. I don't know why. Usually I can't remember exactly who.

"What kind is he?" Leanne asked. By now she was down on one knee, patting Larry on his head and neck. His tail thumped, and his eyes lit up.

"Who knows? What's your guess?"

"Hmm." She cocked her head, so Larry did too. "Oh, how cute. Look at him. What's his name?"

"Larry." He glanced at me when he heard his name.

Now she finally looked closer at me, too. "That's not a dog's name. Why would you name a dog Larry?"

"It's kind of personal. I don't even know you."

She stood up and held out her hand. "Leanne Kristof."

"Karl Gatlin." I shook her hand. "I'll tell you what, If you guess the one breed I know Larry is, I'll tell you about his name, and as a bonus, I'll tell you why I want to nail Reverend Crowder on a class-two felony."

"Whoa." She stood and took half a step back. "Who are you?"

"I'm a private investigator, and I've been hired by a spiritual teacher who's being threatened by someone. We think it might be Crowder."

Larry was confused. Where were his pats? What was going on?

"Who's the teacher?" Leanne asked.

"I don't usually share that information."

"I don't usually keep talking to people who are stalking me."

"Good point." I thought it over and decided that Aria wouldn't mind. "It's Aria Piper."

A series of emotions washed across Leanne's face. I couldn't decode them. Was she suppressing a grin in the midst of it all? That would be strange.

"Hold on," she said, pulling a giant phone out of her olive canvas messenger bag. She pressed a single button—the number was in there already, whoever it was.

"Hello?" she said into her phone. "It's Leanne Kristof. There's a man in front of me who says he's a detective working for Aria Piper." She listened intently for a while. Gradually her face softened. "Okay, yeah. I'll do that."

She hung up and reached for Larry again. He snuggled up to her. "I'm going with Vizsla and ridgeback," she said.

"We have a winner. I'm pretty sure about the ridgeback part." I wanted to ask her about the phone call, but I let her play it out the way she wanted.

"So why is he named Larry?"

"I had a brother named Larry. He died when I was nine and he was six."

"God, I'm sorry. I shouldn't have made you tell me that." Her wide mouth turned down at the corners. I interpreted this as empathy, not guilt.

I liked Leanne. She was a nice person. And a major dog lover. "It's okay," I said. "No one ever makes me do anything."

"Let's sit." She gestured to the bench.

"Sure."

We settled in, and for some reason Larry left us both alone and lay on the grass behind the bench. Leanne gazed at me evenly. She was in no hurry, and I wasn't going rush her. I still didn't know what the hell was going on.

"The thing is," she eventually said, "Aria's my therapist. Or she was, I should say."

"Oh." I was surprised. I imagine my face reflected that.

"So I'd love to help. I just had to be sure you were being straight with me. That was her on the phone."

"You're okay talking about this?"

"Yes. Aria can't break confidentiality about me, of course, but I can do whatever I want from my end. And I'll do everything I can. She's the reason my life works now. Aria's amazing."

"I agree. That's great."

I was still playing catch up with all the implications of this revelation. It looked as though Aria knew a lot more about Crowder than I'd thought, even if the information was privileged. Maybe his beef with her wasn't about real estate, after all.

"Crowder is dangerous," Leanne said. "It's not just sex. He's a hypocrite about everything, and he's the most ambitious person I ever met."

"How does such a creepy guy like that get his hooks into people? Why do people join his church?"

"He's charismatic." She swiveled to face me more directly. "Here's something Aria said to me about somebody else, but it totally applies to Crowder. He believes his own bullshit. Do you know what I mean?

His lies don't come across as lies because when he says them, he believes them himself."

"I understand."

"And he's got big money behind him. I don't know where it's coming from." She tucked a strand of straw-colored hair behind her ear.

"How do you know about the money?"

"I hired your competition back when I filed charges against him. Monterey Bay Investigations. Sorry. I ran out of money before they got very far."

I thought about this for a moment and then filed it away to look into later. "Do you know what happened at Aria's spiritual center yesterday?"

"No. What?"

I filled her in about the murder. I don't think it really sank in. She was responding to what I said as if it were the plot of a book or a movie. That's how I used to be before I'd gotten into this line of work.

Then she provided a detailed account of her molestation. It was hard to hear. It had been much more than a grope. It reminded me why I wasn't cut out for counseling. By the time she was done, I wanted to get in my car, drive to Santa Cruz, and beat the hell out of Crowder.

Chapter Seven

On the way back to Santa Cruz, Larry and I stopped off for lunch at a Mexican restaurant in San Jose, owned by a grateful former client. The guy had a beach house in Capitola—just south of Santa Cruz— and somebody had been vandalizing it whenever there was a full moon. I caught the perp, who was not a werewolf. Those were just the nights he happened to have off.

We ate in our own private dining area, also known as the storage room since I wasn't about to slap a vest on Larry to be in the dining room. Surrounded by shelves and stacks of boxes, it felt cozy in there. Safe. Silvio made us two custom lunches—extra salsa for Larry.

When I finished my red snapper enchiladas, I called and checked in with John Ratu.

"Karl! Nice to hear from you, bro."

"How's it going down there?"

"Everything's fine, but people are real upset about the media. Have you seen the papers?"

"No, I forgot to look."

"It's bad. They called them a cult, and the TV said Aria was an enigmatic guru."

"She just doesn't want her picture taken," I said.

"I know. Aria's wonderful. I'm definitely in love."

"If you keep this up, I'm telling Lotus."

"Aw, man. Don't do that. She's the best thing that ever happened to me." He realized what he'd said. "Of course, your sister is a great person too, Karl. I'm so glad I married her, even though it ended the way it did."

"Yeah, yeah. Anything else I should know?"

"They found out who the body was."

"And?"

"It's just some guy. Nobody knows him."

"Is he a gang member?" I asked.

"I don't know."

"Could you be any less helpful, John?"

"I don't know. Maybe."

"Do you know the victim's name, at least?"

"Hold on. I wrote it down."

There was long pause.

"John?'

"Yes."

"You're driving me crazy."

"Sorry, mate. Here it is. Wayne G. Sharp. That mean anything to you?"

"No. How'd they figure it out?"

"I don't know. I was there when they told Aria, but she didn't ask them that."

"Okay, John. Just keep her safe."

"You bet," he promised.

I called Aria next and filled her in on my progress so far. I didn't always stay in close touch with clients during an investigation, but it felt right with her. It was strange telling her about my conversation with Leanne, since I was sure Aria knew much more about her than I did, even if she couldn't acknowledge it.

I thought of something. "You knew I'd find out about the abuse and talk to Leanne, didn't you?"

"Of course."

"What else have you orchestrated here, Aria?" I didn't mean to inject an edge into my tone, but I could hear that I had.

"Are you defecting to the evil-guru camp, Karl? Do you think I'm using you somehow?"

"Hardly. But if you know anything more that isn't privileged, I need to know it, too."

"There are things I could talk about with you, Karl, but you don't have the background to understand them."

"Try me." I had no idea what she was talking about.

"Okay, here's the condensed version: physical events have associated energy phenomena, and the two arise simultaneously. I can sense the energy patterns and then infer the corresponding circumstances."

"You're right. That doesn't make any sense to me. But I'm not asking you to explain how you know things—just what you know."

"They're intertwined," she said.

"Why do I get the feeling you're not working with me here?"

"Karl, I'm requesting that you trust me to tell you what's relevant to your work, and to withhold from you that which wouldn't be appropriate."

"I hear you. I guess we'll see how that goes." We agreed to talk the next day and said our good-byes.

Matt was taking the nap I wanted when I got back to my office. Not for long, since Larry romped in ahead of me. Reunions trumped naps in Larry's world—as long as the naps weren't his.

I told Matt about Leanne and my phone calls.

"That's interesting. I'll look into Crowder's backers," he told me when I'd finished. "And Aria called here and left me the victim's name on the machine."

"Yeah, I got it from John. Let's talk more later." I gestured for him to get the hell off my couch.

"Okay."

I sat at my desk and ruminated about the case. This was a lot like thinking, but less productive. After about ten minutes, the phone rang. Matt got it after two rings.

"Yo, Karl," he called. "It's for you. It's Reverend Crowder."

I probably should've gathered myself and called him back later, but instead I struggled to my feet and picked up my landline. I knew Matt would be monitoring the call from his desk, too.

"Hello. Karl Gatlin here."

"Good afternoon. This is Gary Crowder. I assume you know who I am?" His voice was pleasant but had a no-nonsense quality to it. He wasn't going to waste words on me.

"I certainly do."

"I believe it would be a good idea if we met."

"Why might that be?"

"I'd prefer to explain in person," Crowder said.

"All right."

"I'll be at my ranch tomorrow morning—down in Corralitos. Would that be convenient?"

"Sure." I was winning the fewest words war, so I had some to spare. "Would you mind if I bring my dog?" I had Larry for one more day before Matt took him back to Adele's.

"Please do, as long as you think he'll get along

with mine. Shall we say nine o'clock? Let me give you the address." It was on Browns Valley Road, not far from the Glaum egg ranch—a local landmark.

"See you then."

Matt ambled in. "That was interesting. What do you think he wants?"

I shrugged. "Probably he wants to find out what I know, but maybe he wants to tell me his side of things or warn me off."

Matt nodded. "How do you think he knows about you?"

"That's a good question. I have no idea."

"You think Larry likes Airedales?" Matt asked. "Crowder's got a pack of them, according to an article online."

"We'll find out."

I was sitting behind my desk, and Matt was standing. He took his time studying my face as he sat down in the chair across from me. He did this periodically for no discernible reason. Perhaps he liked to assess my mood, although I wasn't a moody guy.

"You want to hear about the victim?" he asked.

"Sure."

"Wayne G. Sharp was a local, born and raised in Santa Cruz. He worked as a financial advisor, and he came from a famous family." He looked up at me expectantly.

"Don't tell me. He's a Kennedy."

"A Zoppi."

"The fishing people?"

"Yeah. His cousin still owns two of the restaurants on the wharf, a fleet of boats, and a ton of property. It's his mother who was a Zoppi. She married a guy named

Sharp. Apparently, back then, his not being Italian was a big deal."

"What else?" I asked.

"Well, Wayne wasn't part of Aria's community, he wasn't a member of Crowder's church, and he had no criminal record."

"So no connection to a gang?"

"It doesn't look like it." Matt shook his head and then poked a finger into his ear and wiggled it around.

I'd given up talking to him about this. To me, ears were something you messed with in private. Matt argued that if a body part wasn't associated with a fluid such as mucus, saliva, or urine, then it was fair game. "What about ear wax?" I'd tried once.

"It's a solid," he'd said. "A cusp solid, I grant you."

That was as far as I got. It had been one of the more absurd conversations we'd had, and that was saying something.

"Was he a missing person?" I asked.

"No, and that's odd. His wife said she didn't notice he was gone."

"How'd you find that out?"

"You don't want to know, but my information's reliable. Georgia Sharp said they live in different parts of a big house. I looked it up. It's giant, actually. And they're legally separated."

"Where's the house?"

"In Pasatiempo." This was a gated community just up the hill from town. The homes were grouped around a famous golf course, designed by the same guy who'd created Augusta National, where they played the Masters tournament.

"Where'd he get the money for that?" Even the least expensive property up there was worth well over two million. A giant Pasatiempo home would go for at least six.

"Not from his wife and not from his job. He wasn't particularly successful in his career, and she's a schoolteacher from a middle-class family. It's probably an inheritance from his mother, but for some reason I couldn't find any record of it." He looked away as if he expected himself to know everything.

I repressed my urge to comment on this. "What else did you find?"

"He was a Mason, a golfer, and a recovering alcoholic."

"Any kids?"

"No."

Larry decided to get up and try to climb into Matt's lap at that point. After fighting him off, Matt continued, narrowing his eyes and glaring at Larry.

"They have a vacation home up at Lake Tahoe and a time-share on Maui. He drove an Audi A8. None of the other Zoppis live such a lavish lifestyle. Anyway, it's the only thing out of the ordinary I could dig up."

"How'd they identify him?"

"They found the head." Matt grinned incongruously.

"Where?"

"I'll give you a hint: woof!"

I pondered that for a while. Matt woofed again. Larry woofed back. "That sounds like the king of terriers," I finally said. He would only have asked me to guess if the answer was pertinent to the case.

"Yup."

"You were holding out on me."

"Yup."

"Crowder's ranch, huh?"

"In his barn. One of his Airedales found it."

"Just where Pastor Gary hid it, huh?" I said sarcastically.

"Yeah, right." His sarcasm was subtler than mine.

"Matt, you could've led with this. I just talked to the guy, didn't I?" I could feel a frown pulling down hard on the corners of my mouth.

"That wouldn't have been nearly as much fun. You should've seen your face when I barked."

I took a few deep breaths. This was just the kind of nonsense I'd instructed him to eliminate from his repertoire. As it happened, there was no harm done this time. "Do you think the police know more about this?" I asked. My voice was calm, and I hoped my face didn't reflect my irritation. What would be the point? If I let everyone who irritated me know it, I'd end up dealing with the fallout from that all day, which would probably compound the feeling.

"The police know exactly what we know. No more, no less." Matt held his features perfectly still.

"Ah." That was alarming. Apparently, he was hacking the police computers.

"So what do you want me to do next?" Matt avoided my gaze by glaring at Larry again, who for his part was staring at a bug on the window pane.

"Go home. What time did you get here today?"

"Six a.m."

"Go," I told him.

He nodded and took off.

Larry was bereft.

"What about me?" I asked. "I'm still here."

He fell back to sleep. Larry's grief, however deep, was short-lived. It was his indifference that endured.

Chapter Eight

I woke up early the next day, a tad hungover from the two beers I'd swigged at dinner. Now that I was older, I felt worse after two than I used to feel after four. I knew I ought to give up drinking entirely, but who could eat my cooking without numbing a few taste buds first?

To give Larry his best chance to play nice with the Airedales, we walked farther than usual after breakfast. A tired dog is a good dog.

It had been foggy on the walk, but when we set out in my Mazda for Crowder's ranch, the sun broke through, creating sparkles on the surface of the bay. You could see across the Monterey Bay from our street, if not from my condo itself. Monterey and Pacific Grove stared back at me through a bit of post-fog haze. I couldn't make out individual buildings across the nineteen-mile gap, but I could see where the hills of the peninsula left off and the Santa Lucia Mountains loomed behind them. Sailboats and fishing boats skated across the choppy water in the foreground, and I spied several large vessels in the open ocean beyond it all.

I lived near the mouth of the San Lorenzo River, and wherever I headed, the first part of the trip took me along the cliffs above Seabright Beach. I could've bought a bigger condo inland—Adele and I had sold our place and split the profits—but like the real estate agents say, it's all about location. I had no regrets, and Larry loved it.

The ride down south was ordinary enough until we turned off the freeway at Freedom Boulevard and began to wind our way through a series of small farms. A black pickup truck came up fast on our tail and leaned on what must've been an aftermarket horn. It was so loud, Larry howled in pain. Sometimes I got stubborn in these situations, but in this case, to save my dog's hearing, I slowed and pulled over into a turnout to let the asshole get by me.

That wasn't the deal. The driver veered off the road too, blocking my car. As the big truck squealed to halt, I drew my gun and held it low in my lap. Several cars zoomed by. They probably just assumed I had a mechanical problem and a good Samaritan had stopped to help me.

Two small, dark-skinned men climbed out. I immediately thought of the fabled Honduran gang.

"Stay calm," I told Larry. Sometimes that worked, sometimes it didn't.

Both men's hands were at their sides, but the one on the left had his fists clenched and the one on the right was wearing a shoulder holster under a loose blue flannel shirt. They both wore new jeans with the cuffs rolled up. Oversized cowboy belt buckles gleamed in the light—a bull's horns on one and a set of spurs on the other. Bull guy sported black work boots, and spurs guy wore a pair of brown cowboy boots. They looked Hispanic.

I decided to wait in the driver's seat so I could keep my pistol hidden. Larry began barking frantically. He didn't like them at all.

"Good morning," the one with the fists said in heavily accented English as he approached my window. The other one split off and headed for Larry's window, which wasn't good. If I pulled my gun on my guy, the other one would be behind me. On the other hand, Larry had his head out the halfway open window and was snarling and snapping. That guy wasn't going to able to get close to the car.

I rolled down the driver's side window. "What can I do for you?" I asked cheerily. The more I misrepresented myself as some clueless milquetoast, the more advantage I'd have if things got messy.

A fierce-looking acne-scarred face stared at me. Even the guy's forehead was pitted. He was probably in his mid-thirties. He didn't seem fazed by the crazy dog next to me.

"You can shut the fuck up and listen," he said. I would've preferred an angry demeanor to what I got—a businesslike approach. He didn't raise his heavily accented voice or add anything to the words themselves. If you didn't have to work yourself up to be threatening, then you probably were already.

I mimed closing a zipper on my lips. The guy was puzzled for a moment. Why wasn't I scared? Was I too stupid to understand what was going on?

Then he continued. "We work for somebody who doesn't want you working for Crowder. So turn around and go home."

"Who's that? Who are you working for?"

"Shut up. If you ignore this warning, you're gonna get hurt bad."

"You should threaten to hurt my dog, too. I love my dog. That would really motivate me."

Again, he was momentarily confused. "Okay, we'll kill your dog. You happy?"

"Yes. Very good. If a job's worth doing, it's worth doing well."

"Fuck you," he said. Then he called to his partner. "Show him the gun."

The guy responded in Spanish, which I happened to know. "What?" he said. "I can't hear you with this fucking dog."

My guy repeated himself.

"Larry!" I called. "Quiet!" I wanted both men to be able to hear me. Fortunately, Larry obeyed.

The second man pulled out a new 9mm Glock and waved it around. Maybe that kind of thing worked on somebody, but not me.

"Nice gun," I said. "But I like mine better." I raised my pistol and aimed it at the man on my side of the car.

He didn't flinch, but he held himself rigid. He'd had guns pointed at him before.

"Mine's smaller," I said. "But if your friend shoots me, you'll die too."

The man called to his partner again, this time in Spanish too fast for me to follow.

"Okay, okay," he said to me. "The gun's gone. We'll be on our way now."

I took a peek behind me. My sightline was clear since Larry had settled down in his seat. The gunman—another very ugly dude with similarly scarred cheeks—had his hands up. He was smiling an unconvincing smile.

"Have him step over next to you," I told the one by me.

"Sure. No problem."

As the second thug came closer, I could see that what I'd mistaken for scars were facial tattoos—a cascade of small blue tears on his cheeks. Prison work. When they were both beside me, I addressed my guy. "So I'm going to ask you again. Who sent you?"

"Go ahead and shoot us if you want." He was serious. I'd heard the bravado version of this statement before. I knew the difference.

"Maybe I will." He didn't flinch. I considered my options. Both men waited patiently as though however things turned out was all the same to them. Maybe you didn't join a gang like theirs until you didn't care about a long life anymore. "Okay," I told him. "Here's what you can tell your boss. I already have a client, and I have no interest in helping Crowder with anything."

"Who's your client?" The guy wasn't a quitter—I'll give him that.

"You've got some cojones on you—asking me that. Now get the hell out of here."

They sauntered back to the truck, making a big show of how they weren't scared. Then they took off, tails of gravel shooting out the rear wheel wells of their truck.

I wrote down the plate number, called it in to Matt, and asked him to call Cardenas and fill him in. I was late for Reverend Crowder.

It took a while for the adrenaline to leach out of my system. I hadn't needed to pull my gun in a long time. I wondered why they'd threatened me. I hadn't found out squat yet. Maybe they knew some squat was coming.

Chapter Nine

Crowder's ranch didn't look like much from the road. The off-white mission-style house sat behind several horse-free horse paddocks. Everything looked old. Not quaint or historic. Just old.

Three unshorn Airedales tore across the dirt field to meet us at the gate. Larry barked his happy bark. That was a good sign.

I pressed the recalcitrant call button on an ancient metal intercom that was nailed to a fence post, and someone immediately buzzed us in. I was afraid that one of Crowder's dogs might run out onto the road, but none of them expressed any interest in doing anything but barking back at Larry. What a crew. The biggest one was about three-quarters Larry's size, and the runt was only about a third. They all seemed like real characters. When you don't trim an Airedale's fur, it grows out like a snaky brown and black afro, or maybe a dense bush native to somewhere like Borneo.

We drove up the long gravel driveway as they ran along both sides of us like marauding Native Americans in a 1950s movie. This was a big event in their universe. I hoped it wouldn't be too big a one in mine. I just wanted to have a chat, evaluate Crowder, and move on.

An African-American guy almost as tall as John Ratu and maybe two-thirds as wide met us up at the rambling one-story house. He had his arms crossed, which accentuated his taut biceps, and his steady gaze in the midst of all the excited dogs impressed me. He didn't give a rat's ass what they did. All his attention was on me. I wondered why a pastor needed a bodyguard.

I opened my door, but before I could climb out, Larry scrambled across my lap and leapt out to meet his new friends. The Airedales started chasing him, but everyone's tail was wagging. None of them were fast enough to keep up with him. Larry was a wonder in motion—a slimmer, furrier, smellier version of John. If they ever invented canine rugby...

"Good morning," the man said. "You're late." He had a Chicago accent, which you hardly ever heard in our area. His spread-out nose dominated his well-worn face, and his brow was scarred in several places. Maybe he'd been a boxer.

"Sorry about that. There was an incident on the road. I hope you haven't been standing here waiting."

"I have. Come with me." This guy was obviously angry. I decided that I didn't like that any better than the businesslike deal, after all. Maybe this was because he was so much bigger than the guy in the truck.

"And you are?" I asked.

"The guy you're going to follow. Let's move it."

Aria would not want this man on her land, I thought. If my showing up late was enough to set him off, how did he handle himself when something more challenging came his way?

When we got to the wooden front porch, he turned to face me. He'd gotten over his anger already, which seemed weird. The leathery skin on the bottom half of his wide face was littered with thick but spotty stubble. His nose had been broken more than once and tilted to the left. His eyes were a bit dead but weren't all the way at the Balkan hitman end of the I-don't-give-a-shit-about-anyone spectrum. I could imagine him smiling when he played with his kids. I couldn't imagine him smiling at me.

"Oh yeah," he said. "I need to ask you if you're carrying." His bass voice was a bit raspy like he was recovering from a cold.

"I am. I've got a permit."

"You'll need to surrender your weapon." We stood right in front of the oversized redwood door now, but apparently I wasn't going through it.

"No," I said. I didn't figure I'd need it, but I also wasn't going to do things on Crowder's terms—or this guy's. He was rude.

"That's not acceptable." He raised his voice slightly and then filled his lungs with air. This accentuated his barrel chest.

"Fine. We'll leave." I called Larry, and he came tearing back, trailed by the pack of dogs.

"Sit!" the big guy called. All the Airedales sat down. I felt like doing it myself; the guy mustered quite a commanding voice.

Larry stood next to me, panting.

"Leaving is not acceptable, either," the guy said. "I can take that gun from you."

"I doubt it. Larry, growl," I commanded.

He went into pre-attack mode, his eyes narrowing and the thin ridge of fur on his back rising. Then he began to snarl and growl. His teeth were bared, and slaver formed around them. Although I knew it was an act, I always felt a stab of fear whenever Larry went at it. I guess our species was hardwired that way.

"Whoa," the guy said, raising both palms in the air. He wasn't as alarmed as I expected, but my point was made. "Lemme check with Pastor Gary."

He ducked into the house, and I told Larry to stand down. "Good boy," I said, patting him on the head. The other dogs were all still sitting—and Airedales are a headstrong breed. Impressive.

Gary Crowder came to the door. "Sorry about that," he said. "If you're more comfortable remaining armed, that's fine."

He looked even better than his photos, and I could see what Leanne had meant about his charisma. I liked him immediately. I had no reason to, but I did. He was warm and personable, or at least he was successful at projecting that in just two sentences. And he smelled great—like an herb garden.

I held out my hand. "Karl Gatlin."

He strode across the porch and hugged me before I realized what he was doing. I guess it was some Jesus Is Everything deal. Larry barked.

"It's okay, boy," I told him. It wasn't. It was creepy.

He stood back. "Let's go sit on the back patio," he said. "I can offer you fresh lemonade. We can watch the dogs play. That's a beautiful animal you've got there. A ridgeback mix?"

"Yes."

"Play!" he called, and all his dogs went wild again.

Larry took off. He headed for one of the corrals beside the house this time. A pond sat beside it, and I knew he'd leap into it once he'd heated up enough.

"Are your horses okay with dogs?" I asked.

"Oh, yes. Come this way."

We walked around the near corner of his house, and I was struck by the fact that he hadn't led me through it. He could've been embarrassed about how messy it was, or maybe he wanted to keep me separated from his bodyguard. On the other hand, maybe he had something to hide.

The back of the house was spectacular. Here's where Crowder had spent his home improvement money. A pergola supported a blooming wisteria vine, and clusters of purple flowers soared above a flagstone patio surrounded by a low yellow stucco wall. Several sections of the wall were topped with foot-tall figurines—the twelve apostles. They were painted in the same colors as Da Vinci's *Last Supper*, which I'd seen in Italy on my honeymoon.

A Spanish-style outdoor fireplace, a huge barbecue pit, and a recessed hot tub in a corner alcove completed the scene. We headed for a semicircle of white rattan chairs. The lemonade sat on a glass-topped table between them.

"You've got a beautiful place here," I told him. "I didn't appreciate it until you brought me back here."

"Thank you. I've put a great deal of sweat equity into it. Please…" He pointed to one of the chairs.

I intentionally sat in a different one. On my terms, I thought. Crowder noticed. I tried the lemonade. It was damned good.

"Let me get right to it," Crowder said. "I know you're a busy man." Then he took a sip of lemonade instead of getting right to it. He drank carefully, as though he tended to drop things, or perhaps he wasn't sure if he'd used too many lemons making it. I found myself staring at his hair, which was impossibly, perfectly groomed. A wig? Primping in the mirror every fifteen minutes?

"I need your help," he eventually said. I tore my attention away from his hair and focused on his hazel eyes. What had been a four on the dog-eyes compassion meter before I met him now looked to be a two. Crowder had probably practiced for his photo.

"Why's that?"

"I'm being threatened."

"Tell me about it."

"It's a man on the phone. I have a recording if you'd like to hear. He tells me that he might kill me if he feels like it. He's very cavalier."

Crowder didn't sound particularly concerned. "Aren't you scared?" I asked.

"Oh no. I trust in the Lord—in this life and the next."

"Do you think the guy is serious?"

"I have no idea. He sounds crazy. You probably know better than I do about what crazy people are capable of." He raised an eyebrow and threatened to wink.

Again, I was struck by the reverend's likability. He'd just revealed to me that he'd run a background check on me. There was no other way for him to be aware of my abortive counseling career. Yet he still seemed very caring, down to earth, and reasonable. Even with those eyes. I didn't want to like him, but I just couldn't help myself. It was spooky.

"So why get help if you don't care if you die?" I asked.

He smiled. It didn't run very deep. "I didn't say that, Karl. I said I wasn't fearful. I care about staying alive because I have important work to do."

"What work is that?"

"There's a new era coming—a dark time. It's already started—I'm sure you've noticed. Some of us need to keep the Lord's light shining. If I'm not around, the people who count on me may not make it."

"Make what?"

"The Rapture." His smile was real now. He looked like he was on ecstasy. All we needed were hundreds of twenty-somethings and a DJ, and we'd have a rave.

I watched the dogs for a while. They were playing alpha versus submissive dog games, rolling on their backs, nipping one another. All I needed to do was watch a dog to feel positive about the world. Even a glimpse of one of those little mutant breeds that look like furry toads could do the trick.

"What about your brother?" I asked. "Why wouldn't you call the chief of police for help?"

"Unfortunately, we're estranged." His baseline expression was back—the charming one.

"Why is that?"

"Karl, I know it's your job to ask questions, and I'm happy to answer them. But I want you to take note of the fact that I'm being open with you. When I take my turn and I ask you questions, I expect reciprocity. Can I count on you for that?"

"No."

He frowned. I don't think people defied him very often. "Do you find my request unreasonable?"

"I'm not going to make some blanket agreement with you. You might ask me something ridiculous."

"Yes, I see your point. But there's an issue of fairness here."

"Life isn't fair—not for more than about two minutes in a row, anyway. I think we both know that. I'm going to act in whatever way is in the best interest of my client. That may entail sharing information with you or it may not."

"You already have a client?" He raised his voice. "Why didn't you tell me that?"

"There you go again. You're not entitled to an answer to that question, either. You're not paying me, and you're not my friend. Being personable only gets you so far, Reverend Crowder."

He looked away, frowning again. Perhaps whoever had run the background check on me hadn't interviewed anyone who knew me personally. I was famous for being a pain in the ass in these kinds of situations.

I sized him up further. He wore a white button-down shirt, spotless white jeans, and black cowboy boots. His posture wasn't very pastorish. He slumped, and his head was tilted forward. Perhaps he had a physical problem. Lost in thought, his mouth was a thin red line, and he didn't have much in the way in the way of lips in the first place. His fingernails were filthy with some sort of black grease.

"Okay," Crowder finally said. "I think that continuing our conversation may be beneficial to both of us, despite your truculence."

Truculence, huh? I nodded.

"The police force's perspective on Jesus Is Everything is that we've cried wolf one too many times and they're no longer willing to mobilize at my request.

I played the recording of the caller to a sergeant, and he said it was an obvious prank. 'Get a life,' he told me."

"Why don't you call one of the big agencies? Why me?"

"Two reasons. One, discretion. The fewer people who know about this, the better. Also, I know something about your recent activities, and it seems as though we share some common interests."

"Like what?"

"I understand you recently spent time at the Santa Cruz Spiritual Center, for example. Our church's destiny is to own that property. We have a legitimate claim to it." He leaned forward and dripped earnestness.

"What does that mean?"

"Well, the matter is in litigation, of course." He paused. "Ah, I see you didn't know that."

"Tell me about it."

"Lydia Zoppi Sharp was a very wealthy woman who owned numerous properties around the county. Her son has been a member of our congregation for quite some time—a very generous member. No church can thrive without a few wealthy parishioners. That's just the way it works, Karl."

I noticed how he worked in my name. And his tone and gestures were all very studied. Crowder was performing, and I was beginning to see through his act.

"Go ahead," I said.

"In the latter stages of her life, Mrs. Sharp became involved with Ms. Piper. She was terminally ill and grasping at straws. She bought what Ms. Piper was selling—reincarnation and all the rest. It was very appealing to a desperate old woman. It's also blasphemy."

"Let me guess. She willed the center's property to Aria instead of to her son."

"Yes. She'd promised various properties to each of her sons, and then she reneged. Legally, you can't cheat your children out of what is rightfully theirs, especially if you're no longer of sound mind."

"Here's another guess. Wayne Sharp was planning to hand over the property to Jesus Is Everything once he'd inherited it."

"No, not Wayne. His brother. Our congregant is Ralph Sharp. You know Wayne?"

"He was the corpse in Aria's well."

Dead silence. His eyes left me as he processed what I'd told him. "Oh dear. I had no idea," he finally said.

"Did you know Wayne, too?"

"He manages—managed—our church's finances. This isn't good."

I finished my lemonade and poured myself more to give Crowder a chance to assimilate the news. Then I called Larry over. He'd been lying in the shallow end of the pond. I needed him to dry off or the carpet in my car was going to smell even worse. The Airedales stayed in the water. All the dogs were exhausted by now.

"Can't you help me?" Crowder asked. Now he seemed scared, but I couldn't tell if he was feigning. "I think I'm going to be next," he added.

"Why?"

He shook his head.

"I heard you were trying to buy Aria's property," I said. "Why would you do that if your church has a legitimate claim to it?"

"I can't go into that, Karl. So will you help me?"

"I can't take your case. I'm sorry. It would be a conflict of interest."

"Won't you reconsider?"

I shook my head.

"What can I do to change your mind?" he asked. "I have access to bountiful resources."

"No means no."

His expression shifted dramatically. "It's that little bitch, Leanne, isn't it? She's at it again, isn't she? I know you met with her yesterday, Gatlin."

Creepy Gary had finally shown up. I stood. "Thanks for the lemonade. I'm sorry I had to bring you such bad news."

"Don't try to take the high ground with me, Gatlin. I know all about you. You're a loser. You can hardly pay your mortgage."

"Gary, you were really convincing at first. I liked you for about fifteen minutes. And you've got great dogs. But the truth is, I know you already have investigators on your payroll, you're full of bile, and you can only keep up the nice guy act for so long."

"Arlin!" he called. The big guy was there in seconds. He must've been lurking just inside the back door.

"Throw this gentleman off my property," Crowder said.

Arlin smiled and lumbered toward me. I decided not to tax Larry, so I pulled out my pistol. "I'll just show myself out."

Chapter Ten

I called Matt from the car and told him to order a pizza.

"What happened down there, boss?"

"I'll tell you when I get back."

"Cardenas' partner wants to see you," he said.

"His partner?"

"Yeah. She says he's off today because of a family thing."

"Okay. See if she'll come to the office after we eat."

"You got it. And Aria called. She said to tell you you're doing great. I don't know how she could know that, but that's what she said."

"Thanks, Matt. I'm going to stop at Adele's on the way back. I'll be there around one."

"All right. Good luck. I found out quite a bit, but I guess I'll tell you later, boss."

"Great. I need to think some things over right now."

I didn't think anything over. I listened to the radio. I needed a break from this case.

My ex lived in a funky rental house on the west side of Santa Cruz, a few blocks from the university. She worked as a nurse at the student health center. This was her day off, and I knew she'd be feeling down without Larry around. Also, I owed her money so I wanted to sign over Aria's retainer check.

"What is it now, Karl? What the hell do you want?" This was how she answered the door. You'd have thought I was there to steal one of her kidneys. Then Larry jumped up on her.

"Fuck! He's soaking wet, you idiot. Do you see what I'm wearing?"

I took a moment to examine Adele's outfit. She'd always spent money we didn't have to establish her personal style, which she called her "visual signature." The first thing I noticed were her earrings, which resembled miniature purple Christmas tree ornaments. This struck me as appropriate. Basically, women punched a hole in a body part and then hung decorations on themselves, didn't they?

Her scoop-neck emerald green blouse revealed the top edge of a lacy black bra, and its sleeves billowed out at the elbows as if to hide bandages, swelling, or some sort of deformity. A shiny purple belt—faux alligator, I hoped—matched her earrings and sat on the hips of her sea-foam slacks. I shouldn't know the color sea-foam or think of pants as slacks, but that's what living with Adele had done to me. Luckily, I'd gotten out before I started describing her lipstick as dusky salmon rose or something.

"He's not soaking, Adele. He's just a little damp. He had fun in a pond." She was madder now. "I love that top," I tried. "It looks great on you."

And it did. Everything looked good on her. She was one of the sexiest women I'd ever seen. She was full-figured, with long, wavy red hair. Her blue eyes were usually a little crazy-looking, but hey, nobody's perfect. Our physical chemistry was the glue that had kept us together all those years.

For my efforts, I earned one of her withering looks. She had an array of them. When I used to care, they ran the show at our house. Adele's emotions trumped everything else on the planet—at least as far as she was concerned.

"I have money for you," I said.

"It's about time. How much?"

I told her. She softened. "I'm sorry," she said. "I'm having a bad day."

"I thought Larry might cheer you up." We both looked at our dog. He lay comatose on the grass beside Adele. "Well, he needs a little rest first," I said.

"What did you do to him?"

"Airedales."

"How many?"

"Three."

"Oh my God. My poor baby." She reached down and stroked one of Larry's ears.

"Shall I leave him with you? We're having pizza for lunch, and Larry doesn't like pizza."

"Okay. If you must. And stop feeding him people food. You know what the vet said."

"Adele, do we really still need Matt as a go-between?"

"Yes. Unless you want to bring a shitload of money every time." She straightened up, put a hand on her hip, and shifted all her weight to the same side. She looked like a cartoon character—the wife who met her drunk good-for-nothing husband at the front door at two a.m. All she needed was a rolling pin.

I handed her the check, and she looked it over. "Who's this Aria character?"

"A client. I can't talk about her."

"You're so unprofessional. A real detective would've deposited the check in the bank and then written me a personal check. I'm not supposed to know who your clients are, you know."

"I haven't had a chance to do any of that because I'm on a big case. I thought you'd want the money sooner rather than later."

"Well, duh. Who doesn't? Look, I've got a ton of stuff to do. Why don't you go solve your 'big case'?" She waved me away with a graceful turn of her graceful wrist. She danced, she did yoga, she'd played high-level volleyball. Once again, I wished I could've screwed a different head onto her body.

"Yeah, okay."

"Thanks, though," she added. Then she looked me in the eye and silently, authentically reiterated her gratitude.

For a moment, there she was—the woman I'd fallen in love with. Then she pivoted and disappeared back into her house. I made a point of not staring at her ass. That was a slippery slope, as they say in AA.

Matt had ordered a large pizza with so many toppings on it, I couldn't see any cheese or tomato sauce. I've always considered some foods to be mutually exclusive with others. Matt didn't.

"Matt," I said. "What kind of pizza do I like?"

"Cheese and onions, Karl. But I thought we needed a little variety." He sat in the green armchair in front of my desk, balancing the pizza box on his lap underneath a half-eaten slice. With his long face tilted down toward his pizza, his buzz cut hair, and his skinny, adolescent-like body, Matt looked like a teenager partying while his parents were away.

"This isn't variety. This is sacrilege." I accepted a slice and then seated myself behind my desk. A bottle of local craft beer sat in front of me. "Thanks for the beer, though," I said.

We both ate quickly and sloppily. Matt spilled more than I did, but the pizza box caught most of it. I watched helplessly as molten cheese slid off my slice and formed ulcerous stains on the papers on my desk. The pizza didn't taste that bad, but I made faces anyway to protest the toppings. It was part of my employee-training program.

Matt let me finish eating—three slices—and then asked me for all the details of my morning adventures, which I supplied. I found that organizing the material as a narrative helped me understand things better. Even if Matt hadn't been working for me, I'd have still found someone to tell.

"Wow," Matt said when I'd finished. "That sounds exciting."

"That's one word for it."

"You're actually good at your job, aren't you?" He licked his fingers.

"You're surprised?"

"Well, yeah. I'm sorry, but I've never thought of you as a guy who could hold his own against gunmen and thugs."

"I've told you about some of my earlier cases, haven't I? You knew I was shot once, right?" Matt was a good friend, but I'd only known him three years.

"Sure."

"Well, I've also shot someone. In the thigh and the shoulder. And I spent several weeks in jail when I was framed for a murder."

"No shit?"

I shook my head.

"What else?"

"That's not enough for you?"

"Hey, I'm reevaluating you here."

"Do it on your own time," I told him. "What did you find out while I was gone?"

Matt sauntered to the front office without answering, retrieved his laptop, and then lay down on the love seat with the laptop on his chest. He looked like a teenager again—one who'd had a few lines drawn on his face to mimic age.

I cocked my head at him. "So?"

"Crowder gets his money from church members and a foundation based in Austin, Texas." He clicked furiously on his keyboard. "I'm still working on what's up with that. I've got some calls in, and I'm doing an auto-hack into the state registry. I should know whose names are on the foundation paperwork by the end of tomorrow."

"What about Wayne Sharp?" I knew almost nothing about the victim, which was a major deficit.

"He's a crook. The feds were about to indict him for laundering drug money. Maybe somebody figured he'd cut a deal and was giving them up."

"Would he?"

"I don't know. I would."

"And he manages Crowder's money, too?"

"Well, I heard you say that."

"Any other connection to Aria?" I asked.

"His niece lives at the center—Ralph Sharp's girl. She's kind of a lost soul. Her mother convinced Aria to take her on as a project."

"Does she smoke weed? Was she homeless?"

"Yeah, that's her. Cate Sharp. I talked to somebody down there about her."

"I met her. She's lost, all right. Maybe her presence at the center is a problem for her dad. He's in Crowder's church, and I think he's part of a lawsuit against Aria."

"Yeah, Ralph's gone down there and kicked up a fuss. He's divorced from her mother, who's a weekend student of Aria's."

"I hope he tries it again now that John's down there." I always enjoyed it when I could help supply corrective consequences to bullying or harassing behavior.

Matt smiled. "I'd like to see that. That reminds me—John called. He said he needs a break tomorrow. Eight to eleven in the morning. He didn't say why."

"I can cover it."

"I'll tell him."

I considered all this. "So Aria withheld more information than I thought."

"It's mostly about who her students are," Matt said. "Maybe her roster is confidential, and her lawyer could've told her not to talk about the lawsuit."

"Maybe," I conceded. "But it's irritating. Clients do this all the time, but I thought she'd be different."

"You don't sound so in love anymore," Matt pointed out. He seemed pleased by this. He'd probably thought that I'd screw up the case because of my feelings for her.

"I guess I don't. When I see her, I feel one way. Then ten minutes after I leave, she turns back into someone I don't really know." I thought this insight might reassure him—if he even needed reassurance. Sometimes my assumptions about people's motives were way off. Once I perceived that a client's sister was hitting on me when it turned out she was just trying to convert me to vegetarianism.

"That's interesting," Matt said. He didn't sound particularly interested, though. His brain had moved on. "Let's see," Matt continued. "What else have I got?"

He played around on his computer, and I rubbed the cancer scar on my temple. I realized I hadn't done it since I took on the case. Maybe I was finally getting somewhere with breaking that habit. Even when I didn't have a new scar to work with, I often ran my finger along the edge of old ones.

"Here you go," Matt finally said. "Get this. The former owner of Crowder's ranch? Crowder's brother, Jim. Before that, it was one of the Zoppis—Lydia's dad."

"That's interesting. What do you think it means?"

"I don't know."

"Did you look into Jim the police chief?" I definitely wanted to know more about him. He was both Reverend Crowder's brother and the guy who'd blocked at least one investigation so far.

"I found out a little. He's kind of too good to be true. Something's not right there. I'll keep digging. And you know how you were wondering about Paul—that administrator guy down at Aria's?"

"No, what was I wondering about him?"

"You said no one there was talking about him." Matt looked up with irritation.

"Oh yeah. So what did you find out?"

"Not a whole hell of a lot. He's gay, like you thought." He pointed at me as though I needed identifying as the "you" in his sentence. "And he's mean to people behind Aria's back."

"You mean employees?"

"Everybody—employees, students, tradespeople. It's only sometimes, though."

"He's unpredictable," I said.

"Yeah. And he owes a lot of money."

"Aha. To who?"

"Credit cards. He's got five, and they're all maxed out."

"What does he spend his money on?" I asked. Spending patterns and debt correlated with all sorts of problem behaviors, which, in turn, correlated to all sorts of crimes.

"I don't know. I can't get into the program that has his billing statements."

"Maybe he's a gambler."

"It could be something innocent like home improvements or healthcare," Matt pointed out.

"What about drugs? Is his behavior erratic enough for that?"

"I don't know. That's a good question."

"Hello?" A woman's voice hailed from the outer office.

"Come on in!" I called back, getting to my feet.

A good-looking woman in her late thirties strode in. She was blond, slim, and wiry—maybe she was a rock climber.

"Karl Gatlin?" she asked, looking at me.

"Yes."

"I'm Detective Sutter. Ann Sutter."

She turned to Matt, who rose from the love seat. "You must be Matt..." She'd forgotten his last name, or maybe she never knew it.

"Yup, I'm Matt," he said.

She turned back to me. "Let's talk."

"Sure."

"I'll be at my desk if you need me," Matt said as he ambled out of the office.

"Have a seat," I told the detective.

She paused at the armchair in front of my desk.

"Oh," I said. "The crumbs. Hold on." I scurried over and brushed them off the green wool seat. "My assistant is a barbarian."

"I heard that," Matt called from the other room. I ignored him.

She sat down and pulled out an iPad. Sutter wore a man's pale yellow button-down shirt and black slacks with a perpetual-looking crease you might cut tomatoes with. Up close, she was prettier, with small features, and light blue eyes with reddish lashes. Her makeup was conservative—subtle—and expertly applied. Tiny diamond studs sat low in her ear lobes, and a thin gold chain snaked down her neck into her shirt. She looked down and then up again after only a moment. "You know you should've called the police immediately after you were attacked on the road this morning?"

"Yes."

"I want to hear about it now." Her voice was a monotone now—no inflection, no variation in volume, and certainly no emotion. Visually, she'd be the best friend of the star in a romantic comedy—the serious one. The goofy one would make fun of her. Vocally, suited up in a metal casing, she'd play the know-it-all robot in a cheesy science fiction film.

I told her what had happened, describing the men and the truck in detail. Aria and I had one thing in common—we paid attention. Sutter asked good follow-up questions, teasing out the whole story.

"So Matt gave you the plate number, right?" I asked.

"It belongs to a truck that's registered to an artichoke farm outside Castroville." This was a town about halfway between Santa Cruz and Monterey that billed itself as the artichoke capital of the world. A giant green fiberglass one sat in front of a restaurant on the main drag.

"So where do we go from here?" I asked.

"I've got mug books, we're going to get employee photos from the farm, and a man's down there now. They haven't reported the truck as stolen, so we'll see. Do you have time to look at some photographs?"

"Sure."

She came around the desk and set up her tablet to run through a series of previously convicted men who may have been my guys. I enjoyed her leaning over beside me. I could smell her hair, which hinted at a citrus-based shampoo. She returned to her crumb-free chair, and I sat back with the tablet in my hand. In short order, I found the guy who'd held the gun. The other one wasn't there.

"Hilario Alvarez." Detective Sutter told me when I held up the gunman's photo.

"Hilario?"

"It's not an unusual Latino name."

"Well, I've never heard it. What's his deal?"

"Hired help. From southern Mexico originally.

Chiapas or Oaxaca, I think. Works out of Salinas. Mostly drug stuff. No known whereabouts." She was slightly more excited now. If you listened closely, you could almost differentiate her from a robot.

"So you'll hunt him down, get him to rat out his buddies, and then lock them all up so I'll be perfectly safe?"

"That's right. But be patient. It could take upwards of half an hour." She almost smiled. I don't know why, but I liked her. She certainly tried to hide out in her role as a cop.

"Oh, well. Would you recommend I take any precautions?" I asked.

"Yes." The robot was back.

"And what would those be?"

"That's up to you, Mr. Gatlin. Now, have you gathered any information that might aid us in our investigation?"

"Probably. You may already know some of it, but I'll let you sort that out."

I didn't tell her everything, but I told her most of it. I left out anything that reflected poorly on Aria, including the fact that she'd omitted information and wouldn't let anyone take her picture—which I knew the police would take the wrong way.

She took notes on her iPad and thanked me. "This should be a big help."

"What's up with Lou?" I asked. "Why is he out today?"

She was confused for a moment. "You mean Detective Cardenas? He let you call him Lou?"

"Actually, he let Aria call him Lou, and I happened to be there."

She nodded. "That makes more sense. He's okay. It's a family emergency, but not his immediate family. Lou told me to watch out for you. He said you're a smart-ass who was likely to withhold evidence. Is that right? Are you withholding evidence, Mr. Gatlin?"

"Of course. Doesn't everybody?"

She didn't like that, and we had a brief, pointless conversation about human nature. We parted on less than cordial terms. So much for honesty.

Overall, I was glad I was able to report my experiences to Sutton, and not Cardenas. A woman lurking behind a robot exterior was a far more intriguing variety of cop.

Matt wandered back in after she left. "I heard everything," he said. "You probably should've closed your door if you wanted privacy."

"No, no. I was hoping you'd eavesdrop. What do you think of her?"

"She seemed competent. And she looked great. Beyond that, beats me. Fortunately, I haven't had much experience with cops." He began to sit but stopped himself and faced me head on. "Listen. I didn't get to finish my report—from before Sutter got here. I found out quite a bit about Sumati—the woman who found the body."

"Let me take a bathroom break," I said.

When I returned, I found Matt fully supine on the love seat, his legs dangling over the armrest. This was a new thing. Was his less and less formal posture progressive? Would he be on the floor next?

"She's from Chula Vista—south of San Diego," Matt said as I resettled myself behind my desk. "She was arrested several times as a teen and a young adult for drugs and petty theft—and once for domestic violence. She scratched her abuser when she was defending herself from getting punched."

"They take the one who's bloody."

"Well, that's stupid. So she goes into a low-budget rehab in Watsonville and tries to push the reset button on her life. This was about eight years ago. It worked as far as the substance abuse goes—and the crime stuff. But she keeps getting together with assholes who hit her."

"That's a tough pattern to break. My cousin went through that. But how in the world did you find all this out?"

"Never mind, Karl. Now here's the other thing. She's always dated Latinos. I guess that's who she grew up with. A couple of her exes were involved with the Sureños and another one was high up in the Norteños in L.A."

"You've got names?"

"Yeah."

"Matt, this is really good work. Don't ever go back to high-tech. You're much better at research than I am."

"Thanks. One of her exes is dead, another's in prison, but I located one who's supposedly living clean now. By all accounts, he's still a total douche bag, anyway. Then there's one who just got out of prison two weeks ago—for beating on Sumati four years ago."

"He got four years for DV?"

"Six, but he's out in four. It was pretty bad. She was in the hospital for a week."

"They should lock these guys up forever."

He nodded. "His name's Bobby Mendoza. He's staying with his aunt in Salinas while he looks for work."

"I might have to go have a talk with him."

"Take John with you. Bobby beats on men, too. And he's good at it."

We wrapped it up, and I called Aria. I'd said I would, so I did. The second thing my uncle had told me—right after "Don't sleep with your clients"—was "Do what you said you'd do." He was right. People judged you by that.

Chapter Eleven

"Hi Aria. How's it going?"

"Karl. Thanks for calling. There's not much new on my end. I'm enjoying life as usual. John's learning to meditate. What have you been up to?"

I filled her in. The story fell out of me. It was my third go-round, and by now the big yellow marker in my head had highlighted the essential elements. This was the same one that ran a circle around whichever woman on the beach was wearing the skimpiest bikini, so I knew I could trust it.

"You're certainly earning your fee, aren't you?" Aria said. "Thank you so much. It sounds as though there are any number of suspects and motives at this point. Is that a fair appraisal?"

"Yes. It's hard to narrow things down. Have you had any more calls, by the way?"

"No, they stopped once I met with you."

I had a fleeting thought that the threats were designed to manipulate Aria to call me—that someone wanted me involved. "The thing is," I said, "Sharp was in your well—not somewhere else. And he had ties to Crowder, dangerous criminals, and two of your students."

"Yes."

"I need to ask you some questions, but they can wait until tomorrow when I'm down there."

"Eight to eleven, I understand?"

"That's right."

"I'm delighted we'll be spending more time together. It will give us a chance to explore our connection further."

Our connection? Maybe that was just a spiritual term, but it sounded to me as though she might be interested in me, too. "Yes, I look forward to it," I said, keeping it businesslike for now. "I'm hoping to talk more with Sumati, Cate Sharp, and Paul as well. Do you think you can arrange that?"

"I'm sure I can. Everyone here seems happy to skip their chores. But you may find Cate difficult."

"I'm sure I will. Is John there? Would you mind putting him on?"

"No worries."

"John," I said when he'd greeted me on Aria's phone. "Would you mind stepping away to somewhere private?"

"Okay."

I could hear him talking to Aria. "Karl wants me to go someplace else. I'll be back in a minute. Don't wander off."

After a long stretch in which I could hear him walking and opening a door, John came back on the line.

"Okay, Karl."

"Do you always talk to Aria that way, John? Didn't I tell you to be polite down there?" I was ready to read him the riot act.

"She told me to be direct with the way I said things. She said she could take it—that she was a big girl."

I doubted that those were her exact words.

"I think," he continued, "she saw how hard I was working to say everything like I was somebody else. She's very kind, Karl. I've never met anyone like her."

"Yeah, okay. I've got a few questions for you. Things that I'd like to know about before I head down there."

"Go ahead."

"Have you gotten to know Sumati?"

"Yeah. I like her, too, but she's a mess."

"What do you mean?"

"She goes in the woods and cries, and she's on her mobile more than anyone else here. Aria tells them not to do that, but she does it anyway."

"Any idea who she's talking to?" I asked.

"Not a clue. I'm not a detective like you, Karl. You want me to ask her?"

"No, don't do that. Does she have any visitors?"

"Not while I've been here, but it's only been a couple of days."

"What about Cate Sharp?"

"Cate's last name is Sharp? Is she related to the man in the wishing well?"

"His niece."

"That sounds like a clue," he said.

"It does, doesn't it?"

"She keeps to herself. She's hard to like, but Aria gets along with her."

"Any unusual behavior from Cate?"

"It's all unusual, Karl. She has problems."

"Okay. What about the other residents?"

"There's one guy with gang tattoos, but he's a great guy. He went to seminary for a while."

"What's his name?"

"José something. Mostly they just use first names here."

"Anything more on Paul?"

"No. I haven't seen him much. He does the business stuff, and Aria does the teacher part. It's pretty separate."

"Okay. That's about it."

"Sorry I can't be there tomorrow," John said.

"What's that about?"

"I'd rather not say."

I was surprised. John wasn't one to hold back anything. "If I come early, can we talk a bit more in the morning?" I asked. "I have some other things to tell you."

"No worries."

Matt knocked on my door and walked in yet again after I'd hung up. He was looking a bit haggard. His thin, pointy face was drooping a bit around the edges— especially the corners of his eyes and mouth. He hadn't buzzed his head recently either, I noticed, and his spiky hair was threatening to fall down flat. If I were a betting man, I'd start a pool to see in which direction.

"Adele called while you were on the phone," Matt told me. "She said to tell you Larry was still wet and he jumped on her bed and...hold on, I wrote it down. Quote: 'He fucking totally ruined my duvet that I got in a wonderful shop in Carmel Valley, and I don't know when I'll get back there again because the drive is a pain in the ass, so you tell that sorry son of a bitch you work for that he's a sorry son of a bitch.' Unquote."

"Thanks, Matt. I wouldn't want to miss a single word of that vital message."

He shook his head. "What were you thinking, Karl?"

"She wasn't always like this." I thought for a moment. "So Matt, how would you feel about sweet-talking Adele into letting you bring Larry over to my place early tomorrow morning? I think I need my wingman with me down at the center."

"I can try. As long as she doesn't think I'm taking sides, we get along okay. I'm not a son of a bitch, at least."

"I would think she'd want you to take sides—hers," I said.

"Yeah, that's true, boss. But I think she also respects the fact that I don't—that she can't bend me to her will."

He ambled back to his office, ostensibly to call Adele. I woke up my computer and looked up the Zoppi family history. Before I got too far, I heard a commotion out front. Then a dumpy-looking guy in a shiny blue suit bustled into my office.

"You are hereby served," he said, slapping down a sheaf of papers onto my desk. His squeaky voice didn't go with his pear-shaped body. His drinker's nose and red, pouchy cheeks certainly did. The guy was two years away from cirrhosis.

"What is it?" I asked.

"You think a process server reads these things?" He pivoted clumsily; he may have been drunk.

"You're not a process server. I've seen you in court," I told him "You're a lawyer."

"Okay, okay. It's a temporary restraining order. If you trespass on Reverend Crowder's land or attempt to assault him again, you're going to jail, Gatlin."

"Who are you, exactly?" I stood and stared him down. He blanched a bit, which pleased me. Making people blanch wasn't my strong suit. Despite my rough, scarred looks, an essential friendliness leaked out of me at inconvenient times.

"Harold Pemmican, attorney-at-law." He squeaked this with pride, as though the name was one of the founding fathers, or maybe a literary celebrity.

Matt had followed him in and stood by the door, although I hadn't noticed him. "Pemmican?" he repeated.

"Pemmican," Pemmican said.

"And you're Gary Crowder's lawyer?" I asked.

"He is both my client and my pastor, gentleman. Now, I'm a busy man. You've been served. I'll be on my way."

He hurried off, looking like he needed to find a bathroom in very short order. I picked up the papers and read them while Matt stood and waited.

"Apparently," I said, "I brought an attack dog with me when I 'invaded' Crowder's ranch. Pastor Gary submitted security-camera video evidence of Larry's 'vicious intimidation of a ranch employee' to some clueless judge. And I 'brandished a sidearm in a subsequent display of felonious aggression.' "

"You did, didn't you?" Matt asked.

His remark didn't really register. "Does this thing matter?" I asked. "Or is Crowder just trying to hassle me or let me know what he's capable of?"

"I have no idea. Let's give it to our lawyer. Do we have a lawyer, Karl?"

"No, he died. His son took over, but I don't like him."

"I know someone. She's good." He held out his hand, and I gave him the papers. "I can drop this off on my way home," he said.

"Great. What else do we need to do today?"

"Zip. It's my turn to send you home. Go home. Put your feet up. Drink a beer. Watch the game."

"What game?"

"Oh, there's always a game. Your pick, boss. By the way, Adele said it's okay about Larry. I can bring him over to your place around seven tomorrow morning. Does that work for you?"

"Yeah, thanks. You're go-betweening this time for work, so make sure you're on the clock. Are you keeping track of your hours?"

"Oh, sure. I have to. I do the payroll and the books. If I didn't track my hours, it'd be like I was back in middle school math class again—I'd only be cheating myself, wouldn't I?"

Chapter Twelve

I did what Matt had suggested, minus the beer and the game. My feet were up as I watched a 1950s film noir with Broderick Crawford and some guy who looked like William Powell but wasn't. I loved the way they talked. It was all out-of-date slang, fueled by a surplus of testosterone.

I slept poorly, dreaming about being chased by lawyers, ten-foot-tall Airedales, and my father. I escaped by jumping off a cliff, which wasn't much of a solution, especially since I never landed. The dream went on and on as I just kept falling. I could remember one thought from the dream: perhaps I could learn to thrive in free-fall.

After that, I was restless, and my knee hurt. I thought about the case while I lay there, but I didn't accomplish anything. It was more like worrying than thinking.

In the morning, I did my physical therapy exercises for the first time in weeks. They probably didn't help my knee much when I only did them sporadically, but I felt a little better about myself anyway. When I had a case, I tended to be a workaholic. Even a little bit of self-care was progress.

I opened my door in response to Matt's knock at seven. Larry was ecstatic to see me, of course. He always was. His tail whipped around in flattened circles, and he jumped straight up in the air, boxing with his front legs, and grunting like a drunk caveman. To the casual eye, his version of ecstatic was probably indistinguishable from a full-blown canine psychotic break.

"Thanks again, Matt," I said as he let Larry off his leash. "I know it's beyond the call of duty to deal with Adele. How'd you talk her into this, anyway?"

Larry ran into the kitchen, having completed his greeting ritual. I didn't actually know what he did in there when he first arrived home. I think he might've been checking for intruders, or perhaps he snuffled the floor for meal debris.

"As it happens," Matt said, "she has a doctor's appointment, a hair appointment, and a date tonight. Also, I told her you were taking Larry to the woods, which is sort of true."

"A date?"

"Yeah. He's a dork."

"You've met this guy?" I felt a twinge, and I didn't like it. I didn't want to care a rat's ass about anything Adele did. My goal was complete disconnection—financially, socially, and especially emotionally.

"He's over at her house sometimes. He's a dentist."

"What's his name?" I couldn't help myself. The words arrived before my internal censor could get to work.

"This isn't healthy, Karl. Let it go."

"You're right. Sorry. Do you want to walk with us?"

"I don't think you have time for a walk." Matt glanced at his very smart watch. He upgraded all his gadgets annually. "You wanted to get to the center early to talk to John in person, right? It'll take you twenty minutes this time of day."

"You're right again." I wish I'd slept better. I'd been planning to use the walk to wake up all the way.

"Have some caffeine," Matt suggested.

"Good idea."

The traffic on the way to the Santa Cruz Spiritual Center was ridiculous. I'd lived in Santa Cruz since I escaped Texas back in the early 1980s. In those days, you could get around town easily—even in what would have been rush hour if they'd had one. Despite the hazards of Highway 17 and the efforts of the liberal local government to block growth, almost all the empty spaces between houses had gradually filled in with more houses. Now, even at 7:15 in the morning, the roads were full of BMWs and other cars I couldn't afford.

Larry didn't care. He liked riding in the car. Bumper-to-bumper traffic just meant he got a better gander at all his new friends in the other vehicles.

The last stretch was spectacular in the morning light. Paul Sweet Road ran alongside Dominican Hospital, curved around a Catholic cemetery, and then snaked its way into the forest. As we tooled through a series of curves and uphill grades, the sun glinted through the redwoods that lined the pavement, creating wild-looking patterns.

This time I parked in the back lot the police had used. The signs with aphorisms written on them were bigger here—visible from the parking space. "We're prepared by the journey to meet the challenges that await us at our destination." That one made sense to me. When I'd short-cutted or leap-frogged my way past a new situation, it had never worked out well. I just wasn't ready to be there. "Give yourself permission to be where you're at." That seemed kind of obvious. Where else could you be? And I didn't like that the sentence ended with a preposition. I had to smile at that. I was criticizing metaphysical beliefs based on grammar—what hubris. The last sign read: "Don't make things happen: let things happen. You can't arm-wrestle life into submission." This kind of passive approach to life summed up my disdain of New Agers. They were a mushy lot, abdicating responsibility for directing their own future. Sure, it was easier to sit around and smoke dope instead of going out and grabbing life by the balls, but where would we be if everyone did that? What if Martin Luther King had sat around on his ass and just accepted segregation? Or suppose Steve Jobs hadn't been a driven son of a bitch?

The center bustled already. Students ambled in twos and threes from building to building, and I spotted Aria and John on a path in the distance.

When I opened Larry's door, he sprinted toward John, whom he dearly loved. The Maori started running toward Larry as well. Nearby students watched the biggest man they'd ever seen run about as fast as they'd ever seen anyone run. Jaws were dropping.

It was a game of interspecies chicken. I'd seen it before. Whoever was more foolish won because whoever was smarter understood the consequences of a head-on collision and eventually yielded. Historically, it was probably a wash between the two of them.

When they got close, John twisted to the side, and Larry leapt into his arms, which would've knocked anyone else down. As the two played together, Aria and

I approached them from opposite sides, arriving about the same time.

"Who is this beautiful creature?" she asked. She leaned down gracefully to peer at Larry at his eye level.

He suddenly held himself still, and the reddish fur that ran along his spine stood up as he stared at Aria. John backed away. I was afraid that Larry was going to attack Aria. I'd never seen him react this way. Then he started crouching and mewing like a cat. It was bizarre. Aria bent down and put her hand out. Larry crawled over to her and immediately rolled onto his back. When she reached forward to rub his stomach, he began to shudder and his eyes rolled up out of sight.

"Larry!" I called. My gut clenched and my fists clenched of their own accord.

"It's okay, Karl," Aria said. "My energy affects quite a few animals this way. It's a kind of bliss for them. Their body doesn't know what to do with it."

I stared at Larry. His eyes were still rolled up in his head, and he was breathing erratically. "Will he be okay?" I asked, not far from the threshold of panic. "I need him to be okay."

"He'll be fine, Karl. Once the energy has a chance to integrate, you'll get your dog back—with some subtle upgrades, I imagine."

"Upgrades?" I found her words confusing—reassuring, but also confusing.

She waved her hand, which I took to mean "You don't really want to know."

And she was right. For a moment, I felt frustrated that I wasn't getting a proper answer, but I also didn't want to waste time on wacky explanations. Larry's health didn't take a backseat to anything, but we certainly had bigger fish to fry than a lot of palaver about "energy integration."

"This trick's a doozy, Aria," John told her. "This is better than the one with the potato."

She smiled. It was an achingly sweet expression.

"What do you mean, 'this one'?" I asked.

"Oh, she does all kinds of special things," John said, looking away and energetically shuffling his oversized feet. He wore bright yellow running shoes, which didn't minimize the spectacle.

"Like what?"

"She asked me not to say, and I promised I wouldn't. Sorry, Karl. I shouldn't have mentioned the potato. Did you want to talk to me?"

"Yeah. How shall we do this?" I tried not to ponder how a potato might figure in a minor miracle.

"I have some things to do in my office," Aria said. "You two could meet outside on the porch. It's a lovely morning."

John nodded. "But let me check the room first."

"Of course."

I looked down at Larry, and he peered up at me groggily. He seemed to be back online. More or less.

"Come on, boy," I said gently.

He struggled to his feet and stood by Aria's side. Then we all walked to her office. A few minutes later, I was sitting with John in the sun on the south-facing porch. Larry chose to remain with Aria. The day hadn't warmed up yet; it was cooler on the property than at the coast. I wore a thick blue fleece pullover and a pair of gray, wide-wale corduroys.

"What's up, Karl?" John asked. He leaned back in his green Adirondack chair and, as always, I wondered if it would give way under him. Mine didn't feel all that sturdy, and I was a mere two hundred pounder.

I told him about all the problem people I'd run into so far and asked him to keep an eye out for them. It was a disturbingly long list.

"I know Arlin—the guy at Crowder's ranch," he told me. "We were at the same dojo for a while. He's okay when he's not working."

"Karate?"

"Kempo. It's kind of the Japanese version of kung fu." He snapped into a fighting position almost faster than I could see. One leg was back, and one was bent and leaning forward. His arms were up, one high and one low. He hadn't formed fists. Two of his huge knuckles were bundled together and protruding. All in all, I got the feeling that one punch with those was bound to disable an opponent—perhaps permanently.

"Are you a black belt?" I asked.

"My teacher doesn't believe in belts. He said we should use suspenders instead. He likes to make jokes." He chortled, which reminded me of a Hawaiian guy I knew from a summer job who giggled at the drop of a hat. Both expressions seemed incongruous coming from such large men.

I studied John's face. His speech pattern so far— the rhythm of it—was a little more fluid than usual. "Tell me, do you feel any different after spending a couple of days here with Aria?"

"Well, it's peaceful here. I feel calmer. Who wouldn't?" He shrugged. "If you're asking me if I'm getting all delirious like Larry, the answer's no." He grinned. "It looks like fun, though."

"What about Aria's students? Do they seem like

advanced people?"

"Some do, some don't. That José guy I told you about is a cool dude. And there's a lady named Jasmine who's happy all the time—really happy. But I've only met the ones that Aria's hung out with. I mean she introduced me to everybody at an assembly—you know, like at school. So they all say hi and everything. But you know me, Karl. I take my bodyguarding seriously. I don't go off and chat people up."

"Sure, I understand. Do you have any pointers for me about protecting Aria while you're gone?"

"Keep your gun handy, mate. If it's one of those drug people—or even Arlin—you've got no chance with them without it. Trust me." John frowned and nodded somberly.

I nodded back. "I guess you'd better get going. Thanks for all your hard work."

"No worries." His New Zealand accent was strongest when he said that.

I walked inside and knocked on Aria's open inner door. She called for me to come in, so I did. Larry was still camped out in there, gazing lovingly at Aria. Maybe I couldn't transmit bliss, but I was no slouch at slipping him forbidden people food. That had to count for something.

Aria focused on an oversized laptop behind her desk. She looked up and gestured for me to sit. Her green armchair was comfier than mine. A moment later, I had her full attention.

"I hope you don't mind if I ask you a few questions," I said.

"Not at all. I'm at your disposal." Instead of closing the lid on her laptop, she slid to the side of her desk and faced me, clasping her hands together on the wooden surface. Her simple black top accentuated her olive skin, which looked as though it would be amazingly smooth to touch. Her hair was down, trailing along one shoulder and cascading down the back of the other. She was barefoot.

"I don't want to keep you from your routine," I said.

"I've cleared space for you, and then I've arranged for you to meet with Sumati, Paul, Cate, and José, in that order."

"I didn't say anything about José."

"You want to talk to him, though, don't you?"

"Yes, but that's not the point."

"What is the point, Karl? That I shouldn't know the things I know? Do you want me to pretend I don't?" She wasn't irritated. Her smile and raised eyebrows demonstrated bemusement.

"No, sorry. So tell me about Paul."

"What do you want to know?"

"His background, who he socializes with, and why he's in such deep debt."

"I didn't know he was in debt," Aria said. "It might be a good idea to ask him about that."

"I will."

She filled me in about Paul, but nothing in his history stood out for me. He'd been a marketing consultant for the agricultural industry. He liked to bowl. He suffered from a neurological condition that affected his muscles and made him fall asleep.

"Do you know the kind of men that Sumati gets involved with?" I asked next.

"Only too well. Several of them have shown up

here, and one had to be hauled off by the police." Aria shook her head, hair dark hair reframing her face. "Sumati's energy embodies several interesting elements. Men get hooked on it—unconsciously, I mean. Have you ever heard her laugh? That's the core Sumati."

"And she has some issue that makes it hard for her to be with a regular guy?" In my experience, that's how it worked. It took two to tango.

"Exactly. That's why she's agreed to stay single for now."

"Do you think any of these exes could be involved in the threats or the murder?"

She thought it over. "I doubt it—at least not the ones I've met."

"Why do you say that?"

"There's no normal answer to that question, Karl. It's just something I know."

"Fair enough." What else was I supposed to say to that? "What about Sumati herself?" I asked. "Do you trust her completely, or could she commit a crime under the influence of some creepy guy?"

"That's another good question. She's somewhat veiled to me, and she has disappointed me in the past, so the most accurate answer is that I don't know."

"What about you? Is there anything in your background that would help me sort this out? Did you know that when I google you, there's nothing before 1996?"

"Isn't that when the Internet became popular—when everyone first started showing up on Google?"

"Good point." I noticed she hadn't exactly answered my question, but I let it slide. She was my client, after all. "I understand you inherited this property from an elderly student?"

"Yes. Lydia Zoppi Sharp."

"The mother of the murder victim?"

"Yes." Her tone didn't provide me with any clue about how she felt about this.

"And there's a lawsuit? This woman's other son is challenging the will?"

"Yes. Ralph Sharp has been appealing the court's ruling for several years. These things move slowly." Now it felt as though she was apologizing that things were so complicated.

"And you have a mother and a daughter as students who are also related to these people?" I shifted in my chair. I needed to move every little while or my knee hurt.

"Yes."

"Do you see what I'm driving at?"

"Of course. This is a rich vein for you to mine, Karl. I wasn't aware that any of it might be related to the matter at hand until yesterday—when they discovered the corpse was Wayne Sharp."

"Can you shed any light on how it all might fit together?"

"I'm afraid not." She shook her head. It was a slow, graceful motion until she got to the end of her neck's range. Then a hitch—or even a jolt of sorts—disrupted things before she got back on track going the other way. I felt mesmerized by the whole sequence. She continued. "I can tell you I don't believe any of the individuals you mentioned are capable of murder."

"Who do you think is?"

"Crowder, his bodyguard, and Lou Cardenas."

"Cardenas?"

"Yes. I don't mean he's involved in this case. I just mean he's a person who's capable of murder," Aria said.

That was interesting. "How do you know about Arlin?" I asked.

"Who?" Aria wrinkled her nose and I wanted to kiss it.

I decided to move on to another topic. She'd probably gotten some vibe or something from my description of him. "Do you think we still need John?"

"I have no idea. Having a bodyguard was your idea, Karl. But if you're asking me if I'm enjoying helping him, the answer is very much so."

"Helping him?"

"Of course. That's what I do." Aria pulled her hands apart and then tilted them as though she were holding an invisible beach ball.

Something occurred to me. "Are you helping me, too? I mean, in some weird way besides answering my questions."

"Did you sleep especially well the night we met? Right now, are you present and invigorated?"

I checked in with myself. I was feeling very alert, and the monkey chatter in my head was noticeably reduced. But the idea of somebody screwing with me without my permission was not okay with me.

"You know," I said, "there's something my first clinical supervisor told me. Well, first and last supervisor. Let's face it, I got canned just a few months later, didn't I? He told me that unsolicited help is interference."

"I agree. What you're experiencing is just the side

effect of someone at your stage of spiritual development being exposed to my type of energy field."

"Like what happened to Larry? Aria, let's not get too weird. I've been tolerant of your beliefs, and I know you think all this is germane to the case, but…" I didn't care to go further with this. I was likely to say something offensive.

She smiled another sweet, gentle smile. "I'm doing the best I can to minimize whatever would be difficult for you to handle, Karl."

Larry barked. I glanced at him, and he barked again—more urgently this time. He was hearing something alarming that I couldn't hear yet.

I stood. "Stay here," I told Aria. "I mean it." I didn't wait to see her response.

Larry and I ran outside and hurtled down the front porch stairs. After a half-dozen steps toward the sound of a powerful motor, I saw it. A humongous silver SUV tore across the meadow, heading straight for us.

Chapter Thirteen

I dove to the side, behind a dangerously slim fruit tree. Larry remained on his feet, barking frantically as the truck bore down on him. I pulled my gun and called my dog, and thank God he obeyed. He was by my side in a flash.

Unfortunately, neither of us sensed the man behind us in time. He kicked the pistol out of my hand just before Larry took him down, but by then it was too late.

The SUV skidded to a halt, and three men piled out. One of them was the guy who'd stopped me on the road—the driver's side guy. None of them held a weapon in his hand. They didn't need them. There were four of them, and I was now unarmed. Presumably, someone was calling this in to the police, but we were out in the boondocks. It might be a while before a car could get to us.

"Larry!' I called. "Heel!"

I didn't want him getting hurt. He was astride the big guy on the ground next to me, but he backed off and sat by my side.

Larry's guy kicked my gun away from me and moved behind us again in case we tried to run. With my knee, that wasn't an option.

The other three stood directly in front of us now. "We meet again," the guy with the acne said. "Where's the woman? Is she in one of these buildings?"

I guess I didn't answer fast enough. He stepped forward and pistoned a straight right to my gut. *Jesus.* This guy could punch. I'd tried some amateur boxing when I was young. Nobody had hit that hard—and this guy was a bantamweight at the most. I doubled over, trying not to retch.

"Hit him again," one of the other men said in Spanish.

Then I heard a primeval bellow—a sound so deep and loud, all of us froze for a moment.

John Ratu sprinted around the corner of the building and tackled the boxer, driving him into the man next to him. Before the other one in front of me could react, John shot out his massive leg and swept the guy's legs out from under him. In about two seconds, he'd knocked down all three of them.

I turned around. "Attack!" I called to Larry, and he launched himself at the guy behind us. I almost felt sorry for him. I headed for my pistol, which was about fifteen feet to the side of me.

The guy who'd punched me cut me off. He'd scrambled to his feet and eluded a roundhouse kick from John, who was now engaged with the other two attackers.

The man crouched on the balls of his feet, looking like a cross between a boxer and a martial artist. I had no doubt he could beat the crap out of me in a fair fight. It was lucky I didn't fight fair.

He didn't either. He pulled a double-edged knife on me and lunged forward, the weapon held low. He was going for my crotch.

I hit the ground and called Larry. We'd practiced this move at the training school we'd attended in New

Mexico. With a running start, Larry leapt onto my back and launched himself. He was about head height when he reached our attacker, who was leaning forward. Larry's open jaws clamped onto the guy's cheek, and he screamed.

I heard sirens now. I got up, retrieved my gun, and held it on the four men on the ground. Once Larry had disabled his foe, he'd lost interest in the whole attack thing. And it had taken all of a minute for John to dispatch the other two, one of whom wasn't moving at all.

We waited for the police. After taking all our statements, corroborated by multiple witnesses, they hauled off the thugs and towed away their SUV. The last cop to go said Cardenas would talk to us later about the incident's "possible relevance to the ongoing investigation in which the aforesaid officer is currently the lead detective." Did they teach them to talk like this? Why?

When it was all over, John, Aria, Larry, and I sat on Aria's porch and drank iced tea. Larry fell asleep immediately. All that adrenaline had exhausted him. He had a cut on his lip and a couple of scrapes on his leg. Otherwise, he was no worse for wear.

"So John, why did you come back early?" Aria asked.

"I was going for a job interview in San Jose. Full time. I'd be in charge of a whole security shift. I never get enough bodyguard work, and I'm sick of freelance welding. It's hot. It's dirty. It's no way to live." He picked up his glass of iced tea and swigged as though it were a beer—one he needed after a hard day of welding.

"I didn't know you were looking for a job like that. I can help you find one," I told him.

"I wasn't looking. I was thinking of looking, but then they called me."

"And you had second thoughts on the way there?" Aria asked.

"Yeah. It's a good thing I did." He stared at his empty glass, and it occurred to me most human-sized portions would leave John hungry or thirsty.

"Did you think someone might've been trying to lure you away from the center?" I cocked my head and watched him sort through this.

"No, do you think that's what happened?"

"I do," I told him.

He looked at Aria, crestfallen. His shoulders drooped, and he looked as if he might cry.

"I do, too." Aria's soft, present eyes were the picture of compassion.

"I feel terrible. I let you both down because I'm so stupid." John banged the flat of his hand against the side of his head, which would've knocked me off my chair.

"John," I told him, "you saved the day. You're a hero."

Aria reached out and touched his upper arm. "And Karl was here. You didn't abandon me. It's just that he's not as good a bodyguard as you are."

This struck me as a brilliant thing to say.

"Yeah, that's true," John said. "He wasn't doing too well when I got here, was he?"

"No, he wasn't," Aria agreed. "What were your second thoughts?"

"Protecting you is the best job I've ever had. I love

it here. I'd live here if I could."

"When this is all over," Aria said. "We'll talk about that."

"Really?"

"Really." Aria reached out again and this time her hand lingered on John's forearm.

His face slowly melted into a profoundly relaxed state. I hoped he wouldn't roll onto his belly like Larry. He hopped up and emphatically embraced Aria.

"Don't break her," I said. "She's the client, John. We need to get all her money first."

Chapter Fourteen

I decided to go ahead and conduct the interviews Aria had set up. Despite the delay, everyone was still available.

I walked Larry to the car and settled him in. He tolerated short stretches in there reasonably well. Some people were uncomfortable with a big dog in the room with them, and I didn't need to charm or intimidate anyone. As far as I knew, anyway.

Then I called Matt from the parking lot before I got started. After I told him what had happened, he promised to "take a peek" at the latest police investigation. I was beyond the realm of deniability about his hacking now. I don't know if this made me a conspirator in a crime, but it certainly wouldn't make the authorities happy if they found out. On the other hand, with gang members beating me up while trying to kidnap my client, pissing off the police didn't really register on the adversity Richter scale.

Matt provided additional information about the people I'd be meeting with, but the big news was our new lawyer had gotten back to him already. If the temporary restraining order was converted to something more permanent—six months or a year, for example—I'd have to surrender my gun. People with restraining orders against them in California aren't allowed to possess firearms.

"Hire the lawyer," I said. "Fight it."

"You got it, boss." His "bosses" tended toward the ironic, but this one was almost deferent. Perhaps a case like this was sobering him up.

Larry gave me one of his "Why are you torturing me?" looks when I abandoned him and headed for the empty dorm room Aria had arranged for me to use.

Sumati was my first interview. I sat on a bare single mattress, and she sat across from me on another one. The floors, walls, and ceiling surrounded us with unfinished tongue-and-groove fir. It was a room for a monk or maybe an attic retreat for a ninth grader who wanted maximum insulation from his parents. The former would take it as is, while the latter would need about a dozen sexy posters to render it livable. At least in my day. Now it might be graphics of video-game characters for all I knew.

Sumati wore a pinkish floral print skirt and a thin green sweater. She smelled like fresh earth. Perhaps she'd been working in a garden. Her hair was still a frizzy mess, but I could see a bit more of her heart-shaped face this time. Deep grooves ran from her snub nose down to the corners of her mouth, and shallower wrinkles lined the expanse between her eyes as if she had spent a lot of time trying to decipher bad handwriting. Sumati's somewhat almond-shaped hazel eyes held my attention, despite her inability to make eye contact. If you subtracted the toll of a hard-lived life, she'd be attractive, even pretty.

"Thank you for meeting with me," I said. I used my soft interviewer voice. Even if I needed to play hardball, it worked better to start friendly and ambush later.

"I'm happy to help. You want to know about my ex-boyfriend Bobby and the others, right?" She practically shouted this, as though loudness proved her willingness.

"Has he contacted you since he was released from prison?"

"He calls all the time." Sumati self-consciously lowered her volume. "I know I shouldn't answer, but I feel sorry for him. Like anyone else, he's doing the best he can."

"He's a violent criminal, isn't he?"

"Oh, I wouldn't say that."

"He put you in the hospital, Sumati."

"Well, I was part of that fight, too. I knew if I came home late, he'd go off on me, and then I did it anyway." Her eyes finally met mine. There was defiance in them. And a vulnerability lurked just below that.

"You're talking about this as if it were a couples issue—a problem you could solve by saying or doing the right thing. It isn't. It's a felony. He committed a crime, and you were the victim."

"I know, I know. That's what everyone tells me. But it doesn't feel like it." Her tone was whiney, and she glanced to the side.

"How does Bobby feel about the center—about your being here?"

"Not good."

"Could you elaborate?"

"I don't want to get him in trouble. He says a lot of drastic things about everything. That's just his personality."

"Do you think Aria would want you to tell me?" I asked. This was my ace in the hole with all her students. Surely they wished to follow her lead on things.

"Yeah, okay. He said he'd burn the place to the ground before he'd let me stay much more." She was outright mutinous now, in her power for the first time. It seemed odd since this was her most damning admission and her main goal seemed to be to protect the son of a bitch who'd beat the hell out of her.

Guys like Bobby were another reason I'd proven to be an ineffective counseling intern. I couldn't put aside my strong urge to drop these guys off a high cliff, maybe with chainsaw-wielding women waiting at the bottom. It had been hard for me to work with anyone being mistreated. Emotional reactivity in a therapist constituted static interference in a session.

"When did Bobby say this?" I asked.

"About two weeks ago. But he didn't mean it." She collapsed into herself again. Her voice was weak, and she sounded as though she were merely hopeful her words were true.

"Have you told the police?"

"No, but they know about him. Detective Sutter is real sharp. She was here yesterday."

"Could that have been Bobby's voice on the phone—the guy who told you to look in the well?"

"It didn't sound like him at all."

"He could've disguised his voice or gotten a friend to call," I said.

"Oh, I don't think so." Once again, her words were unconvincing. In fact, all her answers seemed suspect—clearly, she was an unreliable reporter at best. If she were modifying the truth, though, why did she tell me about Bobby's threat?

Sometimes fabrications or misleading answers told me more than the simple truth did. The magnitude of the performance helped differentiate a case's cast of characters, too—who had a strong reason to conceal or mislead, for example. Also, the particulars of a dishonest answer tended to illuminate a suspect's motives, and motive was the key to sorting out a healthy percentage of cases.

I sensed I wasn't going to get any further by pushing Sumati about Bobby. "What about the others?" I asked.

"What others?"

"Your other exes." I gentled my tone and invited her to relax.

"Sometimes I hear from Carlos Muñoz when he wants to borrow money. Like I'd give that loser money." The unvarnished Sumati was leaking out now.

"Is he local?"

"No, he moved to Seattle about four years ago." She shook her head, sending her frizzy hair back and forth across her face like a hirsute windshield wiper. I was reminded of Aria's recent head shake. It was hard to get her out my mind.

"Anyone else?" I asked.

"No."

"If you were me, what else would you ask?"

"That's a weird question."

"Yes. Do you have an answer?"

"I suppose so. I guess you should ask me about José Vega. He's got Norteño tattoos."

"Okay. Tell me about José," I said. "I assume we're talking about the José who lives here at the center?"

"Yeah. The Norteños and the Sureños are always fighting, and if he was in the Norteños, that means he's an enemy of Bobby and those guys that were just here."

"The men in the SUV were Sureños?"

"Well, I'm pretty sure. When the police had me look them over, I recognized one of them. He was Carlos's neighbor in Watsonville. But sometimes these guys join new gangs or do things on their own."

I stood up. "Thank you again." I needed to keep things moving to make sure I spoke with everyone.

She ambled out, found Paul, and sent him to me. I sorted out what I'd learned while I waited. Not much, I concluded.

This time Paul wore a sky-blue skullcap. It looked less ridiculous than the oversized fedora. It might've been crocheted, but I always mixed that up with other kinds of knitting. At any rate, it had small, symmetrical holes in its loose weave. I was again struck by how well-proportioned Paul's face was. He could've been the leading man in a European film about a jewel thief or a count. His long, thin nose sat elegantly under liquid brown eyes. He'd shaved amazingly close. Where would you even get a razor that was that sharp? Maybe a barber had done it.

Paul wore a tailored gray suit, with a cream-colored shirt and a black silk tie. I couldn't imagine why. Whimsical socks counterbalanced his bank manager look—bright blue waves crashing onto a glittery gold beach.

I didn't know that much about the local gay subculture, but I imagined he was still a hot commodity in the dating market. He settled uneasily on the edge of the mattress across the narrow aisle from me.

"So you're in debt," I began. "Tell me about it."

"Why do you think that?"

"Let's not play games. I know you're in debt. I want to know why."

"That's none of your business."

"Wouldn't Aria want you to tell me?"

"It's none of her business, either," Paul said. "What I do away from here is my business."

"It's mine, too. Whether you like it or not. And I'll find out. Don't kid yourself. I'm good at this."

"Screw you." His words were aggressive, but his face and body language remained placid. I guessed that either ambivalence or his illness was at work here.

"You know, when people act this way," I told him, "I can't help but think they have something to hide."

"Think whatever you want." He crossed his arms and glared at me. Now his words and body posture were congruent. It represented a stronger stance. He really didn't care what I thought.

"Is it gambling?"

"No, I don't gamble. It's nothing like that."

"It's not drugs or anything criminal?"

"Of course not."

"Well, at least we're narrowing it down," I said, as much to myself as out loud. Another idea popped into my head. "Are you being blackmailed?"

"That's ridiculous." His protest was even more emphatic now. Had he reached a saturation point with my line of inquiry or had I struck a nerve?

"Maybe you're in the closet, and someone's threatened to out you," I said.

"Maybe you're an idiot. I'm out to everyone but my family back in Iowa. And I don't give a crap about what they think at this point." His glare was fiercer now, as though he were building up to some dramatic action—maybe stalking out of the room.

"Well, if you don't tell me, I'm going to keep thinking it's something along those lines."

He let out a big, dramatic sigh—as though he were performing in a high school play. "All right. Fine. If you must know, it was charitable donations. I've got a soft heart, and I get carried away."

He seemed to be telling the truth despite the unlikelihood of his story. "Great. I appreciate your cooperation. Why didn't you just tell me since it's something so innocent?"

"It's a boundary issue. I've been pushed around my whole life by people like you. And before you ask, which charities I give to is none of your business, either."

He was calmer now, but he still had an attitude. I wasn't going to dance that dance again and rile him up. Apparently, I symbolized a class of people who'd bullied him, probably for being gay. "I see," I said. "Now what about the lawsuit?"

"Which one?"

"There's more than one?"

"There are three at the moment. A place like this attracts them."

"What are they?"

"Well, there's the one about the ownership of the property itself. I understand you already know about that. Then Ralph Sharp has a separate one claiming we've brainwashed his daughter."

"Cate?"

"Yeah. The North Koreans couldn't brainwash

her," Paul said. "I don't think she even has a brain."

"What's the third one?"

"It's from a former employee—my predecessor as head administrator. The guy was hopeless; I had to clean up his mess. That case has been dragging on for years."

"Why?"

"Because the legal system is broken. It's all about money now."

"No, I mean why is he suing?" I asked. "Is it about unlawful termination?"

"Oh no. He says Aria sexually harassed him." He leaned back and appraised my reaction to this absurd claim.

It was probably the most unlikely thing I'd heard yet. And I'd heard some crazy things in the last couple of days. We talked more, but Paul didn't have anything else helpful to say.

Cate was up next. She bounced in about five minutes after Paul left, bracelets jingling—three on each wrist. She seemed to be in a good mood—for her. She stood still just inside the doorway and peered around the wood-clad dorm room. She wore her overalls again, which she hadn't washed in a long time, if ever. Her streaky blond, braided hair snaked down her back. I was again struck by the harmony of Cate's compact features and her bright blue eyes.

The overall package reminded me of several French actresses. I wondered, not for the first time, why French actresses tended to be slim and have small features while French actors were often oversized and sported large, distinctive features, especially noses.

"This sure as hell beats doing chores," Cate said.

"Hey, this is a cool room. It's a lot bigger than mine. Do you think they'd let me switch?"

"I have no idea."

I suddenly felt uncomfortable, and I remembered the last time I'd been in a room solely furnished with beds, with a woman I didn't know. It had been a job interview in a hotel room when I was fresh out of college—an out-of-town company that paid very well. The interviewer had been a distractingly beautiful executive, and I found my mind wandering to the point that I completely misunderstood a question, answered inanely, and blew my chances. Woman plus bed equaled potential sex, however inappropriate. Now, at forty-two, this awkward moment with Cate passed without mishap.

"You said you were Aria's friend," Cate said, "so you've got influence with her, right? You could get me a better room."

"I'll tell you what. I'll do my best to get you this very room if you cooperate in our interview."

"It's a deal." She sat cross-legged on the bed, and she made the full lotus position look easy. It wasn't. Despite her claims to have not bought into the program at Aria's center, she'd meditated a lot—or I suppose she could've been a gymnast.

I'd caught a break on the deal we'd struck. Cate had walked in and immediately provided me leverage. "Were you close to your uncle?" I asked.

"Wayne was an asshole. Now he's a dead asshole."

"That's kind of cold, don't you think?"

She shrugged. "There was some stuff when I was little. I don't want to talk about it."

I knew what that meant. "Okay. What about Ralph

Sharp—your dad?"

"We don't get along."

"Is he an asshole, too?"

"Not really." She paused and thought for a moment.

Her face softened, and I saw intelligence—and awareness—in her striking eyes. I sensed some of her problem behavior stemmed from spinning out responses too fast. If a thought popped into her head, she blurted it out, no matter the consequences. If my mind was a magic eight ball, hers was a tilt-a-whirl. This served as a recipe for pissing people off, getting fired, and sabotaging relationships.

"My dad just lives on this other planet where Jesus is micromanaging everything," Cate finally said. "If you pray to Jesus the right way, he'll get you a new car. Shit like that."

"How long has he been involved with Crowder's church?"

"Maybe three years, but before that, it was some other guy. I mean, my dad tries to be a good person and all, but he's no better than anyone else."

"What do you mean?"

"He's got a temper. He yells, he throws things. And he cheated on Mom for years before she found out. I'm not one to judge—God knows I'm making a mess out of my life—but a hypocrite's a hypocrite."

Cate rocked from side to side. She seemed pleased by her ability to characterize her father. And perhaps by her disclosure about her own problems, as well. In my experience, when self-centered people admit to a character flaw, they tend to feel inordinate pride.

"So you're not close to Ralph?" I asked.

"Not now. He's been down here, but it was fucked up."

"Tell me about that."

Cate let herself fall sideways onto the bare mattress. Now she sprawled as if she were watching a teen movie at a pajama party. I felt a momentary twinge of sexual connotation again and then it passed.

"We got to yelling, and he grabbed my arm," she said, "so José came over and talked to him. My dad shoved him, but José didn't fight back."

"Do you think anyone in your family is involved in these crimes?"

"I doubt it. They're mostly all talk. I've got another uncle who's way weird, though. If it was anyone, it'd be him."

"What's his name?"

"I forget."

"You forget your own uncle's name?" I asked. "Is he on your mom's side of the family? Does he live out of state?"

"I think he's my mom's brother. I'm not sure. He's supposed to be way crazy."

"Well, I'll check him out. What else can you tell me? You're here, you're smart, and you're watching these people all day. What do you think?"

"You can tell I'm smart?" Apparently, she thought she was too but didn't expect anyone else to notice. Perhaps she worked to keep them from knowing. As a young adult, I enjoyed watching people underestimate me.

"Oh, yeah." I nodded as sagely as I could.

"Most people can't." She smiled and sat up again, this time with her feet on the floor and her small, long-fingered hands on her knees. Our conversation had become much more interesting to her.

"You and me," I said, "we're sneaky smart."

Cate's face relaxed into its natural position, which I hadn't seen before. Her smile was tentative now, and her arched eyebrows sat lower over her eyes. I could see what was behind the tough girl act for a moment. She was young for her age. And scared.

"Well," she said, recovering and masking herself again with a frown and an aggressive tone, "if I were you, I'd look into that Paul guy. He's not very spiritual, and I'll bet he's up to something. Also, there's a guy who's been around for an hour or two now and then. He seems like a real perv. He tried to pick me up even though he's a fucking fossil."

"An old man?"

"Not old old. Just way too old for me."

"Do you know who he is?"

"No."

"What does he look like?"

"Like that guy that played Thor in that movie—only skinnier."

"Thor, the Nordic god?"

"Yeah. Sorta."

"So he's blond and fair-skinned?"

Cate nodded.

"Do you know who he sees when he's here?" I asked.

"Aria."

Was this something else Aria was withholding? I had no way of knowing if the man's presence was relevant to my investigation. This was one of those investigations where each step of the way, I uncovered additional questions instead of arriving at answers. In my experience, there would be a tipping point when things would start heading in the other direction.

Cate didn't have anything else relevant to add, although she told me quite a bit about her last boyfriend, whose feet smelled horrible no matter how much he washed them. Once she got rolling, it was hard to stop her. I guessed she didn't have anyone to talk to who she trusted. I couldn't imagine why I'd made the cut. Was it just my throwing a compliment or two her way? Maybe it was my outsider status.

I promised I'd talk to Aria about Cate's room, and then she took off to find José.

At this point, I was expecting José might be a big help with the gang element. I didn't know much about them beyond what I read in the paper.

José came in and shook my hand, looking me in the eye. I got the sense he was really seeing me. And he was extremely calm and poised. He reminded me of Aria in that way.

He spoke first. "You're thinking my tattoos make me a suspect, right?"

Soft-spoken, with a slight accent, he was probably in his early fifties. Other than the tattoos on his neck and arm—crudely drawn symbols I didn't recognize— he could've been an accountant. None of his features stood out, and I imagined that if he wore a high collar and long-sleeved shirt, his mild expression and quiet composure relegated him to the background of people's attention. All in all, José was nothing like the former thug I expected to meet.

"Originally, yes," I answered. "Gang members have tattoos, right? But everybody I talk to says you're a saint."

"Well, that's nice to hear. I certainly didn't start that way."

I gestured to one of the beds and sat on the edge of the other.

"I'd prefer to stand," José said, and then shrugged. "My back."

"Sure." He stood at formal parade rest—like a soldier in an old British war movie. The stance embodied deference but also its opposite. Clearly, he'd do what he needed to, independent of what I thought about it. "You were a Norteño?" I asked.

"Yeah. For nineteen years. I joined when I was fifteen down in East L.A."

"And there are chapters in Salinas and Watsonville?"

"Yeah, but it's all the same gang everywhere. And there's more of them in prison than on the streets. It's the same with the Sureños."

I studied him as directly as I felt I could without offending him. People with intense life stories usually carried clues about who they were now in their habitual expressions and facial wear and tear. In José's case, an excess of loose skin hung off his chin and neck as though he'd been much bigger when he was younger. It wasn't the kind of fatty tissue I associated with former bodybuilders. Maybe he was just in the midst of a serious diet. Wrinkles stretched horizontally from the corners of his brown eyes and mouth, edging closer to the perimeter of his face than I would've expected from someone his age, which was probably mid-fifties. And his teeth were a jumble of mismatched shapes and colors. Clearly some of them were inexpert add-ons—a remedy for losing teeth from fighting? A car accident? Former meth users had awful teeth, but I didn't get that vibe from José. If it were me, I'd have prioritized a few trips to the dentist. José looked like a refugee from 1940s British National Health. With darker skin, of course.

I didn't learn much from my inspection, other than the fact that the guy seemed to inspire me to think about British people. I guessed that this was more about me than him.

"What's the difference between the Sureños and the Norteños?" I asked.

"There isn't any. They're all violent, greedy assholes. They just wear different colors and protect different turf."

"They're both in the drug business?"

"Yeah. They're competitors. They distribute and sell whatever's the most profitable product at any given time." He relaxed his stance a bit and shifted his weight to his right foot.

"And they're hierarchal?"

"I don't know that word."

"Is there a hierarchy, I mean? Like, is there one guy at the top who calls the shots?"

"Oh, I see. Yeah, absolutely. In my day, all the main guys were operating from prison cells—mostly up at Pelican Bay."

This was California's highest security facility. Apparently, it wasn't secure enough.

"Do you know about the Hombres?" I asked.

"Yeah, I heard. My brother still lives in Salinas. They're bad news. Did you know Honduras is the most dangerous country in the world right now?"

"Really?"

"Yeah. I heard it on NPR." Great, I thought. My gang expert was getting his information from public radio. "The drug cartels are running things there," he continued. "They shoot people in the street, and nobody does anything."

"Do you think they're involved in this murder?"

"No. Why would you ask that?"

"Well, the missing head and hands. And those guys in the SUV."

"Those were Mexicans—from Oaxaca. I heard them talking. But I can't think of any reason any of what's happened here involves drugs. Why would it?"

"I'm just trying to explore all the possibilities. And you're my gang expert."

"If you really want to know what's going on, talk to Victor Gonzales down in Salinas. He's on the task force there. We used to work together. You can tell him I said to call." José got out a notepad and a pen from his back pocket. "Here—I'll give you his number."

"Thanks. What line of work were you both in?"

He looked down at me on the bed and smiled wanly. "We were hit men."

I didn't know what to say to that. Had he has just confessed to me he was a murderer? And outed another one? Maybe I'd misheard him. Could he have meant he was a hip man? A ship man?

He watched me. "We killed people," he said. His voice was gentle—wistful. "No matter what I do from this point forward, I'll never balance out my karma. I'll probably come back as a cockroach, or worse yet, a Republican." He gestured expansively to the sides and then winced.

I couldn't smile at that. I was still working on accepting what I'd heard. My gut churned, and I suddenly felt less real. It was weird. It wasn't that I was experiencing the world around me as illusory. It was just me. I guess it was a mild form of dissociation—standing outside myself and observing what I was up to.

I jumped up into the refuge of my mind. Was I safe now that I knew José's secret? Did this put him at the top of my list of suspects? Hardly. What kind of current murderer tells you he used to be one? Which led to the next question: why would he tell me? How could this be in his best interest? Was he intimidating me—letting me know not to fuck with him? That didn't fit either.

"You shouldn't go around telling people that," I finally said.

"I don't. Aria told me to be open with you." He gazed at me evenly. "And I do what she says. That's why I'm sitting here with you instead of sitting in a cell. I do what she says."

I was silent. "Can you help me figure out what's going on around here?" I finally asked. I certainly didn't want to know any details of his former career.

"It's amateurs. Trying to make it look like they're pros."

"Why do you say that?"

"The big show. You don't leave a body in a wishing well unless you've got a damned good reason. Look at all the potential witnesses here. You could throw the guy in the ocean. Instead you skulk around this property and hope nobody sees you? I don't think so. It's stupid. And why would a gang be trying to scare anyone here? The only one I can think of is me, and they know that would be a waste of time."

150

"Why's that?"

"Look at me." José raked a hand down his torso.

"What do you mean?"

"You can't see it? I've got cancer. I'm dying."

I could see it now. The way he held himself was a response to chronic pain. I guessed bone cancer or something else widespread. I'd also ignored the dark circles under his eyes and a pallor that was hard to catch in a Hispanic man.

"I'm sorry," I said.

"It's okay. I'm ready." What I had perceived as a calm demeanor was actually resignation. Who knew who the guy was when he wasn't dying?

"How much time do you have?"

"A few months. It'll get bad in a few more weeks."

"Jesus," I exclaimed.

"No, it's got nothing to do with him. I'm through with him."

Chapter Fifteen

I was worn out by the time I passed one more aphorism sign walking back to my car. It was apt. "Death is profoundly mundane."

I let Larry out to run around and pee, and he obliged. While he was busy, I called Matt to ask him to order Chinese food, but he didn't answer, which wasn't like him. I wasn't worried—there were a host of innocent explanations—but it was one more thing to wonder about.

After loading an extremely reluctant Larry into my Mazda—I lured him with a hunk of power bar I found under the brake pedal—I drove to the restaurant and ordered kung pao tofu for myself. It was the only time I ate tofu, which I consider to be a neighbor of salad on the food pyramid. John had introduced me to the spicy dish years ago, and now I was hooked.

I tried not to think about the case, and I was completely successful for all of thirty seconds. José was a spiritually evolved hit man. Paul was a jerk. Cate was hiding inside herself. Sumati still had relationship issues.

What else? My gut ached from the punch I took from the SUV guy. Somebody wanted to kidnap or hurt Aria. And there were new people for Matt and me to check out—Cate's third uncle, the creepy visitor guy, and a Salinas cop—José's former "coworker."

I had probably forgotten something, but these were the recent developments that came to mind as I scarfed down the hot food.

I used to take tons of notes when I was conducting an investigation, but with my eyes down on my pad or tablet, I missed too much. The good stuff was subtle, often nonverbal, and I couldn't afford to miss it. The last time I took assiduous notes, a suspect reached for a samurai sword on the wall behind his desk while I had my head down. As he shouted, "Die, you son of a whore!" I began to write that down. Fortunately, it had been a novelty sword the guy had won at a carnival, and the cheap blade had broken off on my shoulder. It hurt like hell, though.

So now I didn't have access to every little thing that happened after a whirlwind day. Matt teased most of it out of me afterward, though. I called him again. Still no answer. Now I was worried. He was one of those guys who was in love with his phone. When he'd first gotten his current one, I'd caught him fondling it.

I distracted myself by returning to thinking about the case, even though what I really needed was something to distract me from that. I was struck by the fact that all the suspects and witnesses manifested certain traits when I first met them, and then turned into someone quite different by the time we were through talking.

Sumati became more neurotic. Paul got ornerier. Cate revealed her soft underbelly. And José turned out to be a former hit man, for God's sake. And dying, to boot.

I suddenly realized something obvious. José had nothing to lose. What did it matter if he confessed to me or if he was still killing people? It was like giving notice at work and then staying on as a lame duck for a while. If you screwed up, what were they going to do, fire you? Maybe he held a grudge against Wayne Sharp and he was squaring things before he died. On the other hand, there was no evidence tying him to the victim, and personally I liked the guy. He was clearly a spiritual guy now—kind of like a junior Aria.

It was hard to picture Cate playing a role in any of this, so at the Santa Cruz Spiritual Center, that left Paul and Sumati's exes as viable suspects. More likely, the killer or threatener was someone I hadn't run into yet. I noticed my resolve to focus solely on the threatening phone caller had pretty much dissolved. Murder cases sang a siren song to the ears of any investigator, and no one had lashed me to any masts.

I didn't like Crowder for the murder for a variety of reasons. Would you hide the head of your victim at your ranch and then call the police when your dog found it? Nothing beyond Aria's word tied him to any of this until he made that call to the cops. So someone was trying to frame him. Also, as much as I didn't like the guy, Crowder just didn't seem capable of ordering a killing.

I hadn't met Ralph Sharp yet, but what kind of monster kills his own brother? Cate had hinted that Wayne had molested her, and maybe this warranted a father's revenge on that scale. I'd try to determine if Ralph had found out recently. Otherwise, all the Sharp stuff was about money.

Whoever had hired the SUV thugs was a definite suspect. Perhaps one of the Oaxacans would give him up. It wasn't hard to come up with a motive if a gang leader was behind this. Wayne Sharp had been about to be arrested and might've ratted out his confederates. In the drug-dealing world, the bar to justify violence was set pretty low.

But I still wasn't clear about the connection between Aria and any of this. If the well had just been a dumping ground for a random body, then why lure John away and come for her?

And if the original threats—Aria's and Crowder's—constituted separate crimes from the murder, then why would the killer leave her a torso and send him a head?

Matt finally called me back.

"Where have you been?" I asked. "I was starting to get worried."

"The police hauled me in for questioning. They found the victim's hands buried in the flowerbed outside your condo—with Wayne's watch still on his wrist.

"What?"

"Yeah, I know. There was a fingerprint on the face of the watch too, which they haven't matched to anyone yet. So the cops came to the office looking for you, and then they decided I was the next best thing."

"Cardenas and Sutter?"

"No. Uniformed guys. But Cardenas was waiting at the station. His head almost exploded when I wouldn't tell them where you were. That guy needs an anger-management class."

"What were the hands doing in my flower bed? I mean, how did anyone even know to look in there?"

"The police received an anonymous tip. Somebody told them they were walking by at night and saw you digging."

"And why would I be doing that?"

"Isn't it obvious? You were protecting your girlfriend Aria—conspiring to hide incriminating evidence."

"Oh, yeah. I forgot about that. You hear how that sounds, right?"

"I was just trying to give you a feel for the ridiculous shit they were pulling at my interrogation. Remind me not to dismember anyone, would you? It's not worth it."

"I'm sorry about that, Matt. What did you tell them?"

"Pretty much everything except where you were. I wanted you to have a heads-up before they came at you. Anyway, I still don't know for sure where you are. Are you still at Aria's?"

"No. Fung Shen."

"Tofu time, huh? You're such a New Age dude, Karl."

"What do you make of the print on the watch?"

"It probably doesn't have anything to do with the murder. It's practically a perfect one right on the glass crystal. Who'd be dumb enough to leave that on there?"

"I don't know," I told him. "Where are you now?"

"Back at the office. What are you going to do?"

"I guess I'll call Cardenas. I've still got his card."

Matt shifted into a higher gear and spoke much faster. "I found out something about the foundation in Texas—the one that backs Crowder. It's administered by a money-laundering bank in Austin—the same one Wayne Sharp was using."

"That makes sense. Crowder told me Wayne

handled the church's finances. Good work."

"And I checked into the history of Aria's property," he continued. "She doesn't own it herself. A nonprofit called Enlightenment Services does."

"Who are they?"

"I don't know yet. It's probably just something she set up herself. You could ask her."

"Sure. What about the lawsuit?"

"Sharp and Crowder have a case. The old lady was starting to lose it around the same time she altered her will. She was savvy enough to have a doctor sign an affidavit that she was of sound mind, but nobody can find the guy now. Supposedly he retired and moved to Costa Rica. Anyway, adult children have strong rights in California estate law, and numerous people heard her promise the property to Ralph."

"Thanks, Matt. I'd better make that call to Cardenas."

"Right. Talk to you later."

Chapter Sixteen

"Yeah?" Cardenas answered.

"It's Karl Gatlin. I just heard about the hands."

"Where are you?"

"A Chinese restaurant in Santa Cruz."

"Come on down here to the station. You might want to bring a lawyer."

"Give me ten minutes."

I felt sorry for Larry. More car time loomed. I tried to explain, but I got a look I think he learned from watching those TV commercials about shelter dogs. I can't stand to look at those, but he always did.

The police station was modern, with a wildly inappropriate public art installation out front. It was a stylized insect surfing on Saturn's rings, for God's sake. I'd heard that at cop conferences across the state, Santa Cruz officers were called SBSers—Space Bug Surfers.

The inside was spacious, with enough room between each of the desks in the bullpen that you could actually hear who you were trying to talk to. In the old station, which was just an annex at the picturesque City Hall, it had been so crowded, you had to shout at one another from four feet away.

The desk sergeant escorted me through the bullpen to one of the interview rooms at the back of the building. This room hadn't been designed to be pleasing to the eye. The bare walls were light green cinderblock, except for the obligatory one-way glass mirror. There was a long metal table with two matching chairs on either side of it. The fluorescent lighting seemed especially oppressive in there.

"Here you go," the sergeant said. "Take a seat. The detective will join you shortly."

He closed the door behind him, and I heard it lock. That wasn't good. I decided to stand while I waited so I'd be upright when Cardenas got there. I'd been through this before. You needed to hold onto your power however you could.

He stalked in a couple of minutes later, nodded, and sat down, so I did too. He held some items that he placed on the table: a bottle of spring water, a spiral notebook, a digital recorder, and a metal key ring with about twenty keys on it.

"I assume you talked to your assistant and you know the score?" Cardenas asked.

I nodded. He glared at me with bloodshot eyes. He looked thoroughly worn out. I noticed he almost had a unibrow. The ends of his black eyebrows were microns from each other on top of his wide nose. How had I missed that before?

He leaned forward and spoke aggressively. "So your idea of staying out of our way is getting a restraining order against you, brawling with known criminals, concealing evidence, questioning witnesses before we can get to them, and telling your assistant not to cooperate with us. Am I missing anything?"

"Quit busting my balls, Cardenas."

"I haven't even mentioned the victim's hands, Gatlin? You want to see them? You want to see if they look familiar?" He started to get up—as if he were going to go get them.

"You know as well as I do there's no way I buried anything at my place."

"We've got a witness."

"No, you don't. You got an anonymous tip from whoever planted them there. And I can tell you when that was. It had to have been after 8:30 this morning."

"Why's that?"

"My dog. There's no way Larry walked right by there without smelling them. We left the condo at 8:30."

"You named your dog 'Larry'?"

"That's what you picked up on here?"

Cardenas shook his head and threw his arm to the side. It was kind of a "what am I gonna do with this guy?" gesture. "So you're saying they did it in broad daylight," he continued. "In front of all your neighbors?"

"Everybody leaves for work by 8:30 except for the guy who lives behind me. And I've got an alibi from nine o'clock on."

"Yeah, I heard about all that," he said, shaking his head as though he didn't believe me. "But here's the thing. You're creating your own alibi by telling me this story about your dog. How do I know you're not making it up?"

"Give me a break. This is ridiculous."

Cardenas smirked. "Yeah, I know. We've found out more about this since your receptionist paid us a visit. You're a pain, but you're not an idiot."

"So this is just sadism? Is that your thing, Cardenas?" I could feel my face heating up and reddening.

"What do you make of your fingerprint on the watch crystal?" he asked, as though I hadn't said anything.

This was such bullshit. Why should I have to answer any questions? "Maybe I put it there because I'm an evil murderer and I want everyone to know."

"Well, it wasn't yours," he said. "So we can cross that off."

"Quit screwing around, Cardenas. Why don't we compare notes and see if we can help one another?"

"Yeah, sure. You go first. Do you mind if I record it?

"Not at all. You probably know what we've come up with until today, right? Matt would've told you."

"Humor me."

"Okay."

I took him through it, as well as I remembered. The reason cops in this county trust me is I'm usually willing to share information. Cardenas asked questions and took a bathroom break once. I didn't tell him about José's past or a few other details that didn't seem to be any of his business.

When I was done, I took a bathroom break myself and checked on Larry. Detective Sutter was just driving up.

"That's a beautiful dog," she said, displaying more personality than she had the whole time she'd been in my office.

"Thank you."

"Does Lou know you're out here?"

"Probably not."

"You'd better get back in there," she told me.

She was right. Cardenas was waiting impatiently,

playing with his keys. But he was surprisingly
forthcoming once he started talking about the case.
Probably because he wasn't making much progress
either. Both of us were finding out all sorts of things,
but neither of us knew what the hell they meant.

The police had identified three of the four
assailants at Aria's center. They all worked for the
Sureños off and on. None of them were gang members,
and none of them were talking. Ralph Sharp, Gary
Crowder, and Crowder's bodyguard, Arlin, all had solid
alibis the night of the murder. Aria's sexual harassment
suit was weird, Cardenas said. Ray Lundquist, the
former administrator of the center, had accused her of
various outrageous things, which should've been easy
to disprove. But Aria hadn't expended any energy
defending herself. And the lawsuit wasn't worded the
usual way. It wasn't clear if the guy was trying to win
the suit, get a settlement, or just harass her.

"Maybe Lundquist has an inexperienced attorney,"
Cardenas said. "Maybe Aria's not taking it seriously. I
don't know. But I think it's worth looking into."

"Definitely."

Then he told me about Wayne Sharp's business.
Besides a complex money-laundering scheme (which
he explained and I didn't understand), Sharp also ran a
fledgling Ponzi scheme (which I understood), and he'd
defrauded the IRS (which I knew only too well). In my
defense, the IRS considers incompetence to be fraud.

"Who'd he screw over with the Ponzi deal?" I
asked. "Was anyone pissed off enough to come after
him?"

"We're checking that out. For now, my money's on
the gang he was laundering for. We think it was

probably the Barrio Azteca."

"Who? I thought he was involved with the Hombres from Honduras."

"No, these guys are based in Texas. They started in an El Paso jail, but they've got branches in half a dozen other states now and they farm things out sometimes—especially to La Linea and the Sureños. They like to behead people, by the way. Their main income is from smuggling cocaine in from Ciudad Juarez. Most of them are U.S. citizens, which really helps them out. They make so much money, they have to launder it all over the place."

"How could someone like Wayne Sharp and a Texas gang get together?" I could feel my brow furrowing. I felt like a bad actor—some guy in a silent movie.

"We don't know, but something you told me might be a big help."

"What's that?"

"The bank in Austin. The one with connections to Reverend Crowder and Sharp. I'll get Sutter to talk to the Feds about it. She's got a buddy over there in San Jose."

It was hard to imagine her having a buddy anywhere. "What about the head? Could you determine the cause of death from it? And what did Crowder have to say about it being in his barn?"

"It was a single shot to the temple—a nine-millimeter handgun. And obviously Sharp's head was planted there—the same as your hands."

"Does the murderer think you're stupid?"

Cardenas shrugged with his entire torso, which was an effort for him.

A man in his late forties came into the interview room without knocking. He was tall, with a barrel chest, a round face, and a big presence. Pink blotches marred his porcelain-white skin, especially on his cheeks. His stern expression seemed to be his default setting. He reminded me of a character actor whose name I couldn't remember—one of those guys who played a politician on *Law and Order*.

"Good afternoon, Chief," Cardenas said.

Chapter Seventeen

Jim Crowder nodded and then turned to face me. "Karl Gatlin?"

"Yes." I stood and shook his hand as he introduced himself.

He was wearing a charcoal-gray suit with a white shirt and a dark red tie. My first impression was positive, despite the semi-scowl he sent my way. I remembered I'd felt the same way about his brother, though. At first.

"Why don't we sit back down and chat?" he suggested. It was a gentle order.

We did. Cardenas and Crowder faced me across the plain wooden table. The police chief turned and looked at his detective. "Is he cooperating?"

"Yes, sir. He's been very helpful." Cardenas nodded emphatically.

I appreciated this.

"That's great. So he's confessed?" the chief asked.

Taken aback, all I could do was stare. Did the chief know anything at all about this case?

"Uh, no sir. He doesn't seem to be guilty of anything. We're working together on the case."

"I see. Detective, I wonder if you'd mind stepping out for a few minutes. There are several things I'd like to go over with Mr. Gatlin." This was another order disguised as a courteous request.

Cardenas wasn't happy about it. "Sir, with all due respect—"

"Get out," Crowder said. His tone was steely now.

"Yes, sir." Cardenas took off, leaving his stuff on the table, including the digital recorder, which was still running. If he got caught, I guess he could claim he forgot to turn it off.

"So, Gatlin, I understand you've been harassing my brother," Chief Crowder said in a studied, neutral tone.

"No. Would you like to hear what actually happened?"

"Your side of the story? Sure, go ahead. I should warn you, though. I saw the video."

"The reverend invited me down to his ranch, ostensibly to hire me, although I doubt that was his real motive. I got into it with his bodyguard, which was partly my fault, and when the guy threatened me, I used my dog to scare him off. After that, I had a conversation with your brother, which ended poorly. I think he was upset I wormed more information out of him than he got out of me."

"Can you prove any of this?"

"Well, I don't walk around with a camcorder, but my associate Matt can vouch for the fact that Crowder called me and asked me to go down there. He was on the line, too."

"I see. Let me explain something to you. Gary bends the rules sometimes. He's ambitious, and some people don't like that." Crowder leaned across the table and smiled for the first time. I didn't like his smile. I didn't want to be his friend. "But he's a good man," he continued. "You don't have to worry that he's mixed-up in this murder."

"I appreciate your input." I tried to radiate gratitude instead of annoyance. "But your brother's name keeps popping up, and I'm not going to ignore that. He could turn out to be the piece that leads me to the real killer—who's probably a gang member, by the way. I know your main interest and mine are the same in this case—to apprehend whoever's responsible. That's got to take priority over treating a family member with kid gloves."

"Certainly. But don't overstep your role with Gary. That's my advice. As you know, he'll slap a lawsuit on you at the least provocation. And his man Arlin is a bit of a loose cannon. I wouldn't want you to get hurt."

I studied his face. Was this advice or a veiled threat? I couldn't decide. Crowder held his oversized features still. I got the feeling he was in performance mode and had been ever since he'd entered the room. I don't think he truly reacted to what I said. He stuck to a script.

"Thank you, Chief. I'll keep that in mind. Anything else I can help you with?" As if that was what was going on.

"I want you to know my policy of cooperating with private investigators doesn't apply to you. It's intended for the organizations in town that have sometimes been invaluable to our force." He paused and scowled again. I got the sense this time that he was working at it. His acting was fraying around the edges. "I've got my eye on you," Crowder continued. "I don't know how you won over my detective, but I'll be instructing him to throw the book at you if you fuck up. And you will."

"What book are you going to tell him to throw? The Bible?"

When I finally drove off with Larry, he wouldn't even look at me. I couldn't blame him. Between the restaurant and the police station, this had been the longest stretch I'd ever locked him in.

By now, it was 3:30. It was cloudy and sixty-five degrees. We'd entered the dry season, so there wasn't much chance of rain, but it was gloomy. After three weeks of sun, I was spoiled already.

I realized I didn't have to be anywhere in particular, so I made a couple of right hand turns to head to the dog beach below West Cliff Drive. I owed Larry some fun. This was the only beach in town where dogs were legally allowed to run free, so there were always playmates for Larry. I broke the off-leash rules elsewhere, but most dog owners didn't.

As a result of changing direction, I noticed I was being tailed by a silver Ford sedan—fairly new—and whoever was driving it was quite skilled. He stayed two cars back, hiding behind a full-sized pickup.

I wasn't sure how to handle it. I certainly couldn't outrun anyone in my little car. I could roust the guy and find out who he was. Or I could let him follow me for now since I wasn't doing anything secretive. I could also call the police, but it occurred to me that the tail might *be* the police—someone Chief Crowder had assigned to monitor me. If that were the case, I didn't want to tip them off that I knew about them.

I finally decided to just go about my business and deal with whatever came up. In hindsight, I think the fact that I was armed affected my judgment. I tend to feel safer than I really am when I have the capacity to shoot someone seven times.

We were down on the beach about ten minutes

later with fifteen other dogs and dog owners. I recognized a few of them—the male Akita with the short bald guy, the Jack Russell with the lesbian couple, and the skinny mutt with the Goth girl. The Akita and Larry had tangled a few times, but as long as no one was stupid enough to bring food, they maintained a truce.

Larry and I began by playing ball. I kept a gazillion tennis balls in the trunk because he always abandoned the ball at some point, and I was too lazy to go collect it myself. On this occasion, he gave up our game after ten minutes and began chasing a black Lab, which didn't work out because he always caught him right away. When a pack of small dogs decided to chase Larry, I could see his delight. He'd get a big lead on them and then double back and race through them. Then they'd chase him the other way.

I scanned the cliff top behind us regularly for the first twenty minutes and then began talking to the bald guy. My tail was probably up in his car listening to the radio while he waited for us to return to ours.

The bald guy's name was Jerry, it turned out, and he was a bartender, which was why he could take Zeus the Akita out in the afternoon.

A shot rang out, and I hit the deck. "Get down!" I shouted to Jerry and the others. Most of them did. The next shot kicked up the sand by my hip. The guy was zeroing in on me with a rifle from up on the cliff. The altitude made it a tough shot, but any decent marksman was going to nail me soon.

There was no cover at all on the beach. I sprinted for the freezing water as more shots rang out. Then I ran awkwardly through the shallows and dove in under a crashing wave. I had to fight my way through to deeper water. Already, my clothes felt like they weighed forty pounds. A moment later, while I hid underwater as long as I could, I sensed a big body near me. When I came up to the surface about ten yards from where I'd plunged in, Larry paddled next to me for all he was worth. I heard another shot, and I submerged again.

No one swam or surfed without a wetsuit in April in water this cold. I wouldn't last long.

I don't know if Larry was trying to save me or he thought we were playing a new game, but he swam directly overhead and started scratching the hell out of my shoulders. If the bullets or the water temperature didn't kill me, my dog might.

I shoved him out of the way to get to the surface again, and I emerged behind him on the bay side. I don't think the shooter saw me. There were no shots, at least.

Larry wasn't a great swimmer, and a bullet could hit him, too. For that matter, he wasn't much better insulated than I was against the cold water. Would he be okay?

I took a peek next time up, and I couldn't see anyone on the cliff, so I decided to chance swimming in. With all the cell phones in the world, no shooter in his right mind would stay up there long.

I struggled through the surf. My wet clothes tried to drag me down, but I made it. Larry managed to get back to shore right behind me. We were both shivering. It didn't take long in the bay to chill you to the bone.

"Holy shit!" Jerry said. He was standing by the edge of the water. He grabbed my arm and helped me out. "Somebody go get a towel or a blanket!" he called.

I slumped onto the sand, and Larry lay down next to me.

"Who the hell are you?" Jerry asked. "Why was somebody shooting at you?"

That reminded me to check on my gun. It was still strapped in its hip holster, under my shirt. But it was probably ruined, I thought. I heard multiple sirens.

"Is everyone okay?" I asked.

"Yeah. We all just lay on the ground, and the guy shot into the water. Did you get hit at all?"

"No. Most bullets can't penetrate more than a couple of feet in seawater."

"Oh."

I heard a woman to my right providing a running commentary on her phone about what was happening. If she was talking to the cops, they'd arrive with some understanding of the situation. That would help. "So that's why I'm going to be late, Susan," she finished. Oh well.

Larry shivered so badly that I decided to give him a horizontal bear hug to help him warm up. I imagine we were quite a sight—two wet messes cuddling on the beach.

An out-of-breath older man brought a couple of beach towels, and they helped. Then a minute or two later, the police showed up with wool blankets and emergency medical gear. Larry was happy to have several blankets piled on top of him. I peeled off my wet clothes under mine.

"Check Larry first," I told the cop with the first aid kit. The guy wouldn't, so I clutched my blanket to ward off his examination.

"Okay, okay," he said. He was tall and slim, with short strawberry blond hair and freckles. His spotless uniform must've been tailored. It fit him perfectly. Was he hoping to meet his princess charming on the job? The guy took a look. "He's got some cuts and scratches, but nothing major."

"Those are probably from this morning," I told him.

"Is it true you're the guy that fought off those four Sureños out in the redwoods?"

"That was the two of us, plus a friend."

"You're all heroes down at the station," he said.

I hadn't noticed that when I was there. "John Ratu was the real hero," I told him.

"Home-run John? I'll have to buy him a beer after the next game." He looked at Larry again. "The problem is the water's filthy. Your dog's going to need an antibiotic because of those open cuts."

"Can you do that?"

"I'm not supposed to—it's an EMT thing, and that's if you're a human—but what the hell. I've got a big dog too, so I know the approximate dose."

After insulting Larry further with a needle jab, he checked me out and determined that other than low body temperature, I was fine—which I already knew.

Detective Sutter strode into view. "Let's get you two into a warm police car," she said.

I was shivering more now, probably more due to an adrenaline response than anything to do with temperature. "That sounds good," I said. "You don't mind Larry being in there?"

"Who's Larry?"

"My dog."

"Oh, sure. Somebody said he swam out and saved you. So nothing but the best for Larry."

Chapter Eighteen

I called it a day after Sutter and the other cops were through with me. I'd endured my full share of violence and mayhem. I was also sick of dealing with the police, who asked an insane amount of redundant questions. If I hadn't seen the shooter the first three times they asked me, why would I have seen him the fourth time?

I drove home in my blanket, which garnered me a few stares at stoplights, but this was Santa Cruz, home of every sort of eccentricity imaginable. Some of these people were probably taking fashion tips from me.

At my condo, I took a long hot bath, although I'd never used the tub before for anything but wrestling with Larry on dog-washing day. When he heard the water running, he started to bark. When I clambered in and left him alone, his tail went wild. I'd also set up a space heater in the bathroom; Larry curled up on the tile floor in front of it, hogging all the heat.

I called Matt from the tub.

"Where the hell have you been?" he asked. "Cardenas hasn't been questioning you for three and a half hours, has he?"

"No, I took Larry to the beach, and somebody took some shots at me."

"Holy shit! What'd you do?"

"I ran in the water and almost drowned."

"Good thinking," Matt said. "There's less blood

that way."

"Anyway, I'm done for the day."

"You don't want to hear what I found out?"

"Not if it can possibly wait."

"Should I come by and pick up Larry?"

I'd forgotten it was supposed to be Adele's turn. "Yeah. That'd be great. If I'm still in the tub, just open the front door and call his name."

"Sure. We don't have to talk tonight."

"Good." I was kaput.

I fell asleep in the tub. I didn't even hear Matt when he came to pick up Larry. I was a human prune when I woke up at nine p.m. Mr. Wrinkles heated up a frozen pizza, watched a terrible movie on TV, and then fell asleep again before it was over.

****

I felt like myself in the morning. Because I'd gone to bed early, I woke up correspondingly early. I did my requisite exercises and even threw in a few extra. Then I caught up on my personal email, made a decent breakfast, and shaved for the first time in several days. I even beat Matt into the office.

"Hey, what are you doing here?" he asked when he wandered in twenty minutes later.

"Detecting. What about you?"

"Yeah, me too. This is quite a case, isn't it? It's about time we had some excitement around here."

"I've had enough. Listen, I need to call John. Then I want to hear whatever you dug up yesterday."

I called my Maori colleague. "We need to go on a field trip," I told him. "On short notice." I'd concocted the plan on the drive into the office.

"What about Aria?"

"Can you get Chen to cover? I don't want to go to Salinas by myself."

"Lemme call him. I'll call you right back."

Chen was a martial arts whiz I contacted when I needed two guys. He wasn't my favorite person in the world because he hardly ever said anything.

The phone rang a few minutes later, and I grabbed it before Matt could. "Good news," John said. "He's sitting around playing Scrabble."

"Chen?"

"He's a champ, Karl. He can be here at the center in an hour. Does that work?"

"It's perfect."

While I'd been dodging bullets the day before, Matt had made an annotated list of everyone associated with the case on my whiteboard. He'd mounted it across the room from my desk so clients wouldn't be facing it. I knew Matt didn't have a problem remembering who was who. The list was for me. I strode across the room and studied it.

At the Santa Cruz Spiritual Center, we had Aria, Paul Webb (the administrator), Sumati (the body finder), José Vega (the ex-gang saint), and Cate (the pain-in-the-ass daughter of Lois Sharp). The rest of the Sharp contingent: dead Wayne and his estranged widow Georgia, brother Ralph, who was an Everything is Jesus church booster, and the mystery uncle. On the Crowder side, we had Pastor Gary and police chief Jim and his wife. Then there was Bobby Mendoza, Sumati's ex who'd recently been released from prison, and Victor Gonzales, the gang task-force guy who José had steered us toward. Lastly, we had Ray Lundquist, the former spiritual center's administrator who was suing Aria for harassment.

Matt had listed several others in a separate category he called "auxiliary." I didn't agree with whom he'd put on this list, but I wasn't going to argue. Here he'd written Leanne Atkinson, (Reverend Crowder's accuser), Arlin (the bodyguard at Crowder's ranch), the guys in the SUV, Lou Cardenas, and Sue Sutter.

Then we had the gangs. There were the Norteños who were allied with the Hombres but didn't seem to be directly involved in the case. The Sureños were certainly in the mix, if only because of Wayne Sharp's laundering, and they were also at war with the Hombres, who were crazed Hondurans trying to break into the area. Then the Barrio Azteca was a Texas crew backing the Sureños against the Hombres. Neither of us knew much more than that about the Latino gangs, and obviously we weren't capable of dealing with any of them beyond writing their names on a whiteboard.

I beckoned Matt into my office, sat at my desk, and told him my plan to head down to Salinas with John to talk to Bobby Mendoza and Victor Gonzales. Then he sprawled onto the couch and filled me in on what he'd been up to the day before.

Lois Sharp—Ralph Sharp's ex-wife and Cate's mother—had been cooperative when Matt had reached her on the phone. She'd painted a remarkably balanced picture of her ex, given the circumstances. According to her, Ralph was just a mixed-up guy doing the best he could. He fell under the sway of a series of opportunist pastors. That was his main problem. Well, that and the lying and cheating.

On the other hand, Lois had nothing good at all to

say about the murder victim. She'd provided story after story about Wayne Sharp's greedy self-centeredness.

"I've got background on the guy who filed the harassment suit against Aria, too," Matt told me next. "Ray Lundquist was only running the office at the center for four months. Before that, he worked at the Boardwalk supervising the kids they hire to run the games. He's a Canadian originally, and he's in even more debt than Paul Webb."

"Then how could he afford lawyer's fees?"

He shook his head. "I don't know. He's a coke addict, too. That's where his money goes, and that's why he keeps getting fired."

"Why would Aria hire an addict who was coming from a low-end job? That doesn't make much sense. And where does he live now?"

"He's down in Watsonville—in a bad neighborhood. But he works in Salinas."

"Where I'm going today," I said.

"Right. He's the parts guy at a Hyundai dealer."

"Make sure you give me the address before I leave."

"Sure." He paused and then spoke again. "I know you need to sneak up on that Bobby character, but don't you think you ought to call José's friend Victor to arrange to meet him down there? You can't just waltz into a task-force office."

"Yeah, I called Victor from the car. He's meeting me and John at Casa Maria at one. He says he's busy, and the only free time he has is at lunch."

"I'm surprised he's willing to see you at all." Matt melted into the couch's seat cushions again. If he'd been wearing the same brown color, he might've been invisible.

"When I mentioned José's name, he wanted to help however he could. He basically cast another vote for the guy's sainthood."

Matt started to tell me all the police news, but I let him know he didn't need to because Cardenas already had.

"He told you about their investigation?" he asked.

"Yeah, I was surprised too."

"Here's something else interesting." Matt sat up just a bit. Apparently, only interesting topics could improve his posture. "You know how Aria has no history back past a certain point? I don't just mean on Google. I mean even when I dig deep."

"Uh huh."

"I think it's because she used to have a different name."

"A maiden name?"

"Probably. Next time you talk to her, ask her what it was, would you?"

"I'll see what I can find out. I'm not going to grill her." Aria had made it perfectly clear that she'd decide for herself how much to tell me.

"Have you seen the newspaper?" Matt asked.

"No."

"You're all over the place. And you have a hero dog who fends off drug dealers, rescues people, and takes a great photo."

"Are we on the front page? Will this kill my undercover work?"

"It's front page all right, but your photo doesn't look like you, so don't worry."

"Oh, that's good," I said.

"It's much better-looking than you are."

"Thanks for sharing, Matt."

"All kinds of media people called here last night and left a ton of messages," Matt reported. "I checked them while you were on the phone with John. I'll get calls today, too, once they all drag their lazy asses out of bed. Not everybody's a go-getter like me. What do you want me to say? Do you want to talk to them?"

"No. Just be boring."

"Boring?"

"Yeah, like those athletes that just thank their mom or God."

"Okay. Maybe I'll thank Larry's mom," Matt said.

"Good thinking." I stood up. "I assume there's more, but I've gotta go."

"Anything special you want me to do today?"

"Just keep digging. I think we need to know more about Ralph Sharp and Gary Crowder in particular. Aria's property must be worth millions, and they're the ones involved in that. She told me the first day she thought Crowder's church was behind the threats."

"The property's worth 6.2 million. That's the current assessment."

"Matt, you need to tone down the hacking. We're both seriously screwed if you get caught."

"Oh, it's not me," he said. "All the hacking is done by a mysterious, brilliant guy in South Africa who routes it through the Hungarian embassy in Malaysia. He just happens to look like me."

"Whatever. Just be careful. Don't forget this is just a job—it's not worth going to jail for. I've been there. You wouldn't like it."

****

I was running late—I had to stop for gas—so I called John and told him to meet me in the parking lot at Aria's center. It was about a fifty-minute drive to Salinas.

"Chen's here," he reported when we rendezvoused. "Aria says he has intriguing energy."

"What do you think that means, John?"

"Beats me. I don't get what she's going on about half the time, but it still feels awful good being around her."

John wore his usual voluminous black shorts, and he had on a black polo shirt, too. He looked like he was ready to run onto the pitch for the New Zealand All Blacks. He almost had, back in his prime. He'd made the team until a day before the final cut, and then an injury had sent him back to the minor leagues.

After my Mazda, the inside of John's SUV felt like an auditorium. He helped foster the illusion by turning on loud music.

He was a fan of conjunto music, of all things. The Tex-Mex accordion tunes were kind of peppy, but when John started singing along in heavily accented Spanish, I shouted a protest.

"It's happy music," he told me, turning the stereo down a hair. "Plus we're going where a lot of Mexicans live, right? It'll get us in the mood."

"I need to tell you about the people we're going to meet. And how I envision your role."

"Envision, huh?" He turned the music off. "Okay, Karl. Tell me about it."

I filled him in, stressing that we weren't looking for trouble and we wouldn't start any. But if someone came at us…

Verlin Darrow

****

Bobby Mendoza was our first interview. Matt had found his aunt's address in Salinas where he was supposedly staying, which turned out to be a new two-story stucco home in a middle-class subdivision that had recently been carved out of outlying farmland. An attractive young Latina woman opened the door after I rang the bell.

"Hi." I said. "I'm Karl, and this is John."

John smiled his giant smile, and she smiled back at him. She was probably twenty-one or so, with an alert face and clear brown eyes. Her almost flawless skin was marred by one zit way up on her temple. She smelled like lavender.

"We don't need anything," she said. "And I'm a comparative religion major in college, so you can forget about any missionary work."

"Oh, I'm sorry," I said. "I should've explained. We're checking up on Bobby. Is he here?" I hadn't said we were parole officers. If that's what she wanted to believe, that was up to her.

She looked at John again. "Now I see why you've got the mountain with you."

"Hey," John said. "That wasn't very nice."

"Sorry." She grimaced. "I try to be clever sometimes, and it comes out wrong."

"What do you compare religions to?" John asked.

She had to think that one over. "Each other."

"So is he here?" I asked.

"No. You'll find him down the street at the bar with the blue sign—I don't remember the name. And when you do, tell him that Dolores is going to kick his ass for eating all her yogurt."

John walked into the El Rio Bar and Cantina first. Everybody stopped talking. They couldn't see me standing behind him, and I couldn't see them, either. When he moved to the side. I stepped up beside him. Everybody was staring at us. I felt like we were in the Old West.

There were three men at the bar and two pairs of men at small round tables. Matt had printed out Bobby's mug shot, and I'd shown it to John. Bobby was the guy at the end of the bar nearest us. He wasn't as creepy in real life as in the photo, which surprised me. Usually it was the other way around. His conspicuously round face circumscribed small, close-set eyes and a nose that had obviously been broken a few times. I wondered if Sumati was responsible for any of its crooks and turns. Half a beer and most of a sandwich sat in front of him.

The place was a dump. The furniture was worn out, and it had been cheap in the first place. Everything was dirty, especially the windows. The bartender looked like a Latino Steve Buscemi. And there was conjunto music playing, which was an odd synchronicity. We weren't in Texas. Mariachi was the king in Salinas.

"What the hell are you?" Bobby called to John. "You're not black, and you're not Hispanic. Are you a Samoan or something? What the hell is a Samoan doing in here?" He slurred a few of the words and spoke louder than he needed to.

"I'm a singer," John said in his New Zealand accent. Then he began singing along with the music. The whole bar began laughing.

John waltzed over to Bobby while he kept singing. When he was standing next to him, he stopped singing and put a huge hand on his shoulder. "My friend would like a word with you."

"Fuck off." Bobby thrust his arm up to knock John's hand away. His arm bounced off him. Then he tried to wriggle free from under the hand. John gripped more fiercely, and Bobby's face tightened.

Everybody in the bar got up quietly and sidled out. The bartender reached below the counter.

"No," I said, showing him my gun. He backed away and held his hands up. He wasn't scared, though.

Bobby was gathering himself to try something, but John stepped away before he could. Then our reluctant interviewee swiveled on his old-fashioned chrome barstool and faced me. We were about two steps apart.

"Who the hell are you, and what do you want?"

"We're investigating the murder at the Santa Cruz Spiritual Center," I said in a normal tone of voice. I'd let John do the menacing. "Because of your relationship to Sumati—"

"Joyce," he corrected.

"Fine, Joyce. Because of your relationship to Joyce, I have some questions. My very large friend and I are hoping you'll answer them."

"I might," he said petulantly.

Then he launched himself at John. Bobby was quick. Even drunk, he was very quick. He ducked under John's first punch and almost got to him before John stepped to the side and popped him in the ribs with his other hand. Bobby slid sideways and then turned to face him again.

"I'm armed," I said. "Let's play nice."

Bobby balled up his fists. "I don't give a fuck. This asshole is going down."

He rushed John, throwing a series of punches. The big man flicked each one away with his forearm and countered with a backfist that caught Bobby above his ear. I'd told him to hold back and make sure Bobby stayed alert if he had to put him down.

John followed that up with one of the most graceful things I've ever seen. He leapt about three feet in the air and pirouetted, lashing out his left leg. He tapped Bobby in the right earlobe. Then the instant he landed, he jumped again, this time flicking Bobby's other ear with his right leg. And it all happened so fast I could hardly follow it.

"Shit!" Bobby said. "Okay, okay. I get it. You're some kind of Australian Bruce Lee."

"I'm a Kiwi, mate." This seemed to upset John much more than being attacked.

"I don't know what that is, but okay. Sorry. Jesus."

He limped back over to his barstool. The bartender had slunk out the back door while I was watching John.

"So what do you want to know?" he asked. He grabbed his beer bottle and swigged the remainder of it.

"I want to know what you know," I told him. "Let's start with Joyce. Have you seen her since you got out of prison?"

"Yeah. Once she came down—we sat right over there." He gestured to a table in the far corner. "And we've been meeting in the woods at the center at night. I bring a blanket. I love her and she loves me. I don't care what that witch there says. We're good for one another."

"Were you there the night somebody stuffed that body in the well?"

"What night was that?" Bobby looked down at his

shoes. He was a terrible liar.

"I have a feeling you already know. Do you want my friend to help you remember things?"

"Okay, yeah," he said hurriedly. "We were there. I'm telling you all this because I didn't do anything wrong and neither did she. The sooner you catch those guys, the better. I don't want Joyce getting caught in any crossfire."

"What guys? Did you see men at the well?"

"Yeah, two of them. First, we heard them. They dropped something and made a noise. We weren't real active right then, so we got up to see what was what. There were two Anglos at the well, holding the stiff."

"How could you tell they were Anglos in the dark?" I asked.

"The way they walked. Like they had sticks up their asses. Also one said, 'Good grief.' That's about as Anglo as you can get."

I was excited. I was catching my first big break in the case. "What else can you tell me about the way they looked?"

"They were both fairly tall. One had a hat on. They wore dark clothes. And they drove away in a pickup truck."

"And Sumati—I mean, Joyce—saw all this, too?"

"Everything except the truck. Once I saw what was going down, I sent her back."

"Why didn't the two of you step forward?"

"I'm not supposed to leave the county without permission. Salinas is in Monterey County, and the spiritual center's in Santa Cruz County. It could mean two more years."

"What about Joyce?" I asked.

"Well, she doesn't want to get me in trouble. I told you. We're in love. But also, she didn't want her teacher knowing because she thought she'd get thrown out for seeing me."

"So there was no phone call telling her to look in the well?"

"No, that was my idea." He turned around and tried to finish his beer, which he already had. Then he swiveled back. "Look, here's why I'm talking to you. The real reason. Joyce called me and said you were okay—you wouldn't rat me out. She said I should tell you everything if you found me because you were going to find out anyway." He pointed at John. "She told about this monster, too. She said he could take me, so I had to try him."

"You're full of surprises, aren't you, Bobby?"

"Yeah, I guess so."

John spoke up. "Better buy more yogurt, mate. Dolores is on the warpath."

"Oh, okay. Thanks."

When we turned to go, two big Hispanic guys came in the front door. One held a kid's baseball bat, and the other one was dangling a motorcycle chain.

"You need any help, Bobby?" the bat guy asked.

"No, I got it handled. They were just leaving. And whatever you do, don't fuck with the big one."

Chapter Nineteen

We had time to hunt up Ray Lundquist—Aria's accuser. The Hyundai dealership was easy to find. They'd created an auto mall on the frontage road next to 101. All I knew was the guy was supposed to look like Thor, but how many employees were likely to resemble Hollywood's version of a Norse God?

The place was dead. No car shoppers, no parts customers, and only three of the eight repair bays in action. We stepped into the small, spare lobby of the parts department. Lundquist stood by himself behind a long, high counter, wearing a name tag that read "I'm Ray and I have a big Hyundai smile for you!"

"Can I help you two?" he asked. I got the feeling he thought we were a gay couple. I don't know why.

"We'd like to ask you a few questions," I said, as John and I drew closer.

"Sure. I can help you with pricing, making service appointments—whatever you need."

He was, in fact, a Scandinavian-looking guy—tall, thin, blond, with chiseled features—the next step beyond craggy. He wasn't quite good-looking, but he wasn't bad. There was no visual evidence he was a drug addict. He seemed genuinely friendly, but of course that was his job and maybe he was just good at it.

"It's about Aria Piper," I said.

Lundquist's eyes flicked from myself to John and

then back again. In that two seconds of movement, the customer-service vibe leached out of him. His eyes fixed on me and narrowed. "Oh, I see—the murder. Well, I knew the cops would find me eventually."

I didn't disabuse him of the idea that we had badges in our pockets.

"Hey," he said to John. "Aren't you John Ratu?" Now he was excited, or acting like it to distract me and get his feet under himself.

"I am."

"Wow. I saw you play, man." He was authentically delighted. "You kicked ass on that tour of Canada in 2004. Whatever happened to you? I thought for sure I'd see you on the All Blacks at the World Cup."

"I got hurt."

"Knee?"

"Kidney," John told him. "I pissed blood for two weeks."

"Whoa. Tough luck. At least you've got two, huh?" He paused, and his light blue eyes narrowed again. There was cunning back in there—not on the surface, but not far back. "So now you're an American cop? How'd you pull that off?"

"Well, I'm a citizen because I married this guy's sister. He does all the detecting, though. I'm not a cop. He just likes having a really big guy standing next to him when he goes someplace like Salinas."

I was proud of John. He'd picked up the trick of not lying about who we were but not revealing anything that could hurt us, either.

"So what do you want to know?" Lundquist projected unconvincing, earnest innocence, which he had good reason to peddle, guilty of the murder or not.

After all, the guy was a coke addict.

"Why haven't you stepped forward?" I asked.

"My lawsuit doesn't have anything to do with this."

I did my best to sound like a cop. "I'll be the judge of that, Lundquist. Where are you from in Canada?"

"Ontario. I was visiting family in Vancouver when the rugby team came through."

"You're a fan?"

"Always have been. It's a bigger sport north of the border. Rugby's like American football without the pads and helmets. You can see all the sweat and blood. You should check it out."

I nodded. "So why is your lawsuit dragging on?"

"She won't negotiate." He shook his head ruefully. "I don't want to go to court. To be honest, I don't have the money for it. I could barely scrape up enough to put the thing together."

"You feel you have a good case?"

He cocked his head and stared at me. "Wait a minute," he said. "There's something off here. Aren't you supposed to introduce yourself and show me your badge? Who are you, anyway?"

"I'm a private investigator. Karl Gatlin." I reached for my wallet to pull out a card.

"Well, fuck you," he said. "I don't have to talk to you."

"No, you don't. It would be good idea, though. The cops don't know about you—yet." I was lying, of course.

"That's blackmail." He glared at me and leaned over the counter. I think he felt safer than I wanted him to feel with the barrier between us, and clearly he was pleased to be able to muster an accusation.

I turned to John. "Do you think that's blackmail, John? I'm thinking it's more like extortion. Maybe the threat of violence nudges it up the legal ladder a little. I don't know."

"What threat?" Lundquist asked. He wasn't scared. He was confused.

I pointed at John. "He's my enforcer."

John cracked his knuckles and tried to look fierce. He wasn't a particularly good actor, but Lundquist backed up a step and held his hands up.

"Look," Lundquist said. "I don't want any trouble. Don't make me call the police."

"You won't. You're probably holding, aren't you?"

His eyes widened, and he involuntarily moved back another half a step. "Okay," he said. "I'll tell you what, I'll sell you information. How about that?"

"Why should we pay you for something we can get for free?"

"Oh, you won't get this. And it's definitely got something to do with the murder." He smiled smarmily, as though his information were extremely salacious. Wayne Sharp screwed goats? God knows why that popped into my head.

"How much?" I asked.

"Ten thousand." Lundquist seemed comfortable again, which was unfortunate.

"That's ridiculous," I said.

"Bill your client," he said. "They'll be happy you did."

Apparently, he didn't care who it was. Most people would've asked by now. Maybe he knew I wouldn't reveal my client's name, anyway.

"Why don't you tell me and then I'll see what it's worth?" I said.

"Now you're the one being ridiculous." He had a point, but under the circumstances I couldn't help but negotiate.

"Well, give me a hint," I tried.

He thought it over. "All right. Here's your hint. It's about Miss Goodie-Two-Shoes's past."

That's all he would tell us, even after several more threats of bodily harm—which I wasn't ready to act on. Needless to say, I didn't pay him. Why would Aria pony up that kind of money for information about herself? It was an interesting development, though.

****

On the way to see Victor Gonzales at the Mexican restaurant, I talked things over with John instead of letting it all rattle around in my brain.

"It's funny he mentioned the word blackmail," I said.

"Why's that?"

"That might be what his lawsuit is—disguised blackmail. What if he knows something about Aria that could ruin her career?"

"It's not a career, Karl. It's a calling."

"Yeah, okay. But suppose he did." I turned in my seat to glance at him. "It wouldn't take much to ruin her. You have to be above reproach to do what she does."

"I don't know where you're getting this from," John said.

"Well, I knew her before she became the Aria you know. She wasn't always so special. And I heard of another case once where a ridiculous lawsuit was just a blackmail attempt—settle with me or I'll spill the beans."

"I don't like this idea, Karl. She's our client, not a suspect." John's tone embodied hurt, as though I'd dissed his mother or told him his ears were too big.

"I'm not saying she's guilty of anything, John. It's just that she might have a skeleton in the closet that figures into this."

"Well, I don't know."

We were at Casa Maria already. "We'll talk more about this later," I told him.

Gonzales was waiting for us in a red Naugahyde booth. The restaurant was by no means upscale, but compared to the El Rio where we'd found Bobby, it merited stars in the Michelin guide. For one thing, it was spotlessly clean. It sat in a strip mall next to an Ace hardware.

Victor Gonzales was a big guy, although with John in tow, big guys looked medium-sized at best. His Asian-looking face, like many indigenous Mexican-Americans, featured high cheekbones and a bony brow. He also had one eye missing. He didn't have a glass eye or an eye patch, just an empty socket. It was unnerving.

Victor recognized us. Someone besides Matt had been googling. He stood and shook our hands as we introduced ourselves.

"Am I hearing a Kiwi accent?" he asked John.

"North of Napier," John told him. "You've probably never heard of Napier."

"I've been to Napier—and Hastings and Te Mata. I love your country. It's the only place I've ever been where the people are sane and haven't ruined the environment."

John beamed at him. "Thanks, mate. Te Mata is my people's place. It's sacred. You went up to the top?"

"Yeah. I could feel the energy up there. Very powerful."

John was grinning from ear to ear now. Victor had made his day.

"Why in the world would you come live here?" Gonzales asked him.

"Why else? Love." He gestured at me. "It was his sister." By now, John and I were sitting side by side in the booth. He had three quarters of it, and I was squeezed against the wall.

"You still together?" Victor asked.

"Naw. She kicked me out years ago. I used to have some problems."

They paused, and Victor looked at me.

"We really appreciate your help," I told him.

"I haven't helped yet. José gets you in the door. What you have to say may or may not get you any information."

"Fair enough. We're investigating several crimes up in Santa Cruz."

"Yeah, I saw you in the paper this morning. Well, I recognized your name. The photo was much better-looking than you are."

"Why does everybody keep saying that?"

"Because it's true," John said. "You should use that photo on a dating site, Karl."

I spoke to Gonzales again. "So the murder was at the center where José lives, and he suggested we talk to you about the possibility that it's drug or gang related—maybe people from Salinas. What can you tell me about the Sureños, the Barrio Azteca, and the Hombres?"

"Quite a bit. Who are you working for?"

It felt appropriate to waive confidentiality again. "José's teacher," I told him. "Aria Piper."

"I met her," he said. "She's a remarkable person. In fact, the energy she puts out is kind of like what I felt in New Zealand. Not at Te Mata, John—that was stronger. Do you know what I mean?"

John shook his head. "I'm not an energy person, Victor," he said. "I don't even really know what you're talking about."

"My mother was a medicine woman," Victor told us. "A Tarascan from Michoacan. Did you know we were the only people the Aztecs never conquered? They tried like hell, but they couldn't do it. Anyway, everybody in my family is energy sensitive. Somebody like Aria probably got her deal from meditating or off a guru, but mine was from my ancestors."

This was a likable guy. It was hard to imagine Victor killing anyone. It occurred to me that José might have been lying.

"You know," I said. "I get the feeling José called you about us." Having been through that with Bobby, I was wary of whatever pre-knowledge of us our interviewees had.

"Yeah, he did. I was checking to see if what you said matched up with what he told me. And so far it does." He leaned back, which I interpreted as the onset of approval. I felt glad I'd brought John along to this meeting as well. Clearly, his interchange with our one-eyed interviewee had made a difference.

"Speaking of lunch," John said, which of course we hadn't been, "how come nobody gave us menus or wants to take our order?"

"I told them not to. Did you notice nobody's sitting near us, either? They do what I say because they think I'm still a Norteño. It's been quite a few years, but people remember. Y'all can eat after we talk."

The "y'all" seemed significant. "Where are you from?" I asked.

"Texas, originally. El Paso. Of course, everybody else in Texas thinks it's part of New Mexico."

"Why's that?" John asked.

"Just look on the map, big guy."

"I'm real hungry," John told him. "How about some chips, at least?"

Victor beckoned to the waitress, an older overweight woman. He made an obscure gesture that must've meant chips in local pantomime, because a minute later we had two bowlfuls of handmade tortilla chips and fresh salsa. They were delicious. Of course, without any drinks to dull the heat of the peppers in the salsa, they represented a double-edged sword of pain and pleasure.

"Okay," Victor said. "Here's the deal. The Hondurans are trying to muscle into several areas, including here. The Norteños are willing to work with them, which is probably stupid. Sooner or later, the Hombres will turn on them. On the other hand, the Sureños have struck an alliance with Barrio Azteca."

"Their cocaine supplier?"

"That's right. The Aztecas aren't that interested in expanding in this direction, but they want to keep the customers they have. The Hombres bring their own stuff in on boats—from the Caribbean side of Honduras. If they get going, Barrio Azteca's in trouble."

196

"Do the Aztecas have men up this way?" I asked.

"Yeah, they've sent the Sureños reinforcements. It's likely to get ugly soon."

"Since you're from El Paso, did you run into the Aztecas growing up?"

"No. They're newer. In my day—in my neighborhood—it was join the Norteños or get your ass kicked every day. I got tired of that."

"How did you go from your role in the gang here to being on the gang task force?" I asked. John was hogging the chips, and I grabbed a handful before they disappeared.

"What role is that?" His lone eye narrowed, and he held himself still.

Oh shit, I thought. What have I done now?

John rescued me. "José said you guys were bad dudes," he told Gonzales. "That you messed up a lot of people."

Victor studied me, and I gave him my most harmless, amiable look—kind of a cross between a village idiot and a chimp at the zoo. Or so I imagined. I probably should've practiced it in front of a mirror.

"They always have a token ex-gang member on the force," he finally said. I let my breath out. "They can't make me a regular cop, but I make a living. Plus I go around to schools and scare the hell out of kids. Most of them join gangs anyway."

"What's your take on the situation up our way? Is it your gangs?" I asked.

"You know, it could be, but I think I would've heard something. I've still got lots of friends in low places. And I don't see why they'd dump a body at the center. That's not their modus operandi."

"I thought it was," I said.

"No, they pick locations that send a specific message. If they leave a body at a school, maybe that's where the other gang leader's kid goes. You see what I mean?"

"I do," I said. "What about the leaders? Who's in charge?"

Victor shook his head. "I can't tell you that," he said.

"What else can you tell us?"

"You'd better watch your back, Karl. Those cowboys that came at you at the center—the Oaxacans—they're idiots. Freelancers. Some bigger idiot hired them. But if any of these gangs decide they want you dead, you're dead. Believe me, I know."

"What about the shooter at the beach?" I asked.

"I'm thinking that wasn't gang related, but it's hard to know. They operate a little different up your way."

We talked for another ten minutes, but it wasn't until the end of the third bowl of chips that Gonzales told us anything else useful.

"One more warning," he said. "Don't trust anyone you haven't known at least two years."

"Why's that? That seems a little extreme."

"That's when the Sureños started infiltrating some unlikely contexts—police forces, politicians—who knows what. They can offer bribes on a scale you can't imagine, and they've been recruiting non-Hispanic members for the first time."

"So you're saying some of the people I've been dealing with might be working for the gang?"

"Or they might even be in the gang. It's an alarming development. So far, we've flushed out a building inspector in Watsonville and a CHP officer. And of course, there was Wayne Sharp—their money guy. Well, the Aztecas' money guy, and the two gangs are in bed together for now."

John spoke up. "How can you tell if someone's on their side? I've met a lot of nice people over the last two years. I'd hate to give them all up."

"You follow the money," Victor told him. "Maybe they have a boat they can't afford. Maybe they're driving a Tesla. That kind of thing. Obviously, the police can only go looking for that when there's a reasonable suspicion. We're bound by the law on our side. The gangs do whatever the fuck they want."

"It sounds like frustrating work," I said.

"When we catch one, they bring in two more from Texas or Mexico. And every month or so, another psychopath gets out of the joint and starts back in. I know these guys. Other than José and me—and one other guy who's dead now—nobody goes straight. Nobody turns into somebody you'd turn your back on. Nobody seems to get it into their thick skull that there's another way to live."

"Why did they let you go?" I asked.

"José and I quit together. They'd have had to kill both of us, plus all my brothers, or the survivors would've taken them out. And believe it or not, they're still scared of a couple of old farts like us. We have reputations."

"You must've been a piece of work," John said.

Victor nodded. "I was and I am," he said. "And now I gotta go. Tell Edna you want the *chiles rellenos* with the green sauce."

Chapter Twenty

The *rellenos* were the best meal I'd eaten in a long time. John devoured two portions and a massive hunk of flan.

I closed my eyes and tried to relax in the SUV while John drove us back to Aria's. I was earning my fee on this case. By the middle of each afternoon, I was exhausted.

While conducting an interview, I paid attention the same way a therapist would. It was how I'd trained and I was good at it, but staying that tightly focused for hours took its toll. With most cases, I conducted one or two interviews a day and made a half a dozen phone calls. The rest of the time I communed with the computer screen. I'd hardly glanced at my monitor in days, and every thug in town was trying to beat me up, shoot me, or frame me.

The more I thought about the case, the more I felt overwhelmed and discouraged. The fucking thing was so complicated and messy. Who did I think I was? Sherlock Fucking Holmes? There were just three of us. Myself, Matt, and John. How could we possibly sort it all out?

Aria was waiting for us in the parking lot, standing next to my car. Maybe she'd been doing a standing meditation by the car for the last three hours. Who knows? She hugged John after we disembarked and then gazed at me. Her green eyes were soft but also penetrating.

"Do you have time to talk, Karl?" she asked. "And would you like a hug?"

"Yes and yes," I said, moving into her arms.

She pressed against me with all her being, and I felt loved. The love poured out of her heart and into mine. An infusion of compassion and hope and just raw energy, I was revitalized by it. In a moment, all I could feel was an intense buzzing in my chest. I couldn't think. I couldn't move.

I have no idea how long we stayed like that, but eventually Aria let go and moved away. I stumbled, and John held me up.

"You'll be all right in a minute," he said. "This happens a lot when she hugs people."

I turned in his arms and hugged him too. It wasn't something I'd planned. I just did it. John laughed and hugged me back. Aria waited to the side.

He was right. A moment later, my motor skills came back online. But I was still in some sort of altered state, and I wasn't tired or discouraged anymore. I was also beginning to understand why so many people signed up to be Aria's student.

Aria took my hand and wordlessly led me to her office. I didn't feel a need to talk. Once inside, we sat across from one another in matching wooden chairs. I gazed at her, and she gazed at me. Again, I had no idea how much time passed. I wasn't thinking. I was just there.

Finally, she spoke softly. "How are you feeling?"

"Very well." My voice was hoarse. I cleared my throat. It didn't help.

"That will go away in a few more minutes. I hope you don't mind," Aria said.

"Mind?"

"I'm imagining that when you agreed to a hug, you didn't know what you were in for. To be honest, I didn't either."

I smiled. My mind was still very quiet. I could've talked, but it didn't seem necessary.

"This would be a good time to listen to Mozart." She stood up and fiddled with something beyond my field of vision. I could've turned my head, but I didn't feel a need to do that, either.

Then I heard the music, and I immediately began crying. Aria reseated herself across from me and cried too, a sweet half smile on her gentle face. The orchestra was achingly beautiful—almost too much to bear. And Aria was too. In that moment, she was the most beautiful sight I'd ever beheld.

Her soulful brown eyes were bottomless wells of love. I could see the love wasn't merely personal. She radiated a kind of universal, even impersonal, love. For a moment—too brief to be sure it was real or imagined—I saw a golden glow around her head. Then it was gone.

By the time the music ended twenty minutes later, after many unbidden tears, I felt like normal Karl again, other than a sense of enhanced peacefulness and a mild aversion to forming words. I would've had to invoke a less trustworthy part of my brain to speak, and I was in no hurry to do so. I missed super-calm Karl already.

"It's not abiding now," Aria told me, noticing what I'd noticed. "But what you experienced is always available to anyone, and it can be your baseline."

I nodded. I had an urge to thank her, but the words didn't emerge. That was fine.

"Now, we have some business to attend to, don't we?" she said.

"Yes."

"I think it's time that you reported on your progress, don't you?"

"Yes."

"Are you ready to say more than one word at a time?"

"Yes, I am."

"Okay, now we're up to three. That's great." Aria sat and waited. Her half smile expanded to the full-bore version. I noticed she'd returned to her ordinary visage. Not perfect. No glow. Just one of the most attractive women I'd ever met, and apparently something special in the spiritual department.

I lurched into a report. She had a right to know what I knew. Once I got rolling, the words came out about as well as usual. Nothing I said seemed to surprise or alarm her. She didn't ask any questions. She just listened for twenty-five minutes. I finished with a reminder. "I trust you'll remember to tell me whatever I need to know—about your past or anything else."

"I will," she said. "How is Larry?"

"He's fine." My tone of voice was most of the way back to ordinary Karl. "I'm sure his cuts and bruises hurt, but he never pays much attention to things like that." Then I realized something else. "I was like a dog before, wasn't I? Dumb in a good way."

Aria tilted her head and thought a moment. "I suppose so. I've never thought of it that way before."

"How are you holding up?" I asked. "I haven't

noticed any visible signs of stress lately, but you must have some."

"I'm fine now. I'm fascinated by the way things are unfolding. And your story was gripping."

I stared at her, and she gazed back calmly. Fascinated? Gripping? This wasn't a screenplay. We were living this so-called story. "How about your people here?" I asked. "The SUV incident must've been disturbing."

"It was, but we're all okay. That just happened to be their life curriculum yesterday."

Once again, her cavalier tone seemed inappropriate. And "life curriculum" was a fatalistic metaphor at best. Did she believe that to be the literal truth? Was there a big teacher in the sky writing a personalized lesson plan for everybody?

"And your weekend students?" I asked. "I assume the police talked to all of them?"

"For the most part. One man disappeared because he had outstanding warrants. Another one is on a retreat in Hawaii."

I realized it was Friday. "The extra students will be coming tomorrow?"

"Yes. We're carrying on as usual."

"Do you think it would be a good idea for me to talk to any of them?" I certainly couldn't afford to interview all of them.

She considered that. "No, I don't. But I'll call you if that changes."

"Great."

We paused and just looked at one another again. I was surprised how comfortable and natural I felt with her, despite her off-the-wall philosophy. Maybe it was because her point of view kept her from being judgmental. She wasn't going to reject me because of a momentary lapse of manners or common sense, and that let me be me. Aria was like an anti-Adele—no mines to set off and no fireworks in store for hapless transgressors.

Aria finally broke the silence. "I think that's all we need to do today. I have students to meet with. Give me a call if there are any new developments I need to hear about."

"Sure."

****

On the trip back to the office, whatever she'd done to me began slipping even further away. On the one hand, I was returning to comfortable, solid ground— what I knew. But it was also disappointing on a deep level. I think I was hoping more of the tranquility had stuck to my ribs.

Matt was napping again on my couch. He was so asleep, I had to shake him to wake him up. "I'm seeing a pattern of what you do when I'm not around, Matt."

"Gimme a break, boss. I think I'm coming down with something. I don't feel right."

"Oh."

"I did get some work done, though," he said in a nasal voice. "Why don't I tell you about it in case I run out of energy and have to go home?"

Matt told me he'd hit a wall checking into the main suspects in the case, so he'd gone back and dug up more on some of the peripheral people.

"You never know," he said. "And I'm glad I did."

"Am I going to be glad, too?"

"I think so. I looked into Leanne Atkinson's

background—the student who accused Crowder? She was adopted as an infant from out of state and grew up as the only child of a well-to-do couple over in Los Gatos."

This was an upscale town nestled against the foothills on the other side of the Santa Cruz Mountains. It was a good place to grow up—the high school sent scores of kids to Ivy League schools, and every grade level still offered music and art classes.

"On top of her parents' money, she inherited more from an aunt when she was fifteen," Matt continued. "Apparently, this was somebody she didn't even know. Talk about a charmed life."

"When did she find out she was adopted?" That was always a big piece of somebody's psychology. If she knew early on, that was a lot different from having her self-professed birth mom show up at her wedding. I wasn't clear on why Leanne's childhood was relevant to our case, but I knew that Matt would get around to that.

"The thing is, I don't think she knows. At least, I can't find anything about that."

"I don't get why you're telling me this." I was running out of patience.

"Here's the part that ties in. When she was a senior in high school, she won a full-ride college scholarship."

"So?"

"She didn't have good grades because she partied too much. And she's not a minority and her parents aren't poor."

"So they gave money to someone who didn't deserve it."

"No, here's the thing. It was the Enlightenment

Services Foundation that did it—Aria's people."

That grabbed my attention. "Maybe it was because Leanne was Aria's therapy patient," I said after a moment of thought.

"Isn't that unethical?" he asked.

"Very."

"Let me play junior detective for a minute," Matt said. "Suppose it was a payoff to Leanne for entrapping Crowder or making a false complaint? Was there already bad blood between Aria and Pastor Gary back then?"

"Not that I know of. That's rather far-fetched, Matt."

"Yeah, I know."

"Could there be a family friend on the board or something?" I asked.

"I'm looking into it. So far, everybody seems legit. It's a who's who of local spiritual people—not Christians, but everybody else. They've even got a for-real Tibetan lama—well, sub-lama, I guess."

"What else did you find out?"

"Nothing more about her, and I don't know that she matters, anyway. But here's a piece of news. Apparently, Paul from the center has a lover and they meet in a motel in Scotts Valley, but nobody knows who he is. I'm thinking maybe that's where the money goes. Do gay guys buy each other jewelry and stuff?"

"Beats me. Maybe watches. But motel bills mount up, too," I pointed out.

"Also, he's originally from Salinas." Matt's voice was weakening. I had to strain to hear him. "That may not mean anything, but it makes me want to find out more. That's where all the bad guys come from so far."

"I agree. Check it out."

"I researched Sutter and Cardenas and all the other cops we talked to, but I didn't find out anything that concerns us. Unless you care about archery. Sue Sutter is a national level archer."

"How about the bank in Austin? Did you find out anything else about that?" I asked. There were so many threads to follow, it was hard to keep them all straight. I looked forward to when we could start discarding leads and focus on the meat and potatoes of the case.

"Oh, yeah. I corroborated the fact that the bank itself was dirty from a couple of law enforcement databases. Besides Sharp and three other money launderers, they're administering a bunch of phony foundations to help people dodge taxes."

"Including the one that feeds the Jesus Is Everything church?"

"It wasn't on the list I saw, but maybe. Crowder's sugar daddy—the guy signing the foundation checks—is a Texas billionaire you've probably never heard of. He spends a fortune trying to keep his name and likeness out of the news. His wife is the one in the limelight. She used to be a Philadelphia Eagles cheerleader. Apparently, she chooses where the philanthropy money goes." Matt breathed heavily after this longer report.

"Why would they want to support Crowder's church? And what's this guy's name?"

"Brent Bonheim. His wife is Nana. And I have no idea why anyone would give money to that church."

Matt was fading. He was still reclining on the couch, but now he'd sunk farther into the green cushions. He looked as though he couldn't fight gravity anymore. I'd never seen him like this. He was a blob.

"How are you feeling?" I asked.

"Not good."

"Go home. I'll answer the phone. If you feel better later and you want to work, you can do it from home."

"Okay." He struggled to escape the couch and wobbled out of the room.

Detective Sutter called me a while later. We'd spent time together after the shooting, and she was friendlier now. "I have news about your shooter," she said. "Several witnesses picked guys out of a slideshow. Do you know a Frank Buccanfuso?"

"No, I'd remember that name."

"Other witnesses picked out a man named Carl Steiner."

"Nope. I don't know that name, either."

"You know the drill. We've got too many witnesses," she said. "Two others said they saw the guy, but he wasn't in our array. And a woman identified one of the first officers on the scene as the shooter."

"The average person doesn't pay attention to much. It's like they're sleepwalking."

"I agree, Karl."

So we were on a first-name basis now. Would she be asking me out next? Had she succumbed to my craggy charms?

"Did he leave shell casings?" I asked.

"Yeah, he left in hurry. .223 caliber. Eleven shots."

"I guess I was lucky."

"Yeah. So anyway, we've got officers hunting for both suspects," Sutter said. "When we corral them, I'll call you so you can breathe easier."

"I appreciate that, Detective."

"Sue. Call me Sue." She paused a moment and then spoke more slowly. "You're all right, Karl. I wasn't sure about you at first."

"Well, when I met you, I thought you were a robot," I told her.

She laughed. "They call me that behind my back at work. And Ice Queen, too."

If it were me, I wouldn't be laughing at that. "What do you make of Aria?" I asked. Now that we were buddies, I thought it might be helpful to get an outsider's perspective. I'd been studiously avoiding thinking about my weird energy experience with my client. As much as I could dismiss Aria's ideas about life in general, I certainly couldn't deny that her energy or whatever could make good things happen.

"I think she's for real in the spiritual department. My sister was in a cult, and that was way different from the vibe at Aria's place. But that doesn't mean she lives like a saint. Do you know most famous gurus are scoundrels in one way or another?"

"Like what?"

"Women, boys, money—you name it. On the one hand, they're teaching and helping. But something makes you feel above the law, or least like you're exempt from ordinary morality."

"You're a deep one, aren't you? What are you doing being a cop?"

"I couldn't figure any other way to get hit on all day and paid like crap."

"Deep and cynical, too." This conversation was going to some unexpected places. "Why are you letting your hair down with me?" I asked.

"Am I? I don't know. I guess I trust you. Do people

210

tend to trust you?"

"You know, they do. Maybe it's because I'm trustworthy. But are you sure you're not just wildly attracted to me because you saw me in my sexy wet blanket?"

"That's definitely not it."

"Are we at the stage," I asked, "where I ask you what you're wearing, and you lie and tell me all you have on is sexy black underwear and stiletto heels?"

She laughed. "I don't think so. Don't push your luck."

"I was totally naked under that blanket, you know."

"Okay, okay. Enough. Getting back to Aria, my point is I haven't ruled her out as a suspect. Who knows for sure what anyone's capable of?"

"Not me."

It was time to call it a day again, but on the way home, I stopped at the only gun shop in town to let Jay take a look at my oceangoing pistol. I'd been going to him for years. He was an older Polish-American from Wisconsin with a disturbing comb-over and a bushy, gray mustache. He always looked as if he'd just eaten something that had gone bad.

"What did you do with it after you got out of the water?" Jay asked me. He already knew about the beach shooting.

"A cop told me to take it apart and put the pieces in rice."

"That's for cell phones, but it's not the worst thing you could've done. Did you put it back together after it dried out?"

"Yeah. And most of it was still pretty well oiled. So that's good. But I haven't tested it."

"Let's shoot a few rounds into Zelda," he said. They'd made Jay tear down the range he'd built out back, so now he used a bullet-absorbing pad affixed to the wall of his storeroom. I don't know how it worked.

He loaded the Sig Sauer's clip, we both put on earmuffs, and he fired three rounds into the pad. In the enclosed space, the noise was still deafening.

"It's fine," he said. "But come back to me when you want a real gun. This thing's okay if you're carrying concealed, but that's about it."

"You know what they say, Jay—the smaller the gun, the bigger the..."

"Nobody says that, you idiot. Now go home."

I did.

Chapter Twenty-One

I called Chen first thing the next morning. "I need you to follow somebody," I told him. He'd done this for me before. And Chen and John had worked as a team on several other cases. I could trust him.

As I lay in bed that morning, I'd decided to find out more about Paul the administrator and his mystery lover. Why was he hiding who the guy was? Why be at a motel instead of one of their homes? Was the lover a married man? Were they even lovers? There were other reasons to meet someone at a motel—a drug deal, for example. And was this connected to his debt? People do all kinds of things when they're feeling money pressure. Plus, I didn't like the guy's hats.

"Okay," Chen said. "I'll follow whoever you want."

"How'd it go at the center yesterday? I'm sorry I didn't get a chance to talk to you."

"It was fine."

"What did you think of Aria?"

"Nice lady."

"Chen, why don't you talk more?"

"No reason."

"Did you get hit for talking when you were a kid?" I asked.

"Don't go there."

"Is it a spiritual thing?" I knew he approached

martial arts as though it were a religion.

"It's just me."

"Okay, I can respect that."

I gave him the details about Paul and told him to be careful. I called and checked on Matt next.

"I'm a lot worse, boss," he said. His voice demonstrated his words. It was quite weak and thin, like a ninety-year-old man who some caretaker had forgotten to feed. There was a little whininess there, too.

"What do you think you have?"

"Flu, maybe. I've got a fever and all the rest. I'm really sorry."

"Is Rachel around?" His girlfriend had a big heart. I liked her a lot.

"Yeah. She's taking the day off to take care of me."

"I wish I had somebody like her."

"You will, Karl."

"Take care, Matt. I'll just muddle along without you."

"Muddle away."

When I got to the office and checked the landline messages, which was normally Matt's job, I found six from the media, one from my sister, and one from Jill Kepler, who identified herself as my lawyer. I hadn't even known her name. I realized how much I counted on Matt. He was more like a partner than an employee these days.

I called Ms. Kepler. "Hi, this is Karl Gatlin."

"Hello. Jill Kepler. Thanks for calling back. It's a little odd that you're my client and I haven't met you, but your associate has been very helpful."

She sounded sharp, enunciating her words economically, but perfectly. I wasn't distracted by her southern accent. "Good," I said. "What's the deal?"

"I looked at Reverend Crowder's temporary restraining order, and it's not very strong. It states that you were trespassing, when you have a witness who will corroborate that you were invited. Unholstering your gun is a 'he said, she said' situation—they don't have video of that. And however your dog misbehaved, there's no established pattern of harassment and no proof of ill-will."

"Great. So what happens? Will some other judge void it?"

"No, it's not that simple. The complainant has the right to a hearing, and you and Matt will have to testify if Reverend Crowder insists on his due process."

"If?"

"Yes. I've been in contact with the church's secretary, and she told me he'll drop the order on two conditions. I think it's a good idea to agree to them. They're not unreasonable, and it'll save you time and money."

"What does he want?"

"He wants you to go see him again and apologize. He even said your dog was welcome. The other thing is he plans to write you an apology, as well, and he'd appreciate a written acknowledgement from you that you received it."

"That's a little wacky, isn't it? Does all that have any legal ramifications?"

"Only if you incriminate yourself when you apologize. Just remember you're not there to confess or assume responsibility. Make it personal. Say something like 'I'm sorry for any distress my visit may have caused you.' If he pushes it, go a little further. It's worth the risk to avoid going to a hearing."

"Okay, I can do that. What about his letter to me?"

"I'd guess that's a religious thing—penitence or whatever. It has no legal meaning unless he's dumb enough to void his complaint with a confession of his own."

"Okay, good."

She continued. "Matt also wanted me to look into prison sentences for hacking. Is he there?"

"He's home sick." I didn't want to hear anything about that. "How about you call back Monday? I think that one can wait."

"Sure. Anything else?"

"No. Thank you so much for your help with this—and for picking up the phone on a Saturday."

"At least you weren't calling from jail," she said.

"Not yet," I told her.

I tried my sister next. She was probably worried about me. The media coverage of the murder had certainly trickled down to Santa Barbara.

"Kim, it's Karl."

"What the hell is going on up there?" She was angry, as usual.

"It's a gnarly case."

"That's not much of an answer, is it?" Kim raised her voice, angrier now. "I've left messages on your cell phone for two days. And John won't call me back, either. He was a worthless husband, and he's still just as worthless. I deserve to know what's going on."

"Sorry. I haven't been checking my phone. And let's leave John out of this, okay?"

"You need to quit this case." She was ignoring everything I said.

Kim was my older sister, and since the day I was born, she'd been trying to boss me around. For most of our childhoods, our mother drunkenly careened through a series of abusive boyfriends. Our father was never in the picture—whoever he was. Kim had appointed herself head of the household, which was her and me and a succession of dogs that ran away when nobody fed them. In response to her childish mothering, I organized my personality around resisting being controlled. The kid version of this had merely been clueless; the adult version was proving to be more deleterious. On the other hand, without an out-of-control mother and a bossy sister, I probably wouldn't have developed much self-awareness. Why bother with that if you don't have to?

"In fact," Kim continued, "you need to get out of this business altogether."

"We don't need to have this conversation right now, Kim."

"Yes. We do. How do you think I'd feel if you get yourself killed tomorrow and I hadn't said anything? You have a master's degree, for God's sake. You're bright, and you work hard. Think of all the things you could do instead of hanging around with violent criminals. It doesn't have to be counseling. What about teaching? You'd be a great teacher, Karl."

"Kim, I gotta go."

"You don't want Mom worrying about this, do you?"

"Go ahead and tell her if you want." I'd learned the only way to keep from being manipulated by my sister was to stop caring about whatever she used for leverage. Sure, I'd prefer my mother be spared from worrying about me. But that wasn't up to me. Kim would tell her or she wouldn't based on her own criteria—the way she connected the dots in her mind. I hung up on her as she started in again.

Of course, she had a point. The case was out of control, and I seemed to be in everybody's crosshairs. I didn't even know why.

I called Crowder's church, and his assistant answered. "This is Karl Gatlin. When would it be convenient for the reverend to meet with me?" I asked. "I owe him an apology."

"You certainly do," she said. "Let's see, obviously tomorrow is out."

"Obviously?"

"We're a church. Tomorrow's Sunday."

"Oh, of course." I'd just outed myself as a heathen.

"How about later today? Reverend Crowder usually finishes writing his sermon by late afternoon. I know he'd like to settle this as soon as possible."

"Shall we say five?" I suggested.

"Yes. Meet him in his office at five. Do you know where our temporary location is?"

"I'll find it."

Temporary, huh? Were they expecting to win their lawsuit and move onto Aria's land?

I decided to go to Ralph Sharp's house. Maybe I could get a gander at the guy even if he wouldn't cooperate. As the victim's brother and Pastor Gary's follower/bankroller—let alone a Zoppi—he interested me. The old family money could well be an element in the case since both Aria and Crowder's properties had once been Zoppi owned, and the former was in dispute because of that.

Ralph's take on brother Wayne-the-sinner's lifestyle might be illuminating as well, especially if he knew whatever had happened to Cate at Wayne's hands. Perhaps I could get him rolling by asking about Aria and her Satanic hold on his ex-wife and daughter. He sounded like a guy who enjoyed a good rant.

Even if Ralph Sharp didn't want to talk to me, I might find out something important. The way uncooperative witnesses chose to repel me could be telling. If he went the police route, would he call 911 or Chief Crowder himself? Would he try to toss me out on his own? Threaten a lawsuit? Maybe he'd politely usher me out, clapping an arm over my shoulder. An AWOL teen had employed that once right before he'd kneed me in the groin. You learn the hard way in my business.

Sharp lived partway up the hill that ran from the wharf to the university campus, on the west side of town. Because of the panoramic views, the homes in that neighborhood were pricey, but most weren't monstrously large or pretentious-looking. If I were rich, this was where I'd be shopping for real estate in my Aston-Martin with my beautiful real estate agent by my side. Larry could sit in the back seat for once.

A newish Lexus sedan sat in the driveway. A pink one. That was different. I rang the bell, and an attractive, exotic-looking woman in her thirties answered the door. She might've been Filipina.

"Yes?"

"I'm so sorry to bother you," I said. "I was hoping to talk to Ralph about his brother's death."

"Why? Who are you? Are you wanting a story for

your paper? You can't have one." Her rapid English was heavily accented. Her first language was definitely Spanish, but there was something else mixed-in—probably Tagalog.

"Oh, no, ma'am. I'm trying to find the killer. I'm a detective. My name is Karl Gatlin."

"Oh, well, that's different. I'm Mrs. Hazel Sharp—Ralph's wife. He's out, but maybe I can help you."

"I hope so. May I come in?"

"Oh, of course. Where are my manners?"

She led me to an expansive living room. All the furniture was new. I sat on a beige leather love seat, and she perched on the edge of a matching chair across from me. Hazel Sharp was small and self-contained. Her face was a mask of congeniality, and I suspected what was behind it was reasonably congenial, too. Some people play a role that's similar to who they are.

She was also very pretty. Not sexy at all, but pretty. Her features mimicked those of a ten-year-old girl, although she looked to be in her late twenties—quite a bit younger than her husband. Having sex with her would've felt like pedophilia.

"I didn't know Ralph had remarried," I said.

"Oh yes. We are newlyweds," Hazel proclaimed. "Four months of happiness."

"Let me guess. You met at church?"

"Yes! Reverend Gary introduced us. Do you know our pastor? He is a great man." She was happy as a clam now. I was reminding her of wonderful things. My impression of youth and innocence was supported by her words and tone.

"I've been to his ranch, and I'm seeing him this afternoon," I told her disingenuously. Clearly, this woman did not read the newspapers or online media and probably didn't know much about her husband's affairs. Otherwise, she would've known my name or recognized me from my photo in the Sentinel.

"That's very good," she said.

"Have you been in this country long?"

"Two years. My aunt lives here. Maybe you know her. Consuela Crowder?"

This was Jim Crowder's wife, I remembered. That was a major piece of information. "I know Jim," I said, "but I haven't had the pleasure of meeting your aunt." I felt I'd schmoozed enough, so I tried a more germane question. "Mrs. Sharp, were you aware of your brother-in-law's illegal activities?"

"Oh, no. We didn't see Wayne too much. He was very busy. But he sang and told jokes at our wedding. It was very fun. If he lost his way and Satan's will took root in him, we can only pray for mercy now that he has passed."

I didn't know what to say to that. I decided to try something else. "Does your husband talk about the lawsuit—about his inheritance?"

"I most certainly do not!" a voice boomed from the doorway. Ralph strode in the room. "Hazel—go upstairs. This man is not our friend." He glared at me as she scurried off, her head down.

Ralph was well fed, and his black suit hugged him tightly. Perhaps his new wife was a good cook. A patchy fringe of graying hair sat above his large ears. I didn't like his nose at all. It was too small for the rest of him. But there was intelligence in his green eyes.

"This is unacceptable, Gatlin. I should call the police." His voice was a deep baritone, firm but under control.

"Your wife invited me in."

"Probably under false pretenses. Hazel is easily fooled by your sort. She has a big heart, and she expects everyone else to have one, too. She and I will be having a talk about this. And that's on your head."

I felt a twinge of guilt. Hazel's body posture as she slunk off hinted at spousal dominance or abuse. How would she fare once I'd left? "Congratulations on your nuptials," I tried. "Your wife is a lovely woman. I didn't come here to take advantage of her. I didn't even know she existed."

"That's a likely story. You're a detective, and you didn't know something like that? Why am I even talking to you? Get out!" His tone was imperious now. He expected obedience, and this time he'd get it from me. He had every right to toss me.

So Ralph liked to push people around and didn't feel he needed any help to get the job done. And his naive, immigrant wife was the niece of Jim Crowder's wife. It struck me that practically everyone in this case was only one or two degrees separated from everyone else. It was like a spider web with each suspect living along a spoke that connected to the middle, as well as to adjacent threads. The question was: who was the spider in the middle of the web?

Chapter Twenty-Two

From Sharp's, I headed to an early lunch. I called Adele to see if she wanted to join me. She said she would, just as soon as Larry started solving calculus problems. She also told me I'd broken her favorite garden trowel and she'd never forgive me for that, even though it had been two years ago.

I liked to go to an omelet place and eat eggs for lunch. It was the rebel in me. I also enjoyed spending time with Rita, who I'd briefly dated before I was married. She was fun, but she drank too much and believed there were elves everywhere. Eventually, I couldn't take it.

"Rita," I called, as I walked in. "I'll have my usual."

"You don't have a usual," she said, running over to give me a dirty hug. She claimed she was the world's sexiest hugger—that she'd won a contest in Las Vegas. Rita rubbed herself against me while she stroked my ass, and then stood back to judge the result. I sported an obvious erection.

"Gotcha," she said, waltzing off to pick up an order.

After scarfing down a perfectly cooked omelet, I headed down to Aria's center. I wanted to talk to Sumati about what her boyfriend Bobby had told us. He'd provided an eyewitness account, but I wasn't sure if he was lying. The weekend students would be there too, including Cate Sharp's mother, Lois.

This time, there was no place to park. I drove back out onto the street, found a wide spot on the shoulder, and hiked in on the long gravel driveway. When I approached the path leading to Aria's office, a man stepped up from a stool. His name tag said he was Greg.

"May I help you, sir?" he asked. He was a squatty little sixty-year-old with bushy, black eyebrows. He held himself as though he were a midlevel communist bureaucrat.

"Are you the greeter? Like at Walmart?"

"Sir, I'm the weekend security director. We can't have just anyone wandering around here. Now please state your business." He was maintaining a reasonable tone, but it was clear he didn't like me. I guess the Walmart crack hadn't helped my cause. His officiousness wasn't helping his.

"I thought John Ratu was on the job here." I softened my tone. I didn't need to alienate the guy.

"You know John? He's working under my supervision," Greg told me.

I got out my cell phone. "John, can you meet me by the sign that says, 'Yield gracefully to what is?' "

"Sure. Aria's meditating with everybody. She's safe for now."

While I waited for John, I ignored Greg the greeter and thought about this latest sign. It seemed way too passive. Were we all supposed to bow down to whatever was going on around us, regardless of how screwed up it was?

In a minute, John strode around the corner of the

building. He towered over both of us, of course. The top of the officious man's head reached my friend's midsection. John wore his customary black shorts, but this time a brown T-shirt stretched across his expansive chest. An abstract graphic adorned the shirt, along with a short poem: "We are like complex, completed origami. Our task is to unfold ourselves and return to the simple, blank sheets of paper we once were before we were us." After reading it, I could see that the rainbow-colored graphic depicted a stylized origami swan beginning to unfold itself. Did they have a souvenir store on the grounds?

"What's up?" John asked me. "Hi Greg," he added.

"Greg here was telling me how he's in charge of security and he supervises you."

"Now that wasn't exactly what I…" Greg began.

He was interrupted by John's laughter. "That's a good one—Greg supervising me." He couldn't stop laughing.

"What's going on?" Greg asked. "I'm just trying to help out here." He held his hands up in supplication. They were chubby little things with sausage-like fingers.

"It's okay, Greg," John said. "This is my real boss. And Karl, lighten up." He gave me a playful cuff on the shoulder. "Come on, I'll walk with you."

"Okay, sure." He led me back around the corner, and we walked toward to a stone bench in front of the dining hall.

"I like your shirt," I told him. "Is that your new philosophy? We're all folded paper?"

"Nah. It's one of those Aria sayings—did you know she makes them up herself? Somebody here makes shirts out of them and sells them really cheap. I spilled juice on my polo, so now I'm an ad for...well, whatever this shirt means."

"Gotcha." I noticed that John's accent was strong that day. It seemed to come and go. We'd reached the bench, and we hunkered down onto it.

"Whatever you do, don't go in there." John pointed to the door of the dining hall. "That's where they keep the salads." He laughed again, and I joined him this time.

We sat silently for a minute or two. I found myself listening to the birds, which I didn't usually do. It was almost as if they were singing harmony with one another. I could smell the redwoods again, too. The aroma was distinct from pine—subtler, less fresh, and more complex.

"I need to talk to Sumati," I finally told John.

"She's in there meditating with everyone else." He swiveled his big head to look at me. "It's good you don't want to see Aria. She's got a really full day."

"How long before they're finished in there?"

"I dunno. Maybe fifteen minutes. We could go in and sit in the back."

He noticed the look on my face—probably a wince or even a grimace.

"Come on, Karl," John said. "It'll be good for you."

"Okay, fine." I hadn't tried meditating in a long time. Maybe it would be easier now. And if I didn't feel like trying it when I got in there, I could observe the weekend students instead and get a feel for who was who.

John silently let us in the hall, and we sat against

226

the back wall next to the double doors. I stretched out my legs to baby my bad knee. Nobody looked up or paid any attention to us. The spacious room was almost full. Aria sat up front on a little stage, and everyone else rested on purple yoga mats on the clean hardwood floor. Some sat cross-legged, some didn't.

Aria herself sat in a full lotus position with her eyes closed. She wore white yoga pants and a long-sleeved black T-shirt. Her feet were bare. She looked absolutely calm and relaxed, with yet another sweet half smile on her face.

I was struck by her skin, olive-toned and flawless. Maybe I was too far away to see any imperfections. I don't know. And her figure was trim and very much in proportion. The line from her shoulders to her hips was an especially graceful curve. She was just achingly beautiful in the natural light coming through the refectory windows.

I remembered what Matt had said when I'd first described Aria to him—that the way I saw her demonstrated my feelings. I wondered if my current perceptions were being skewed by my heart—and whatever Aria had done to it. I still hadn't fully come to terms with what had happened when she'd hugged me.

I decided to close my eyes and meditate. My mind raced around like a ferret on speed—or whatever street drug was available to members of the weasel family. It was horrible. After a few minutes, I opened my eyes and watched people instead. I decided Lois Sharp was the snub-nosed redhead sitting a few rows behind Cate, who assiduously picked her nose the whole time I watched.

Eventually, a gentle timer chimed. Probably some

Buddhist catalog company sold mellow timers.

Aria said, "Thank you," just loud enough to hear, and everyone gathered themselves and stood. No one spoke as they filed out of the room.

I followed Sumati outside. "Excuse me," I said. "I think we need to talk again."

She turned to face me. "Yeah, okay. I knew you'd be back."

"Bobby told you I'd been to see him?"

"Yeah." She shifted her weight back on forth on the balls of her feet. Sumati tried to look me in the eye and managed to get as close as my forehead.

"Shall we go to the group room again?" I asked.

"Okay."

We didn't talk on the short stroll there. I listened to the birds again. They sounded even happier now.

When we'd settled on pillows in the spare space, across the circle from each other this time, Sumati launched into it. "I'm so sorry I lied to you. I was protecting Bobby. The thing is, what he told you is what's true."

She then told me the exact same story in the exact same words. Obviously, she'd been coached. And her attempts at eye contact were even less successful now. I had an idea. "Let's go see the spot in the woods where you were," I said. "That would be helpful to me."

"Uh, okay." She wasn't happy about this.

We walked to the edge of the tall woods, which wasn't far, and hiked a well-worn trail for about twenty yards. Shafts of sunlight pierced the shaded, needle-strewn ground, and the trees' scent was much stronger now. Quite a few of the redwoods sported carbuncle-like burls at their bases, which my mind sought to turn into faces. I knew evolution favored whoever was a whiz at facial recognition, but all I came up with was a cartoon character or two. I guess my line was doomed to die out sooner than most.

Sumati stopped suddenly and then pretended to be lost, glancing around with a big, fake frown. "I'm not sure," she said.

"Try."

She walked to her left into a ring of young redwoods—they group around their long-gone mother tree—probably gauging how far she and Bobby could've been and still heard a noise from the well. Sound carried in a redwood forest because there was almost no undergrowth—just complex patterns of fallen needles from the tree themselves. Redwoods ooze something that poisons sun-seeking competitors. Their sap made them virtually fireproof, too. Remarkable.

When she'd picked a spot, I asked her if she was sure—she was—and then I searched for any evidence that someone had laid a blanket down. I made a big show of this, following some imaginary protocol.

"Nope." I said. "It wasn't here."

"I guess I'm wrong, then." She stared at her shoes.

I faced her with my arms crossed. I could sense her uneasiness. "How often are you in this forest?" I asked.

"I walk here every day."

"So it would be fair to say that you know it well?"

Sumati nodded, and her eyes darted up and to the side. She was close to cracking. This wasn't someone who lied a great deal.

"I know you're lying, Sumati. Let me remind you that I work for Aria. I'm here to help her—to help the center. I'm not trying to get you or Bobby in trouble. If you cooperate with me, everything will be fine. If you don't, I can't make that promise."

"Okay, okay. Let's go back inside. I don't want to talk about it here." She pivoted and almost ran along the slim path behind us. I tried to catch up, but she sped up to stay in front of me. My knee told me to let her.

Back in the group room on our not very comfy meditation pillows, the truth spilled out of Sumati. "We weren't in the woods." She sounded relieved to tell the truth—and it was obviously the truth. She'd shoved her unruly hair out of her face, and she gazed at me evenly. "We were fooling around in Bobby's car," she continued. "We saw two guys drive up without their lights on. So Bobby snuck out of the car and followed them while I stayed down low in the car like he said. Bobby can get upset if you don't do what he says. But he's working on that. He's taking an anger-management class at the Y. I'm so proud of him."

"What happened next?" I asked gently. She was on a roll. I didn't want to inject myself into her narrative.

"After a while, I heard their truck start up and then leave. Then Bobby came back. He said they'd put something in the old wishing well, and the next day I should go over and pretend to look in it and say somebody on the phone had told me to do that. See? That was Bobby doing right. He didn't have to tell me to go find the body. He did it because it was the right thing to do. He didn't want that poor man in the well to just rot or something."

"What do you mean, 'pretend to look in it'?"

"He said to keep my eyes closed when I leaned over—that I wouldn't want to see what it was."

"So you never actually saw the body?"

"No. He saved me from that."

"And the police didn't figure out any of this when they talked to you?"

"No. Bobby and I practiced a lot. I lied a lot better that day—to you, too. I'm a good liar if I get a chance to rehearse." She leaned back and smiled just a bit. It was a perverse sort of pride, I thought.

"Why did Bobby make up the story about the woods?"

"Well, it's not technically his car. He borrows it at night sometimes. It used to be his car so he still has a key."

"Can you think of any other reason?"

"No. Bobby works on a need-to-know basis—like in a spy movie."

After a few more questions, it was clear she could add nothing useful on that subject.

"Have you seen a creepy guy who comes from offsite and meets with Aria?" I was thinking of how Cate Sharp had described who I suspected was Lundquist, but then I remembered Sumati had been at the center long enough to know him as the previous administrator. "I'm sorry," I said. "Let me ask about Ray Lindquist instead. Have you seen him on the property lately?"

"Yeah. What a jerk. He's nothing like my Bobby."

"What kind of an administrator was he?"

"He was okay at first, but then he was terrible. He used to hit on me all the time, and he was lazy." Sumati shook her head, and her dark hair fell back over the left side of her face. It was so dense and frizzy, it took a while to get there and bounced upon landing. "I don't know why Aria put up with him for so long," she continued. "He turned into the worst boss ever."

"Do you know why he still meets with Aria?"

"No."

"Okay, that's it. Thanks, Sumati."

"Don't tell Bobby I said all this, okay?"

"I won't." I didn't want that on my conscience. "Is there anything else I ought to know about what's going on around here?" I asked.

"You know I work for Paul, right?"

I nodded.

"Well, his personality has changed. It was gradual at first, but the last few weeks, he's gotten...Well, not as nice. He's impatient. He yells a lot. It's not like him."

"What do you think is going on?"

"I don't know. I know his disease is supposed to be progressive, so maybe that's it."

"What's the name of his condition?"

"He told me once, but I don't remember. It's a long name. You could ask Dr. Venkatesh. That's his neurologist."

"It doesn't work that way, Sumati."

I asked her where I might find Lois Sharp that time of day. She told me to try the bench by the side of the women's dorm—where she usually visited with her daughter before her appointment with Aria. I hadn't realized Aria segregated her students by gender, but it made sense.

Chapter Twenty-Three

Sure enough, there they were. Cate was talking a mile a minute, and her mother—the woman I'd picked out in the meditation hall—was listening.

"Good afternoon, Cate," I said as I got closer. "I don't mean to interrupt, but I need to talk to your mom." I turned to the woman. "You're Lois Sharp?"

"Yes. And I'm happy to help you, Mr. Gatlin. Cate, honey, can you give us a few minutes?"

"Whatever," Cate said. She marched away, reaching in her pocket for a joint. She was wearing her overalls again, but this time she had on a black tank top under the worn denim, and her blond hair was down.

"Please." Lois patted a spot on the bench next to her.

The former Mrs. Ralph Sharp was attractive in a matronly way. Her outfit didn't ward off the impression of premature middle-age, but it suited her. She wore a navy pantsuit and a white button-down shirt. Her low heels matched the suit's color exactly, and her auburn hair was up on top of her head in an oversized bun. She could've been a wedding planner or a departmental secretary at a university. She smelled like cats.

"Thank you," I said. "I won't take up too much of your time."

"Don't worry about that. I've been looking forward to talking with you. I knew you'd get around to me."

233

Her eyes were bright blue and alert.

"Why's that?"

"I'm the only one in a position to speak freely and knowledgeably about the Sharp family. And I think you need to know everything I know. I wasn't entirely comfortable on the phone with your associate a few days ago. At that point, I didn't know who you people were."

"Okay, great. What can you tell me?"

"Ralph was a decent husband until his break." Lois Sharp's tone was neutral, and she kept her eyes on mine.

"Break?"

"He thought he was having visions," she explained. "The doctors and I understood them to be delusions. Ralph's brother was schizophrenic and suffered from similar symptoms, although his were much worse. He thought he was the Messiah."

"This was Wayne?" Why hadn't anyone else mentioned this?

"No, the other one—Chet."

"I don't know anything about Chet," I said, "other than Cate mentioning she had a third uncle. Is that who we're talking about?

"Yes. Nobody talks about him. They're a very proud family. Last I heard, they were warehousing Chet up at Napa State Hospital. He might be dead by now, but I suppose there's an outside chance some new med helped him and he's out."

"So what were Ralph's visions?"

"He saw red flaming letters in the sky, and they told him what to do. It was only for a week or so, but he was never the same after that." Her tone was sad now, more for him than herself, I sensed.

"Did they tell him to become religious?"

"More or less. He was supposed to get involved in some holy mission to usher in a new era. From my reading, this is common with a grandiose psychosis."

"So he found Crowder?"

"Eventually. He tried some other churches first and gave them money we needed for other things. He wouldn't listen to me. When I said anything sensible about his new religious fervor, he told me I was doing Satan's work."

Those were the exact words of the threat Aria had reported. I thought about Ralph's voice. That matched up, too.

"Is Ralph capable of making threats over the phone?" I asked.

"Absolutely. In fact, I've heard him do it numerous times. He's a bully, but not in person. I guess he's a cowardly bully, if there is such a thing."

"Thank you for that. That's very helpful. You know, I met your ex and his new wife this morning. They're an odd couple."

"He found someone willing to be completely submissive. He thinks that's what the Bible says about marriage—that men should be in charge. It's another reason I had to leave him."

"I understand his new wife, Hazel, is Consuela Crowder's niece?"

"Yes. Consuela is a lovely woman," Lois said with a smile. "I've known those Crowders for many years."

"Are you bitter about how your marriage turned out?"

"Just a little at this point." She turned to face me

more directly. "It was an ugly divorce. And when Gary Crowder introduced Ralph to little Hazel—well, that was kind of the last straw." She winced at the memory.

"Was Ralph a good father to Cate?" I asked.

"Not really. He never took the time to get to know her. She's always been difficult, but she's our only child. He could've tried."

"What about Wayne?"

"He was hard to warm up to. He was just too much of a narcissist."

"Do you mean that in the clinical sense?"

"Actually, I do. I'm a social worker," Lois said. "Clearly, Wayne had a personality disorder. He was outrageously arrogant. Everyone else on the planet was only an object to be used by him."

"I have a degree in clinical counseling, but I never got a license. Remind me of the difference between a narcissist and a psychopath."

"Oh, I don't know. I guess it's a matter of degree. Wayne never chopped people up or—" She realized what she was saying and stopped abruptly.

"That's okay. I understand. What about his widow, Georgia? She won't talk to us—or the press." Matt had made absolutely no progress in this arena.

"She's extremely passive most of the time, with an occasional profane outburst." Lois shook her head. "I don't mean she's submissive like Hazel. It's beyond that. It's like she doesn't have any preferences at all. After a few years, I put my foot down with Ralph. No more socializing with Wayne and Georgia. They were like some horrible wrestling tag team. If Wayne wasn't being offensive enough, Georgia would say something inappropriate and ruin our evening."

"Anything else?"

"A favor."

"Of course."

"You've talked to Cate. You must've formed some impression of her. Aria speaks highly of you, and I'd love to hear what you think. What can Aria and I do to help my daughter?" Lois tilted her head and waited expectantly.

I thought that over. I wanted to help, but I wasn't sure I had anything useful to offer. "Well, I'm no expert, but obviously she's mad at the world. Probably there's hurt behind that. And I think she gets overwhelmed by her feelings and then acts out to get out from under them."

"I agree." She nodded emphatically. "So what should we do? I'm scared she's totally lost her way. I know she wants to leave the center."

"I think that's bravado. I'll bet she stays here for a while. But the main thing is you can't cheat her out of her hard lessons. Cate's got a rough road ahead of her, and she's the one that has to trudge down it."

"So what's my role?"

"Let her trudge," I said. "And love her."

****

I arrived early for my five o'clock meeting at Crowder's church, which was in an unattractive industrial building. Well, part of one. The other half was an herbal tea company. I could smell the sharp tang of peppermint, jasmine, and cinnamon in the parking lot. Even pleasant odors become nasty when they're too intense. I felt mildly nauseated.

The interior of the converted warehouse was relatively church-like, with wooden walls and plush brown carpeting. The ceiling was high but not terribly inspirational. The heavens here were metal struts supporting a corrugated tin roof. I wondered if anyone could hear Crowder's sermons on a rainy day.

The layout was simple. The front doors opened up to a shallow lobby that spanned the width of the building. To the left were several offices, to the right was a meeting room with the door open, and straight ahead was the sanctuary—an auditorium, basically. It held about six hundred seats—chairs, not pews. A giant wooden cross towered over a simple white altar at the far end of the room. It looked like mahogany or rosewood—nothing you'd squander on a Jewish criminal back in the day.

An unmanned desk sat in front of the offices to my left, and half a dozen institutional-looking chairs were grouped to the side of it. While I contemplated prowling around the less public parts of the church, Crowder's assistant returned, so I headed over to her. She was a severe-looking, older woman with a regal bearing. She reminded me of an English actress whose name I couldn't remember.

"Hello," I said. "I'm a little early."

"And you are?"

"Karl Gatlin."

"Take a seat."

She put her head down and began reading something while I still stood in front of her desk. Maggie Smith, that was the actress. Only upon closer examination, the resemblance was faint.

I sauntered over to one of the chairs—the furthest one from Miss Friendly. No one walked by. I closed my eyes for a moment.

"Look who we have here," someone boomed.

I'd fallen asleep. I looked up. It was Jim Crowder.

"I didn't expect to find you here," he said. "Do I need to arrest you for violating a restraining order, Gatlin?"

"Once again," I said, "I was invited."

He reached out and patted me on the shoulder. It was creepy. His thin smile was even creepier. "Gary told me," he whispered.

I stood up. "You know, I didn't expect to see you here, either, Chief. Are you hanging out with your brother on the taxpayer's dime?"

He lowered his voice so the secretary couldn't hear us. "Screw you," he said. Then he smiled again and walked away.

"Karl," the other Crowder called from his doorway. "Reverend."

I strode over to him and hugged him the way he'd hugged me when we met. He was even more uncomfortable than I'd been. It was satisfying.

Then I walked past him into his office and peered around the spartan and tasteful decor. A variety of Christian-oriented artwork perched on several shelves—a ceramic vase with fish symbols on it, a small portrait of John the Baptist, and a multicolored folk-art cross from somewhere in Central America. El Salvador? I'd seen that style somewhere before.

"Have a seat, Karl. I hope we can repair this rift between us."

I sat in front of his huge maple desk and he sat behind it. His tan western suit fit him perfectly. He waited, his face impassive. I was struck again his amazing, rigidly erect hair.

"Sure," I said. "Let me start by apologizing. You invited me to your home, and I responded by antagonizing and then threatening your bodyguard, which was rude and unnecessary. Sometimes I have a problem with taking orders from people."

"That's very gracious of you. And many people have that problem—even when the orders come from God Himself. It's certainly something you can work on if you wish to."

"Thank you. I'll look into that. Speaking of bodyguards, where's Arlin?"

"He is no longer in my employ."

That was interesting. Had some danger passed so he didn't need him anymore? Had Arlin screwed up somehow?

"Now let's get on to my apology," Crowder continued. "I've drafted a letter, and I'd like you to read it. Then I'd like you to look at a letter of acknowledgement I've drafted."

"This seems unnecessarily elaborate, but if that's what you want, sure."

He passed me the two letters, which were on expensive vellum. His apology was detailed. In formal language, he expressed remorse about swearing, misrepresenting "certain facts," allowing his employee to mistreat me, and "letting God down."

The acknowledgement letter was just that. I signed it despite still feeling a bit mystified by the whole thing.

"Are you out of danger?" I asked. "Is that why Arlin isn't with you?"

"I'm not comfortable discussing that. I know it's your job to ask questions, but it wasn't a good idea for me to answer them last time."

"Let's put the past behind us," I said. I wanted Gary to believe whatever game he was playing was working—that I liked him again, or whatever. "We share some common interests," I continued. "You mentioned that last time we spoke and I think you're right, so perhaps we can work together to resolve things." I had no idea what the interests or the resolutions might be, but it sounded good to my ears.

"I'm sure we do. Good luck with your investigation. Now I have some church business to attend to. I'm sure you can find your way out."

He stood and held out his hand, which I shook. Dismissed, soldier.

****

I called Matt from the aromatic parking lot. "How are you feeling?" I asked.

"A little better. I worked a couple of hours, but I didn't turn up much. What's new?"

"I need you to check out a few leads." I gave him a laundry list of things that had come up that day. "When you're feeling well enough, of course," I added. "I'd do it myself, but I'm out here in the trenches facing mortal danger at every turn while you're ensconced in bed being spoon-fed chicken soup by a beautiful woman."

"Repartee is beyond me right now."

"My God, you really are sick."

I headed home from Crowder's. Falling asleep in the waiting room was, ironically, a wake-up call that I was working too hard again. Maybe someone like Aria could stay on the go and pay close attention all day long, but I couldn't.

Chen called just as I finished a rather pathetic frozen dinner. For one thing, the peas weren't even close to being round. Dented, discolored vegetables were the least of it, actually, but what could I expect for three and a half bucks?

"What's up?" I asked.

"Paul Webb was easy to follow. He met a guy at a motel in Scotts Valley. They were only in there for an hour and a quarter. But the other guy wasn't gay."

"How do you know that?"

"Gaydar."

"What?"

"*I'm* gay."

"Oh." I was surprised. I guess there'd never been a reason for Chen to share this before.

"So the guy was Latino," he continued. "And he was carrying a big gym bag. He brought it in, he brought it out. Paul Webb went in with nothing and came out with nothing."

"So you don't think it was a drug deal?"

"It could've been, but no."

I'd never heard Chen talk this much. His voice was educated and smooth. "So then what did you do?" I was hoping he'd followed the second guy and maybe found out who he was.

"I followed the guy Paul met. He drove to an import store in Watsonville. A nonprofit for poor people."

"Like Goodwill?"

"No, it's all artists' stuff from Mexico, and the profits go to kids down there." He didn't seem to have an opinion about this one way or the other.

"Ah." That would be a good front for a drug-smuggling operation. If it wasn't one, on the other hand, it sounded like a worthy charity and I'd have to do my Christmas shopping there.

Chen kept talking, unprompted. "So I went in after a while and asked for a pamphlet or whatever they had. If that didn't help, I was going to ask to talk to the manager because I didn't see the guy from the motel up front."

He stopped. This was more like him. Apparently, I needed to prime the pump at this point, so I did. "But they had literature?"

"Yeah. He was right there in the pamphlet. He's the director—John Bishop."

"I thought you said he was Hispanic."

"Well, he looks like he is. Maybe he was adopted."

"That's great work, Chen."

He gave me more details. I'd look into it in the morning.

I turned in early and dreamt that everyone in the world was gay but me. In the dream, I didn't mind. It made me feel special.

.

Chapter Twenty-Four

"Rise and shine!" a man's voice called roughly.

Who the hell was in my bedroom? I opened my eyes about the same time they flicked on the overhead light—three Latino men. I had this weird sleepy idea for a moment that I was a racist because I thought so many of the bad guys in this investigation were Hispanic. Than my adrenaline kicked in, and I was completely awake.

The man on the left held a revolver on me while the one on the right came over and took my gun off the nightstand. A short, wiry guy in his late forties stood in the middle. He had the dead eyes that placed him all the way at the bad end of the bad-guy spectrum. He also had tattoos of crosses all over his neck.

The guy was too damned casual. Like Aria, he displayed no tension or worry on his face, but his version was chilling. Clearly, it was because he didn't give a shit about me or what I might do. All in all, he was the scariest person I'd run into in a long time.

The other two were probably the second and third scariest. They were bigger and looked dumber, which wasn't a good combination. In my experience, ignorance was a major element in violent behavior. If you couldn't think your way out of an iffy situation, then you tried to assault your way out.

Here they were in my house—with me still under

the covers. If I'd only had Larry, I thought. A mouse couldn't have snuck in with my boy on the job.

"You know who I am?" the middle guy asked.

"No."

"That's good."

He didn't have much of an accent. He watched me for a while. He probably won every staring contest he ever competed in—his gaze was piercing. I was at his mercy, and that seemed to be a quality that was quite strained in this case, Shakespeare notwithstanding.

"So who are you?" I asked. "What do you want?" I knew they weren't there to kill me or I'd already be dead.

"I run the Sureños out of Salinas and Watsonville. My name doesn't matter."

"Are you here to confess?" I don't know how I came up with that. I guess part of me knew I'd fare better if I gained the guy's respect.

He smirked. "That's a good one. You've got cojones, pal."

"I guess so."

"You're nosing around, and I don't like it." His tone was still casual. I was an annoyance—a bug—not a threat that required his A game in the intimidation department. On the other hand, his two sidekicks were working hard at prison-yard stares. "We're hoping to get to kill you," they said with their eyes.

The leader continued. "I'm here to tell you—man to man—the Sureños don't have anything to do with this."

"Why should I believe you?"

"You think I do this all the time?" He clenched his jaw, and his voice was steely now.

"No."

"We're not involved, and I don't want us involved. If they find your body at your mother's house after we kill her, which is what'll come next, then we're involved. I can't let you keep fucking around, and I don't want you dead, so what's left?"

"A man-to-man talk?"

"Exactly." He nodded, and somebody inhabited his eyes for a moment before they deadened again. "Some people I trust said you were okay," he said. "So here I am. Now, what are you going to do?"

"I'm going to believe you and look elsewhere."

"Good. And if you're bullshitting, I'll know it. We have people everywhere."

"I believe that, too."

"Leave him his gun," he told the guy on his right. "He's gonna need it."

"Wait a minute," I said. "If you know I need my gun, it sounds like you know who's behind this. Why not tell me? If it's a rival gang, don't you want them to go down?"

He'd started to walk away. Now he stopped and looked at me again while he thought that over. "I'll tell you this," he said. "I don't rat people out. I don't care who they are. But you might look a little further south than us."

"Okay, thanks. I appreciate that."

They left. My gun had been deposited on the bureau across the room. Here was another reminder that at any moment, from any direction, anything could happen.

I shook with residual adrenaline as I followed my morning routine, and I considered what the leader of the

Sureños had said. His logic made sense. They'd have taken a more lethal approach if they were responsible for Sharp's murder. He was telling me I was an inconvenience they preferred not to deal with. And I believed him. Obviously, they weren't innocent, per se. They were just busy committing other crimes instead of this one.

And Honduras was south of Mexico. The guy was definitely aiming me at the Hombres. That was clear.

****

Rachel—Matt's lover—stopped by with Larry.

"You are a girlfriend and a half," I told her, giving her a hug. Rachel was solidly built. She could've played inside linebacker for a player-strapped high school. It was like hugging a man who happened to have a squishy bosom and smelled like herbal conditioner. She wore black-framed glasses and bright red lipstick. Sometimes she wore bright red glasses and black lipstick. She was a tricky one.

"Yeah. Going to see Adele is way above and beyond the call of duty," Rachel said once she'd stepped back. She gave full-body hugs, but only for an instant. It was kind of a cross between an East Coast and a West Coast hug. "She thought I was involved with you," she continued, "even though I explained the deal about five times."

"I really appreciate this." Larry was jumping all over me, so I got down on my good knee and communed.

"You sure love your dog, Karl," Rachel said.

"I do. How's the patient?"

"Lousy. I mean, he's a lousy patient. He complains nonstop. But he's feeling a lot better this morning. I'm

247

off to work today. Thanks to your crazed ex, I'm late."
She was a paralegal at the courthouse. It suddenly
occurred to me that she might be Matt's source of
inside information.

I saw her off and got on the computer for a while. I
was planning to drive down to talk to John Bishop—
Paul's motel buddy—at his charity store in Watsonville,
but it wouldn't open up for several hours. I started by
researching Ray Lundquist—the guy with the
harassment lawsuit against Aria. We didn't know
enough about him.

As he'd told us, he was Canadian, from a small
town in southern Ontario near Hamilton. He had a
record up there, which made me wonder how he was
working in the U.S. Was he an illegal immigrant? It
was a lot easier to be one if you were white. The police
didn't stop you once a week for going two miles an
hour over the speed limit.

Lundquist had never been violent. His arrests were
for fraud and petty theft, and he'd only been convicted
once—back when he was twenty-three. His brother was
in prison up there for beating a guy to death in a bar.
Nice family.

I tried the newspaper archives in the area and hit
pay dirt. Ray had been famous for a while. At first, his
name had been withheld because he'd been a minor and
he was supposedly the victim of the crime. But later,
he'd tried to cash in on his notoriety by coming out to a
magazine, and then all the newspapers had covered that.

He'd been a junior in high school when his English
teacher had slept with him and gotten caught. By all
accounts, she'd had a drinking problem. Her photo was
fuzzy—the early part of the archive had originally been

microfilm—but she looked quite attractive. Her name was Lina Piatanesi. She'd only been twenty-four. I examined the photo with a magnifying glass to see if I recognized a younger version of someone local. It wasn't Aria or anyone else.

Piatanesi got a year in prison. She also got pregnant, and apparently the baby was Lundquist's. She gave the girl up for adoption—while serving her sentence—and she found a way to disappear once she was released. I don't blame her.

What I'd found explained why the adult Lundquist had taken the sexual harassment route with Aria, whatever his game was. He'd been through it before. He knew how it worked.

I was fairly sure he was trying to extort money from her. He probably knew she had plenty of it—the foundation's finances weren't secret. And she'd told me upfront that paying my fee wouldn't be a problem. Matt's investigation had verified that.

But I couldn't see how Ray Lundquist tied in with the murder. Now that I was fairly sure Ralph Sharp had made the threats, and that Wayne had been laundering drug money, it was hard to see how Lundquist fit into any of that.

This happened a lot in an investigation. I'd dig around for one thing, and I'd uncover a secret or two that was unrelated. In most cases, they were relatively benign. Sometimes I'd tell my client everything I found, and sometimes I protected the innocent, if there were any. I played it by ear.

In this case, I wondered why Aria wouldn't want my help with Lundquist. I guess if his lawsuit had no basis at all—and I couldn't imagine it did—then the only threat here was the hassle and expense of Aria having to defend herself. But then I remembered she was a spiritual teacher, and if Lundquist went public with something even slightly embarrassing, her reputation might be irreparably damaged.

Aria had told me she wasn't actively seeking students—the right ones found her. So if a scandal scared off some new people, maybe that wasn't a big deal. But wouldn't a scandal interfere with her current students' progress? I knew she was dedicated to them.

Larry was bored and antsy, so we went for a long walk on the beach. He had a great time chasing birds. I let things percolate in my mind. Sometimes insights bubbled up when I didn't go after them. This tended to happen when Larry and I were walking. A couple of things did break the surface, and I made a note to follow up on them later.

I called Matt when we got back to my condo and told him to check deeper into Gary and Jim Crowder's backgrounds. Why wasn't the reverend married? If Chen could be gay, Gary could be. Maybe he was being blackmailed about that. And where had brother Jim been stationed in the military? Had he met his future wife over in the Philippines? Did he have any skeletons rattling around that we hadn't discovered yet? His behavior with me suggested something was up. For that matter, why not look into both Consuela Crowder and her niece, Hazel Sharp? What did we really know about them?

"I'll be fine, boss," Matt said when I was through. "Don't worry about me." Then he coughed a very fake cough.

"I already talked to Rachel. I know you're feeling

better. Work from home today if you need to."

By now, it was time to head to Watsonville. I'd checked the Folk Arts Cooperative website; they were open on Sundays. I saw John Bishop's photo, too. He didn't look Hispanic to me, but he did look like a nice guy. He might not be at the cooperative on a Sunday, but if he wasn't, I'd talk to whoever was. I needed to get to the bottom of whatever Paul's deal was. If he was using hard drugs, Aria needed to know. He was an integral part of her center.

I brought Larry, of course, who wore his shiny green service vest. I was going schmoozing, and I needed my wingman.

Watsonville lies in the middle of a fertile valley south of Santa Cruz, about halfway to Salinas. It's a twenty-minute drive on Highway 1. The city's proximity to the more Anglo towns in the county gave it an economic advantage over Salinas. It saw an influx of new homes and money from people pushed out of Santa Cruz proper by ever-rising property values. In turn, this squeezed the largely Hispanic population economically, many of whom had moved on to less-green pastures in the San Joaquin valley. You could rent a decent home for a third of the cost in Stockton, Modesto, or Lodi. The farther from the ocean, the less exorbitant the cost of living.

The day was sunny and cloudless, and the quality of the light etched the outlines of the road signs and the other vehicles. Some days were like that, or at least they seemed that way to me. I could never tell if this was an external phenomenon or a perceptual shift within myself. I'd given up trying to choose between the two, and now I simply enjoyed the experience. Everything looked bigger and more three-dimensional too. Could the sun do that?

I found the storefront easily, and as always, parking wasn't a problem in downtown Watsonville. A mall with box stores had set up shop on the outskirts of town a decade ago. Bye-bye local businesses. Half the storefronts were boarded up, and most of the remaining merchants were peddling dollar items, discount travel back to Mexico, or the like. My emotional support animal and I walked to our destination and wandered in. Larry was on a leash for a change.

"Oh, what a beautiful store," I said to the man behind the counter. It was Bishop.

"Thank you. That's a beautiful dog, too. What's his name?" His voice was smooth and gentle. He could've been a kids' TV show host. Not Mr. Rogers. Maybe one of the ones that showed cartoons.

"Larry. Would you like to meet him?"

"Oh, yes. I'm a dog lover. Always have been. Will he behave himself off his leash?"

"Yes."

I released Larry, and he ran over to where Bishop had come around the corner and was bending over with his hand extended. My wingman was getting us off on the right foot. I'd been surprised at first at how disarming a friendly dog could be in my line of work. Now I just worked it.

Bishop was a solidly built guy in his sixties. He wore a white Mexican wedding shirt and khaki pants. His long, wrinkled face displayed no remarkable features. He could've been an extra in a movie about Midwestern farmers—maybe while his kids' show was on hiatus.

Larry loved the guy. I was beginning to think this man had nothing to do with drugs. Perhaps Chen's gaydar had failed him and Bishop really was Paul's lover.

"How long have y'all been here?" I asked.

"Just a year and a half."

"How did you get interested in all this?" I gestured to the racks of wood carvings, hand-embroidered blouses, and silver jewelry. The store was small but packed with brightly-colored arts and crafts.

"I was in the Peace Corps in Chiapas."

"I don't think I know where that is."

"It's the southernmost state in Mexico, just north of Guatemala. It's poor, and the government neglects it because the population is mostly indigenous, so it's suffered from years of revolutionary violence. Do you have an interest in Mexico? It's an amazing place."

"I'm becoming much more interested lately." I stick to the truth when I can.

"I met my wife there. Many of these pieces are from her village." He walked past me to a shelf with several painted mirrors. Larry followed him. "Sylvie's brother made this," he said, holding up one of the mirrors. Its light blue frame featured colorful, whimsical animals. Some of the painted figures were fictional hybrids such as a horse with a jaguar's head and a pig adorned with chicken feathers.

"It's gorgeous," I said. "But I'm worried you won't make a go of it here. Downtown Watsonville isn't exactly thriving."

"No, but we want to support our community. And I doubt we could afford the rent up where the tourists are."

"I hope I'm not keeping you from your work. I'm just naturally nosy." This was true too. If I weren't a private investigator, I might have asked all these questions anyway.

"No, no." Bishop rose from his crouch and released Larry from his ministrations. "Obviously, business is slow. Visiting helps pass the time." Larry sprawled sideways and appeared to immediately fall asleep.

"Have you thought of supplementing your income with something else?" I asked carefully.

"Like what?" He cocked his head and narrowed his eyes. Would my question have triggered suspicion in an innocent man? He continued to watch me closely as I spoke.

"Well, there must be other things to bring back from Mexico that have more value to some people," I said, trying to soft-pedal my approach.

Bishop stepped back and surveyed me from head to toe now. I was wearing fairly new jeans, a blue Henley, and black running shoes that I never ran in. To my eye, I didn't look like a drug dealer. I could've been DEA, I suppose.

"Who sent you?" he asked.

"Paul Webb. I'm sorry I didn't get right to it. I don't know how this works." That seemed sufficiently vague to cover all the possible bases. The ball was in his court.

Bishop peered at me intently, compassion in his eyes now. "Are you in the early stages? I don't see any symptoms."

I was beginning to understand. "Yes, but it's progressive, of course."

"And you've tried all the mainstream treatments?"

"Yes. Nothing's worked. You're my last hope."

"I don't do any treatments here. Did Paul tell you how much it is?"

"I have a confession," I said. It was time to come clean. "I'm a private investigator working for Paul's boss."

"Aria? You work for Aria?"

"Yes."

He strode behind the counter and dialed a landline. "Aria, there's a guy here with a scar on his cheek who says he's working for you."

He listened for a minute and then beckoned me over. "She wants to talk to you."

I walked over and took the phone. "Aria?"

"Karl, I appreciate your hard work, but John is a good man doing important work. I sent Paul to him. He's importing medical treatments the FDA is dragging its feet on approving here, and they might save Paul's life."

"What is it?" I asked.

"It's an infusion from Germany. It's perfectly legal in most of the world, including Mexico."

"So Paul's face droop, his falling asleep, and his personality changes are all part of a life-threatening neurological disorder?"

"Exactly. This branch of the investigation is a dead end. If it weren't, I'd have told you about it. You need to start trusting me. You're going to waste a lot more time if you don't."

"Yeah, okay."

"And buy something expensive while you're in there. Put it on your expenses for the case if you want."

"Sure." I gave the phone back. "I'm sorry, Mr.

Bishop. I didn't understand the situation."

"Apology not accepted. I don't appreciate subterfuge." He folded his arms across his chest and glared at me.

"I'd like to pick out some items while I'm here."

"You're not going to make this right by buying things. I'll bet that's not even a real service dog, is it?"

"No."

"That's reprehensible." He walked around the corner of the counter and stooped to pet Larry again, dismissing me. I wandered around the store and selected several pieces, including the mirror that Bishop had shown me. When I got to the counter, he wouldn't sell it to me.

"Pick another one," he said. "You don't deserve Julio's work."

The thing is, he was right. It was one thing to lie to criminals—or even suspects. That was just part of my job, the same as it was for cops. If this demographic felt free to lie to us and we didn't, it gave them too much of an advantage. What I'd done felt slimy, though. I needed a shower and a stiff drink.

Chapter Twenty-Five

Instead, Larry and I decided to visit Matt at home. It was Larry's idea, really. When we approached Matt's freeway exit, he started barking furiously.

"All right, all right."

Matt lived in an old two-story Victorian house on the east side of Santa Cruz. When he'd been rolling in high-tech money, he'd gutted the inside and created vast open spaces and soaring ceilings. It was like something out of *House Beautiful* magazine.

We let ourselves in. Larry raced off to find his friend. I lay on the black leather couch in the great room. I'd tried to call it a living room once, but Matt had corrected me. What was the difference? $200,000, he'd told me.

He stumbled in with Larry a minute later. He was wearing gray sweatpants and a green sweater. Dark circles pouched under his brown eyes and his mouth was a ragged line—almost a wince. Matt eyed my indolent pose and told me to make myself at home.

"Thanks. I love this couch. It's the best." Larry climbed up onto it, seconding my opinion. He settled down at the other end of the leather expanse, nudging one of my legs out of his way. Ordinarily, Matt would've kicked him off any his obscenely expensive furniture.

"*Mi casa es su* intrusion," Matt said.

"I don't think that's a Spanish word."

"Ask me how I'm feeling," he said. I did. "What do you care?" He fell down onto a matching love seat across from me. When Matt landed, the cushion tossed him sideways. He lay where he'd been thrown, tilting his head to square his horizon with mine.

"Was that satisfying?" I asked.

"Which? What I said or getting comfy?"

"The former."

"Yes, it was. I'm good to go now."

"I just met with the guy Paul's been meeting at a motel," I told him.

"Was he hot?"

"Not my type. And not gay. And not a drug dealer. And not even a slightly bad person."

"Then what the hell is he?"

I explained.

"Well," Matt said, "he's still smuggling and acting as an unlicensed doctor or infuser or whatever."

"True. What did you dig up this morning?"

"Your instincts were good. I think Crowder's gay."

"Gary?"

"Yes, of course. Brother Jim has that Honduran wife."

That took a moment to register. "Honduran?" I sat up.

"Honduran," Matt reiterated with more energy now. "Some kind of ethnic group down there. Jim Crowder was a military policeman at Palmera Air Base outside Tegucigalpa. He met Consuela in the city. Her dad was a doctor."

"I didn't know we had a base down there."

"It's only about six hundred people," Matt told me,

rubbing his temple as though he had an insect bite. "The Honduras Air Force Academy is on the grounds. They used the base for CIA ops back in the day. Now they run counter-drug missions."

"I heard the drug cartel—the Hombres—was pretty much running the country."

"It's bad. We could have 600,000 troops down there, and it probably wouldn't matter," Matt agreed.

"So let's back up a minute—from before you started showing off. Why do you say Gary's gay?"

"I just got off the phone with two people in Oklahoma and one in Southern California."

"On a Sunday morning?"

"I told them I was a reporter looking for any old associates of Crowder who no longer attend church services."

"That doesn't sound like it would work. How'd you even find these people?" I asked. I reached down to pat Larry, who had slithered up the couch and shoved his nose into my thigh.

"You don't want to know. And mostly it didn't work at all. But a guy that went to Bible college with him said he was 'irregular.' "

"Did you check to see if he was talking about his G.I. tract?"

"I did. Then another one said he saw Crowder in a gay bar once."

"Hardly definitive. And let's be clear that neither of us is homophobic. We're looking into this because of the blackmail angle."

"Of course. But hang on, I've saved the best one for last."

"Don't tell me. He held his pinkie out while he

sipped tea at the opera?"

"Crowder had an affair with a fellow teacher at the school where he taught down south. A guy." A self-satisfied smile unfolded on his wan face.

"Why didn't you just tell me that in the first place?"

"You don't understand narrative arc, Karl. You never have. I was building up to it."

"Wait a minute. What about Leanne Atkinson? If Gary Crowder was gay, what would he be doing molesting her?" I asked. I stopped stroking Larry while I pondered. Now his cold nose was snuffling mercilessly in my crotch.

"Ever heard the word 'bi'? Or maybe she's lying," Matt said.

"Maybe. The main thing is Crowder's hiding something that could ruin him."

Larry finally gave up and lay down on a nearby Persian rug.

"Yup," Matt agreed. His lower volume demonstrated that his energy had ebbed again.

"Okay, let's get back to Jim Crowder. Do you think the Honduras thing is significant?"

"I don't know. Back then, there wasn't a drug scene down there. But it's still uncanny, isn't it?"

"Yeah, first it looks like the bad guys might be Hondurans and then lo and behold, the chief of police has all kinds of ties to the place. Wait a minute. I just realized I've been building an inadvertent narrative arc."

"You can't do them inadvertently."

"Well, anyway, I forgot something big that's similar to you holding back your best evidence." I told him about the Sureños in my bedroom.

"How could you possibly forget that?"

"Maybe my purported forgetting was really part of my complex narrative arc."

"Maybe you are the strangest boss in the world," he countered. "I don't know what to say about the Sureños' wake-up visit. I guess your take on it is probably right. They're warning you off in an uncharacteristically nice way because they don't want attention from the cops. Maybe they've got something going right now that's especially important to them."

"Maybe," I conceded. "Hey, what about Hazel Crowder—Jim's new wife? Did you find out more about her?"

"Honduran, too. She's Consuela's niece like we thought."

"No, I mean she represents a more recent connection to the place. She came up here during the drug era, right?"

"That's right. What do you think? You met her."

"I can't imagine she's involved in anything, but like you said, 'Who knows?'"

"Oh, here's another thing," Matt said. "Cardenas called and told me to have you call him back. You're not answering your phone, are you?"

"No. I've been too busy. Unless it's you, I've been letting calls go to voicemail."

At that point, Larry decided to hop up and race to the front door for no apparent reason. Then I heard gunshots. From a handgun. And from close by—maybe in Matt's driveway.

"Get down!" I called.

I ran to a window as a white BMW sedan zoomed

away. I sprinted outside. A body lay facedown beside my car at the end of the driveway.

I couldn't see who it was—or if the guy was dead or not—so I flipped him over. It was Victor Gonzales— the task-force guy. He was definitely dead. He'd been shot just above his missing eye and in the neck.

Matt was right behind me, calling 911. "Tell Cardenas to come," he croaked to the dispatcher. "It's his case."

"Oh shit," I said, looking at Victor's ruined face.

Chapter Twenty-Six

Larry was upset. He'd never seen or smelled a human corpse before. I sat on the driveway next to him and held him while he shook. Matt wasn't doing much better. Maybe he could've handled a murder better if he weren't sick. Maybe not.

The cops arrived within ten minutes. One of them had been the first responder at the beach shooting, too—Casey, his name was. Dennis Casey. I felt cold as soon as I saw him. I guess the association of the freezing water of the bay and his Irish mug would endure for a while. I'd never seen the other patrolman before. The ambulance pulled up right behind them, siren screaming, but it didn't matter.

Casey wasn't happy with our answers to his questions. We should've had some idea what Gonzales was doing there. We shouldn't be investigating things we had no business investigating. And apparently, I should've been able to see the BMW's license plate. It was like the guy had a template in his head of how things were supposed to be, and he blamed us for not matching it.

Casey's very fair skin and short, light brown hair lent him a youthful air. Dark freckles looked out of place high on his cheeks. Beside them, his watery blue eyes were set deep in his face. He was about five foot seven and definitely suffered from short-man syndrome. Casey reminded me of a kid who'd cheated off my test in middle school, precipitating both of us flunking.

He asked us quite a few questions that weren't particularly relevant to the murder at hand. I think he was interested in what it was like to be a private eye. I couldn't imagine why else Casey would want to know who John and Chen were. For that matter, how did he even know about Chen? Had I become so notorious down at the station that everyone was swapping stories about me?

His partner, Thompson, a younger athletic-looking African-American, did crowd control. The crowd consisted of half a dozen neighbors, a couple of gawkers in cars, and two Jack Russell terriers who kept trying to run through the crime scene to get to Larry.

Cardenas and Sue Sutter drove up in an unmarked sedan about twenty minutes into all this. Cardenas immediately banished Casey to interviewing the neighbors.

The detectives took us inside to talk. Larry had calmed down by now. He trotted alongside me back into the great room and lay down on my feet.

Matt and I sat on the couch together, and the two detectives sat across from us in the love seat. Sutter spent some time examining the interior of the house. She wore a tan blazer over a yellow top and khakis. I saw a few wrinkles at the corners of her eyes I hadn't noticed before. The light from Matt's skylights highlighted the lines on everyone's face.

Cardenas wore designer jeans, a gray and white wool poncho, and black cowboy boots. He looked like a Rodeo Drive version of a Hispanic Clint Eastwood in a spaghetti western. Had he been working undercover or was this his Sunday best?

"We need to compare notes again," he said. "Not just about this murder."

"I agree," I said. "And I'd be happy to go first."

Sue placed her recorder on the glass coffee table between us without asking. I didn't mind. I detailed what I'd discovered since we'd last met. Matt chimed in with background information, withholding any facts he'd gleaned from illicit sources.

"I gotta admit," Cardenas said, "you're doing better than we are. Most of these people won't talk to cops. What did you make of Rivera?"

"Who?"

"The top Sureño—the guy in your bedroom. You're lucky to have survived that meeting, you know. If it hadn't gone his way…"

"I thought he was smart and dangerous. He had a presence."

"Yeah, that's what I've heard. What about our victim here? Victor Gonzales? Did he seem nervous or scared when you talked to him in Watsonville?"

"No, quite the opposite. My impression was he was confident and good at his job. Talk to John Ratu if you want to see what he thinks."

"Maybe Gonzales was too good at his job," Sue said.

"So you're sure he wasn't worried?" Cardenas asked, ignoring his partner. "You know he walked away from the Norteños? And he's been working with the cops."

"Yeah, I know, but that was years ago and…Oh shit."

"What?" Sue asked.

"I just remembered something. Victor said the reason he wasn't worried about getting killed was he had a pact or something with José—you know, the ex-gang guy at Aria's center. And with his brothers, he said. If anything ever happened to him, they were going to come after whoever was responsible. We need to call John—to tell him to hold onto José before he finds out about this and goes off. I know he's supposed to be spiritual now, but he's got nothing to lose. He's dying."

"Call John. I'll get a car over there," Cardenas said. We both grabbed our phones.

"I'll go look for him," John told me. "I'm sure you're wrong, though. He's one of my favorite people here."

"Just do it."

"This could be a bloodbath," Sutter said. "As it is, there's a delicate balance between all these gangs."

"Do you know what Gonzales was working on?" Matt asked.

Cardenas leaned forward. "He was trying to get an undercover cop into the Hombre gang. It was somebody from Honduras who works a beat in San Francisco. Gonzales came up to Santa Cruz to get us to manufacture a fake rap sheet. He said the police forces in Salinas and Watsonville had been infiltrated. He was even worried about ours, if you can believe that. I've never even met anyone from Honduras."

"Yes, you have," Matt said. "Hazel Sharp and Consuela Crowder."

"The chief's wife is Honduran? You're shitting me. He tells people she's from Mexico City."

"She went to school there. A private boarding

school. But she grew up in an upper-class family in Tegucigalpa."

"That's very interesting." Cardenas glared at me. "You could've mentioned that, Karl."

"I can't remember everything. Especially after I just saw somebody's face with a bullet hole in it."

He waved his arm around. It was vintage Cardenas.

"So maybe Victor was on his way here to tell you something," Sue said.

"Maybe," I said. "But it doesn't add up. Why wouldn't he call or go over to my house? How could he know I was here at Matt's?"

"Maybe he put a homing device on your car," Matt mused. "Did he leave the meeting down in Salinas before you did?"

"Yeah, but cops don't do that without a warrant." I looked at the detectives. "Right?"

"*We* don't," Sue said. "But those task-force guys do sometimes. They handpick people who are willing to cut corners."

"Did you find his car? He didn't follow me here on foot."

"No, we didn't."

I thought it over. "Then it wasn't a drive-by," I told them. "Victor wasn't here already. We heard the shots—and Larry heard something else first—and then I ran to the window. By then, the car was almost out of sight. The bullet wounds were from close range, right?"

Cardenas nodded. "No more than a few feet. Who's Larry?"

My dog was up on his feet now, licking Sue's hand. He seemed to like her. "This is Larry," she said.

Cardenas grunted. I'd noticed the longer a

conversation, the more of a caveman he became.

I continued. "They didn't have time to stand in the driveway, shoot Victor at pointblank range, and then get back in their car and get down the road so fast. I think you'll find they shot him while he was still in the car and then pushed him out—while they were moving."

Matt spoke up. "All of which begs the question: why do it here?"

"It's probably another warning," Cardenas said. "Although I don't know why any of these people want to warn you instead of just popping you."

Sutter voiced her opinion. "I think there are two groups here. One wants to kill you—or at least they did two days ago at the beach. The other one's more interested in scaring you off. Like with Sharp in the well, they could've picked anywhere to do this latest shooting, but they decided on Matt's doorstep."

"It wouldn't have been hard to find out that he worked for me," I said. "And his home address isn't a secret."

"Everything's not always about you." Matt pointed at me, belying his statement. "Maybe they were scared of what I've been digging up."

"Maybe."

John called me, and I took it. "I can't find José. I don't think he's here. Somebody said he was meeting a friend for lunch, but they don't know where."

"Are the police there yet?"

"I don't think so. No, wait a minute. I hear a siren."

"Go look in the woods. I think he walks in there. And have the police search the buildings again."

"Sure, Karl. But what about Aria? I can't leave her

alone."

"Good point. You stay with her. Send some of the students out to look."

"Okay, yeah. No worries." He sounded worried for once, though.

"John can't find him?" Sue asked after I'd put my phone down.

"It sounds like José's gone out to lunch with a friend. Let's keep our fingers crossed."

"What about the Gonzales brothers?" Cardenas asked.

"I think they're all back in Texas," Matt said. "I did some research on Victor before Karl met him. It would take them a while to get here once they hear the news."

"So where do we stand?" I asked Cardenas.

"I'm thinking." He gestured randomly again. At least it was random to me. "Give me a minute."

He took about three. Larry came over, and I scratched him behind the ears for a while. Matt slumped down in his corner of the couch. He didn't look good. Sue Sutter stared at her hands in her lap, which were so tangled together, it looked as though she'd have trouble getting them apart again.

"Go to bed," I told Matt after a while.

"No," he replied softly, all energy drained out of him.

"Okay," Cardenas finally said. "Here's what I think. Reverend Crowder and his people want Aria's property, and Lundquist wants her money. Meanwhile we've got Wayne Sharp mixed up with a drug cartel that's probably connected to one of these two. I don't know which one. I know Reverend Crowder and Ray

Lundquist both seem like unlikely allies of Latino gangs, but that's what the evidence points to. Sharp was in the process of cutting a deal with us about his criminal activities, by the way."

Cardenas paused to see if we were paying attention, then, satisfied that we were despite Matt's obvious stupor, he continued. He held his arms down with some effort. Apparently, he was working on his gesticulating problem. "So we've got rival gangs fighting turf wars over their drug business. It looks like the Hombres are the most aggressive ones, so maybe they're behind the attacks on you, Karl. But none of them would hesitate to kill Wayne Sharp if they knew what he was up to."

"And dismember him?" I asked.

"That probably points to the new kids on the block," Sue said. "Unless the Sureños or Norteños are ramping up to show the Hombres they can be just as ruthless."

Cardenas continued. "One of the guys from the SUV attack at the spiritual center—the skinny one that John beat up—has talked. He's more scared about his wife and kids' welfare with him in prison than he is about his employer. They were hired by an Anglo he didn't meet. He said our friend Franco—the one you fought—was the guy who brought him onboard. So that piece isn't gang-related and probably goes back to Aria's land or her money."

"We're still working on Franco," Sutter said. "But he's one of these guys with a so-called code of honor. What do you make of him, Karl?"

"When they ran me off the road. I got the impression he was scared of his boss—that it was a gang leader."

"That was probably an act." Cardenas pointed at me, paused, and then wagged his finger. "You're not going to believe this, but one of the things we found out about Franco was that he was in an improv group in Ciudad Juarez before he became involved with drugs and crossed the border. At the station here, he had some rookie convinced he was somebody else. He almost escaped."

"It's hard to imagine any of these people doing ordinary things," I said.

"Everyone's got a past," Sue pointed out. "Some of us get a rocky start and straighten out. Others go in the opposite direction."

"What about Georgia Sharp—Wayne's widow?" Matt asked. He was alert again. "I couldn't find out much about her, and we can't locate her, either."

Sue spoke up. "I talked to her, and she's a strange one. Very timid. She and her husband supposedly lived in different parts of the house, and she was planning to divorce him. And that's what it looked like in their mansion. I suppose that could explain how unaffected she was by his death. When I interviewed her, she mostly just acted nervous about my getting dirt on the carpet."

"If Wayne was a big crook," Matt said, "then she must've known about it—or participated. Did you look at her as a suspect in the murder?"

"Of course." Sue cocked her head and squinted. "I felt like I was talking to somebody who was guilty—of something, anyway. But she has a solid alibi, and she actually stood to make much more money if she divorced him than if he died. He'd made a new will."

"And she knew about it?" I asked.

"Yeah, she did. Wayne Sharp brought her to his lawyer's office to watch him sign it. The guy was a real piece of work."

"Anything else?"

"Georgia Sharp is also extremely passive. She agreed with practically everything I said, even when I made up something completely ridiculous to see how she'd respond. And she offered me some of her medicinal pot. Talk about clueless."

"Maybe she was high," Cardenas suggested.

Sue shook her head. "No, it's more than that. Anyway, she's staying at her sister's. We gave her permission. It seemed like she might be next on the hit list, and her sister's got a different last name and lives down in Big Sur. I'll give you the address, Karl. Maybe you'll have better luck with her than I did."

"There's something called Dependent Personality Disorder," I said. "These people are practically incapable of acting on their own and controllers like Wayne have radar for finding them. I've seen the dynamic in action. It's like a lion picking a vulnerable animal out of a herd."

"That fits," Sue said.

"Did you know about the third Sharp brother?" I asked Cardenas. "I only found out recently, like I told you."

"Yeah, Chet. But he disappeared. Wayne and Georgia checked him out of Napa State Psych Hospital about three weeks ago for what she called an 'outing,' which is kind of weird based on what Sue just said. If the Sharps were estranged, why would they do that together? Anyway, he ran off on their watch. The hospital confirmed the story."

"Maybe family stuff trumped their enmity," Matt suggested.

"Not with Wayne," Cardenas responded. "He always did what he thought was right for Wayne, even if it screwed everybody else over—including his family. I met the guy once."

"You didn't tell me that, Lou," Sue Sutter said.

He shrugged. "It was at a party at the chief's house. Jim's brother Gary was there, along with Wayne and Ralph. This was maybe two years ago. Wayne started off the evening as a self-centered son of a bitch. As he drank, he got worse—meaner and more abusive."

"To his wife?" I asked.

"No, she wasn't there. She was supposed to be visiting family back East, which doesn't make much sense in hindsight. Wayne brought a date—some Vietnamese girl. He was married, and he brought a date. It was just a horrible scene. Julia and I left after a couple of hours, and we haven't been back to Jim's house since." He turned to me and Matt. "My wife doesn't tolerate that kind of shit. In fact, if I even say the word 'shit' in the house, I'm totally up shit creek."

Matt spoke up. "I admire your ability to say 'shit' that many times in a sentence about not saying the word shit."

"You look like you're running a fever," I told him. "He's sick," I told the others. I was concerned about what he might say next.

"Yeah, I better go to bed. Sorry," he said to Cardenas.

"No, no. That was funny. Don't worry about it."

After Matt stumbled away, Cardenas continued

273

talking about Chet Sharp's disappearance. "The three Sharps were staying at an upscale winery near Healdsburg—one of those places that's like a resort. I don't see how Chet could enjoy anything like that, but his shrink said he'd been off Haldol and on an experimental drug for a couple of months."

"How'd he manage to disappear?" I asked. "Somebody on psych meds for schizophrenia can't usually manage something like that."

"Well, you'd know more about that than I would. Maybe they weren't giving him his pills like they were supposed to. Years ago, he did some pretty wild stuff when he wasn't taking them. Sometimes he'd even pretend he was nuts when he was doing fine so he could avoid prosecution and get sent to the hospital."

"I visited someone in Napa once," I said. "I'd rather go to jail."

"Anyway," Cardenas continued, "Wayne and Georgia woke up the second morning they were there, and Chet was gone. They called the police and the hospital, but he hasn't been seen since."

"You still don't believe in coincidence, do you?" I asked.

"Nope. Sharp is a crook, his wife's strange, and his little brother's crazy. Then one brother disappears, and the other one turns up dead a couple of weeks later. I'll find the connection. It's been a dead end so far, but I'll find it."

"So Chet is Wayne and Ralph's younger brother?" I asked.

"You know, I don't really know. I was assuming," Cardenas said. "You know, from the way Ralph talked about him."

Sue spoke up again. "Lois—Ralph Sharp's ex—told me something interesting about Chet. She said Georgia dated him first—before his initial breakdown—and then she switched over to Wayne."

"That was a long time ago," Cardenas said. "It's gotta be twenty years at least."

"Yeah," Sutter agreed. "You never know how far to go back with this kind of thing. For some people, the past is the past. Other people never forget."

"What do you think about our finding out that Gary's gay?" I asked. "How does that figure into this?"

"It probably doesn't," Sutter said.

"I agree," Cardenas said. "Personally, I thought he was anyway."

I thought it was odd neither of them considered this to be a significant clue. "Have you looked deeper into Aria's background?" I asked. "I know she's my client, but with murderers running around, I think we need to turn over every stone. Matt and I haven't come up with anything about her early life."

"We haven't either," Cardenas said, "and we've got access to all sorts of databases you don't. It's suspicious."

Larry wriggled like a fish at this point, and I extracted my feet from under him. He was unusually restless. Perhaps it was a delayed response to encountering a corpse.

"What about her social security number or old driver's licenses?" I asked.

"Everything starts when she came to California in 2002," Sue said. "It's strange, and she refuses to explain. We can't compel her."

"So we all agree she's got something to hide?" I

glanced at each of the detectives in turn.

"I'm not so sure," Cardenas said.

"He's sweet on her," Sue said.

"It could be she's just a private person," he said, glaring at his partner. "You know, with boundaries and all that. I mean, what could a person like her have done that she wouldn't want us to know?"

"I have no idea," I said. "And I wonder why Aria would hire an investigator if she was trying to hide things. That's like going into a counseling office and trying to keep the therapist from finding out what your problem is."

"Suppose the threats scared her," Cardenas said. "And when the police wouldn't help, maybe she picked the agency with the worst reputation in town to keep down the odds that anyone would find out her secrets. No offense."

I considered that, putting aside the implied insult. "None taken. That actually makes sense. Aria knew me years ago when I was really incompetent at my job. The sensible thing to do would've been to contact a big agency. And Aria is very sensible." I thought for a moment more. "Speaking of the police not helping her, is there a pattern here? When Leanne Atkinson accused Gary Crowder years ago, the case was dismissed. When Aria called about her threats—more than once—it went nowhere. Is this Jim's doing?"

Sue answered me. "Well, if the chief knows his brother's gay—and he must—then why would he believe a woman who claimed he molested her? Her-word-against-his cases never go anywhere, anyway, even if everybody's sexual orientation is lined up right."

"Gary could be bisexual," I said, channeling Matt.

"Do you have any evidence of that?" Cardenas asked.

"No."

"Let me ask you this," he said. "If someone told you they were being harassed by your brother, and you loved him and thought he was a really good guy, would you believe them?"

"Probably not," I said. It occurred to me that the two detectives wanted to believe their chief was honest. I would if I were them. "I've gotta say that putting all our cards on the table and working together was a terrific idea."

"That was Sue's doing," Cardenas said, gesturing with his thumb at his partner.

"Getting back to Aria," I said. "Let's brainstorm about what her secret might be—assuming she has one that's relevant to the case. I'll get us started. She could be a Nazi war criminal."

Sutter laughed. Cardenas frowned.

I glanced at him. "I'm setting the tone. Let's think outside the box and not worry about what sounds reasonable."

"Okay," they said together.

"She could be a fugitive—maybe she was in a radical political group," Sue tried.

"She could've worked in a slaughterhouse," I said. "She could have the blood of countless cows on her hands, so cutting up a body would be child's play for her."

"What's wrong with a slaughterhouse?" Cardenas protested. "My brother-in-law operates one. It's honest work."

"Lou, you're not getting into the spirit of this," Sue said.

"All right, all right. Maybe Aria was a stripper or a hooker," he said.

"Now you're talking." I looked up and let my mind wander. "She could've been a drug addict, too."

"Or a spy," Sutter said.

"Or maybe a superhero," Cardenas tried. "Aria Piper could be her mild-mannered secret identity."

"Way to go, Lou," Sue said. "That makes me think of one. What if she stole someone else's identity, and she's not really her?"

"Okay," I said, "here's one to end on. What if she had plastic surgery, and she's really Jimmy Hoffa—or Elvis?"

Chapter Twenty-Seven

Needless to say, our brainstorming didn't amount to anything. I guess we got carried away with the creative aspect of it. But it had been the most fun I'd had that day.

When the police had finished tagging, bagging, interviewing, and all the rest, I made a couple of egg-salad sandwiches in Matt's kitchen, ate one, and left the other one with a note for the patient. Then Larry and I headed down to Aria's. I needed to see her again.

More than anything, I needed a barometer reading on her. Would she seem as wonderful as before? It was easy to think uncharitable thoughts about her when I was off the property, but I hadn't been able to reconcile them with my direct experience of her. Presumably, at this time of the day—late afternoon—she'd have some time free. If not, maybe she'd make some once I told her there'd been another murder.

It wasn't hard to find a space in the main parking lot this time. Most of the Sunday day-trippers had gone home. I called John to see where he and Aria were, and he told me she was in her office with her last student for the day. He and I could talk while she finished up.

He met Larry and me on the wooden porch. They had a more muted reunion this time. Larry jumped around with John for a minute or two but then crashed.

Every time I saw John, he was bigger than I

remembered. Well, wider, really. And his mobile facial features varied a great deal. Today, his nose seemed to be longer than usual and his eyes browner. In general, he looked like his face had been flattened a bit, too. I don't know how he did that. Maybe it was just a reflection of his mood. Or mine.

We sat at the far end of the porch from Aria's window after Larry settled down. I spoke first. "You never found José, right? Otherwise you would've called."

"Yeah. You think he's okay?"

"I don't. If he was having lunch somewhere, he'd be back by now, wouldn't he?" I told John about Victor and the pact.

His mouth set in a hard line and his brow furrowed. "What'll we do, Karl?"

"There's not much for us to do. The police are handling it. But I'll consult with Aria. She may be a help with this. Now I've got a question for you. Do you think you're still needed here?"

"I don't know, but can't I stay until you catch all the bad guys?"

"If Aria doesn't mind paying."

"I'll do it for free."

"Well, then of course, John. I only get to tell you what to do when I'm paying you."

A slim Asian woman in sweats stepped through the door alongside us. She was crying. She stumbled past us, her head down, and then trudged toward the dorms.

When the woman was out of earshot, John said, "That happens a lot. I don't know what goes on in there."

I strode into the building after telling Larry to stay

outside with John. I didn't want the distraction of dealing with his response to Aria's energy. One ecstatic dog incident was enough.

Aria's door was open. "Karl, what a lovely surprise. Come on in." She stood and came around the desk to hug me.

I held my hand up. "Maybe later," I said. "I think we need an unaltered Karl to start with."

"I understand."

Aria stayed on my side of the desk, and we settled in simple wooden chairs about five feet apart. She wore an embroidered white dress that looked as though it came from Bishop's folk-arts shop. Yellow and purple threads danced around the neckline, and a series of tight green spirals cascaded across her chest. I liked it a lot. I was about to tell her so when I saw her legs for the first time. They were spectacular. I especially liked her taut calf muscles. Maybe wearing the dress was a Sunday thing. I couldn't imagine how she could meditate in it.

For the first time, Aria looked tired. It wasn't her face that told me, it was her body language from the waist up. She was holding herself upright with effort.

"Let's start with José," I said, and I told her about Victor Gonzales's murder and the concerns I had. "Were you aware of any of this?"

"The history, yes. Everything but today's events. I imagine José has assembled an arsenal and will kill as many of the Hombres as he can." She said this in her usual matter-of-fact way.

I was shocked. "You don't seem too concerned."

"Of course I am, but I have no control over this."

"Couldn't you call him and tell him not to do it?" I asked with heat. "He'd probably take the call if he saw it was you. He's ignoring everyone else's efforts to contact him."

"Perhaps he would. I don't know. But I don't interfere in my students' lives. Even when they ask me to, I don't tell them what to do."

"Why not? Don't you sometimes know better what they ought to do?" Ordinary conversations with Aria always seemed to slide into the philosophical realm. I was trying to keep people alive, not debate how to help troubled students. If I couldn't talk her into taking action, more people would die.

"What's 'better'? What's 'ought to'? These are just stories in your head, Karl. Can we really second-guess someone else's life curriculum? It might look horrific from our vantage point. So?"

"Look, I understand what you're saying. Sort of. But this situation isn't much different from what we learned as therapists—and you still are one, Aria. When it's life or death, it's our duty to save lives. José's homicides are going to lead to his getting killed, too. He knows that, so it's really just a complicated suicide. Do you usually let people commit suicide?" I was working hard. A less-than-well-thought-out argument wouldn't have any traction with Aria.

"Karl, I've considered this type of scenario before. I agreed to abide by certain rules as part of my credentialing as a counselor, so in that sphere, I adhere to a duty to maintain life. But here I answer to a higher power. Believe it or not, my heart tells me not to control other people's lives—no matter the provocation. I'll tell you what, though. If you want to speak to José, I'll call him on my phone and then hand it to you. Say whatever you wish. I have no interest in controlling you, either."

"That would be great. Thank you."

She dialed and handed her cell phone to me. José answered.

"It's Karl Gatlin," I told him. "Where are you?"

"Is Aria there? I'd like to thank her and say good-bye."

"José, listen to me. We're going to nail these guys the legal way. I'm getting close. Rivera—the head of the Sureños—came over to my house this morning. He's helping."

"Rivera, huh? I appreciate what you're doing, Karl. I'm glad you're on the case for Aria's sake. But here's how the system works. If they catch anyone high up in a gang, the son of bitch will just keep running the show from prison. Nothing changes. Plus, if I don't do anything, Victor's brothers are all dead. There's no way to protect them from the Barrio Aztecas back in Texas. Those animals would love to take out all the Gonzaleses as a favor to the Sureños."

"It's suicide. You can't survive this."

"That's fine. You think I want to wither away? And my karma's fucked, anyway."

I gave up and handed the phone to Aria.

"Hello, José. How are you feeling? Uh huh…I understand…Thank you. It's kind of you to think of me in this moment…Of course…I love you, too…Good-bye." She hung up the phone and gazed at me evenly.

"So now he's off to commit multiple murders," I said.

"It's up to him, Karl. It sounds like he will." I must've been making some sort of awful face. Aria winced and then continued. "Let me try to explain my understanding of how things work—what's behind the drama we all face periodically."

"I think we have other things we need to do. Maybe later."

"Bear with me." She held up a slim palm and dipped her head. "I need you to understand a bit more about why I do what I do. You don't need to sign up for my perspective, but the distaste you're displaying for my choices is going to interfere with our work—and whatever else we might prove to be to one another."

That last line hit me like a freight train. Really? She felt something too? She seemed sincere, she was lovely, and I'd been alone too long, all of which contributed to the hope that suddenly welled up in my chest. But wasn't it convenient that she presented the possibility of my being with her at that moment? Was she reeling me back in because I was starting to think clearly? I felt the hope suddenly morph into resentment as I thought this. It constituted a rude shift, and I also found myself resenting the loss of my newfound hope.

"Go ahead," I said. For four days, I hadn't managed to dissuade her from doing anything she wanted to do. For someone who said she didn't like to be controlling, she was certainly stubborn about getting her own way. Her tone was bugging me, too. On the surface, it was soft and loving, but she never let go of her teacher role. She was always the one who had the answers, and I was always the clueless dunce who needed teaching. For God's sake, this was an investigation and I was an investigator. Did she think that assigning herself the moral high ground somehow made her better at my job than I was?

"You're operating under a false premise, Karl. You

think all this is real." She motioned with her arm across the breadth of the room.

"Your office isn't real?"

"Nothing is," she asserted, smiling ruefully. "I'm not. You're not. Everything we perceive is an illusion. So there's no death, and there are no murders. It just seems as though there are."

"It sure does. That's crazy, Aria. Do you hear herself?" I could feel the pitch of my voice rising.

She smiled her full-bore, devastating smile at me. I deflected it with a frown.

"There's no separation," she continued. "There are no individual people, and there are no discrete forms. There's only oneness. And the oneness is an energy—a consciousness that generates illusion."

"Why? What's the point?"

"There's no point to any of it—in human terms. The game is beyond meaning, beyond words, and beyond thoughts."

"You honestly believe that people getting murdered is just a game?" My disbelief was embodied in my tone. Who could take their beliefs that far?

"I do and I don't. It depends on where you stand when you look at it. I'm encouraging you to stand where you can see life and death as aspects of a bigger picture that you don't understand."

"Let's get back to the case," I said. I'd had enough. She nodded.

I reported all the new developments. I even threw in a few of the brainstorming ideas about her—just for fun. As usual, she listened closely and didn't interrupt. I thought I saw a small, odd reaction while she was listening to some of the nutty ideas about her past, but I wasn't sure.

"I don't suppose you want to fill me in about your mysterious history at this point?" I finished.

"I don't."

"It can't be all that bad. Are you protecting someone else?"

She gazed at me. Nada.

"You must be tired," I said.

"I am. And I still have a talk to give this evening."

"I'll let you go. I'm sorry if I was rude. I've got a lot on my mind and I'm tired, too."

"Of course."

We stood. "I'd shake your hand," I said, "but I don't want to take any chances with all this energy crap."

"That's probably wise."

Chapter Twenty-Eight

John persuaded me to call Chen and get him to hustle over to relieve him so he could take me out to dinner. Larry would stay on the property and visit with Chen, whom he liked.

"You need cheering up," John told me. "And I need a break. A break with Mexican food in it." He rubbed his hands together as though to warm them up for a physical task—dipping tortilla chips?

"Have you been living on salads?"

"God, no." He reeled in disgust at the thought. "Aldo makes me special food. But he's still limited to vegetarian ingredients. Aria doesn't allow any meat on the property."

"Why not?"

"It's a spiritual thing, Karl." This was about as helpful an explanation as what Aria had said. But at least John was more concise.

We took John's SUV. Chen had made it over in record time. He drove a crotch rocket—an extremely fast Japanese motorcycle.

"Did you know Chen's gay?" I asked as John tooled to El Charro in Soquel. The traffic was light, and it felt like rain was looming.

"Of course. I think it came up the first time we had a long talk."

"A long talk with Chen?"

"What? He doesn't talk to you?"

"Not much."

"Well, he's a funny guy. But you should see him fight. He's better than I am. He's the best I've ever seen."

"I didn't know that either. What else am I missing?"

John paused to dodge a bicyclist who'd decided he was entitled to be in the middle of our lane. "He's from Idaho. His family raised sheep. And his partner is the mayor of Los Gatos."

"You're kidding, right? Chinese-American shepherds? In Idaho? And the gay lover of a politician?"

He nodded. "No, it's all true. How could I think up things like that?"

"Tell me more about yourself, John. I'm getting the feeling that unless someone's a suspect in a case, I don't know much about them."

"Do you know my favorite color?"

"Green?"

"Nope."

"What about my brothers and sisters?" he asked.

"Uh, one of each?"

"Nope." He shook his big head slowly from side to side. "Now, Karl, at this point you're supposed to ask about what you didn't know. That way, you're showing interest, and people will tell you things."

He filled me in about his life as we finished the drive over. I felt like a jerk for not already knowing about his six siblings, his father's diabetes, and his brief career as a Maori rap singer.

John loved El Charro, but it was too authentic for

me. For the most part, California Mexican restaurants don't cook with lard. I often felt sick after I ate at El Charro, although I must admit everything tasted great going down.

A tiny Asian hostess met us at the door. She was about twenty and cute as a...well, as whatever would be whimsically descriptive without being racist.

"It's you," she said to John. "King Kong."

"I prefer being called Godzilla."

"Who?"

"Kong it is," he said. "You have a table for us?"

"Always, big guy."

She led us to a corner table at the back of the small dining room. We sat down and began devouring the chips that waited for us in a brown plastic dish on the red vinyl tablecloth. I ordered a Negra Modelo from our older Hispanic server and John had an iced tea. When the drinks came, we ordered food as well.

The inside of the restaurant was a time capsule. Nothing had changed in thirty years. The walls and ceilings were festooned with brightly colored Mexican souvenirs—the kind of things you'd buy in a border town for your kid. Well, before those areas became so dangerous. The music was an endless loop of mariachi songs. I hoped John wouldn't sing along.

"I thought about moving to Mexico when I broke up with your sister," he said, noticing my gaze. He almost never used her name.

"Or vice versa."

"You mean Mexico moving to me?"

"My recollection is my nameless sister broke up with you."

He waved his King Kong hand. I half expected him

to scoop up a nearby woman and haul her off to his lair. It was the beer doing the thinking. I was already on my second one, and we'd been at El Charro about ten minutes.

"Well, anyway, I almost moved to Mexico," John said. "I love the culture and the weather. And it's cheap, too."

"Whereabouts?"

He told me the different towns he'd visited, but also that, ultimately, he'd decided against any of them.

"Why's that?"

"They made fun of me because of my size. Not like Kitty." He pointed at the hostess. "That's just in fun. Down there, the kids follow me around and laugh and throw stones."

"I'm sorry, John."

"It was bad enough growing up. I don't need any more of that."

The food came, and we ate without talking. I kept drinking. What was the point of an authentic Mexican dining experience without beer and tequila? My phone rang when I was almost finished. I saw it was Matt.

"I better take this," I told John.

"Sure."

I stepped outside and answered it. It was cooler now and drizzling. I huddled under the eave of the restaurant's roofline, my back flattened against the ridged composite shingles.

"Karl," Matt said, "I finally heard back from my contact on the Enlightenment Services Foundation's board—you know, Aria's funding source. About Leanne's scholarships?"

"Yes, go ahead."

"Well, I thought you'd want to know while you were down there in case you wanted to bring it up with Aria. Are you still at the center?"

"No, but I've got to get back to retrieve my car." My mind wasn't too sharp. I concentrated hard to follow him.

"Here's the thing. It was all Aria. She picked Leanne, she convinced the others that Leanne had some special spiritual qualities, and then she kept the scholarship money flowing. I don't know why. Leanne didn't even apply for one."

"Maybe Leanne really is special. I was impressed by her. But what matters is what Aria thinks. She had a chance to get to know her in their therapy sessions, right?"

"That's true. Maybe it's not that weird."

"The thing is, Aria's got a lot of strongly held ideas about things. I got a snootful of them today." My mind was wandering. I shouldn't have tried to work while I was drinking.

"Like what?"

"Matt, I'm eating dinner with John, but here it is in a nutshell: Nothing's real. Nothing's separate. It's all just energy playing a trick on us. Can you believe it?"

"Karl, that's what half the world believes."

"You're kidding, right?"

"No, those are the key concepts of Hinduism and Buddhism. It's not wacky at all. Rachel believes those things."

"Well, she probably doesn't go around trying to convince other people it's true."

"Just me," Matt said.

We hung up. I lurched back inside.

"Sorry, John."

"That's okay. It's work. If you were on the phone chatting up some other ex-brother-in-law, that'd be different." He smiled and watched me.

"You know, John, it always cheers me up to be around you," I said. "You've got such a good attitude. All those 'no worries' you say. You really mean them, don't you?"

"Sure. Life's not as serious as everybody thinks. In my culture, we have fun and let things roll. Here's something my grannie used to say: if you get out of your own way, good things happen. How are you going to do that if you're worrying?"

"Tell me, when you look around, do you think all this is real?" I asked.

"Naw. Nothing's real. Everybody knows that."

****

John drove us back to the center twenty minutes later. When I stepped out of his SUV, headed for my car, and stumbled on the gravel, he grabbed my arm.

"Give me your keys, Karl."

"I just had a few beers."

He held his hand out. I knew John. We'd been through this before years ago when I'd had more of an ongoing problem. He wasn't going to take no for an answer. I handed him my keys.

"Chen can take me home on his bike," I said.

"Not without a helmet."

"Well, then you can drive me."

"Let's go see how Chen's doing. He only signed up for an hour. He might have something else to do."

We started walking. I was perfectly steady. Three beers wasn't drunk in my universe. I'd just slid on the gravel, which could've happened to anyone.

"So what's your plan for me if he has to go and you have to stay?" I asked. "Should I sleep in your car? Bed down with Aria? Or maybe Cate?"

He stopped and grabbed my arm again. This time it hurt. "Listen to me, Karl. You had four beers, not a few. And a margarita. You'd better behave yourself."

"Yes, sir." We started walking again. "Where are we going, anyway?"

"Everyone's gonna be at the meditation hall. Just ahead of us. And I'm serious about you behaving yourself. I'll pick you up and carry you out if I have to."

"Got it." Four beers was not a big deal, either. I didn't need supervision.

We ambled in the back door. Chen was leaning against the wall just to our right. John stepped over to him, and the two of them whispered to each other.

I hadn't seen Chen in the flesh since I took the case, and blurry or not, he exuded a physical poise that told the world he could kick anyone's ass if he felt like it. Maybe he didn't say much in words—at least to me—but his body language reminded me of those martial arts teachers in old kung fu movies. How could I have not noticed this before? Chen held his slim, tautly muscular frame in a state of continuous physical readiness. And could someone have such strong facial muscles that they held his features in place? Chen's hard-edged visage epitomized the opposite end of the spectrum from John's loose, active face. I felt like clapping as I watched him. Bravo, Chen!

I gazed around. Much like the last time I'd visited the meditation hall, fifty or sixty people held themselves like shoddily made statues of the Buddha on the polished wooden floor, arranged in neat rows. How did they manage to get the spacing so exact? Tape on the floor? I pictured silver duct tape with bright red writing: "sit here," "sit here," "sit here." Then I imagined being the one who had to churn out all the little signs. What a pain. Aria probably made them do all sorts of things like that just so they'd get worn down psychically and accept all her crazy ideas. Spiritual boot camp.

Aria perched on the stage like last time, looking great. A sprinkling of hot yoga babes sat in the crowd in front of her, and some wore pretty skimpy outfits, but Aria stood out on a lot of levels. How could someone look so graceful just sitting there? Well, I thought, if Chen could do it, so could she.

I was obviously a little buzzed. Bravo, Chen? Yoga babes? Little pieces of tape on the floor? My regular brain was back in there somewhere wondering who was coming up with that crap.

"Go sit down," John told me when he returned. "Meditate a while."

I didn't think about it. I just did it. Well, the sitting part. Standing was getting harder by the minute, anyway. I grabbed a spot in the middle of the pack, making several people break ranks and scoot across their imaginary duct tape.

At first it was boring, hunkered down, doing nothing. So I watched Aria for a while. She sat straight and held herself absolutely still. That was boring, too. Then I closed my eyes and tried to meditate. Maybe I'd do better this time, I thought.

I realized after a few minutes that trying to

meditate wouldn't work. I needed to just sit without trying—without thinking about what was the right way to do it. These ideas arrived in my head unbidden. Perhaps my usual filtering system had been compromised by alcohol.

So I sat. I had no idea for how long. It was like I was asleep or unconscious after a while, but I wasn't. On the other hand, I wasn't exactly awake, either. Maybe the beers made me more susceptible to whatever was happening in the hall around me. I don't know. When I opened my eyes, Aria and John were standing in front of me. Everyone else was gone.

"Hi, Karl," Aria said. "How are you feeling?"

I had no clue. I checked in with myself. "Excellent. "I'm excellent." I was completely sober and quite calm. My legs hurt, though, especially my knee.

"He'll be fine to drive himself home in a few minutes," she told John. "That would be the best thing for him."

"Are you sure, Aria?" John gazed at her with concern and then glanced at me with even more.

"Yes."

I wasn't so sure. Excellent or not, I still felt way different than my usual self. Improved, I guess, but different. I had no idea how that translated to driving or anything else.

I stood and said good night to both of them. They insisted on walking me to my car. "Where's Larry?" I asked on the way to the parking lot. I should've been alarmed that I'd forgotten about him, but I wasn't. I'd left him with Chen when John and I had gone out to eat.

"Matt came and got him," John said.

"Matt? He's sick. Why would he do that?"

"Karl," Aria said, "you were sitting for four hours."

I stopped in my tracks. That didn't make any sense at all. "Really?"

"Yeah," John said. "And Matt called and said Adele was raising hell. She said she was supposed to get Larry tonight. Aria said we shouldn't wake you up, so Matt came up with a plan to come and get Larry."

"Oh. Thank you." I didn't seem to be having any emotional reactions to what I was hearing.

We'd reached the car. John gave me my keys and a huge hug.

"I love you," he said.

He'd never said that before, although I knew he did.

"I love you too, Kong."

When John released me, I stepped forward without thinking and hugged Aria. It was totally different this time.

A jolt of electrical energy shot up from the base of my spine. When it got to my head, it whirled around for a moment and then kept going—through the roof of my skull. It was hot and buzzy—not quite electrical but very strong. I was still connected to it, but it was also shooting out into the world, connecting me with everything, even the stars in the sky. Then I passed out.

Chapter Twenty-Nine

This time I woke up in a bed with a very firm mattress. I felt rested, as though I'd had a full night's sleep. I turned my head and saw a digital alarm clock on a bedside table. It was 4:16 a.m. This was a very dark space. There were no LEDs from other devices or appliances piercing the black.

I could hear loud insect songs. And I smelled cookie dough. I must be in Aria's bedroom, I thought. John must've carried me in.

I was lying on my back and my knee ached, so I turned onto my side and bumped into someone, who shifted away from me. I realized I was naked and she was, too.

"Aria?" I said.

"You're back." She seemed wide awake. "I hope you don't mind being in bed with me. I thought it would be best under the circumstances. It wasn't a good idea for you to go into samadhi and then hug me immediately afterward."

"I wasn't thinking."

"And I should've stayed out of range. I'm sorry."

"I have a few questions," I said. And an erection. "What's samadhi? What happened to me?" I couldn't see Aria, but I was extremely conscious of her presence next to me.

"It's just a very deep meditation. I apologize for

using jargon. I try to avoid it."

"Were you and John standing in front of me for four hours?"

"No. I brought you out of it when it was safe. People can stay in that state for days."

I was avoiding the obvious sixty-four million dollar question. Why were both of us lying naked in her bed? "Why would something like that happen?" I asked instead.

"Karl, what you're really asking is, 'Why am I me? Why is my internal energy configured the way it is?' I don't know."

"And the hug?"

"Tell me about your side of it. What happened for you?"

I shared all ten seconds of my conscious experience—the energy racing up my back and out of the top of my head.

If anything, my erection was bigger and harder now. I could feel the heat of Aria's body lying scant inches from me.

"That's a type of awakening energy," she told me. "It lives at the base of everyone's spine. It's called kundalini. Google it."

Google it? She was a spiritual teacher and she was advising me to get my answers from someplace like Wikipedia? I realized my last thought was almost a normal one. I wasn't in a weird state anymore. Well, not too weird, anyway. I still felt different in some subtle way.

"You might have digestive difficulties for a while," Aria said. "The sudden onset of kundalini is tough on the physical body. Ordinarily, it's released gradually—

as seekers engage in practices on their spiritual path."

I was conscious of the phrase "physical body." Since Aria always spoke so precisely, apparently she thought there were other types of bodies. I couldn't think of any.

"And of course," she continued, "you're wondering about being nude in bed with me."

"Well, yeah."

"When you became overwhelmed last night, you needed to be near my energy to stay tethered to the physical realm. And I needed to sleep. I was exhausted. For some reason, the energy connection works better with no clothes. A teacher once told me that inanimate objects have karma, too, and that they interfere with things. Anyway, you were in danger, and now you're not. It worked."

"Danger of what?"

"Not coming back."

"Dying?"

"Not exactly. Why don't we forget about all that? I'm cold. Would you like to hold me?"

"For spiritual purposes?"

"No. I have something else in mind."

One thing led to another. A half hour later, I broke my cardinal rule of detecting. I made love to my client.

The only energy I experienced was the transcendent joy of a long overdue orgasm.

****

I awoke to the sight of Aria's nude figure stretching by the side of the bed. It was still dark out, but she'd switched on a torchiere by her side of the bed. Her smallish breasts were thrust forward as she pulled her arms behind her. The dark nipples were slightly askew—the right one was higher and more to the outside than the left. Her navel didn't seem to be centered, either.

It had been so dark when we'd made love, I only knew how she felt to my touch. Now I was surprised to see her belly was flat. It had felt so warm and soft in bed, I'd expected it to be more rounded. And her thighs were thinner than they'd felt.

Aria's dusky skin looked just as smooth and creamy as it felt. As she turned and bent forward, her dark hair cascaded over her shoulders. This was the first time I'd seen it loose. It was thick and wavy.

Aria saw me watching her and kept stretching. She was probably doing yoga, but I'd never been very good at distinguishing that from regular stretching. She wasn't the least bit self-conscious. Maybe she didn't identify with her body. What did it matter what you looked like if you didn't think you were real? I wasn't sure which of Aria's wacky ideas had stuck to my ribs, but the concept that life was just an illusion was certainly at the forefront.

"How did you sleep?" she asked.

"Well. And you?" I felt awkward. I hadn't been in this situation in many years, and never with someone like Aria—if there even was someone like Aria.

"Great."

"How long did we sleep?"

"Only an hour. It's six fifteen. I'm very late." She kept stretching, regardless.

"You don't seem too panicked." I felt fully rested, which seemed odd.

Aria smiled and finished her routine. Then she came back to bed and nestled against me. "They probably think I'm dead," she said. "I've never been late before."

"Let's make you even later." I kissed her and one thing led to many others.

She was a wonderful lover—giving, intuitive, and remarkably skilled. We went slowly this time, building up to an even more satisfying climax than the night before. She shuddered for all of two minutes when she came. Maybe being spiritual enhanced your pleasure. I certainly couldn't take credit for it.

I didn't know what the ramifications of being lovers were going to be, but they'd have to damned awful to counterbalance the heaven of being in Aria's bed.

While we dressed after showering together, I found myself back in work mode. Even as I formulated my line of questioning, I knew it was inappropriate to ask anything in that tender moment. But I couldn't stop myself.

"So do you think there's something unusual about my energy? Is that one of the takeaways here?" I asked.

She peered at me. "Absolutely. I felt it the moment I met you in your office," she said.

"Like you did with Leanne Atkinson? Did that happen with her? Is that why you awarded her those scholarships?"

She froze. She hadn't seen that coming. For a few seconds, she turned away, hiding her face. Then she pivoted and looked me in the eye. She was crying.

I felt like a creep. "I'm sorry," I said. I moved to hold her, and she pulled away, turning her head again.

"God damn you," she said to the other side of the room. Then she faced me again. Her green eyes were fierce. "If you must know," she said. "Leanne is my daughter."

Aria left hurriedly, without uttering another word. I finished dressing and walked to my car to go out to breakfast. I didn't want to go home.

On the way to the Sunrise Cafe, I thought about what I'd learned from asking my inappropriate question.

First, I'd reminded myself I was still capable of being an insensitive asshole. The fact that this persona had appeared in a post-coital context seemed significant. Maybe I'd been pushing Aria away because I was scared of intimacy. Or her energy. Or just something big and new.

I wondered for a moment if the case was more important to me than Aria was. In a way, the case *was* Aria. My original mandate had been to keep her whole, after all.

I'd also learned what the connection was between Aria and Leanne. I doubted it had anything to do with the murders, but at least that itch had been scratched. Leanne had been adopted, and Matt believed she didn't know who her birth mother was. So Aria would've had to have given her daughter up early on. Why?

This was the way my mind worked. Practically all the answers I stumbled onto—or forced out of new lovers—led to new questions. Until the case was finally solved. Or it wasn't. I'd endured some notable failures.

The other takeaway might've been the most important. Aria had shown me she was still a human being—someone with hurt and anger and all the rest. She'd even sworn at me.

I was tremendously relieved by this. There was no

way I could be in a relationship with an enlightened superperson. It was bad enough she knew so much more than I did about metaphysics, was about a hundred times nicer than I was, and looked a hell of a lot better. If she also lived beyond the domain of feelings and never misbehaved, there'd be no prayer for us.

Of course, there might not be any, anyway. I didn't know how forgiving Aria was, or if she'd even be interested in trying to forgive me. She'd done nothing but try to help me since I'd taken on the investigation. And then we'd made love. What did I do next? I ambushed her. If I were her, would I forgive me? Probably not.

For my part, I still wasn't sure about her, either. She was mixed up in murders, she withheld things from me, and her variety of spirituality was unfathomable to me—and possibly delusional.

I hardly tasted my breakfast. Whatever benefits I'd gained from the samadhi and the kundalini seemed to have vanished, although I wasn't hung over.

Matt called me as I was walking out of the cafe. "Karl, how are you doing? Did they turn you into a permanent zombie?"

"Unfortunately, I'm still me."

"You looked like somebody else last night. You should've seen your face while you were sitting there."

"Why? What did I look like?"

"Your face was completely blank," he said. "It was like nobody was home at all. Aria said not to worry, but it looked to me like you'd checked out for good."

"I don't remember anything about it," I told him. A street guy approached me for money and I waved him away.

"I'm at the office," Matt said. "Are you heading in?"

"You're not still sick?"

"A little. It's tolerable."

"I'll be there in fifteen minutes. Thanks for your help with Larry last night. Did we mix up the schedule with Adele?"

"I don't think so. She was just being a dick."

"Isn't that a gender-specific insult?"

"I don't know. Just get your ass down here." He hung up on me.

I called Aria and left the most heartfelt apology I could muster on her voicemail. It couldn't hurt. She called me back almost immediately.

"Karl, I didn't listen to your message yet. I assume it's an apology?"

"Yes."

"Can you meet me for dinner tonight? I'd like to tell you about my early life—about my daughter."

"You don't have to, Aria. It's none of my business."

"It's time. You're right."

We arranged to meet at a health-food restaurant at six. I drove to the office. It looked as though I hadn't entirely ruined my chances with Aria.

Chapter Thirty

First, Matt and I chatted about the case. We didn't need to speculate about Aria's backstory since she was going to tell me anyway. He had lot of good ideas about our cast of suspects, their motives, and how we might proceed.

I thought again about taking Matt on as a partner. The notion was growing more attractive every day. He'd been helpful on the simpler, nonviolent cases I'd taken on since he came onboard, but he was proving his mettle on this one. How far along would I be if Miriam was still answering the phone and doing her version of research?

Matt also told me the non-news of the case. There was no sign of José, and he hadn't attacked anyone yet. But all of Victor's brothers had disappeared in Texas, and one was here for sure. There were four of them. The cops hadn't made any progress on the beach shooting. They'd found the suspects that various witnesses had identified—Buccanfuso and Steiner—but both had airtight alibis. It looked like Bobby—Sumati's ex whom John had fought in the Salinas bar—was dealing drugs for the Sureños, but Matt hadn't been able to dig up any details. Further research into the Crowders and the Sharps hadn't yielded anything useful. And John had nothing to report from the Santa Cruz Spiritual Center.

Matt agreed that Georgia Sharp—Wayne's widow—was a key character in this drama. "If she's so passive," he added, "maybe you can get her to answer self-incriminating questions."

He supplied me with Georgia's sister's address in Big Sur, which was about a two-hour drive, south of the Monterey Peninsula. I decided to take another road trip to meet her. I wished it was a Larry day so he could go, too.

If Georgia had holed up in, say, Modesto in the Central Valley, I don't know if I would've made the trip. That two-hour journey feels like five. But the latter part of the drive to Big Sur is phenomenally scenic. They film car ads on Highway 1 where the forested mountains sprawl down to meet the sea. And Big Sur itself is even more spectacular. Most of it's a state park, with steep hiking trails through the redwoods.

I was at the stage of an investigation where poring over the facts I'd collected so far wasn't likely to be helpful. I could go out and collect new ones—which I was en route to doing—or I could let it all float around in my head and once again see what my subconscious presented. Sometimes this process was comical. I'd whistle a song for ten minutes before I noticed it was "I Shot the Sheriff," "Cocaine Blues," or something else germane to a given case. Other times, fragmentary thoughts would pop in my head. I'd learned to trust these, too. I made a vow to explore any thoughts I had on this trip, regardless of how irrelevant or off-base they might seem to be.

After Matt got back to work at his desk, I checked my voicemail, ignored every message, and then did the same with my email. Following a brief trip to the bathroom, I jumped into my Mazda and hit the road. The longer I waited, the more traffic I'd hit on the way home.

It was warmer than it had been the last few days and partly cloudy. Or maybe partly sunny. I think those two phrases were created by a cabal of evil meteorologists to drive us all crazy.

After a few miles, I tuned into KPIG, an Americana station out of Freedom, California. They played some hardcore testosterone-infused stuff just to establish their reputation as outlaws, but they also played obscure artists the other stations ignored. These made even the locally produced ads worth tolerating. Where else could I hear western swing, bluegrass, folk music, and 1950s rhythm and blues back to back?

First up was Tim O'Brien. The next good one was Buddy Miller. As I passed Watsonville, the deejay even played Hank Williams—"Setting the Woods on Fire."

My life has never been the same since I heard Hank on the soundtrack of *The Last Picture Show*. His voice was like a shiv in the metaphorical prison yard of my life. It pierced the armor around my heart, and I cried for the first time in years.

I explored the various thoughts about the case that bubbled up as I continued to drive, but nothing added up to much. I was glad I'd been through this before. In the beginning of my career, I'd agonize, trying to force something to the surface. Now, I knew it would come when it was ready—like an overdue baby.

A few miles south of Watsonville, I drove through rich farmland, eventually passing Castroville and then the old Fort Ord military base. When they'd shut it down, 22,000 people suddenly disappeared from

Marina and Seaside. Parts of those communities were still ghost towns.

The traffic picked up as I passed Monterey and Carmel. Then I hit the spectacular home stretch. It was hard to concentrate on the winding road when each turn brought another panorama into sight. There were waterfalls, cliffs, rocky islands, and sandy, inaccessible beaches. Even the road itself was worth viewing, with long concrete bridges across canyons, and multiple hairpin turns. I remembered driving that stretch for the first time when I was nineteen. I had nightmares for months. It was gorgeous but also extremely dangerous.

This reminded me of Adele. That was her, too.

Georgia Sharp's sister lived in the middle of nowhere. I drove through the town of Big Sur and took a left up a rough dirt road into the hills. Two dirt roads and long driveway later, I could see the place ahead of me. Thank God for GPS. It was a faux log cabin, with a shiny prefab metal garage, and a nondescript wooden shed set off to the side and behind it. The array was set squarely in the middle of a small greenish meadow.

I drove on in. There were no cars or people in sight. If they'd gone into town—and there was nowhere else to go—they'd probably be back soon.

I tried to park the car out of sight, but most of it was still visible from the driveway. It was the best I could do.

Then I got out, stretched my legs, and walked up the rickety wooden steps to the porch. I knocked on the front door. No answer. I pushed open the unlocked door and called out. Nothing. So I went in.

I was taking a chance I wouldn't ordinarily take, but I'd driven a long way. First, I found the back door so I could glide out that way if someone came home. Wandering around a back yard represented a different kind of intrusion than getting caught inside someone's house. People got cranky about that, but they didn't usually call the cops.

Then I started snooping. There was evidence that two women and a man lived in the house, but the man either didn't own much or his principle residence was somewhere else. Georgia's clothes were strikingly different from her sister's, assuming the sister matched the cabin. One closet was full of jeans and flannel shirts and sweatshirts. The other one held matronly dresses, shoes with heels, and even a few floral hats.

It was also easy to differentiate which end of the dining room table Georgia had been using. A pile of estate paperwork, house deeds—they'd owned three—and letters from several lawyers sat in a sloppy pile. Underneath a bank statement was a first-class ticket in Georgia's name to Chile—a one-way flight in five days. In the margins of the attached itinerary, someone had scrawled, "Call and get seats together." That was interesting. I happened to know our extradition treaty with Chile was quite weak.

I leafed through the rest of the paperwork, took a few notes, and tried to remember as many of the other details as I could. It looked as though she was trying to liquidate all her assets to fly the coop. With whom? I was betting it wasn't her sister, and I made a mental note to appraise everyone in the case as a potential lover.

There wasn't much else in the house that concerned me, although I did notice the man who stayed there dyed his hair red, which was unusual. At first, I thought the hair dye was one of the women's, but the user had smeared a male-sized red fingerprint on the box. I tore off that corner of the cardboard to take with me.

From the house, I headed to the one-car detached garage, which was far less rustic. It was butt ugly, in fact. It looked like a stunted mobile home, replete with two-tone aluminum siding—lime green and white.

I went in the side door and could barely stand in there. Neatly stacked junk—mostly furniture and boxes—littered the far side of the concrete floor. The other half of the garage was a jumble of similar-looking items. Someone had just tossed these in. Either Georgia's sister was schizoid, or two people had participated in filling up the space. From the dust on the organized side and the lack of it on the other, I deduced the mess had been added recently. By Georgia?

When I opened several boxes on each side of the garage, though, I saw it was all a single individual's junk. It could've been the man's. Gender-neutral items such as books, stereo speakers, and landscape paintings comprised the bulk of the items. If it were the man's, it might explain why he'd made such a small footprint inside the house.

I left the garage and headed for the shed, but I didn't get far.

A woman's voice rang out. "Hold it right there."

They'd snuck up on me. A brown pickup truck was parked about fifty yards up the driveway. This was why I needed Larry.

Georgia and someone who was probably her sister stood by the side of the house. The sister held a shotgun. Aimed at me.

"Who the hell are you?" she asked. She wore denim overalls, a black turtleneck, and hiking boots. She looked like she'd been in the military. It was the way she held herself. Her dark eyes projected fierceness. An act? I couldn't tell.

"Karl Gatlin," I said. "I'm sorry for the intrusion. Let me give you my card." I started walking toward her, planning to distract her and take the gun away, but she fired it over my head. I froze. "I'm looking into Wayne's murder." I aimed that at Georgia, who was a mouse in a red sweater set and white Capri pants.

Her eyes darted to the shed. That was interesting.

"I'm a private investigator," I added.

"Are you armed?" the sister asked.

"Yes."

"Throw your gun and your wallet over here," she told me.

I hesitated.

"Criminals killed Georgia's husband. They're not going to kill her, too. Not on my watch. You might be here to do the job."

I drew out my pistol, held it by the muzzle, and placed it on the ground. Then I kicked it forward. At that range, a twelve gauge would almost split me in half if she had anything nasty in it. I tossed her my wallet next. It held my driver's license, gun permit, and private investigator's license. If that didn't satisfy her, nothing would.

The sister held the shotgun steady. "See if he's who he says he is," she told Georgia.

"Okay." Her little girl voice fit her. It barely carried to me, all of fifteen feet away, although her odiferous perfume certainly crossed the gap effortlessly. She was a nonentity, barely inhabiting her insubstantial body.

"Karl Gatlin," she reported. "He's a California licensed investigator." She discovered the photo behind my license. "Oh, what a cute dog!"

"That's Larry," I said. "I was hoping to bring him down today, but my ex has him."

"Shut up!" the sister said. "We don't need to get chummy with this guy, Georgia. He's trespassing. He's trouble."

"I was just waiting for you. There's no place to park on the road."

"I said shut up!" She waggled the gun.

"Just one last thing," I tried. "I want you both to know I haven't been inside any of the buildings. I just waited outside."

This time the sister's eyes flitted to the shed—just for a second. What was in there?

"Get out," she said. "Don't make me call the cops."

I called her bluff. "I think we should. It's illegal to brandish a firearm in this state, you know."

She glared at me. "That's bullshit. You can do it on private property. And if you're dead, no one's gonna hear about that, anyway. They're going to see you with your peashooter in your hand, a big hole in your chest, and a witness who's gonna tell them how you attacked us."

"You wouldn't do that."

"Try me," she said grimly.

I tried to stare her down. That didn't get me anywhere. I looked at Georgia, who shrugged and smiled as though she wanted me to like her despite whatever was happening.

"I'll tell you what," I said. "If you give me back my gun and my wallet, I'll be on my way. But perhaps I could ask you both a few questions over the phone?"

"Not going to happen," the sister said.

"I think we all want the same thing here—to find Wayne's killer. Am I right?"

The sister ignored me. She turned to Georgia. "Put this asshole's stuff in the trunk of his car. Then go into the house."

"What do you want me to do there, Frances?"

"Clean something, Georgia."

Wayne's widow followed orders and disappeared into the house.

"Are you sure you're sisters?" I asked. "You couldn't be more different."

"I'm not her fucking sister," Frances said. "And If I see you up here again, I'll definitely shoot you."

Chapter Thirty-One

I stopped in town for a snack. I was hungry, but mostly I needed to decompress. If I came up too quickly from the depths of a gun-toting confrontation to the surface of normal life, I might get the metaphorical bends. I imagined they were less painful than the literal ones, but why take a chance?

The restaurant looked like a place where tourists might go after a morning of hiking—if the sun were in their eyes or they'd lost their glasses. It was built in the style of an English cottage, but it had been a poor imitation to begin with and it was shabby now. The dark-green paint was peeling from the shingled walls, and the shrubbery around the wraparound porch was out of control.

I figured a cafe that looked like that would attract a local clientele, which suited me. After I ate, I might find someone who knew Georgia's sister and whoever had been up at the house. The year-round population of Big Sur was only about a thousand people. They probably all knew one another.

The name of the restaurant should've tipped me off about what I'd find inside. MacDharma's. It was filled with elderly hippies wearing the same costumes they'd worn forty years earlier. They all seemed to be friends—people were passing dishes from table to table. I felt as though I were crashing a party. And there were only four menu items that day. Three were salads. I chose the tempeh casserole, which was surprisingly tasty.

I guess I walked in with a chip on my shoulder—left over from my encounter at the house. When a woman at the table next to me asked to borrow the brewer's yeast, I told her I didn't know what she was talking about and returned to my meal.

"The yellowy powder. It's by your right elbow."

"Oh, sure. Sorry."

I handed it over. Her long white hair obscured most of her face, even more than Sumati's had. It was like the hair was talking to me.

"Who are you looking for?" she asked. Her voice was hoarse as if she'd been shouting all morning.

"What do you mean?"

"You're fuzz. You're in here. What's up?"

"Leave him alone," a man called from behind me.

"Yes, Baba," the woman said, as though she were an obedient child.

I swiveled to see who had my grandmother's name. It was a slim, elderly white guy with a bushy white beard. He was completely bald, and his pate was very shiny. I wondered if he polished it. His eyes were brown and very soulful. They reminded me of Aria's. The rest of his face was unremarkable—kind of professorish—in the geology department, maybe. Give him an agate bolo tie; that was all he needed. He wore loose white cotton clothes from head to toe.

"This is a holy man," he announced, pointing at me with an outstretched arm. "Don't be fooled by his appearance." That was a backhanded compliment if I ever heard one. Did they all think I looked like a

Neanderthal?

"I'm Baba Hari Friedman," the man said, striding over to my table.

I stood. "Karl Gatlin," I told him.

I extended my hand, and we shook. I could feel a buzzy warmth radiating from his. Maybe he could feel the same from me. I don't know. A week ago, this would've been one of life's great anomalies. Now it was only a shadow of what I'd felt with Aria.

It also wasn't what I was looking for when I came into the place. The tempeh wasn't either, for that matter. I'd been hoping for a cheeseburger and fries.

"Come sit with me," Baba said. He pointed to a small table in the far corner of the room, where he'd been sitting alone.

"Sure." I was here and I seemed to be talking to a local. Maybe it would work out.

As I passed his followers, carrying the remnants of my casserole, they all stood and bowed down to me. It was disconcerting. This guy said I was special, so now everybody was throwing away their own ideas about me and adopting his. They were a cult, I realized.

"How did you come by your energy?" he asked. "Who's your teacher?"

"Aria Piper."

"I thought I recognized the pattern. Good for you. She's the real deal."

"Pattern?"

"It's all patterns, of course. Energy patterns. You're an interesting character. You have the meridians of a yogi, but I can see that you don't know shit from Shinola about all this. It doesn't usually work that way. And your kundalini has just risen—sometime in the last few days. You should be a mess. Nobody integrates this quickly. What's the deal with you, Gatlin?"

"I wish I knew. And what's Shinola? Something brown?"

"Yeah. It's from before your time. I'm older than I look." Friedman looked to be around seventy.

"How old are you?" I asked.

"Eighty-four."

"No shit?"

"No shit. May I ask a favor? If we work together, I think we can heal one of my people. I haven't managed to do it on my own. It'll only take a couple of minutes."

"What's wrong with her?"

"Post-Traumatic Stress Disorder—from sexual abuse."

"Well, first of all, I have no idea how to heal anybody," I told him. "And I doubt that anything's going to make a difference with PTSD. People go to therapy for years for that, and they still have nightmares and flashbacks."

"Are you willing to try? I'll show you what to do."

"Okay, fine." It was easier to just go along with him

He raised his arm, snapped his fingers, and called, "Amy, can you come over here?"

Amy ran over. She was an attractive woman in her mid-twenties wearing an orange tie-dyed T-shirt and jean shorts. I hadn't noticed her earlier. She resembled a better-fed, taller Cate Sharp, but her attitude was the opposite of the younger woman's. She seemed shy, but she radiated cooperation at the same time. This wasn't a passive person, I could sense, just one who was willing to spring into action if you asked her to.

"Sit here," he told her, pulling up a chair between us.

She did. Then she closed her eyes and sat still. She'd done this before.

"Karl," Baba said, "I want you to place your right hand on Amy's heart chakra and your left one on the corresponding location on the opposite side of her body—on her spine."

I didn't know anything about chakras, but I figured he meant over her heart—which would be partially on her breast. I wasn't going to do that to the survivor of a sexual assault.

"It's *between* her breasts," Friedman instructed, seeing the look on my face. "On her sternum. I'll have my hands on either side of her head. We'll work as a team."

"Why can't I do her head?" I asked. "You know her better than I do."

Throughout this interchange, Amy just sat there. She seemed to have completely surrendered to whatever Baba wanted.

"I work on the mental planes—forming energy templates. You're a heart person. Your spiritual commodity is love."

"Really?" That seemed wildly unlikely to me.

"Really."

"Can we check with Amy to see if she's okay with this?"

"I am," she piped up enthusiastically.

"All right," I said. "Let's try it. What else do you want me to do?"

"That's it. Just put your hands where I said. The energy itself knows what to do."

318

I had a strong urge to bolt, but perhaps we really could help. Stranger things had happened in the last few days. So we put our hands on her. I didn't feel anything at all—besides the sides of her small boobs, I mean.

After a few minutes, Baba took his hands off, so I did too. "It worked," he reported. "She's fine now."

That didn't seem likely. Amy opened her eyes, thanked us, and ambled back to her table.

"Okay," Baba said. "I owe you one. Is there anything I can do for you?"

"You know, there is something. I've got to get back to Santa Cruz, but I'm a private investigator and I'm trying to keep an eye on some people who live up on the mountain." I gave him my card.

"Fascinating," he said.

"Are you and your people willing to help?"

"Tell me more. If we won't be harming anyone, then certainly. It sounds like fun."

I gave him the Reader's Digest version of the case, the address of the sister's place, and the cast of characters who might be up there. I was especially interested in who the man was—the guy with the dyed red hair. I wasn't sure the partial fingerprint I had was enough to find out. I'd let Cardenas or Sutter sort that out.

"They have to come into town sometime," I finished. "I'm not asking you to actually go there. The older woman I described has a shotgun—it wouldn't be safe."

"Okay," Baba said. "I don't know them, but I can put someone down the road from there. There's only the one way in. Give me your cell number, and I'll call when we have something to report. It's the least we can do. You have no idea what a gift you gave Amy today. For some reason, you're mostly veiled from your higher self."

This was one more piece of gibberish to me. Higher self? Since my curiosity was limited at that moment—maybe to insure my continued sanity—I just thanked Baba and said good-bye.

Everybody bowed to me again as I walked out—without paying, as it turned out. The server had to chase me down in the parking lot.

"I don't care what kind of guru you are," she told me. "We're still using money around here, you know."

I gave her a big tip. Then she bowed even lower than Friedman's followers had. "Forgive me, Baba. I spoke in anger."

I invented an I-forgive-you hand wave. It was a cross between a high-five and a peace sign. I was beginning to understand what Aria had said about the pitfalls of being a spiritual teacher. I could get a little too comfortable with all this reverence, and I know half those diners would've slept with me if I'd even smiled at them. Hell, maybe the men would've, too. I was meeting gay guys everywhere I went on this case. That was northern California for you.

Chapter Thirty-Two

So who was Frances—the woman with the shotgun? She'd said she wasn't Georgia's sister, and I believed her. So why was she there? Maybe Frances was taking advantage of Georgia for financial reasons. Anyone with a strong will could probably persuade Georgia to do anything.

My best guess was that Georgia's absent sister was on vacation or something. I hadn't seen any luggage anywhere, so that supported my theory. Of course, it could've been stored in the shed, but I didn't think so. I was willing to bet the jumble of junk in the garage had been stored in the shed until quite recently, and now something or someone was in there. The man with the dyed red hair?

What else might the shed hold? Evidence about the murder? Surgical tools? I couldn't see Wayne's widow cutting off someone's head, but I could picture Frances getting drunk and going for it. This didn't seem nearly as likely as a drug murder, but if those two women were innocent, they sure didn't act like it.

I brainstormed again. Maybe they were kinky lesbians, and they had some sort of embarrassing sexual apparatus in the shed. Maybe Francis stole motorcycles and hid them in the there. It could've been a moonshine still or a counterfeit press. An illegal exotic pet? An arsenal of guns?

Verlin Darrow

I was running out of ideas. And, as usual, the brainstorming had been fun but pointless. Even if I happened onto exactly what was in the shed, I wouldn't know it. Not yet.

As I passed by Watsonville on the way back to Santa Cruz, I turned on the radio again and I sang along to Big Sandy, Hot Rize, and Emmy Lou Harris, a balm to my poor brain, which hurt from all my efforts to make sense out of the Big Sur trip. My supposed mini-vacation from the case at MacDharma's had just generated more weird shit to process.

A couple of hours later, I found myself standing and staring into my closet, trying to decide what to wear to dinner with Aria. I felt like a seventeen-year-old. Did the blue button-down shirt make me look like I worked in a bank? Did the white polo make me look like a doofus golfer? What about my favorite jeans? Did they sag in the butt? Were they too threadbare?

I lay down again for five more minutes and then tried a do-over. This time I grabbed a black polo, the jeans, and a blue fatigue sweater. I was not seventeen. I was just a nervous grown man.

Sprouts Eatery was more upscale than most healthy restaurants, but like a cheap bottle blonde in a film noir, it still showed its salad-affiliated roots. Instead of hip modern art on its bamboo-matted walls, there were close-up black and white photos of all the nastiest vegetables—Brussels sprouts, kale, and bok choy, for example. Also, none of the tables and chairs matched one another. Each seemed to be a handcrafted set from a different Asian culture. Some were wicker, some wooden, and one garishly proclaimed its unknown-to-me heritage in purplish bamboo.

The best thing about Sprouts was the private alcove at the back of the dining room. Aria was waiting for me there, even though I'd arrived ten minutes early. Her dark, wavy hair framed her face, which displayed an expression too complex for me to decode. She wore a dress again. This white sheath wasn't quite figure hugging, but it wasn't schoolmarmish, either. I began smiling as soon as I saw her.

"Is it safe to hug you?" I asked.

"Yes."

She slid into my arms, and I felt a surge of emotion, not energy. I realized that all the fireworks with Aria had kept me from directly experiencing my feelings before. Now, I was aware of affection, lust, and simple joy, with a little excitement mixed in.

"I'll screen my energy when I'm with you," Aria said. "If I'd known about your vulnerability to it, I'd have been more vigilant from the outset."

"Thank you. I appreciate that."

We sat down across from one another at the Chinese-looking black lacquered table. I was struck again by how present she was. She was right there—all of her.

"Any regrets?" I asked.

"About last night?"

I nodded.

"None. You?"

"Hell, no."

We looked into each other's eyes for a while. We were interrupted by our server, a sleepy-eyed young man with long blond hair and several piercings. He gave us menus, agreed to fetch us water, and told us to carry on with our *occhi dolci*.

"What's that?" I asked.

"It's Italian for 'sweet eyes'—the look of love." He tried to demonstrate his words, but he looked like a crazy person getting a mug shot.

"Thank you for that observation," Aria said. "I hope you have someone in your life to look at that way."

"Oh, I do," he said. "I have a girlfriend from Rome. That's how I learned that phrase."

"That's wonderful," Aria said.

He walked away with a big grin on his face.

"You have a way with people," I said.

"When you're in the moment, it comes naturally. So, Karl, what kind of day have you had?"

"I went down to Big Sur to interview Wayne Sharp's widow."

"How did that go?"

"Not well." I told her about the two women and what I'd found—and not found—on the property.

"Please don't break the law for me again," she said.

"I'll keep that in mind. Oh, and I met a guru after that."

"Which one? There are a few down there."

"Baba Friedman."

"Oh, Arnie. He's a real character, isn't he?" Aria shook her head as though the word "character" was only mildly derogatory in her world. In mine, it was code for a major pain in the ass.

"Yeah. He liked my energy," I told her.

"I'll bet he did."

Instead of going into all that, I asked Aria if she was ready to tell me her life story. The server returned before she could respond. Although neither of us had glanced at the menu, we each picked the frittata special he told us about.

"I'm Canadian," Aria said. "From Toronto. I started drinking when I was fifteen. I had my reasons, and most of them were sexual. I'd prefer not to go into that." She paused and gazed at me.

"Of course. Just tell me whatever you want and skip the rest."

"I acted out. I took drugs. I flunked out at school," she told me. "I ended up in court-ordered AA, and thank God it took—for a while at least. After a couple of years, I entered a phase characterized by chronic relapses. When I felt overwhelmed emotionally, I hit the bottle again. Nonetheless, I managed to get through college and earn a teaching credential. My first position was teaching English at a high school in St. George, Ontario. I was lost. I had no idea how tough it would be. Halfway through the school year, I relapsed. Not just with alcohol, but with sex, as well."

"Ray Lundquist," I said. "That was you. You're Lina Piatanesi." I was showing off, but I was also saving her from having to tell me what was probably the most painful part of her story. "But I've seen Lina's photograph, and you don't look like her," I added.

"Yes, I'll get to that. I slept with Ray—once—but that was enough. It was a horrible thing to do. I've never relapsed since."

"You became pregnant?"

"Yes, with Leanne. I probably could have told everyone I had a boyfriend back in the city or something, but Lundquist went public because I wouldn't keep sleeping with him."

"So you ended up in prison? Wasn't that an

unusually harsh punishment? Especially back then."

"Things were different in small-town Canada. And the Lundquists were a prominent family. At the time, I felt so godawful about myself, I didn't fight it. I felt I deserved even worse than prison, and I managed to arrange that. I gave away my baby."

"I'm so sorry," I told her. "I can't imagine giving up a child."

"Yes. I regretted it for many years, but now I think it was best for Leanne. She's grown into a remarkable woman. Who knows who she'd have been if I'd tried to raise her."

"I'm sure you would've done fine. This Aria was always in there, right?"

"You don't know the whole story."

"Please, go on."

Aria gathered herself and continued. "When I was released from prison, I changed my name and moved to British Columbia. Ray found me and threatened to reveal my past. He hadn't been successful extorting sex from me before, but he kept at it, and now he wanted more—marriage. He believed he was in love with me, and perhaps he was."

"Why not just stonewall him and accept the consequences?"

"I was working at a preschool. My grief about Leanne drove me to seek positions in which I could help young children. My history would disqualify me from continuing, and I couldn't bear any more shame."

"What did you do?" She didn't need coercion to tell her tale, but I wanted to stay connected—to be a part of the moment.

"I moved again. And he found me again. And I

moved again. And he found me again. He'd commit petty crimes to cobble together enough money to hire people like you. I was an amateur up against professionals, and I didn't know how to disappear."

"God, what a nightmare."

"It was. But I didn't drink. I just kept working to build a life worth living—which never happened. Lundquist scared off boyfriends, followed me around, and worse. It was hell. If I went to the police, my secret would be revealed. Finally, I met a social worker who helped abused women escape their partners. She'd started a nonprofit in Calgary, and she didn't mind breaking the law if she had to. She took me under her wing."

"So Lina Piatanesi became Aria Piper."

"Yes. I even had plastic surgery—just enough to make me unrecognizable. It was a drastic solution, but Lundquist was relentless. He was obsessed with me, and one of his most recent demands was to tell him where Leanne was. I couldn't let that happen."

"You moved to the U.S.?"

"Yes. I obtained a student visa to get a master's in counseling in Michigan, and then I found a way to stay legally after that. I've been a citizen for eight years."

"You came out to California to keep an eye on Leanne?" I wanted her to know I was attuned to her decision-making—that it made sense to me.

"Yes. The adoption was supposed to be closed, but my attorney found a loophole and they were legally obliged to tell me the details. My daughter lived in Los Gatos."

"Let me guess. Lundquist eventually found the same loophole."

"Yes. As her birth father, he had rights, too. And after sixteen years, I guess he became curious about what had happened to her."

"How did that lead him to you?"

"He wasn't looking for me, but we both attended her high school graduation."

"I met him," I told her. "I brought John with me."

She smiled a wan smile. "I wish I'd been there."

"Lundquist is a worm."

"He's worse. Trust me."

I looked deep into her eyes, speaking to every layer of her. "I do," I said. "I trust you."

I realized our food had never arrived. I beckoned to our server, who scurried over and explained. "Phil grabbed it and gave it to other people. I'm so sorry. Would you still like it?"

Would we still like the dinner we'd come in to eat? Really?

"That would be great," Aria said.

"Okie dokie."

"So now Lundquist is blackmailing you again?" I asked Aria when our server had wandered off.

"Yes. He spent most of his inheritance on a coke habit. When he recognized me—and I'm surprised he did—Ray also recognized an opportunity."

"Is he still in love with you? Are you back to square one with the guy?"

"No. He's moved on from that, thank God. And we negotiated this time. I paid for twenty-eight days of residential rehab for him, and I helped him get situated when he got out."

"The job at your center?"

"Yes. I've worked very hard on forgiveness for the

past twenty years—for myself and for Ray. For his part, Ray seemed to sincerely desire a better life. He meditated with us, he volunteered for extra duties. It went well for a while."

"Let me guess. He started using again?"

"Yes. I understand relapsing only too well. But after a few months, it was clear he wasn't merely incompetent because he was using. His basic lack of integrity came to the fore."

"You fired him?"

"Yes. I had to. I won't go into the details, but he experienced my decision as not living up to my side of the bargain."

"So he filed the lawsuit to extort money?" I asked. "If you settle the lawsuit, you'd really be paying him off to keep his mouth shut?"

"Yes. I've repeatedly told him I'll give him nothing more—no matter what. Leanne is old enough now to handle the truth about her father. And I'm willing to weather the consequences. But Ray's hanging around, hoping I'll change my mind. If he reveals my past, whatever chance he has to get a payoff becomes nil."

"Do you think he'll do it anyway eventually? Maybe just out of spite?"

"I do. And I think that day is looming. He's a vengeful person. In the past, his need to punish others has sometimes trumped his greed. He believes I ruined his life, and you know what? As much as he's tried to ruin mine, he might be right. All of this is the extended price tag of my mistake, not his. He was just a kid."

"Could he have anything to do with the murder?"

"It's possible, but I don't think so. He's never gone to lengths like that in the past. A dismembered corpse as coercion?" Aria shook her head.

"Doing a lot of coke can induce psychosis."

"That's true. I keep forgetting you were a therapist." Aria leaned back and took a few slow, deep breaths.

"No, I never made it that far, but I remember things. That's one of the reasons I'm good at what I do now." That reminded me of something. "Why did you hire me in particular? And weren't you worried whoever you hired would uncover your past?"

"I thought we were simply dealing with threats," Aria said. "It never occurred to me the investigation would prove to be so comprehensive. I've tried to keep you reined in, too."

"You certainly did. I like to gallop, though."

She smiled. "The answer to the other part of your question is a bit embarrassing."

"The 'why me?' part?"

"Yes. Truth be known, I've had a crush on you for years," she told me.

"Really?" I was shocked. Moi?

She nodded. She didn't look embarrassed at all.

"Wow," I said, for lack of any other response.

"That's it? Wow?"

"Yes. I wonder if that's how I get all my cases. Perhaps my craggy looks are too beguiling for clients to resist." I was deflecting my feelings with humor so well, I didn't even know what they were.

"Uh huh."

She seemed disappointed that I wasn't taking her seriously, but what was I supposed to say? A jumble of undifferentiated emotions roiled around in my gut, and I didn't have time for them. I'd been doing a lot of stuffing things away lately, even though I knew they'd show up and bite me on the ass someday.

"Maybe we'd better get back to the case," I said. "Does Leanne know about you?"

"No. We have a close relationship, but it's as therapist and client."

"How'd you manage that? Did you give her a scholarship for counseling, too?"

"Something like that. I told myself traditional ethics didn't apply, and I see now that of course they always do. On the other hand, the arrangement was very much to Leanne's benefit, which is what the spirit of the guidelines is attempting to ensure."

"You should think about telling her. Look at who she's missing out on—the Aria sitting here now. Lina Piatanesi is dead and gone. And if Ray Lundquist is likely to tell her someday, don't you think it's better if it comes from you?"

It was Aria's turn to ponder. She took her time, and her face cycled through various expressions, most of them exhibiting some variety of tension.

"You're right, Karl," she said. "Thank you."

Our food finally came, along with an older man in a suit, who apologized profusely for the delay and offered us free okra, which we declined.

"Eat," I told Aria. "We can talk more about this later if you want."

She nodded, and we were quiet while we ate. When we'd finished, I spoke. "I know this is tough. When you've kept a secret so long, it's hard to let go of it." She nodded again, watching me closely. "Maybe I should tell you a secret, too—so we're even. Let's see…should I go with the second head I hide under my armpit or my career as a geisha?"

"I vote for geisha," she said, not quite smiling. "The head thing is so commonplace. Half my students have extra heads."

I was glad she'd recovered enough to banter. Bantering was my go-to litmus test for gauging someone's emotional recovery—assuming they had a sense of humor.

"Or we could talk about something else," I said. "Like us."

"Are you still thinking there's an 'us' after everything I've told you?" Her voice was soft now and the corners of her mouth trembled. I could sense her vulnerability.

"What do you mean?" I was genuinely puzzled. "Oh, you think I'd reject you for something that happened all those years ago?"

She nodded a tiny nod. The words weren't falling out of her as usual. She still wasn't herself.

"Actually, I'm relieved you're not perfect," I told her. "That might be a deal killer. Your story is what a previous You did. It's irrelevant. Or actually, I take that back. It's totally relevant. It's undoubtedly one of the reasons you turned into the woman I know. So I'm glad it happened the way it did."

"You mean that?" Her voice was still a bit weak, but a wan smile appeared as she spoke.

I checked in with myself to make sure it wasn't something I was just saying to make her feel better. "Yeah, I do," I told her. "Would you even be a spiritual person if you hadn't had to work through all this horrendous crap?"

"I have no idea." She took a moment to push a lock

of hair to the side and tilted her head back. "I generally experience the world exactly the way you just described it. One thing follows another, and the rightness of what's in the moment helps me understand the perfect necessity of what led to it. But it's been challenging to maintain that perspective in this arena."

"There wouldn't even have been a Leanne if you hadn't screwed up, Aria. The world would've gotten cheated out of her."

"I know these things are true, Karl. I just can't hang onto them all the time."

"I'll hang onto them for you." I surprised myself by what I was saying. It was like I'd suddenly turned into a good therapist. "You can come borrow them anytime you need to," I added, feeling a smile break out on my face as well.

She smiled more broadly now, reached across the table, and took my hand. "You're sweet."

"No, I'm not. I'm a hard-boiled private eye. True, I have a heart of gold buried under my tough exterior, and I have a soft spot for dames with legs up to here." I held up my hand as high as I could beside the table. "But sweet? No way, Dollface."

The server thought I was beckoning him and rushed over. "Is everything all right? I hope everything's all right." His boss had lit a fire under him.

"Everything's perfect," I said. "We just figured that out."

Aria followed me back to my condo in her hybrid. Unfortunately, it was currently a pigsty. When I'm on a case, my housekeeping always goes to hell. I could see she did her best to accommodate the mess, but her nose crinkled up when she strolled in. And she rolled her eyes when—lord help her—she needed to use the bathroom.

Once we were in bed, after slowly undressing each other, I told her my condensed life story, which I've never found to be particularly interesting. Even my little brother Larry's death felt banal to me by now. Aria told me about her childhood in Toronto. Her parents were older. She'd been an accident when her mother was forty, a fact that she was reminded of regularly. Her father had been a philosophy professor at York University. Neither of her parents had ever played with her beyond one hand of gin rummy when she was too young to understand the game.

I was surprisingly comfortable lying naked next to Aria and just talking. I had an erection, of course, but it didn't scream at me to do anything. That was new. My penis was generally my second most impatient organ—after my bladder.

We fell asleep in each other's arms without making love. I slept so soundly, I didn't even know she was there. In the early morning, she awakened me by nibbling on my lower lip. We made up for lost time—one of the most delightful interludes of my life.

I'd never had a lover like Aria. Fully present every second, unselfish, sensual, and acutely intuitive, she was also the most beautiful woman I'd ever been with. Inside and out.

Aria needed to get back to the center for morning meditation, and I needed to get to the office to check in with Matt, so once we'd cleaned up and eaten, we parted company with a tender kiss.

Chapter Thirty-Three

When I walked into the office, Matt took one look at me and said, "Holy shit, Karl. Who?"

"What?"

"No, who. Don't go Abbot and Costello on me, bro. Who the hell did you sleep with? Sue Sutter? Don't tell me it was Adele."

"I don't kiss and tell."

"Yes, you do."

"Not when it's true love."

"It's Aria! This is great. You're doing a guru."

"Calm down, Matt. We've got a murder to solve."

"Three."

"What?"

"A Sureño got killed in Watsonville last night, and Cardenas says it's connected to our case. And in case you forgot, somebody shot Victor Gonzales. So that's three."

"Whoa." We walked into the inner office together. "What's the story there?" I asked as we both sat in our usual spots.

"Hondurans, it looks like. They're not going to catch them."

"Why not?"

"They never do. Guess how many Hombres are behind bars?"

"A couple of thousand?"

"Eleven."

"How is that possible?"

"They kill their own people. If anybody gets caught, they murder them."

"Then why are we still alive, Matt?"

"I'm thinking it's because the Hombres didn't kill Sharp. If they had, they wouldn't let us keep snooping. So maybe we need to rule out the Sureños and the Hombres since they're in bed together, so to speak."

I told him about Big Sur and whatever else I thought he needed to know, including Ray Lundquist and Aria—without going into all the sordid details. That was her secret to tell.

"First of all," Matt said. "Give me the fingerprint on the hair-dye box, and I'll see what I can do with it. Second, I'll bet the military lesbian with the gun is a bodyguard. The husband got killed, so the wife's scared. Third, the Friedman guy is clearly insane. If there were anything special about you, I'd know it. You're a schmo like everybody else. And fourth, Lundquist is a cokehead, right?"

"Yeah."

"So who does he get his cocaine from?"

"Why do you ask?"

"Well, here's my idea. Suppose Lundquist owed money to a drug-dealing gang."

"That's a big suppose, Matt."

"Bear with me, stud. I'm trying to tie Lundquist the blackmailer to Lundquist the possible murderer. What makes him a crappy suspect is that he has no connection to Wayne Sharp, right?"

"Yeah, he might want to scare Aria into capitulating financially by putting a body on her property, but that's about it."

"But Sharp was working for the Hombres. They sell coke, and Lundquist uses coke. So if he didn't chop someone up, maybe he still had something to do with the body ending up there. It could've been a way to pay off a debt."

"I thought Sharp was laundering money for the Sureños."

"He used to. Remember, he got a better offer from the Hombres," Matt said. "That's something Sutter found out."

"Launder for us instead, or we'll kill you?"

"Exactly."

"I'll tell you what, Matt. When Chen and I go see Ray Lundquist to encourage him to not bother Aria anymore, I'll check into that, too. But I met the guy, and he doesn't seem right for this."

"Why not take John?"

"He's too ethical. I need mean, or at least a better simulation of mean."

"Ah. Take a look at this," Matt said. "This is the pièce de résistance of my work." He handed me a missing person's flier from the Napa police. It was for Chet Sharp.

"I see what you mean." I leaned back, feeling heat in my chest. Matt may have just broken open the case.

I got on the phone to Cardenas. "I need you to check something out. I can't explain why at this point, but it's important."

"I'll do what I can, but we're pretty sure the Hombres are behind all the murders, Karl. Whatever you're pursuing is probably beside the point."

I explained what I needed, and he promised to get

back to me later that day.

"Be careful, Karl," he told me. "The more progress we make on this case, the more dangerous it becomes for all of us. And there's definitely a mole in the department somewhere. Someone's been tampering with the evidence we've gathered against the Hombres."

"Okay, thanks."

I hung up and turned to Matt again. "You're doing great work."

"Thanks. Here's something else. You know how the Hombres are doing whatever they want in Honduras?"

"Yeah."

"One thing they do is kidnap people—it's a big part of their income, like in Mexico. Consuela Crowder and Hazel Sharp both have relatives missing down there."

"So you're thinking maybe the missing people are hostages to get the chief to look the other way—or even mess with evidence?"

"Maybe. Or maybe it's nothing. Since they come from wealthy families, odds are some of their people would be missing. It's that bad these days."

"Where'd you get this?"

"From Honduran newspapers. They're online. And my computer translates—sort of." He looked down at his laptop. "It says, 'Prominent entities who create wealth have been enduring untoward hardships outside their normal realms of living for the profit of others who do not operate in good faith.' "

"You know, you can download a decent translation app for about three dollars," I told him.

"I like mine. It amuses me." He did seem delighted by the fractured vocabulary.

"So how do we follow up on this?" I asked.

"I'm going to look into any cases Jim Crowder stepped in on."

"He came into the interview room when I was with Cardenas," I said. "Our detective friend wasn't pleased."

"Exactly. That kind of thing. Maybe there's a pattern. And maybe they're making Ralph Sharp do stuff, too—through his wife Hazel."

I thought for a moment. "Somebody told me the Hondurans had infiltrated a lot of organizations here…it was Victor Gonzales, I think."

"Maybe that's why they killed him. Maybe he knew too much about that."

"We're doing an awful lot of speculating for detectives who ought to know solid things about this case by now."

"Did you just call me a detective?"

"I did."

"Cool." He smiled as wide as I'd ever seen. He was like a ten-year-old who'd won the biggest stuffed animal at a carnival.

Chapter Thirty-Four

I picked up Chen at a nearby parking garage, and we drove down to Salinas to see Lundquist. Chen had reverted to one-word responses, so after I told him what I needed from him, we rode silently.

Chen wore old-fashioned shiny black warm-up pants and a snug red T-shirt. Even when he was sitting, he was a bundle of compressed energy. It was as if he were always vigilant, always ready. For what, I don't know.

We pulled into the Hyundai dealership and parked on the far side of the building from the parts department. Matt had called earlier and ascertained that Lundquist was working that day.

Before we could get out of the car, an old Chevy pulled into the spot next to us. It was Bobby Mendoza—Sumati's boyfriend.

I ducked down, and Chen followed suit without needing to be told. I pulled my gun and held it low. Then I heard Bobby open and close his door, following by the sound of his boot heels moving away on the asphalt. He hadn't seen us.

I told Chen who Bobby was, and we formulated a new plan. This time we walked through the showroom so we could approach the parts desk without Lundquist seeing us coming. A salesman started to approach us, and I waved him off. His disappointment was palpable.

There was a place to wait just shy of the room in which Lundquist stood across a counter from Bobby. We could hear them, but they were around a corner from us. None of us could see one another.

"So I need to return this air filter, Pencil Dick," Bobby said. "Please gimme my money back." His voice was rough and careless. Perhaps he was drunk again.

"Bobby, do this right," Lundquist hissed. "I'm at work here." Then he spoke up in a louder voice. "Yes, sir. Let me get you a cash refund."

He was a terrible actor. If even a non-English-speaking mechanic had walked by and heard this interchange, he'd know something was up. I peeked around the corner. Bobby handed Lundquist a cardboard box, and Lundquist handed him cash.

Chen and I stepped into the room.

"Oh, shit," Lundquist said.

Bobby pivoted, and his eyes widened. "This one's not so big." He launched himself at Chen, who stepped nimbly to the side and punched him in the side of the head. Bobby went down hard.

Out of the corner of my eye, I saw Lundquist gather himself to bolt, box in hand.

"No," I said, showing him my gun. I held it on him as I walked over and took the box. As I'd thought, there was white powder in a small baggie jammed into the middle of a hollowed-out air filter.

I heard a thud behind me. Bobby had gotten up and was now down again.

"So here's the deal," I told Lundquist. "We came here to beat the hell out of you. This guy pounding Bobby behind me..." I turned for a moment and pointed at Chen as he seemed to kick a prone Bobby in

341

the kneecap. "He's not as nice as the giant guy was."

I'd told Chen to pull his punches and kicks after the first few. But even so, the sight of him pretending to beat Bobby was grotesque.

"This one kills people," I said. "But don't worry. Now we don't have to. We've got this," I said, holding up the filter box. "And two witnesses who saw your deal go down."

Lundquist's face was frozen, except for his eyes, which darted around frantically.

"If you ever communicate with Aria Piper again," I said, "you're in prison—or worse. If you ever contact your daughter, same thing. If I ever see you again—anywhere, anytime—I'll shoot you. Am I clear?"

He tried to say yes. It took him three tries.

"In fact, I'd like you to move back to Canada. Can you do that for me?"

He nodded. Chen finished his show and leaned against the wall next to me. A woman customer strolled in, saw the body on the floor, and glanced at us. Chen gently shook his head, and she ran off. She moved amazingly fast for an older woman in high heels.

I saw Bobby shift his weight. He wasn't unconscious.

"Bobby," I said. "Don't bother Sumati anymore. I don't care who loves who. If you contact her, I'm putting you back in prison."

He didn't say anything, but he heard me.

I continued with Lundquist. "I'd also like to know whatever you know about the murders."

"Uh, they say it's the Hombres."

"Who does?"

"The Sureños do. Bobby does."

"All three of the murders?"

"Yeah. But that's all I know. And I have an alibi for the Sharp one. Remember?" His voice was shaky. In fact, all of him was shaky. Apparently, we'd found a way to scare him more than his gangbanger dealers had. Perhaps it had been Chen's casual dispatch of the toughest guy Lundquist knew.

"We better go before the cops show up," I told Chen. I turned to Lundquist. "You've got a day to get out of town."

Then we took off.

We'd been lucky to catch Bobby and Lundquist in the act. Usually, I ran into some luck on a case, but I hadn't had much in the last few days. Maybe it was Aria's luck, and we were riding her karmic coattails. I liked that notion, and I liked the idea that I was thinking like a spiritual person for once. If I was going to be with Aria, I'd have to get comfortable coloring outside the lines.

I was speeding as usual on the trip back to Santa Cruz. A police cruiser flashed its lights behind us along a rural stretch of Highway One. I pulled over onto the wide shoulder.

"Let's stay nice and calm," I said to Chen. "This is probably just a traffic stop."

"Sure," he said.

The police car parked behind us, and the lone cop in it clambered out and strode over to my window. It was Casey—the city cop who I'd talked to after the shooting at the beach, and also when Victor had been shot and killed. I rolled down my window.

"Oh, it's you," he said.

"Casey, right?"

343

He looked hungover. His pale face was even paler than last time, and one blue eye was bloodshot. "That's right. Dennis Casey. Do you know how fast you were traveling, Mr. Gatlin?"

"I do not. Where's your partner today?"

"Home sick. You were exceeding the speed limit."

"Yes, I probably was. Just like all the other cars. Why are you making traffic stops outside your jurisdiction?"

"Look, I'm asking the questions here, Gatlin."

"Go ahead."

Just then a white Toyota careened off the road and slewed to a stop in front of us—angled so I couldn't drive away. There were three Hispanic men in it. They began climbing out with guns in their hands.

Casey reached down to his holster and I did, too. I felt good about our chances since there were three of them and three of us. Also, one of us was a cop and one was Chen.

Casey turned the gun on me. "Drop it," he said.

Chen rolled out his door and disappeared, presumably under the car. I was too surprised to do anything.

"Now!" Casey commanded.

I dropped my gun onto the empty seat next to me. The other men fanned out around the car, holding their guns by their sides. Traffic zoomed past us, oblivious to what was happening.

"So you're working for the Hondurans, and now I'm finally going to meet some," I said.

"Shut up. I should've killed you on the beach, Gatlin. You're a pain in the ass."

"Oh, that was you?" I struggled to keep my fear

from showing. "No wonder you were the first cop on the scene. What did you do? Go change clothes in the rest room?"

"Get out of the car," he growled.

I did. He backed away from me and spoke to the men in rapid, fluent Spanish. One of the men said something back. I couldn't follow it. It was some sort of dialect.

All three of the gangsters were burly but quite short. One was extremely ugly with a big squashed nose on an oversized head. The other two could've been brothers. They were younger, maybe early twenties—slim guys with small features. They looked like they did this kind of thing all the time. They were all alarmingly casual.

"You're going with them," Casey told me.

"Let me guess. You were stationed at the air force base in Honduras."

"It's a beautiful country," he said, smiling briefly. "Now move!" He waved his gun in the air like we were in an old Western.

"Is the chief in on this, too?" I asked.

He ignored me.

I didn't have much choice. The Hombres escorted me into the backseat of their dirty white Camry. One climbed behind the wheel—the ugly one. The other two flanked me in the backseat, their guns in their hands. Neither of them had bathed in a long time. The car reeked of sweat and stale beer.

No one in the car seemed to care about Chen. That was just plain stupid, I thought. I turned and glanced behind me as we pulled into traffic. Casey was peering under my car, still holding his gun.

Good luck, I thought.

Chen versus one man? Gun or no gun, I'd bet on Chen.

Chapter Thirty-Five

The driver exited at the first opportunity, crossed over the freeway, and headed back south. I tried talking to them, but no one responded. I don't think I was a person as far as they were concerned. I was a package of walking, talking meat they were delivering.

I wasn't dead yet, I told myself. Either the Hombres wanted to know what I knew, in which case I'd be tortured to tell them—and then murdered once I did. Or I was being held hostage in order to compel someone else to do something. Unfortunately, this much more palatable possibility seemed less likely.

Suddenly, I felt a rush of visceral fear. I hadn't thought myself into it. It was a storm that swept in and settled in my gut. Would I survive this? Would I ever see Aria again?

When we drove by where my car was parked, I saw the patrol car had already departed. Casey could've apprehended Chen, but there was an excellent chance Chen had overpowered him and taken his car.

I asked myself, if I were Chen driving a police car in these circumstances, what would I do? I decided I'd get on the phone while I followed the Hondurans from a safe distance. Maybe I'd call the cops. Maybe I wouldn't trust them. I might call John or anyone else I could think of.

I thought about looking behind us to see if I could

spot Chen, but I didn't want to role model sensible kidnapper behavior. If it hadn't occurred to the Hombres to watch for a tail, so much the better.

We turned off Highway 1 at Route 129, which wanders around south Watsonville and then winds through a mountain pass inland. I was surprised. I'd figured we were headed to Salinas.

The driver turned down a pothole-riddled side street, and then another one. We were now in a truly bad neighborhood. The houses were small and sad-looking—no landscaping, iron bars over all the doors and windows, and no sign of any kids. For that matter, there was no sign of anyone at all. Had all these homes been foreclosed?

We pulled into the driveway of an unpainted cinderblock commercial building in the middle of a row of houses. An old, vandalized sign out front had once read "Pajaro Valley Pest Control."

I was wordlessly guided inside, where half a dozen men sprawled on the rough pine floor. The windows were blacked out with peeling spray paint, and the interior walls had mostly been knocked down, so the water-stained sheetrock ceiling was drooping in several spots. There was almost no furniture. If I were making a shitload of money selling drugs and kidnapping people, I'd hang out somewhere more upscale, which was pretty much anywhere else.

The men in the building looked like younger versions of the ones who'd escorted me in. They were dressed in jeans and T-shirts advertising various inappropriate products—yogurt, Volvos, and Ohio State University, for example. I wondered for a moment what would've constituted appropriate products. Guns, maybe. Or real estate companies that specialized in filthy hovels.

Most of them were only in their late teens. No one was interested in me. Ugly guy shoved me down onto the floor in the corner of the room. Nobody had patted me down, so if I'd had a second gun, I could've tried to shoot my way out. But I didn't. It made me think they were cocky, though. And maybe not too bright.

One of the brothers—I'd decided they really were brothers—sat about six feet away and held a gun on me while everyone else went about their business. This consisted of texting, playing video games on expensive-looking laptops, sleeping, or arguing with one another in the same strange Spanish my trio had spoken.

I figured we were waiting for their boss, or at least someone who spoke English. This was probably a branch office—a garrison for the Hombres soldiers—and someone was on his way from headquarters in Salinas.

I closed my eyes and tried to rest. I needed to be in the best possible shape for what was coming. Of course, I didn't fall asleep. I just pictured all the horrible things coming down the pike.

It must've been at least a half hour before I heard a shot. It came from behind the building. The men scrambled to their feet and rushed to the back door— my guy, too. Then the front door burst open— somebody had used a battering ram—and a guy with an AR-15 started spraying it across the array of Hombres. It was deafening.

Most of them were cut down, but two dove to the side and came up firing. The assault-rifle guy moved to the side and three or four more men poured into the room, firing a variety of weapons.

In my corner, the main danger was from an errant shot, but even the on-target rounds were chipping out shards of cinderblock from the walls and slivers of wood from the floor. These were flying around, ricocheting off everything.

After only twenty seconds, all the Hondurans lay dead in various contorted poses. It was horrific. I looked in the front doorway. There was a fat guy in overalls down there, too.

Blood was spurting out of one Hombre's chest, and another one had most of his arm torn off. The ugly guy was much uglier now—he'd taken two bullets to his forehead. One of the brothers lay on top of the other. Both were riddled with wounds in their lower abdomens. Dark blood pooled around them and ran into the cracks between the pine boards on the floor.

My heart was pounding, and I felt sick to my stomach. It was all I could do to keep from vomiting. The smell of blood was awful. And in that enclosed space, I couldn't escape from the horror.

I checked myself over. I was bleeding from my thigh and my forearm. Fortunately, neither was a serious wound. The one in my leg was a big wood splinter, and the other one represented an odd piece of good luck. An almost totally spent bullet had burrowed itself partway into my arm. It must've bounced around dozens of times before it reached me. I pulled the slug out by the uneven tail that was protruding, burning my finger in the process. I'd need someone to look at the wound soon. It was bound to get infected. But it didn't hurt that much.

Rivera—the head of the Sureños and my morning

visitor several days earlier—strode in the front door, kicking aside his downed soldier. I didn't have a good feeling about what was coming next. After all, what was one more corpse at this point? I'd seen the whole thing, including the fact that Rivera was here at the scene. Why would he let me walk away?

He surveyed the interior of the building, finally spotting me in the corner. His bushy, black eyebrows jumped upward. He hadn't known I was there. In the back of my mind, I'd been holding onto the ridiculous notion that the assault had been a rescue operation. No such luck.

Rivera wore black jeans and a white T-shirt splattered with blood. He was jumpy—he couldn't stand still. His eyes were wild, too. Either he was on speed or he was manic—this was beyond the adrenaline that was making me shake uncontrollably.

Rivera gestured for me to follow him outside. I stumbled to my feet and then almost fell as I slipped on several shell casings. Eventually, I made it out.

He tried to talk to me on the front stoop. I couldn't hear a thing. The gunshots had been the loudest sound I'd ever experienced. I pointed to my ears, and he nodded. Then he gestured for me to follow him to a black SUV. I glanced around to see if running might be my best option. There was a guy standing next to another SUV holding a handgun at his hip. In fact, there was an armada of SUVs parked on the street. The Sureños had come in force, although it appeared they'd only needed a few men to get the job done.

I was still nauseated and felt lightheaded. In lieu of any other viable option, I stumbled to the curb and climbed into the passenger seat of Rivera's vehicle. The two Mexicans who'd accompanied him to my condo piled in the back as their boss climbed in to drive. He tried talking to me again, and this time I could make out sounds, at least. I shook my head.

Rivera pulled away and drove down the street at exactly the speed limit. He calmed down a bit as he took a route I didn't recognize. It became clear we were heading to Salinas on back roads. For a while, I just breathed deeply and gazed at the farmland we passed. I'd been traumatized. Nobody should have to watch all those murders.

Eventually, I tried talking. As I came to my senses, I realized just because I couldn't hear didn't mean I couldn't talk. And if I shouted, so what? I wasn't at the library.

"You can count on me," I said. "You saved my life. I wanted those guys dead, too."

Rivera said something, and I caught most of it. My hearing was coming back. "...I haven't decided yet...For now, just..." He spoke quickly, but he didn't seem to be on speed anymore. I guess it had been adrenaline, after all.

After a few more miles, one of the guys in the back seat bragged to the other that he'd killed two of the Hombres. I didn't have any trouble hearing and understanding their Spanish now, although one of my ears hurt like hell. It was a deep ache.

As a result, I heard the siren behind us, and I wasn't surprised when Rivera slowed down. I turned and saw the flashing lights. It was a police car. There wasn't a shoulder on the rural road, so Rivera drove up onto the edge of a fallow field.

"Don't fuck around," he said to me. "Can you hear

me?"

"Yes."

"If you do, you're dead, and so are the cops. Just face forward, and don't say a word."

"Okay."

I heard two doors open and close behind us.

Rivera told his guys in the SUV to act normal, whatever that meant. "Shit," he said. "It's plainclothes."

"Good morning, sir," Chen's voice said at the driver's side window.

I glanced to my right. John stood by the back door on the other side.

"What's the problem, officer?" Rivera said in a very different accent than he'd used with me. He sounded like an Italian tourist now.

"Could you get out of the car, sir?"

"Why?"

"Because I asked you to," Chen said matter-of-factly. "Are you refusing to obey the direction of a detective while on duty? That's a felony, you know."

It certainly wasn't, but Chen was doing fine.

As Rivera opened his door, John opened the one behind me. "Out!" he ordered in his New Zealand accent.

"Wait a minute!" Rivera called, on his feet beside Chen. "Raul, Al—these guys aren't cops!"

I jumped out of the passenger side of the car just in time to see John dive into the backseat. Chen began fighting with Rivera on the other side of the car. The head of the Sureños could handle himself.

John lay on top of both of the gunmen. His weight pinned the arms of the near one, and he wrestled with the far one from a prone position.

I reached in the back and retrieved the gun from the one nearest me. John managed to hit the other one hard enough to snap his head back against the headrest. Then he took his gun. I hoped they didn't have backup weapons. I wasn't crawling in there to frisk them.

John maneuvered out of the car on my side, keeping the gun he'd taken trained on the men in the backseat. They sat perfectly still, facing forward.

Chen and Rivera were still fighting, which surprised me. I ran around the car with the Colt Python I'd taken.

"It's okay, Chen," I said, as the two men stood apart and eyed one another. "We've got their guns."

His eyelids were hooded, and his jaw was clenched. I'd never seen Chen in full-bore action mode before. Everything about him was tight and all of a piece.

Rivera was looser. He kept shifting his weight back and forth—the way a tennis player moved while waiting to return a serve.

"Why don't you let us finish," Chen said. "This is fun."

Rivera smiled. "Yeah, it is. Who the fuck are you, anyway? This is the longest fight I've had in years."

"Me, too," Chen told him.

Rivera rushed him. Chen tried a leg sweep, and Rivera jumped straight up with his legs tucked. At the peak of the jump, he shot a leg out and caught Chen on the hip. Unfazed, Chen retaliated with a flurry of punches, which Rivera dodged or blocked. It was all happening almost too fast to see.

Then Chen faked a kick with one leg and snap kicked with the other. When Rivera blocked it with both arms extended down, Chen seemed to stumble and began to fall. Rivera was fooled. He slid forward and cocked a fist to deliver a coup de grâce.

Chen had been waiting for that. He leapt in the air and kicked him twice in the face. Rivera sprawled backward. As he was falling, Chen kicked him again in the gut. The Sureño landed hard on the hard dirt of the field beside the car. He stayed down.

"Jesus," he said. "If you can do that…"

Chapter Thirty-Six

Chen had called John from the police car early on, and the Maori had driven down and joined him where he was parked around a couple of corners from the Hombres' derelict hideout. Even in a marked car, Chen had no trouble discreetly following the trio of kidnappers.

They'd discussed whether to call Cardenas and decided to reconnoiter on foot before they did. If the cops showed up, maybe I'd get shot.

Chen and John were lurking behind an abandoned home adjoining the building I was in when the Sureños gathered at the end of the block. Rivera sent men behind the row of houses in their direction. With armed gang members coming up behind them, Chen and John moved forward and overwhelmed the two Hombres guards outside the back door. Then they headed around the block back to the police car.

That's what saved me. With those guards out of commission, the attack's success was assured—with minimal crossfire.

Although my colleagues had no way of knowing if I'd survived, they called Cardenas and followed the first vehicle to leave the scene following the barrage. Lo and behold, there I was in Rivera's SUV.

"Where's Casey?" I asked Chen as I held the gun on the Sureños' leader.

Chen exhibited a rare smile. "In the trunk of the police car. With the release disengaged."

Various cops arrived soon. Many more were gathered back at the massacre scene in Watsonville. The rest of the day was spent with the CHP, the Feds, and all the local police forces. There'd never been any gang activity on this scale in Northern California before. The media was all over it too, but I ignored them as best I could.

Back in Santa Cruz, I didn't get a chance to get a moment alone with Cardenas until 6:30 that evening. We sat slumped in the break room at the police station, eating stale vending-machine food.

"So," I said, "did you have a chance to look into all the fingerprints?" This was one of the favors I'd requested after my meeting with Matt.

"Yeah, somebody switched the cards. Probably Casey, but it could've been anybody willing to take a bribe. And that print Matt gave me matched who you said it would."

"Could it have been the chief who messed with things?"

"Crowder's dirty. But not in a hands-on way, it seems. The Feds arrested him about an hour ago. He hired Casey and gave him gang-relevant assignments that he wasn't qualified for. He looked the other way on a couple of other things, too. That's enough to hold him for now."

"Why would he? His wife?"

"Yeah," Cardenas said in a tired voice. "Consuela Crowder's family is under the gun back in Honduras. It looks like the chief's brother was involved at some level, too. Under the threat of having his homosexuality revealed, Gary brought Hazel up from Central America and shoved her at Ralph Sharp so the Hombres would have leverage with him, too. I don't know why they cared about the guy, though."

"What were Gary and Jim thinking? These guys are maniacs."

"I don't think either Crowder knew the kind of people they were dealing with, although the chief should've. Maybe he thought he knew about Honduras from living there way back when, but things have changed. Gary's just an idiot."

Cardenas paused and watched me. He looked exhausted. I probably looked half dead.

"So what are you going to do?" he asked. "As far as the authorities are concerned, the case is pretty much closed. If you don't do anything, your case disappears, and everybody moves on to all these new gang murders."

"Yeah, I know. But I can't let him get away with this."

"Okay. Call me in if you need to. And be careful."

"I will."

I'd had a chance to call and talk to Matt several times during the afternoon. I'd also responded to Baba Hari Friedman's voicemail, as well as several others.

Matt and Larry were waiting for me at the office. I was joyful to be reunited with my dog, and I began to weep as I hugged him. I guess part of it was still being alive. What a day.

"Crying?" Matt said. "Really?"

I wasn't in the mood for Matt's wise-ass comments. "You know I've seen about ten murders today, right?"

"Yeah, sorry. I've just been bored, and that puts me in a bad mood. Larry's not the world's best conversationalist. Even when I skewer him with passive-aggressive wit, I get zilch."

"Let me tell you what Cardenas confirmed. You're going to like this."

I filled him in, and he tied up some loose ends from his end while I lay on the grimy carpet and played with Larry. We had a tug of war with a giant rubber hotdog. Nothing Freudian there.

"Aria called, too," he said. "She says she's glad you're okay and she went up to Palo Alto today to talk to Leanne."

"I'll give her a call." I reached for the phone.

"No, you can't. She's in something called samadhi tonight. She says it's a deep healing meditation where you don't answer the phone, so I should tell you all her news."

"Please, go ahead."

Matt picked up a notepad. "I want to get this right. Aria told her daughter that she was her mother, and Leanne said she knew but she thought Aria wanted to keep her distance. She even knew who her dad was, and she'd come to terms with that. So they both hugged each other and cried, and it was all wonderful."

"That's great."

"Yeah, she seemed pretty happy about it on the phone. Then I asked her if she was willing to call Leanne and ask her about the molestation charges against Reverend Crowder."

"That's kinda pushy, don't you think, Matt?"

"Well, it just didn't fit with what we know about the guy. He's gay, right? And I don't like leaving even little things unresolved. You never know. Anyway, she agreed and called me back later."

"So what did you find out? Now you've got me wondering, too."

"Leanne had a gay male friend who was molested and wouldn't come forward because he hadn't come out to his family. Crowder knew that, which was why he'd picked him. So Leanne made up a hetero version of the abuse and took it to the cops to ruin Crowder's reputation as much she could. She knew it wouldn't stand up in court, but she felt obliged."

"What a creep. We've got to nail him for something."

"The cops will," Matt said. "Remember how he's connected to that dirty bank in Texas?"

"Yeah."

"They're rounding up everybody tomorrow. They've got him on a number of charges, including tax evasion. Churches are exempt, but pastors aren't."

"Great."

"And José's back."

"Back where?"

"At Aria's," Matt said. "He told her the Sureños did the job for him. All the Hombres involved in Victor's murder were killed at the pest-control place. José and Victor's brothers were set to get going tomorrow, so that's good."

"Do you know what the upshot of all the shootings and arrests is in terms of the local gangs? I asked a couple of the Feds, but they were all too busy to talk."

"The main thing is the Norteños are going to rule for the foreseeable future. The Hombres lost half their lieutenants, and the Sureños lost all their leadership."

"Who else besides Rivera?"

"The other two in the car were his capos."

"Are you getting these terms from *The Sopranos*?" I asked.

"Maybe."

"So now the Norteños are going to run wild?" I asked.

"Pretty much. There's no stopping gangs. Not as long as there's economic inequity, racism, antiquated drug laws, and insufficient police budgets."

"Is anyone likely to come after me?"

"No," Matt said. "The Sureños are going to be fighting amongst themselves for power until Rivera gets to prison and starts running things from there."

"So jail's like a time-out until Rivera gets right back in power when he gets to prison?"

"Yeah. And the Hondurans have bigger fish to fry than you. The Feds are all over them. They're using antiterrorist laws to haul everybody in."

"Did you talk to John?"

"Yeah. He'll meet you at your house in the morning. And we all agree Aria doesn't need protecting anymore." Matt looked at me earnestly, which wasn't an expression I was accustomed to seeing on his face. "If it's okay with you, I think we should give John and Chen big bonuses. I cleared it with Aria. They deserve them."

"They certainly do. I should name my firstborn after those guys."

"Or just change your own name," Matt said. "That'd be better than you having kids. The world doesn't need any more of your DNA running around."

Chapter Thirty-Seven

Larry and I had to fight through a throng of media vultures when we left my office. They'd found me while I was inside. After a bit, I told Larry to growl, and he went into his unnerving act. It was a Red Sea parting after that. I could see the headlines: "Former Hero Dog Turns Vicious."

Paramedics had pulled the two-inch-long splinter from my leg and cleaned out the weird wound on my arm. Neither they or any of the cops had ever seen a bullet do that. I was left with a three-eighths-inch-deep hole that was exactly the diameter of a 9 mm bullet. I felt like spackling it over.

The two wounds took turns keeping me up that night. I told Larry I was giving him a taste of his own medicine when he gave me reproachful looks after being awakened. What a hypocrite.

I called Aria first thing in the morning, but her phone went straight to voicemail. I didn't leave a message. I was disappointed that I hadn't been able to talk to her the evening before, and now she wasn't available again. I felt sorry for myself for a few minutes. Didn't she know how traumatic yesterday had been? Why wasn't I the top priority in her life? Was meditating really more important than my feelings? Then I got tired of that, so I ate breakfast.

After scrambled eggs and frozen waffles, I called

Aria back and left a message this time. "Hi. I'm thinking good thoughts about you. I wish I were talking to you instead of your phone. You probably know from Matt that I'm okay. Give me a call and let me know how you're doing. And congratulations on your reconciliation with Leanne. Uh… I'm not sure what else to say." I paused, and then I got panicky that the machine might cut me off. I don't know why that seemed important. "I love you," I blurted out, and hung up.

Oh, shit, I thought. What had I done? I'd meant it, too. That was the worst part. How long had I known her as our current versions of ourselves? Five days?

Larry and I didn't go for a real walk. We'd be hiking in a few hours anyway—down in Big Sur. This time I was going there with two wingmen. And amateur agents were on location. Hippie agents full of salads.

John came by on time, and we loaded our gear in his big vehicle. He'd drive. I coaxed Larry into the wayback, but before I even got to my door, he'd jumped into the back seat.

"That's okay, Karl. He can sit there. No worries."

We climbed in. "John," I said, "I haven't heard you say that phrase much the last few days."

"No worries, you mean?"

"Yeah."

"Aria says when people are around her, they cut back on their old habits. You don't touch your scar anymore. Even Lou Cardenas doesn't wave his arms around all the time."

"You know, you're right." I told him about Georgia Sharp, Frances, and the shotgun. I wasn't sure how much background Matt had provided.

"I know Frances," John said. "That's Arlin's girlfriend."

"Arlin? The guy who was Gary Crowder's bodyguard?"

"Yeah. They met at the convention."

"What convention is that?"

"The bodyguards convention. It was in Anaheim about three or four years ago. I only went once—when it was in Phoenix. It was pretty boring. And it was way too hot there."

"So she's a bodyguard, too?"

"Sure," John confirmed. "She gets a lot of work from Monterey Bay Investigations. When somebody wants a woman, she's the first one they send out."

"Is she any good?"

"Not bad. Good with a gun. But not a thinker. And she cheats at cards."

I looked at him. "That's good to know." I told him more about the setup down there. Then to pass the time, I asked him about New Zealand. According to John, it was unspoiled and Kiwis weren't paranoid like Americans.

"What do you mean?"

"They're not scared of one another. I mean, a lot people are scared of me at first because I'm so big—at least until they know I'm a rugger. But we ask strangers over for dinner and lend them our cars if they need them. If it weren't for my girlfriend, Lotus, I'd head back there. But she's got her mom and her nephews here."

I decided to take Aria to New Zealand on a vacation, if she took vacations. I realized I didn't know much about her. I wondered what kind of music she listened to and what toppings she liked on her pizza. Did she ever watch TV or go to the movies? For that matter, maybe she'd already traveled to New Zealand and had hated it. How would I know?

It had been a sunny day up at our end of the bay. As we traveled down the coast, the fog grew thicker. By the time we were approaching Big Sur, I could only see a few hundred yards in front of us.

I called Friedman, and we met him in the MacDharma's parking lot. He sat on the front steps with Amy—the girl we'd supposedly healed.

"I don't think it's a good idea for Amy to be involved in this," I said, jumping out of the car.

"Why not?" Friedman asked. "Aren't all the bad guys dead now?"

"There's at least one more."

"Holy crap," Amy said as John emerged from the SUV behind me.

"G'day," he said.

Friedman stepped over, shook John's hand, and introduced himself. "I like your energy," he told him. "It's strong and old."

"Thank you. You seem very nice, too."

Friedman turned to me. "Amy wants to pay you back for helping her. Please let her. She's going to bring you to the trail head back beyond the house. She knows the Santa Lucia Mountains well. She grew up here."

"No one with PTSD should be around violence," I said. "It's triggering."

"I don't have it anymore," Amy said. "And if I'm with that guy…" She pointed at John.

"John," he told her.

"I don't think I'm going to be in any danger. Look at the way he stands. Look at him move. He's like a big cat—a giant cat."

"Thank you," John said. "You look like a nice person, too." He wasn't used to being around folks like this. Aria's students were spiritual-minded, but they were pretty self-contained.

"They're all up on the land," Friedman said. "Set your phone on vibrate, and I'll call you if that changes."

"Okay, fine. Let's get started. Do you like dogs?" I asked Amy.

"I love them."

She saw Larry in the SUV, ran over to it, and opened the back door. He jumped out, and she got down on her knees and stroked him. He liked her, but it was the same way he behaved with five-year-olds. There was some tolerance mixed in.

We piled back in John's SUV, with Larry and Amy in the back seat. She gave John directions and guided him as we backtracked and took a narrow, winding road up a steep, redwood-studded canyon. After a time, the road became gravel, then dirt, then underbrush, and then we hit the tree line.

We all got out, and John and I hoisted our daypacks onto our backs. I told Larry to sit, and he did. It seemed important to have him with us—he'd saved my ass in tight spots plenty of times—but he needed to obey commands.

"I'll have to take you in the first half mile," Amy said. "There's no trail, but it's easy walking between the redwoods. Then I'll show you where the trail starts. I hiked it yesterday because Baba told me to. It's about three miles in, and then when you get to this tree where

I tied a yellow ribbon—on your right—you'll be behind the shed that's on that property."

"Great."

So I told Larry to heel, and we started hiking. He stuck by my side. The real test would be when he saw a squirrel or a deer. I'd put him on a leash if I had to.

This redwood forest was denser than the ones near Santa Cruz, but the trees weren't as tall. There were more bay and pine trees mixed in and fewer ferns. Someone from the East coast would probably think it was the most amazing fairy tale woods he'd ever seen. Out our way, it was just par for the course, with a few small variations from the norm.

"Here we go," Amy said when we'd reached the trailhead. "Good luck. Can I give you both a hug?"

"Sure," we said in unison.

She hugged each of us quite enthusiastically. She did seem very different from the girl I'd met a couple of days ago. It seemed as though her problem pendulum had swung from the PTSD end of the arc all the way to the other pole. I hoped she wasn't doomed to endure poor boundaries and too much trust.

The rest of the hike in was more of the same. Nothing stood out for me, other than Larry continuing to behave himself—even with provocation. Two Steller's jays dive-bombed him. They're big, aggressive birds, but he did fine.

The trail was easy to follow. I'd gone first so my view wouldn't be limited to John's back. I think he had to rein in his normal pace to keep from running me over. We found the tree with the ribbon around 11:30. As promised, the shed and the rest of Georgia Sharp's hideout was just behind it.

Amy, I thought, consider your debt paid off.

Chapter Thirty-Eight

I gave Larry a hard stay command at the edge of the forest. He wouldn't break it unless I called his name. This was something he was good at. When we were at training school, he'd won a competition against forty other dogs, including a police dog and a Pomeranian who had been pretty full of herself. Larry was our ace in the hole. We'd only use him if we needed to. Otherwise, he'd stay safe.

John and I crept forward until we were behind the shed, next to a windowless, white clapboard wall. Close up, it was clear that the shed was very well built. It had probably been the original cabin on the property.

John pulled out Chen's two-piece shotgun from his pack and assembled it. If Frances had a shotgun, John was going to have one, too. It was a beautiful piece—handmade in Italy.

I drew my pistol, and John covered me while I snuck around the side of the shed to the door. I flung the door open, gun in hand. No one was in there. I tapped the wall twice to let John know what was going on.

Clearly, someone was living in the shed. There was an unmade bed, a desk, and several suitcases filled with men's clothes. There was also a slightly warm mug of coffee on a corner of the desk. The mug said World's Best Brother. Someone had drawn a shaky heart on it with a red marker.

I really doubted the guy who'd been drinking the coffee was even in the .001 percentile of good brothers.

I glided back the way I came. "He's here," I told John. "Probably in the house with the two women, but we'd better check the garage."

We did. It was clear. It was time for the dangerous part. I crept around to the front of the house and John to the back. He was awfully big for creeping, but he was also flexible and athletic. If no one happened to be looking out a window in his direction, he'd be fine. Since all the windows were open, we had to be quiet, too.

John hid somewhere back there and then played a recording of animal hooves pounding on the ground through an MP3 player hooked to a portable speaker. This was Matt's contribution. I don't know where he'd found the recording, but from the other side of the house where I crouched, it sounded realistic.

The plan was that John would grab whoever came out to check on things. Presumably, then someone else would come out to check on whoever hadn't come back. That would leave only one of them in the house. We were rooting for Frances to come out first without the gun. With her out of the picture, things would be a lot easier.

No such luck. Georgia came out first. "I don't see them," I heard her call through the open back door. She had such a girlish, unformed voice, I thought she was one at first.

I heard the hooves again. John had either moved to the side of the house or he was aiming the speaker that way.

"I'm going to go look," Georgia said. "I think it's deer." I was surprised she was capable of this much initiative.

After that, silence. Whoever was in the house didn't seem to care much. Some time passed. I told myself there was no rush. My uncle had told me a plan had to unfold—that it had its own pace that you had to cooperate with.

Eventually, I heard Frances in the house. "Goddammit. Where'd she wander off to now?" she growled.

"What are you asking me for?" a man's voice said gruffly. "Go look."

She stomped out of the room. I had no idea if she had her shotgun with her. I decided to try the front door. If John could handle Frances, that left me with my gun in my hand against a man who was probably sitting on a couch reading a book.

The door was unlocked. These people, like most criminals, were not nearly as careful as they ought to be. The man was, in fact, lying on a beige corduroy couch reading. It was a financial magazine.

"Hi, Wayne," I said. "Don't get up." I held my gun on him.

"I'm Chet," he said after a moment. "Who are you?" His hair was red, and he'd altered his features somehow.

"I'm the guy who knows you're Wayne."

"He's very, very, very dead," Wayne said in a squeaky voice, trying to sound crazy. I didn't buy it.

He didn't seem scared. That probably meant Frances had taken the gun with her and he expected her back. He didn't know I had a partner. I pulled a chair over so I could watch both Wayne and the open back door. I couldn't hear anything out there. I had hoped by now that John would've called to me that he'd handled her. Perhaps he'd taken out Frances quietly and was standing on the back porch listening to me talk to Wayne. If I were in that situation, I wouldn't necessarily interrupt us.

"What didn't occur to me at first," I told Sharp, "was that you and Chet were identical twins."

"It's Karl Gatlin, isn't it?" he said. "There are a lot of things that didn't occur to you. You've made blunder after blunder. You're a moron."

There was my man. There was Wayne. "Hey," I said, "you're the one who left the front door open. But here's a question for you. Why put Chet in the well?"

He was confident now he'd gotten used to the idea that I was here. After all, he was smarter than everybody else, so what kind of threat could I really be?

"Two birds with one stone. Ralph told me somebody named José Something was a gangster who lived there. Everybody was going to think I'd been murdered by gangsters anyway, so why not do my brother a favor? He's been battling that witch for years over Zoppi land. Our land."

In my experience, once you get a narcissist talking, it's hard to shut him up. They crave attention and admiration—at all costs.

"When that frame didn't pay off, you decided to try another amateur-hour frame on Crowder, right?"

"Well, I had to do something with my dear brother's head, didn't I? The idiot police hadn't figured out yet I was the one in the well. What's the point of faking your own death if no one knows it's you?"

"And the hands. Weren't you afraid of the fingerprints?"

"I had that covered," he said, putting down the magazine on his lap and sitting up straighter. "Friendly cop. I don't know why they didn't lock you up, though."

"Other people aren't as stupid as you think."

"The fuck they aren't. Take you, for example. Did you know my partner's been standing behind you with a shotgun for the last minute? Why do you think I'm telling you all this?"

"I don't think so, Sharp." In his place, I might've tried something like that too. I didn't take my eyes or my gun off him. "Georgia's out there hogtied somewhere," I said. "My bodyguard's better than your bodyguard."

"Bigger," Francis said. "But not better. Not today."

I slowly pivoted in my chair. Not only was she holding a shotgun, it was Chen's shotgun. I tossed my pistol onto the floor in front of me.

"Where's John?" I asked. She was bigger than I remembered and held the double-barreled twelve-gauge like the pro she was.

"Resting," Frances said.

"And my lovely wife?" Sharp asked.

"Also resting."

Wayne rose behind me and carefully edged around the perimeter of the small living room to stand beside Frances. It was my turn to try something. The longer I could keep a dialogue going, the better my chances were for staying alive.

"You're not going to Chile with Georgia, are you?" I asked Wayne. "You're going with Francis once she assumes Georgia's identity."

"Bingo, Gatlin. You always seem to find out things just a little too late, don't you? She's been my bodyguard the last six months. Well, she started that way."

"So you'll kill your wife, too? And John. And me. And whoever comes after you next? It's not viable. People know we're up here. We recruited local help. Anyway, a guy like you doesn't have the stomach for all that killing."

"I do," Frances said. "I like chopping people up, too. Especially if the payoff is a few million."

"What about Arlin?" I was trying anything I could think of to engage and distract them.

"Who?" Wayne asked.

That was promising. "Her boyfriend—Arlin. You didn't know about him? He's a bodyguard, too."

Sharp looked at Frances, who glared at me. "Shut up," she said. "He's just trying to get us to turn on each other, Wayne."

"I'm thinking she's got a plan a lot like yours." I said. "Only maybe Arlin becomes you, as well as her becoming Georgia. Maybe down in Chile—after she kills you, too."

Wayne kept looking hard at Frances. If he had any doubts about her, maybe he was wondering if there really was an Arlin. The downside here was if Frances thought I was seriously blowing it for her, she'd shoot me to shut me up. Her face reflected her agitation, but her finger relaxed on the trigger of the shotgun—which was what mattered.

I decided it was time. "Larry!" I called, as loud as I could. I knew he'd be listening, and I knew he'd come running if he could hear me. I waited a few seconds and then shouted, "Attack!"

"Very amusing," Frances said. "But—"

Then Larry was on her back. She pitched forward as his claws dug into her shoulder blades, and she landed on the shotgun, which fired a load of buckshot into the wall beside me. Wayne came off of the couch and made a grab for the gun. I kicked him in the head, and he went sprawling into the base of a steel torchiere. It was very satisfying.

Larry bit Frances on the back of her neck and held on tight. She tried to roll away, and the other barrel of the shotgun let loose, hitting Wayne in the shoulder as he gathered himself on the rug in front of me. He screamed.

I called Larry off, and he went running to look for John. Then I held my pistol in one hand, while I speed-dialed Friedman's number with the other. Neither Wayne nor Francis moved. I sidled to the side to keep them both in sight.

"Call 911," I told him. "We need an ambulance and the police. And get up here as soon as you can. We may have some people that need your kind of healing, too."

"What's all that screaming?" he asked.

"It's a very loud dead man," I told him. "Just hurry."

I wasn't sure what Frances had meant when she'd said John and Georgia were "resting." Were they dead? What could she have done to take John down without even making any noise?

Once the police got there, I found out. Georgia had been wearing perfume that had triggered John's asthma. When Frances came out of the house, she'd found him lying on the ground next to a manacled Georgia, gasping for breath. We found his inhaler in Frances's pocket. That was attempted murder on top of all the rest. You can't take an inhaler away from an asthmatic.

Chapter Thirty-Nine

Matt threw a party at his house three days later. I'd made him a full partner, and he was celebrating both that and our wrapping up the case. He insisted on calling it a wrap party—as though we'd just finished shooting a movie.

He invited everyone associated with the case. Well, everyone who wasn't in jail, wished we were dead, or were themselves dead.

Once everyone had arrived, Matt emceed an award ceremony. He'd asked me what I thought of the idea, and I told him it sounded like fun. It also filled in the blanks for the guests who hadn't been involved in the case's various denouements.

"First," he said, standing on top of a rosewood end table in the great room, "the award for biggest dick in the investigation, and I don't mean that anatomically, goes to Wayne Sharp. Unfortunately, Wayne can't be here tonight to accept his award because he's lying in a hospital bed in the jail with a torn-up shoulder. His brother Ralph was planning to accept it for him, but it turns out he's a major dick, too, so he's in the same jail for conspiracy to commit murder. I know some of you who voted for Karl are disappointed he didn't win, but obviously the competition was very stiff in this category this year."

That drew plenty of laughs. I booed.

"Next up, we have the biggest hypocrite category. In a landslide victory, Gary Crowder captured this coveted honor. Karl, of course, was second. Once again, our winner is unavailable tonight as he's in federal custody."

Matt continued. "We have some new subcategories in the bodyguard category this year. The funnest bodyguard is John Ratu. The scariest is Chen Something. I asked him his last name, but he wouldn't tell me. Hell, maybe that is his last name. And the most dismemberish bodyguard is Frances Loomis, our murderer."

He continued in that vein until he'd covered almost everyone.

"Now, on to the major awards," Matt continued. "The best assistant detective honor goes to Karl Gatlin for his help solving this case. I couldn't have done it without him."

We all laughed at that.

"And of course, as I do every year, I've won the best crime-solver award again."

We all cheered. It was Matt's party, after all.

We had a good crowd. Unfortunately, Rachel—the woman Matt wasn't in a relationship with—was out of town for work.

Lou Cardenas and Sue Sutter were there. I thought she looked disappointed when she saw Aria on my arm, but on the other hand she'd brought some musclebound guy she claimed was her husband.

Leanne came too, with her husband. When she wasn't communing with her mother on a love seat by the back door, the two of them danced all night long, and they were good at it. Very good.

Chen was there with his husband, who really was the mayor of Los Gatos. I don't think I heard Chen utter a single word all night. By contrast, Mr. Chen—or whatever you called married gay partners—was extremely gregarious. He also looked like a young Marlon Brando, which rendered him quite popular with a gaggle of clueless women.

Cate and her mom Lois seemed to have a good time. Larry attached himself to Lois. He did that at parties. He picked someone and then followed her around all night. She didn't seem to mind.

Cate talked quite a while with Amy, who was there with Baba Hari Friedman. Friedman turned out to be a fun guy—especially after a few drinks. I guess if you've got your own cult, you can do whatever you want.

I was surprised to see José, who'd gotten a ride from Paul. Both weren't feeling well and didn't stay long. Maybe Aria had told them to come, anyway. This time Paul wore a gray pork pie hat. He told me that he'd gotten in the habit of wearing hats when he was getting chemo for his condition.

John Bishop—the guy with the store in Watsonville—was there with his Mexican wife and a visiting folk artist from rural Chiapas. She not only didn't speak English, she didn't speak Spanish, either. But she was a gifted mime. I had no trouble at all understanding her. She stood about four foot ten.

Sumati was conspicuously absent. Apparently, she'd gone AWOL from the center. Perhaps she and Bobby had run off somewhere—so much for my anti-matchmaking.

Matt had invited Adele—don't ask me why—and

she made a grand entrance with a tall, handsome date. I don't think they were too serious since he couldn't remember her name when he tried to introduce her to someone.

Adele was in a good mood. She said a few snarky things to Aria, told John he looked fat, and whispered to me that it would be a cold day in hell before she ever forgave me for ruining her life. Then she left early before things became epic.

John told me Aria had taken him on as a student. He was excited. His girlfriend, Lotus, didn't seem too thrilled. I hadn't seen her in quite some time, but she sported all sorts of new tattoos, including red calligraphy on her upper arm which was a paraphrase of one of Aria's signs at her spiritual center. "We're all in this together." That had to mean something about her own spiritual commitment.

When a conjunto song came on, courtesy of our host, John danced with Larry and sang along. As far as I was concerned, that was the highlight of the evening.

No, that's not right. The highlight was when Aria told me she loved me. Even a dog dancing a polka couldn't top that.

Oh, another thing. Aria told me she wanted to help with future cases. She and I and Matt and Larry could all work together. I think the body count of this case had alarmed her—as well it should. She wanted to keep me safe.

Who wouldn't want another partner with her skill set? I was a lucky guy. I had the most beautiful dog in the world, a friend and partner who could hack into virtually any database, and a girlfriend twice as enlightened as anybody else's.

Life was good. There was just one major challenge. I had to find a way to become worthy of all this.

Coming soon from Verlin Darrow…

Coattail Karma

A Fantasy Thriller

Published by the Wild Rose Press

A psychotherapist is dragged into a war between spiritual factions vying for control of the planet. Is he Buddha's clone? Has his mentor actually granted him enlightenment? Can the woman by his side kick everyone's ass? As Sid is chased through New Zealand, India, and the redwoods of northern California, his sense of identity dissolves and something amazing takes its place.

A word about the author...

Verlin Darrow is currently a psychotherapist who lives with his psychotherapist wife in the woods near the Monterey Bay in northern California. They diagnose each other as necessary. Verlin is a former professional volleyball player, country-western singer/songwriter, import store owner, and assistant guru in a small, benign cult, from which he graduated everyone when he left.

Before bowing to the need for higher education, a much younger Verlin ran a punch press in a sheet-metal factory, drove a taxi, worked as a night janitor, shoveled asphalt on a road crew, and installed wood floors. He barely missed being blown up by Mt. St. Helens, survived the 1985 Mexico City earthquake, and (so far) has successfully weathered his own internal disasters.

Verlin is also the author of a fantasy thriller, *Coattail Karma* (Fall, 2018). He encourages readers to visit his website or email him to find out more about all his writing.

Learn more about Verlin Darrow at
verlindarrow.com and contact him at
verlindarrow@gmail.com.

Thank you for purchasing
this publication of The Wild Rose Press, Inc.
For other wonderful stories,
please visit our on-line bookstore at
www.thewildrosepress.com.

For questions or more information
contact us at
info@thewildrosepress.com.

The Wild Rose Press, Inc.
www.thewildrosepress.com

To visit with authors of
The Wild Rose Press, Inc.
join our yahoo loop at
http://groups.yahoo.com/group/thewildrosepress/